FATHER OF
DRAGONS

THE BINDING OF THE BLADE

BY L. B. GRAHAM

Beyond the Summerland
Bringer of Storms
Shadow in the Deep
Father of Dragons

BOOK 4

THE
BiNDiNG
of the
BLADE

FATHER OF
DRAGONS

L. B. GRAHAM

P&R

PUBLISHING

P.O. BOX 817 • PHILLIPSBURG • NEW JERSEY 08865-0817

Page design by Tobias Design

Printed in the United States of America

Library of Congress Cataloging-in-Publication Data

Graham, L. B. (Lowell B.), 1971-
    Father of Dragons / L. B. Graham.
        p. cm. —   (The binding of the blade ; bk. 4)
    This book contains two chronicles. A "prologue" precedes the first chronicle which is entitled, "Awake." The second chronicle entitled, "Arise," is followed by an "epilogue" and a "glossary." Each chronicle has its own table of contents.
    Summary: As the forces on both sides are being drawn together toward a great battle, Aljeron and Valzaan journey to awaken the Father of Dragons, to enlist his aid against Malek's armies.
    ISBN-13: 978-0-87552-723-9 (pbk.)
    [1. Fantasy.]   I. Title.
    PZ7.G75267Fat 2007
    [Fic]—dc22

                                                                    2007005360

For Tom and Ella

Who brighten my world and give pleasure to my days

CONTENTS

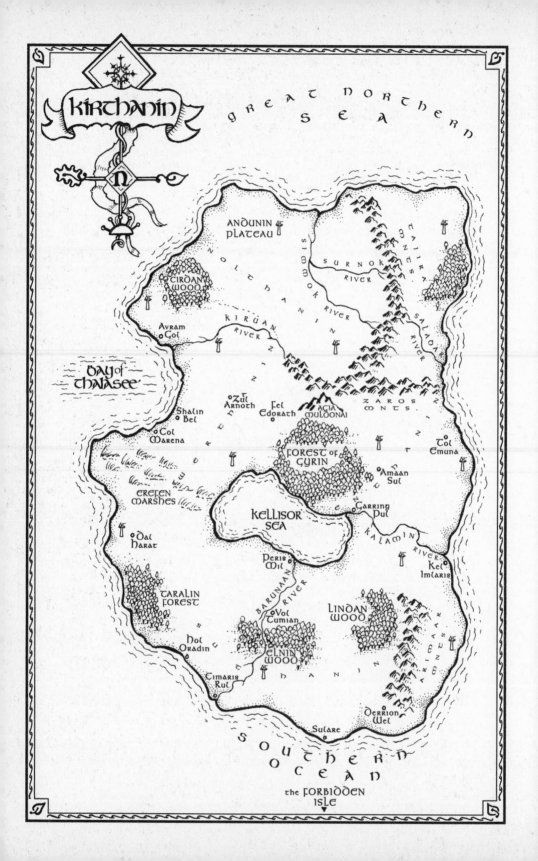

PROLOGUE:
VULSUTYR

THE DECK CREAKED under Vulsutyr's feet. He gazed out over the water as he walked toward the starboard side of the bow. He passed the empty front bench, looking down at the great oar, unused and still. The wind had been steady and strong all the way, a fact that Vulsutyr took to be a good omen. He'd doubted off and on since long before their departure from Nal Gildoroth, doubted that aligning himself with Malek had been a wise choice, but the time for such reservations was past. He was committed, as were his children, and their fate was now tied to Malek's, for better or for worse.

Summer was fading. A cool breeze was stirring above his head as the massive sail billowed in the darkness. Others designed and built these great ships, and he had wondered about the vessels' ability to make headway through the water carrying so much weight. His concerns proved unfounded. Even without his children filling the long rows of benches and operating the oars, they made rapid progress across the wide waters. Not since the dawn of the First Age when he woke to life at the foot of Agia Muldonai and was brought to his island had he seen the shores of Kirthanin. He would see them again now, and soon, and if all went well, he would return again to the place of his beginnings and stand once more upon the foot of the Holy Mountain.

The merest sliver of faint morning light slipped across the waves, and he looked back over his shoulder toward the east. The darkness was definitely beginning to roll back as morning broke across the horizon. He turned back north and peered through the still dim sky, looking for a glimpse of land. He saw it. Amid the various dark shapes that made up the horizon was the unmistakably darker and immobile faint outline of shore. The southern shores of Suthanin lay ahead, though still a fair distance away. It might not be before evening, but today he would set foot again upon solid ground.

As the outline of the land grew clearer, he thought again of the beautiful coastline of his island slipping away in the bright sunshine behind him. He missed the stark beauty of home and the solitary existence he had led there with his children, at least before Malek and the Nolthanim came, and before Malek filled the island with his creations. He wondered again, as he had so many times over the years, what Malek would have done if Vulsutyr had not allowed him to stay. If Vulsutyr and all his children had fought Malek, could they have defeated him and his men? He remembered from the beginning of all things the power and majesty of the Twelve, but he had come to see over the long years that Malek, though still powerful, was not all that he had been.

In the end, none of his questions had answers. He had grown in his own power even as Malek had declined in his, perhaps to the point where he was almost Malek's equal, but he had realized this too late. He had made the pact and kept it, and now that pact had brought him to this time and place. More than that, he had helped Malek create *them*, and they would not have been easily destroyed had Vulsutyr rebelled.

He had been happy on his island, and when this was finished, he would go back there. Malek had talked of Vulsutyr staying in Kirthanin to rule at his right hand, but Vulsutyr knew that Malek would be as happy to see him return to the island as Vulsutyr would be to go. The hunger to destroy and to rule emanated from Malek, and Vulsutyr would be happier as the sole ruler of his own little world than as Malek's lieutenant in the larger domain of Kirthanin. Yes, he would go back, but before he could, he needed to deliver Kirthanin and the Mountain to Malek, which he meant to do as quickly as possible. Seeing Agia Muldonai again was the only part of this whole journey he was looking forward to.

As the sky lightened, Vulsutyr spotted a sail in the distance. He raised his hand to shelter his eyes from the slight morning glare. It was a ship all right, and it had seen them. There was no mistaking that. Vulsutyr realized from the moment he saw the sail that if he could see this much smaller, single ship, then surely they could see the enormous fleet gliding across the waters toward them.

The ship was turning back toward land. He could see it cutting a wide swath as it tried to reverse its course. It would make a run for land to warn what remained of the forces stationed along the southern shore. The dragons and most of the men had been pulled away by the civil war up north, but a small garrison manned Sulare and the surrounding area. There was little these forces would be able to do against Vulsutyr's fleet, but he preferred they had no warning. The ship would need to be overtaken and destroyed.

Vulsutyr moved to the bow and climbed the tall, arcing prow that extended up and outward. He cupped his hand to his mouth as he held to the solid wood with the other. He called with a great shout to the sky, and echoing from the other great ships came more calls and cries. These calls echoed across the water, rolling in like thunder on a cloudless day. Several of his children came quickly from down below, taking up the great oars as they took their seats on the benches. The beater of drums began to beat out the rhythm, and Vulsutyr felt the mighty vessel surge forward under his feet. He smiled. The ship ahead had a sizeable lead, but it would not outrun his children.

Morning turned into afternoon, and they drew closer to the ship as it drew closer to the shore. They were so close now that he could see men scurrying back and forth on its deck. He could see fear in their movements. Their ship was lighter and more agile, but it was losing its advantage with every passing moment.

Now men with bows and arrows were coming to the port side, which was the only side that afforded any angle at all with which to attack. Vulsutyr called to his children who weren't manning the oars to be ready. A small volley of arrows was released, but most fell short into the water while a couple struck the side of the ship. The men on the other ship, realizing they were not yet in range, waited.

It was a strange waiting game. The parties stared at each other across the intervening waves. Vulsutyr in all his might and grandeur stood proudly at the side of the ship, gazing with a fiery intensity at the men who looked back in despair. When the distance between them had been cut in half, another volley was loosed. This time, Vulsutyr's children lifted great wooden shields above their heads to shelter both themselves and their brothers on the oars. The arrows sailed long or struck these harmlessly. Vulsutyr strode across the deck and picked up one of the colossal but empty barrels that had carried fresh water across the Southern Ocean, and walking to the rail, threw the barrel with great force so that it struck and snapped the forward mast of the other ship.

Cries of terror echoed across the water along with the great cracking of the mast as it split and fell, rending the air.

The ship seemed suddenly to turn back toward the pursuing vessels, and almost before anyone was aware of it, Vulsutyr's ship was within striking distance. Instantly, half a dozen of his children leapt across the small gap, their feet crashing through the deck of the other ship. Men leapt from the vessel into the water on either side as Vulsutyr's children smashed the vessel to pieces beneath them. Great chunks of wood fell in every direction as the vessel collapsed. Vulsutyr's children in churning water quickly grabbed hold of the massive ropes lowered for their return. They snatched up the ends and pulled themselves back up on deck.

Vulsutyr gazed down at the flotsam and jetsam as it passed under the prow of their ship. Flesh and wood both succumbed to the mighty pull and were dragged under the keel to be raked beneath the vessel. He looked up to the shore. In much the same way, they would roll over everything and everyone between here and the Mountain.

The sun had fallen beneath the horizon and twilight was fading as Vulsutyr walked along the sand. All around him the hosts of Malek were assembling as far as the eye could see. The children of Rucaran the Great had already moved north from their landing place to scout out the vicinity and bring back word of its defenses. Likewise the Nolthanim and Malekim had assembled in two extensive but coherent masses, preparing for a nighttime march. His own children surrounded him on the beach, waiting for the last of the ships, watching uneasily as it sailed in under cover of dark.

The great dark vessel glided in and ran aground in the soft, warm sand. From up on deck, half a dozen great chains dropped, and two of his children took hold of each chain as the rest gathered round and drew their weapons. The tension in the air was thick, and Vulsutyr felt sweat beading on his brow as he waited with the rest of them.

The creaking of great locks coming undone and massive iron bars being pulled open broke through the still night air. Every other activity came to a halt. Vulsutyr swung his head around and saw the eyes of a myriad of men and Voiceless trained on the dark and unadorned prow.

A handful of his children appeared up above, leaning over the prow's side and motioning to him. He nodded and motioned to his children holding the great chains to commence. Swiftly they responded, pulling with great power as the chains tightened above their heads. For a moment they appeared like a dozen leaning statues trying to pull the ship further aground, when suddenly the top of the ship's prow began to come away from the deck, and the whole front of the vessel fell crashing down into the knee-high water, burying itself in the soft, loose sand.

Those who had been pulling the great chains scrambled wildly to get away from the cavernous opening that they had created, not stopping until they were well behind their armed and waiting brethren. A wide path opened up through the encircling masses, with Vulsutyr alone standing in front of the ship's gaping jaws. He felt his solitude keenly, and stepping in toward the great hole, he also stepped aside, leaving a clear path up the beach.

For a long moment nothing happened, and the gathered crowd stood in silence, waiting. Then there emerged from the vacuous hold a creature almost a span shorter than Vulsutyr but with shoulders much wider and long powerful arms that hung almost to its knees. Eyes as black as the empty night sky stared straight ahead as the lead creature passed by Vulsutyr, less than a span away but with no hint or sign of recognition. A second passed after, just like the first, and so on until all twelve had moved silently by.

Everyone watched them go, and as the first one reached the grass beyond the sand it began to run at a smooth, even pace. The others likewise broke into a run, and before long both their dim and dusky forms and their near-silent footfalls passed beyond Vulsutyr's capacity to track them. They were gone now, unleashed upon Kirthanin like shadowy nightmares sprung from the depths of the world's most troubled dreams. Vulsutyr watched them go and wished them all speed, knowing that whether they were ultimately successful or not, they would not be going back across the Southern Ocean with him, and for that he was glad. Though he had shared in their making, they had never respected him as their maker or harkened to his voice, and he did not claim them as his own. They were no children of his, and if he never saw them again in his lifetime, he would not be grieved.

More than a week later, Vulsutyr and the hosts of Malek were moving north across the open grasslands of Suthanin. They had met with little resistance in that first week, but word of their arrival had gone ahead of them, and men and Great Bear were coming south to meet them, or so the wolves had said. He believed it was true, because the shiny marauders had been flying increasingly overhead. Let them come, Vulsutyr thought. He was not afraid of the dragons. He would reach up and pull one from the sky and rip it open, despite the protection of its scales, and then all of them would know he was not afraid of the fire in their hearts.

The sound of horns up ahead spurred Vulsutyr to start running. It was a battle cry, and his children ran behind him toward the front lines. There they saw men fighting men, and Great Bear battling with Malekim as the children of Rucaran ran among the combatants.

They made their way through the confusion, but as they neared the front, several golden forms dropped from the sky and flew low overhead. Vulsutyr stood tall as his children stooped and ducked all around him. As the wave of dragons passed on, Vulsutyr looked past them to another dragon soaring higher. This dragon was different, larger and purer of color, the gold untainted with any lesser hue. His great golden head stared down, his deep bright eyes searching Vulsutyr's face. It was Sulmandir, Father of Dragons. Vulsutyr had seen him once before flying high above the Mountain. Vulsutyr did not shrink back, but met the gaze of this highborn foe without trembling.

Again the dragons circled and returned, coming this time even lower. Blasts of fire and heat erupted from their mouths, and Vulsutyr's children dove out of the way while Vulsutyr himself stood firm even as fire enveloped him. When the fire and smoke cleared, however, Vulsutyr remained, standing as strong and tall as ever. Now, though, he drew his long bright sword and held it high over his head, the blade running almost parallel to the ground as he clenched the hilt. Vulsutyr's body glowed in the heat from the fire, and as those around him stared, traces of flame ran along his bare arm and rippled along the edge of the sword until the whole blade glowed with fire.

Vulsutyr threw his head back and laughed a deep, majestic laugh. Straightening up, he roared, and the sound of his voice split the sky, echoing across the battlefield. He felt the heat and glow of the fire warm his body and strength surged through him. Fire ran through his veins like blood, and if this was the best the dragons could do, they would fall one by one at his feet as he tore them to pieces.

The small cluster of dragons passed overhead a third time. Again fire and smoke billowed, but Vulsutyr remained focused. The last of them swept above, and Vulsutyr leapt into the sky, striking the tail of the dragon with a sharp, swift blow. The flaming sword sliced the tail clean off, and it fell to the ground with a thump, severed dragon scales sprinkling the ground. The dragon's wings beat harder, trying to maintain his altitude, but he faltered. Vulsutyr sprinted forward underneath him and, leaping again, took hold of the tip of his wing. Vulsutyr pulled, dragging the dragon down from the sky and slamming it into the sun-baked earth.

The dragon did not surrender, raising itself as best as it was able with its massive jaws open to attack Vulsutyr. The fire giant was ready, though, and he easily dodged the dragon's strike, letting the great wide jaws snap harmlessly. Then, with remarkably swift reflexes, Vulsutyr grabbed the dragon's neck as it recoiled. Holding him still, Vulsutyr slid his hands up to the dragon's jaws, and with a sudden jerk ripped the dragon's bottom jaw from his head. The creature bellowed as it fell sideways to the ground, and Vulsutyr drove his flaming sword up to the hilt through his exposed underbelly.

Blood poured through the gaping hole and seeped down the golden scales into the brown grass and thirsty soil. Ripping his sword out in a swift motion, Vulsutyr stepped up onto the now motionless golden form of the fallen dragon and searched the sky. There, high above, Sulmandir still flew, watching Vulsutyr's every move. Vulsutyr's eyes followed him across the sky, unmoved. Sulmandir swept around in a great arc and headed back north across the battlefield. As he did so, Vulsutyr raised his empty hand and clenched his fist in a gesture of defiance. He was Vulsutyr, Father of the Giants and master of fire, and whether the Grendolai succeeded in their appointed mission or not, the dragons would not deter or slow him.

The Mountain loomed large. They had come to it at last, but it was not as Vulsutyr imagined it would be.

The tide of battle turned against them despite all he had done on Malek's behalf. Though the Nolthanim held their own against what remained of the Suthanim, Werthanim, and Enthanim, the Great Bear had dealt serious blows to the Malekim.

What's more, his own children, as strong and brave as they were, had proved less able to withstand the furious attacks of the dragons than he. They moved now toward Agia Muldonai, more in retreat than anything else, visions of conquest and dominion slipping away.

He cursed the creations of Malek for their weakness. Rucaran's children, for all their prowess and stealth, had been beaten back again and again by the steady strength of the Great Bear, as had the Malekim, bred specifically to be their counterpart. Though the Malekim succeeded in the early engagements in inflicting heavy casualties against the forces of Kirthanin, the movements of the Silent Ones had been shadowed doggedly by the Great Bear ever since. Their single-minded dedication freed the dragons to focus on Vulsutyr's children, and increasingly the dragons were able piece by piece to pick off the stragglers, whoever was unfortunate enough to be caught away from the protection of the whole. He watched over and over as the patient and determined dragons kept well away from him and singled out one of his children across the battlefield to be overwhelmed and struck down.

Without a change of fortune, this war would be lost, and along with it his hope of delivering the Mountain to Malek and going home. He had to strike a counterblow. He had to even the odds and take the next battle into his own hands. He would break the lines of the Great Bear and give the Malekim a chance to take control again. He would sweep away the weak and weary men of Kirthanin, who hung onto their swords and their courage with the same weak grip. He would pull from the sky any dragon that dared to come near him, and he would turn the tide once more, single-handedly.

From their left flank, the side farthest from the Mountain, he heard the alarm. He looked up into the sky and saw the now familiar sight of dozens of dragons approaching from the west. The men and Malekim ahead of him broke into a run, as did his own children. They were running toward the Mountain, no doubt hoping to take some high ground and fight this next battle from a position of their own choosing. Vulsutyr ran with them, eager to set foot upon the base of the Mountain once more. He would draw strength from the place of his creation and the object of his mission.

A deep rumble like thunder rolled across the heavens above him, and he turned to see the form of Sulmandir leading the dragon formation closer. He had not seen the dragons' great father in their last few battles, but now he was back. Good, Vulsutyr thought, there could be no better way to turn the tide quickly then to strike Sulmandir down. He pressed onward. This was his day.

The battle raged on. All around him, the lines of Malek's forces were broken or breaking. He had done what he could, but for every time and every place where he broke through and turned back their adversaries, fresh holes in their defenses sprang up across the field. Multitudes of Great Bear kept pouring out of Gyrin. Surely all the draals had emptied themselves entirely, and the full might of the clans of Kirthanin were here to wage this battle, for everywhere he looked the fury of the Great Bear dominated the battlefield. Men and Malekim alike fell back, and only his own children could hold back their line here and there.

The full measure of Kirthanin's human armies must have been similarly mustered, for men kept flowing in toward the Mountain from both the east and the west. They were not as powerful as the Great Bear, but they were not giving ground or falling back. They fought, Vulsutyr thought, as he himself would fight were he cornered before the gates of Nal Gildoroth with nowhere else to go.

Afternoon became evening and the sun hung low in the west. He was weary, very weary. Despite the renewed vigor he had gained with his feet upon these rocks and the Mountain at his back, his strength was fading. He felt hope slipping away with the evening light.

He scrambled higher up the mountainside, just for a few minutes, to regain his composure and to figure out where best to assault next. It was an impossible choice. Everywhere things were falling to pieces. How could he pick one place in desperate need of his presence over another? How could he pick one hole in the dam to plug when the flood was being loosed even as he stood and watched? He had sworn to himself that this day he would turn the tide, but he knew even as he stepped higher up the Mountain that he had failed.

A golden form shot swiftly over his head. He looked up to see Sulmandir bearing down at him with great speed. He threw himself down to avoid the outstretched claws of the Father of Dragons. Dust and dirt covered Vulsutyr as he sprang to his feet, his body bleeding from a dozen small cuts from the small sharp rocks that littered the lower reaches of the Mountain. He looked around him and realized that while he had been moving backward, his children had been pressing forward. He was set apart from his own.

But he was not afraid of the dragons. They could come upon him all they wished. Their fires would not hurt him and their smoke would not slow him. He would find strength in the heat and turn their fire against them. He rose to his full height and watched Sulmandir circle to come in a second time.

This time the dragon did lead with an explosion of flame many times hotter than any with which the others had torched him. It blazed all around him. As the smoke cleared, he looked down at his arms and saw the glow, back again, this time even brighter than before. He drew his flaming sword and held it high. "Come to me, Father of Dragons!" he yelled. "I will cut your heart out and rip your head from your body!"

His voice resonated across the battlefield. Engagements both heavy and light, both fierce and fading, began to break up as all eyes turned to see the duel just getting underway at the foot of Agia Muldonai. Other dragons were circling high in the air, sometimes swooping when it looked like one of Vulsutyr's children might be moving toward the Mountain, using flame and smoke to hold them back, but none of the other dragons approached the Mountain. Only Sulmandir flew close to the giant of fire. Only Sulmandir soared above him, his wings almost touching the Mountain.

A third time Sulmandir dove, flying faster and faster toward Vulsutyr. His wings sent powerful gusts of wind across the battlefield, and Vulsutyr tensed as his golden form drew close. A swift lunge took Sulmandir by surprise, and a mighty thrust of the flaming sword straight up into the sky just missed one of Sulmandir's great wings. The dragon altered his course and sank awkwardly lower in the air before regaining his graceful rhythm and pulling upward.

Vulsutyr raised his empty hand and with a clenched fist shook it at the sky. He screamed, his face contorted with rage and malice. But he was quickly aware that he had misjudged Sulmandir's trajectory. The dragon was not rising above him as he had done the last couple of times. Instead, he cut back swiftly and was accelerating rapidly, directly at Vulsutyr.

Even as Vulsutyr's step forward had caught the dragon by surprise, so Sulmandir's change of pace, coming back immediately rather than circling above and gathering speed, now caught Vulsutyr by surprise. Vulsutyr felt suddenly exposed there upon the Mountain, and with a great swoop downward Sulmandir was upon him. Vulsutyr dodged late, and the sharp talons of one of Sulmandir's claws ripped strips off of his bare shoulder and upper arm. He winced as his blood ran down his back and side. He turned, following his adversary without gestures or cries this time, only concentration. Sulmandir had drawn first blood.

Again Sulmandir circled back around. He seemed, if possible, to be coming this time even faster than he had come before. Vulsutyr stooped, feinting another dodge, but as Sulmandir passed overhead he stood quickly, driving his fiery sword up into Sulmandir's underbelly. Sulmandir's momentum caused the jab through the tough golden scales to become a long, jagged gash as the blade ripped him open. At the same time, Sulmandir's back legs struck Vulsutyr firmly in the chest, knocking him down.

Vulsutyr rolled over immediately and staggered to his feet. He felt a rush of adrenaline. He turned to see Sulmandir just avoid crashing into the side of the Mountain, setting down heavily and awkwardly not far away. Instantly Vulsutyr pursued, scrambling across the loose rocks to finish what he had started. He would salvage victory from defeat this day after all. The death of Sulmandir would change everything.

Sulmandir spun quickly, despite the blood gushing out from underneath him and the golden scales lying loose among the shale and stone. He reared as Vulsutyr approached, roaring with a cry so loud and so fearful that Vulsutyr stepped back. But as the last sound of its echo died away from the Mountain, Vulsutyr felt his courage return. He smiled at his foe and laughed. He too had howled like a beast when he felt cornered and defeated. He was cornered no longer. He was in charge now.

He circled Sulmandir warily, watching to see how mobile the dragon was. Sulmandir moved slowly, perhaps with difficulty. A golden streak passed overhead, and he looked up to see a dragon almost upon him. Quick reflexes and a swift stroke of his flaming sword kept the dragon far enough away that his talons couldn't do him harm.

They're coming now, Vulsutyr thought, trying to save their father. He knew he needed to strike first and strike fast. He didn't want to fight all the dragons gathered there at the battlefield in order to finish the job, and they would be able to get to him a lot quicker than his own children would. He turned back to Sulmandir and accelerated straight toward him, sword raised. Just a couple steps and a powerful stroke and Sulmandir's head would tumble down the Mountain.

A flash of gold flew into view from the side. It was unexpected and lashed his arm, sending his sword clattering to the stones. Sulmandir's tail, razor sharp and incredibly fast had lacerated his wrist and forearm, slicing them open and nearly severing them completely. The pain was sudden and sharp, but he had no time to think about it. Sulmandir himself was now striking forward. If the dragon had moved slowly and with difficulty before, he did not do so now. He struck with lightning speed and precision, one massive claw sinking straight into the base of Vulsutyr's neck, another pinioning his healthy arm to his side. The burning pain in Vulsutyr's wounded arm was immediately eclipsed by the cold bite of torn flesh and exposed veins. Vulsutyr felt the claw penetrate his soft neck and all hope was gone, washed away by a flood of despair. He knew with utter clarity that this was death. His eyes blinked once as the dragon's great golden head drew closer, Sulmandir's wide eyes fixed on his own, peering dispassionately at his prey. Both claws tightened and pushed deeper inside him, and then there was only darkness.

AWAKE

1

DREAMS AND VISIONS

RULALIN STOOD BEFORE the cavernous opening in the side of the Mountain. The loose rock beneath his feet began to slide and he stepped forward, closer, to avoid slipping downhill. He rubbed his sweaty fingers on his cloak, clasping the thick rough fabric until his fingers hurt. A cool wind blew out of the darkness, air that was foul and stale. It was strong enough to toss the hair on his forehead to and fro, and Rulalin raised his hand to sweep some of it out of his eyes. Sighing, he relaxed his grip on his cloak and walked into the cave.

For a while, he was aware only of darkness before him and light behind him, but as the light from the outside faded, he was increasingly aware of dim but constant light from pale blue stones evenly spaced along the base of the wide tunnel's walls. Their light seemed to grow stronger as the light disappeared. He looked back over his shoulder, and the gaping hole in the side of the Mountain was but a pin-hole of light in the distance. He turned and kept going.

The wind kept blowing in his face, and though the foulness remained, he grew almost accustomed to it. He was glad of the coolness in the air as it struck his face, for the tunnel seemed very warm. Sweat was beading on his brow, and he could feel it spreading out in damp circles on his cloak. He thought he'd been here before, but he didn't remember this heat.

He turned out of the large tunnel into a smaller corridor and kept moving forward. He had been walking for some time, it seemed to him, and yet he had seen nothing and no one. It was eerily quiet and empty, and the only sounds he heard were the sound of his feet echoing on the rock and the sound of his exhalation, abnormally loud in his own ears.

He passed by turns through larger tunnels, smaller corridors and spacious halls where the ceiling and sides were beyond his sight. All of it was dimly lit. All of it was vacant. All of it seemed both familiar and unfamiliar at the same time.

Looking down, he watched his feet move, one after the other. He was strangely conscious of the fact that they seemed to be self-propelled, moving without direction from him. He had felt this way before, as though he were sleepwalking in a dream, moving without willing to move, but never as strongly as he felt it now. His feet had entered the cave, and he followed. His feet turned a corner, and he followed. His feet felt their way along the smooth stone floor, and he came after, always, ceaselessly after.

Suddenly, his feet came to a stop before a wide, solid wood door. His hand, as completely beyond his control as his feet, reached out and pushed the door open. It swung back with a loud creak on rusty iron hinges, revealing a large room, though by no means a cavern like some of those he had just passed through. No, this room had walls and a ceiling that Rulalin could see, though it was large. It was like the large halls through which he had passed in at least one respect: It was essentially empty. It was essentially empty but not completely empty. In the middle of the room was a staircase ascending through a hole in the ceiling into darkness.

He walked to the foot of the staircase and paused. It seemed at last as though the will directing his feet had disappeared. He did not move. He stood and stared upward into the darkness. The room in which he stood was semi-illuminated by a pair of faintly burning torches to the right and the left of the door he had entered. As he peered upward, he could see no such light shining above. There were only the stone stairs going upward, ending, and then nothing.

A chill swept down Rulalin's spine, and he felt instantly cold. The heat of the exterior corridors was gone here. The sweat that had poured from him clung uncomfortably to his shuddering skin. He had been to this place before. There could be no doubt of that. He had been up these stairs before, and though he did not wish to ascend them again, he felt his right foot lift off the ground and come down on the first step.

His foot felt as heavy as if it were made of lead, and its echo on the stone bounced around the chamber. His left foot, likewise heavy and awkward, left the ground below him and came back down, equally heavily and with an echo just as deafening. Step by step he ascended, until first his head and then his torso and then his whole self was swallowed in the darkness of the room above. He stepped from the stairs onto the solid floor rimming the large hole through which he had just passed. He saw a chair beside the wall and stepped over to it. As soon as he placed his hand upon it, the light below was extinguished, and he was left in utter darkness.

He froze at first, but when nothing else happened, either good or bad, he sat down in the wooden chair and waited. He sat for a long while, hands folded together in his lap, his head erect, looking straight ahead though he could see nothing in this place. He unfolded his hands and rubbed them on his arms, trying to erase the chill that had driven away all memory of warmth. It remained.

He sat until his eyelids grew heavy. They drooped dangerously close to shutting, and his head started to fall forward before he jerked it upright again. His eyes opened wide, and his body tensed. He was very awake, very alert. Something was different. A voice echoed in the room, but it wasn't his, *You are sworn, and you are mine.*

Rulalin looked up at the roof of his tent. He could tell by the amount of light above him that it was midmorning. The Mountain again. For a long time he had not dreamed at all, at least not that he could remember. He was merely restless, tossing and turning, and according to Soran, sometimes talking as well. Now he was dreaming again, but when he dreamed, it was always the same. There was always the gaping opening that led into the Mountain, always the long lonely walk, always the same dark chamber, and always the inescapable voice.

He rolled over and faced the tent wall. To turn the other way would mean to look at the wooden cage in the far corner, but he didn't want to do that. Of course, it wasn't so much the cage as the figure hunched inside it, but fresh out of his dream, or nightmare, or whatever one would call it, he didn't really want to see Benjiah peering through the slats of his cage at him, not that Benjiah had done much other than sit motionless in the back corner since being brought into Rulalin's quarters.

Outside of their initial brief exchange, Rulalin had neither approached the cage nor addressed Benjiah. It had been his plan to unnerve the young boy with his silence. He had learned the power of silence to throw a man off his guard. Fearing silence, the nervous always said things they ought not to say and later wished they had not said, and Rulalin wanted any and all information he could pry from the boy about the enemy, and about Wylla.

He heard the rustle of the tent flaps opening, and morning light streamed in. Along with the light came a gust of cold air. It might be Spring Rise, but the air still had the chill of winter. He sat up on one elbow, failed to hold back a yawn, and looked over at the silhouette of Soran, framed against the bright outer world.

Rulalin motioned Soran to the small wooden table that sat a span or so from his bed and stretched as he got up himself. Despite his new rank and the benefit of the tent, his muscles were stiff and sore, and he longed for the distant pleasure of a bed and fireplace.

He took a seat across from Soran, who seemed distracted by the cage. His young friend was eyeing it while trying to appear like he wasn't, and Rulalin fought his own desire to look. If young Benjiah was inside, watching them, he might notice Soran's curiosity, but the boy would see none from Rulalin.

"So," Rulalin said.

"So."

"A cold morning."

"Yes," Soran nodded, "very."

"Good thing spring is here," Rulalin said tersely.

"Yes," Soran answered, nodding knowingly to acknowledge the sarcasm, "though it isn't the cold that you notice when you first go out."

"No?"

"No."

"Really," Rulalin said, peering at his friend's face. "What do you notice first?"

"Come out and see," Soran said, standing.

Rulalin rose from the table and followed Soran. He pulled his cloak tightly around him and tied it firmly, stepping through the flaps. The cold of the morning stung his face, but Soran was right. Immediately, all thought of cold or anything else was replaced by the overwhelming realization that it wasn't raining, not even drizzling. Even if the soggy and saturated ground beneath his feet still sloshed with water, the air was dry and nothing fell on his head or face.

He looked up and held out his hands, opened wide. Nothing. The sky was dark and the clouds as thick and sinister as they had been all the way along their long and unending march, league after league, but there was no rain. Rulalin looked from the dark sky to Soran.

"Amazing."

"Yes."

"I'd given up hoping we'd wake up and find the rain gone," Rulalin added, remembering how many mornings he'd risen, bitterly disappointed to find yet another long, soaking day ahead.

"Me too."

"I'll take it though."

"As will I." Soran almost laughed. "As far as I'm concerned, I don't care if it never rains again. I can do without it for a while."

"Agreed," Rulalin said, but his thoughts were drifting away from the conversation even as he said it. "I suppose if I'd really thought about it, I should have seen this coming."

"How so?"

"The Kumatin," Rulalin answered. "If the rain was meant to bring flooding, to turn the rivers into roads for the Kumatin, that mission has been accomplished. Now that the enemy has crossed the Kalamin into Enthanin, the river is a barrier to our pursuit. Cheimontyr is holding back the rain even as he summoned it, all to aid his own purposes."

"Do you think the rain will return once we get across?" Soran asked, the disappointment evident in his face and tone.

"Maybe not," Rulalin said, trying to be hopeful. "After all, we realized long ago the rain couldn't go on forever unless Malek meant to drown the world entirely, which wouldn't make sense. He's a destroyer all right, but he means to rule something. Maybe the rain was always destined to end once the Kumatin made it all the way inland. Maybe this was always the plan, and the setback facing us now at the river is just a coincidence, a momentary delay of little note."

"Well," Soran said, pointing at the mobilized camp, scurrying with activity in the direction of the river, "if it is of little note, there are certainly a lot of hands and heads at work down there trying to figure what our next step is."

"Yes," Rulalin conceded, "I can't see how we are going to get across quickly either, but I'm sure Malek and Cheimontyr and Farimaal will think of something. I'm just glad it's their problem, not mine."

"What do you think will happen?"

"I don't know. I think the Vulsutyrim will cross the river and bring the abandoned boats back. That would be the logical first step, but most of the vessels are small and will only carry men and wolves. The giants can swim across, though the waters are deep and rough. It's the Malekim that are the problem, the Malekim and our supplies. Even if we could start right away, it would probably take a couple of days to get everything across. So, I think we can relax a little bit. We're probably going to be right here for the foreseeable future."

"I'm not complaining. We could use the rest."

"We could."

"Besides, it isn't like the head start will do the enemy much good anyway. They are still outnumbered and overmatched."

"Perhaps."

"Perhaps? Do you doubt it?"

"Did you see the wall of earth that shut us off from them?"

"Yes," Soran started, seeming a little frustrated by Rulalin's point, "but I fail to see the relevance."

"Why?"

"Why? Because, as you said yourself, the wall of earth, as far as we know, was the work of that boy in your tent with the help of Valzaan's staff."

"I think it was Valzaan's staff. I don't know for sure."

"Perhaps not, but it makes sense that it would have been. How else could the boy have done it?"

"I don't know. I'm just saying it might not have been Valzaan's staff."

"Even so, the boy is our captive now. If he could wield great power at will, why is he stuck in a wooden cage? Surely you're not afraid of him?"

"Soran, I don't know what to make of him or of any of it, and that is what scares me. When the wall of earth collapsed, revealing only the boy and the shards of the staff, it made no sense. How could that boy, a child really, hold back Cheimontyr? How could the Bringer of Storms be thwarted by a boy not yet of age? Even if he was holding Valzaan's staff, how is it possible? Valzaan himself could not do this. At least, he didn't. When we overran Zul Arnoth, he could not hold us back. Even on the beach above Col Marena, the power he wielded couldn't save his own life."

"No, and Benjiah has yet to save his. He is here after all and as likely as not his life is already forfeit, even if he keeps it yet a little while."

Rulalin didn't answer. He had thought already of the possibility that he might not be able to save Benjiah, and it worried him. How would Wylla react if Benjiah was dead or beyond Rulalin's power to save when they reached Amaan Sul? He had not planned for this, and while he saw that Benjiah's capture could ultimately be the very thing he needed to help his plan succeed, it could also be the very thing that brought his dream tumbling down.

"Look," Rulalin eventually said, "all I'm saying is that what the boy did was remarkable, staff or no staff. If power equal to Cheimontyr's remains, either in him or in a staff or in anything, who knows what else can happen? If it can happen once, perhaps it can happen again."

"I just can't see it," Soran said softly, almost whispering. "As we couldn't have seen what he just did a few days ago."

Rulalin thought back upon his first glimpse of Benjiah after the chaos and confusion of that day had begun to settle down. He had looked so small and pale, a limp body being carried by a couple of men like a fallen soldier being moved from the battlefield. His fair hair was soaked with sweat and matted to his head, and his dangling hands were being dragged across the slick, wet grass. Who could have believed, even then, right after the fearful display of power, that its like could have come from him?

Rulalin suspected that the whole discussion of whether the power had been Benjiah's or the staff's was wrong-headed. Such power was almost certainly too much to attribute to either or even both working together. Such power pointed beyond its user to its maker, beyond Benjiah to Allfather.

It was a chilling thought, disrupting any notion Rulalin had, whether conscious or not, of Allfather as a distant figure unconcerned with the unfolding events in Kirthanin. If He had bequeathed such great power to Valzaan and then to Benjiah to oppose Malek and his forces, then why could He not do so again? Even as Malek had given Cheimontyr power to control the weather, maybe Allfather also could grant to others the power to defeat His enemies.

Rulalin, however, quickly countered this in his own thinking. If Allfather had the power to defeat Malek and end his quest to rule Kirthanin, why hadn't he done it years ago? Indeed, why had Malek been allowed to live at all once his rebellion had begun and his intent had been made known? Perhaps Allfather was not stronger than Malek, as had been commonly taught and believed, and perhaps even if Allfather was more concerned with the affairs of Kirthanin than Rulalin had previously thought, maybe it didn't really matter. Surely Allfather must lack either the power to stop Malek or interest in what he was doing, or else He would have squelched this uprising long ago.

Rulalin was largely comforted by all this, but not entirely. Valzaan had talked to them of this all those years ago in Sulare, saying that Allfather had both the power and the desire to see Malek defeated but had reasons of His own to let the foretold ages of the world come to pass. Valzaan said that the end was not in doubt, even if the events between now and the end might be. Valzaan's belief and conviction, as confident as it was, didn't necessarily make these things so. After all, the old man had been blown helplessly into the sea. Still, Rulalin found it impossible to dismiss his words entirely, because for him, given what he had done and was doing, it would be especially painful if Valzaan turned out to be right in the end.

"I wonder," Rulalin said, realizing as he did so that Soran almost certainly would have no context to understand the question he wanted to ask. "I wonder if our betrayal of Kirthanin is forgivable. I mean, in an ultimate sense, not just if the men and women we've betrayed can forgive us."

Soran looked sharply at Rulalin. "What do you mean, 'in an ultimate sense'? I don't follow you."

"I mean," Rulalin answered, trying to be patient even though his natural tendency would be to react to the challenge in Soran's tone, "if it really is true that one day we'll have to give a reckoning, an accounting for what we've done, you know, to Allfather or something, could we be forgiven?"

"I don't need to be forgiven," Soran said.

"You don't?" Rulalin asked, surprised at the coldness in Soran's voice.

"No, I don't. I did what I had to do to save my city. If Allfather even cares about any of this, what right would He have to condemn me? He had His chance to save Fel Edorath. He had His chance to stop Malek if He really cared to. It would be a bit hypocritical for Him to leave Malek alive and well in the heart of the Mountain and then to get bent out of shape when we joined Malek to keep Him from destroying our city, wouldn't it?"

"Maybe we were supposed to value Allfather's commands and our faithfulness more than our lives," Rulalin answered, his quiet, sober tone increasingly at odds with Soran's growing vehemence.

"That's just stupid."

"Is it?" Rulalin answered, not entirely concealing his anger at the insubordinate speech. "I mean, you talk as though we actually saved Fel Edorath. Fel Edorath isn't saved. Fel Edorath is divided and by now, probably empty and abandoned. Some follow Malek, and some follow Aljeron. Some died with us, and some died against us. The city is empty, and its unity broken. What kind of city have we saved, exactly? We've saved nothing so much as our own hides."

"You're just in one of your moods again," Soran said.

"Maybe I am," Rulalin answered. "Then again, maybe I'm not. Maybe what we've done, what I've done, maybe it is so reprehensible as to be beyond forgiveness. Maybe when I walked into the Mountain I walked beyond the reach of mercy. Maybe when I swore that oath, I gave Malek more than my allegiance."

Soran didn't answer. He didn't even look at Rulalin. He stood with his arms folded, staring in a different direction, as though he hadn't even heard what Rulalin had said. Rulalin sighed.

"I won't bother you with my thoughts on the matter any-more," Rulalin said at last, letting the anger that had briefly seized him go. He put his hand on Soran's shoulder. "I'm sorry. Most likely, I'm asking questions without an answer any-way. What we have done, we have done."

It was a strange day for Rulalin. He wanted, almost above all, to keep well away from the hustle and bustle of the parts of their encampment closest to the river. He didn't want any part in the brainstorming, planning, or work that their new predicament would mean for them. As long as he was suc-cessful in having no role in any of these things, he could bear no responsibility for any failures along the way.

The easiest way to stay out of that mess would have been simply to stay in his tent. Ordinarily, he would have taken a seat at his small wooden table with his back to the tent flaps so as to appear busy and unavailable, just in case any-one would come by with anything but a direct message for him. He could have justified this seclusion all the more eas-ily since the cage with their recently taken captive of war was also in his tent. Who could have questioned his loyalty to duty if he had shut himself up all day to keep an eye on the boy?

The boy, though, was just the problem. Rulalin had no idea if his own silence was succeeding in unnerving Benjiah, but Benjiah's silence was unnerving him. He couldn't help but imagine that Benjiah was keeping careful watch on him. He didn't plead for his life or beg for water or food. He didn't lash out at the cage or his captor. He just sat, quietly and as far back in the shadows as he could.

Consequently, Rulalin found it impossible to remain in-side the tent. The day, then, was an endless succession of movements out into the camp and then back into the tent when he thought he had been spotted and might be called upon by Tashmiren, Farimaal, or one of the other captains. While outside, he moved briskly from one place to another, trying to look busy and preoccupied. While inside, he sat at his small table, ill at ease and dying to go to the cage to see what its occupant was doing.

By late afternoon, he finally realized that the situation was untenable. Benjiah needed to stay under his care, which meant he needed to stay nearby, but he could not stay in the tent. That much was certain. He would have the cage re- moved after dinner, but first he would speak to Benjiah.

As darkness fell upon the camp, Rulalin approached his tent with dinner in his arms. He had procured two loaves of bread and some salted meat that wasn't too far gone. Once cooked, the smell of being slightly off had gone away, and compared with what many in the camp would be eating that night, Rulalin knew he couldn't complain.

He paused at the entrance to his tent and waited for the man behind him to step inside first and place the pitcher of cold water and cups on the table. He followed, setting the food down carefully.

"Thanks," he said to the man, who bowed and exited.

Not waiting for nerves to set in, he picked up one of the loaves and a hunk of the meat and carried them to the cage. He stooped and peered in. The pair of torches now burning on stands sent flickering rays of light through the slats. Ben- jiah sat in the back corner, watching Rulalin.

"Dinner," Rulalin said calmly, placing the food between the bars and setting it down on the floor of the cage.

Benjiah didn't answer and didn't move.

Rulalin walked back to the table, picking it up and moving it over to the cage. He set it down and returned for his chair. When he had settled in, he started to eat his food, pouring a cup of water and setting it likewise between the slats.

"See," he said a few moments later as he swallowed a mouthful of bread, "the food is quite all right. If I wished to kill you, I would have done so already."

Benjiah didn't move at first, but as Rulalin continued to eat, saying nothing further, Benjiah crept over and took the things Rulalin had set down. He took them and returned to the corner, where he set about tearing into the food hungrily.

Rulalin finished his dinner and sat back, watching the boy eat. Benjiah remained as he had been, sitting quietly, eating, staring out of the cage at Rulalin. Rulalin felt the uneasiness coming over him. He was irked. It was the boy who was supposed to be feeling unnerved, not him.

Rulalin leaned forward, across the table. "The wall of earth, did you raise it?"

Benjiah chewed on his supper and didn't answer. Rulalin returned his stare. He had known he might not get answers or cooperation this time. He would still ask the questions, though. Who could know which question might be *the* question, the question that would open the flood gates and get the boy talking?

"Was the staff Valzaan's? I thought I recognized the shattered fragments as they were being burned."

He emphasized the last few words clearly, and yet, if the boy was at all disconcerted by the fiery fate of the staff's remains, he didn't show it. He lifted his cup and drank.

"How'd you come by it, anyway? No one else want it?"

Silence.

"I don't suppose it matters anymore, though, does it? The prophet's staff is gone, just like the prophet. What power it might have contained is now lost forever, like its former owner."

Benjiah put the last piece of bread in his mouth and chewed. When he had finished eating, he drank what was left of the water and set the cup down.

"Would you like some more?" Rulalin asked, raising the pitcher and filling his own cup. He lifted the cup then and drank.

Benjiah neither answered nor moved.

"Aren't you afraid for Amaan Sul and for your mother?"

Benjiah shifted his position somewhat, but Rulalin couldn't tell if it was his question that had gotten to the boy. He thought that perhaps he had seen a bit of Benjiah's interior wall come down, but if he had, Benjiah's quick recovery had kept him from being certain of it. To be sure, the boy regained the same look of calm he had worn all the way through the brief dinner and interview.

"If you are afraid," Rulalin said, slipping out of the chair and stooping by the slats of the cage, "Don't be. As far as it lies with me, I will see that no harm comes to her, or to you—if you help me."

Benjiah had followed Rulalin's move from the chair to the ground beside the cage, but still he did not reply. He sat, and he watched.

"Think on it," Rulalin finished, standing again and moving the table off to the side. He walked over to the flaps and called to the soldiers waiting outside. He then turned back to the cage. "Don't worry, you aren't going far away, but I thought some fresh cold air might help you to think clearly so you can be more helpful the next time I ask you my questions. Enjoy."

The soldiers entered the tent, and securing the cage carefully on all sides, they lifted it from the ground and carried it out into the night.

Benjiah felt the cold keenly as the men carried the cage outside. He had heard Rulalin talking about it with the man he called Soran that morning and felt it sweep in as the flaps opened, but the tent had been a relative refuge. Now he was outside, and he felt for himself the chill as it penetrated his thin tunic and pants. He had lost his cloak somewhere in the process of being moved into the enemy's camp, and he doubted that his captors would be very sympathetic to his current predicament.

The cage bounced up and down as the soldiers carried it, and he worried that too much of this might make him sick. He needn't have been worried though, as his ride was fairly brief. Not thirty spans away from the front of Rulalin's tent, a couple of supply wagons sat empty. The soldiers set the cage down beside these, and all but a pair of them moved off through the camp. The two that appeared to have been given the task of guarding him took seats on the edge of one of the wagons nearby, turning their backs on him.

Sitting, he drew his knees to his chin to try to stay warm. At least he wasn't wet, he thought. Then he realized what was different. There was no rain. Under the cover of the cage's solid roof, he hadn't noticed it at first. He held his hand out of the slat and felt the beautiful absence. No raindrops spattering on his skin or drumming the wood. The night was cold but dry, and he hoped that the rain had ceased to fall on the other side of the river also.

Benjiah's heart rejoiced. He realized of course that it was entirely likely that the cessation of the rain was Cheimontyr's doing, but he still took the end of the storm as a blessing. That plus the coming of Spring Rise, even if it didn't yet feel like spring, were signs of hope no matter how small, and he needed them now more than ever.

He peered up out of the bars at the nighttime sky. He could see no stars. The rain had stopped but the clouds remained. He sighed. He would have liked to see the stars, and even more so the sun the following day, but perhaps he'd have to wait for that. It would be worth it when it came, of that he was sure.

As he thought about the sun, shining brightly in the sky, he found it hard to see the return of the sun as anything but defeat for the enemy. Perhaps the rain coming and going was at Cheimontyr's command and part of his plan, but there seemed to be something antithetical about the sun to the giant's being that made Benjiah doubt the Vulsutyrim would let it show itself if he could help it.

He shook his head, leaning back against the slats. That was silly. Whatever Cheimontyr desired, surely the Nolthanim at least, if not the Malekim and Black Wolves, would desire the return of the sun some day. Of course, Benjiah realized that if Malek's hosts prevailed in this war, the future of Kirthanin would be charted according to Malek's own personal desire, not that of any of his servants. To that Benjiah could not speak or even hazard a guess. What Malek might want or not want with regard to the sun, Benjiah did not know.

Benjiah looked up at the solid roof of the cage. He thought of all the days and nights he had walked, ridden and slept without covering above his head. League after league, he would have paid almost any price to have shelter, and now that he was a captive in this cage, there was no rain.

Reflecting on being inside the cage brought to mind Rulalin's offer: protection for Benjiah and for his mother, though at a price. As he thought about what Rulalin had said, he honestly didn't know if the condition "if you help me" applied to the entire offer or just to himself. Rulalin might have been saying he was going to help Benjiah's mother, regardless. There was no way of knowing now what the man meant, and even if Rulalin's intentions were clear, how could Benjiah trust him? The man had killed his father in Sulare in cold blood; why should Benjiah think his own life would be spared?

He thought of his mother and Amaan Sul. What remained of the men under Caan and the others would arrive safely, he hoped, but he would not be among them. That would be hard for her, but she would have to be strong and clear her mind for the decisions before them. Amaan Sul was not a city built for sieges, especially not of the kind Malek's hosts would bring. Benjiah couldn't imagine how the city would escape, especially if he was here, rendered useless, seemingly without any of the power and strength he had so recently wielded.

He tried again to summon some form of it to push apart the slats of his cage, but he felt nothing. The light and heat that had flowed through his body beside the river and in the dragon tower did not come. Perhaps the power had come from the staff, or at least through it. Whatever had happened, he could not summon any miraculous deliverance. He hadn't even been as yet successful in connecting with a windhover to see what was going on in the world. Perhaps he had served his purpose. Perhaps Allfather was finished with him.

He lay down. Still cold, he curled up on his side. He didn't really believe, deep down, that Allfather would just abandon him. He had known that staying on the southern shore of the Kalamin might mean capture or worse, and he had stayed willingly. He would face what came next with courage and without fear, knowing that Allfather could deliver him if He chose but that He was not obligated to do so.

His mind drifted again to his mother. Rulalin had spoken about her with a strange earnestness. Benjiah had felt the man playing with him, testing him as he asked his questions. He had known that Rulalin would like answers, but that he hadn't really expected any. Benjiah had known this before the men came strutting in to carry him out, but his relocation had certainly confirmed it. His punishment for failing to respond had been determined before the interrogation began. And yet, when Rulalin had slipped from his seat and stooped by the cage, staring in, Benjiah had seen in his eyes something else. If he had not known better than to trust Rulalin, he would have called it sincerity. The more he thought about it, the more he thought he was right. Rulalin had probably believed that he was offering Benjiah comfort, but his comfort was not comforting. The last person in the world to whom Benjiah would entrust his mother's safety and well being was Rulalin Tarasir. Surely the man knew that. Maybe that was why he had added that Benjiah's own well-being and possibly his mother's might depend on Benjiah's help. That part, at least, had likely been intended as a threat. Rulalin must know that he need not remind Benjiah of all people what he was capable of. If he could aid Rulalin in order to save his mother and yet maintain his honor, he would, but Benjiah couldn't imagine such a scenario. He would need to be careful with this man, who seemed to want to show Benjiah in successive moments that he was a friend, and then remind him that he was the family's greatest enemy. He would need to be careful indeed.

The rain was pouring. Benjiah stood upon a plain, and all around him the rain fell heavily. It wasn't night, but the sky was dark. Lightning flashed horizontally through the clouds and thunder rolled across the sky.

The plain disappeared, as did the rain. Instead, Benjiah found himself in darkness, total darkness. He was dry and hot, his clothes soaked with sweat. A surge of unbelievably bright light illuminated everything. His own eyes were almost burned by the intensity of it. Then, as quickly and as the light had come it was gone, and Benjiah was no longer in darkness.

He was squatting in a cage. He knew the cage now. Every line on every slat seemed familiar. He reached over with his fingers and felt the rough sides of the slats nearest to him. He ran them down along it, and a sharp jab of pain erupted in his fingertip as a long slender splinter sunk under his skin.

The cage also disappeared. The great white city emerged all around him. It was always this way. Always the rain. Always the light. Always the cage. Always the city. This time, though, when he closed his eyes the city did not disappear. He waited.

He was always given a glimpse and only a glimpse. Every time he had tried to move or turn around, the city vanished. He stood still now, his eyes closed, enjoying the incomparable feel of warm sunlight on his face, wondering how long it and the city would remain.

After a long time, he decided that he might as well try. He turned slowly, looking at the buildings that rimmed the great open square. They didn't go away. He kept turning. Soon he had turned so far that he could no longer see the portion of the city revealed at first. He had his back to the square entirely, and off in the distance, rising above the other buildings, he could see a great hall-like structure towering. He was curious to go see it, but he didn't dare move. He was afraid that he might lose this.

He couldn't turn much more without moving his feet, so he decided to risk just the smallest of pivots. He shifted his weight and slid his feet ever so slightly. Nothing changed. He kept turning so that he was now facing back onto the square. A long, low wall ran in a gigantic circle in the center of the square. It had probably housed a reflecting pool or something like that once, or perhaps it would again one day.

Having turned all the way around, the vision of the city did not disappear. He had moved his feet a little bit; dare he move them more? He took a step into the square. His feet echoed on the smooth, white pavement. The sound died away, but the pavement remained, as did the city erected upon it. He relaxed and began to walk, slowly but surely, moving across the open square to the low circular wall.

He bent down and felt the smooth stone. The splinter and the pain were gone from his finger. When he looked more carefully, he could see no trace of either, or of the blood that must surely be flowing from the wound. The rock was warm but not hot, and his fingers lingered upon it.

He started to walk beside the wall. The pavement inside the circle seemed just like the pavement on the outside. He felt the urge to cross over the wall.

Do not cross over, a voice said inside of him.

"Why not?" he asked out loud.

Because you are only meant now to see this place. You are only here in seeming. When you are really here, you will know what to do.

"But how can I come here? I've never seen this place before and don't know for sure where I am."

You will come here the same way you have gone everywhere your path has taken you.

"How is that?"

I will bring you.

"What am I to do?"

Here the sacrifice is to be made. Here the blade will be laid down. Here the binding will be broken. Here will be both the end and the beginning, and all things will be made new.

A rumbling shook the ground and Benjiah was thrown to his knees beside the wall. The ground and the city quaked, but neither was destroyed. Water exploded out of the earth beyond the wall and flowed like a great waterfall in reverse up into the sky. Benjiah looked up as a wall of water fell cascading upon his face.

2

FLOODWATERS

TAL KUVARIN ALLOWED his good hand to dangle in the water beside the skiff. This was no small act of the will, as the floodwaters were still murky, allowing little visibility below the surface except in rare glimpses granted to the attentive eye. This cloudiness in the water combined with the image of the great black beast that had come slithering up the Barunaan made it an act of faith to allow his fingers to dip below the surface. Even thinking about it now made him want to snatch his hand back to his chest, but that would be giving in to an irrational fear. He wanted to demonstrate not least of all to himself that despite the inexplicable events of the last week, he was not trapped by that fear.

He looked up from the water's surface and glanced about him. For almost as far as the eye could see, the water's surface was smooth and placid. Only the occasionally protruding rooftop or piece of random floating furniture signaled anything amiss in this body of water, which a week ago had been no body of water at all, but the center of Peris Mil.

Glancing back over his shoulder he found Garin, his bushy black beard streaked with grey and large muscular arms rhythmically stroking the oars in their locks, looking silently at him. He knew that Garin would go as long as he wanted to go, that he would row until night fell upon them if asked, but he also knew that Garin would be wondering by now whether it was wise to keep going. They had been out twice already today, searching as best as they were able in different quadrants of the flooded town. Where exactly, though, had they already been? With no streets or signs to mark their way, it was hard to know if they had been in this precise place before. Everywhere they went there were buildings protruding in varying degrees from the water with the same or similar collections of floating debris, the flotsam and jetsam of lives washed away in one terrible day.

His whole life he had lived in Peris Mil, but he'd never seen a day like that day. The rain had been falling for months, of course, and flooding was a problem already. They had some success in diverting the runoff and holding back the rising Barunaan. Floods were nothing new to a town born of the Barunaan, so work on the river wall began long before the first floodwaters came. Long and mighty, the great wall and all its devices for relieving water pressure grew with the rising challenge. For a long time the town was confident of its ability to stay ahead of disaster.

Their confidence began to flag a few weeks earlier, when materials for the wall and equipment to handle the challenge presented by its ever-increasing height began to dissipate. A break in the town came a few days before the actual break in the wall. Tal could almost imagine he had heard it, an audible groan and sigh that ran like a fissure through the streets closest to the river, up into the town center and beyond. Suddenly, townspeople gave up hope and were flowing out of the town even as the water welled up outside the wall, waiting to flow in. It will be soon, Tal thought when he saw people spilling out of their homes with hastily packed cases and, in some instances, whole carts of belongings.

In the end, most of these carts were abandoned. People left behind the cumbrances that would have drowned them as surely as if they'd been tied to them and dropped into the Kellisor Sea. They made their way one by one through the teeming masses up and out of town, heading on foot beyond the eastern perimeter until they believed they had reached ground high enough to be safe.

At least, most of them squeezed out in this way. Some remained, because they believed in the floodwall, or because they believed the flood wouldn't reach their home, or because they couldn't leave behind the things they treasured, things which by now had been swallowed by the angry river. Tal and Garin were in search of these who had remained behind.

"I think we should go a little further southwest, just to see what we can," Tal said to Garin.

"It will be dark in a couple hours, maybe less," Garin said, continuing to row.

"I know. We'll see what we can, and then we'll head back."

Garin nodded.

Tal turned back. He had seen the wall break, though from a distance. Having had the presence of mind to drag several boats, including the small skiff they were now using, out of Peris Mil in advance of the mass exodus, he had remained with Garin near the town's edge in one of them, hoping to be of service to any who fled at the last minute. Pieces of stone and rock shot into the town with remarkable force, crashing with sounds like thunder into the buildings they had been erected to protect. It was as if the wall had held as long as it could and all at once surrendered to the unconquerable force of the river. Through the great holes water erupted, cascading into the low-lying areas of Peris Mil by the docks.

This state of affairs lasted only a few moments, for as they had watched, a great section of the wall was ripped in half by a pair of massive black hands. A great and fearful form rose above the top of the wall, the enormous head of some nightmarish creature in the flooded Barunaan. Hysterical screams echoed throughout the town as water poured in like a raging waterfall. The rest of the river wall crumbled with little resistance, and the raging water came behind it, smashing to bits the closest buildings, some already weakened by the stone projectiles the river had spit out. Onward the wall of water came, sweeping over many a fleeing man or woman, though Tal and Garin were able to save a few. Eventually the water had come as far as they were, and their small boat was buoyed up by the rising tide. At moments that day, Garin lost control of the boat and they were tossed about by the floodwaters in such a way that Tal had wondered if they would themselves be victims of it.

At one point, as they swirled around and around, caught by some strange whirlpool between two buildings, he looked up at the silhouette of the great dark creature as it towered above the town. The waters were leveling out, and he saw the creature from his exposed midriff and above, shiny and slick as it stretched upward out of the Barunaan. He remembered it all too well. *What in the name of the Mountain is that?* The thought came at that moment and never really left. By the time Garin got the boat under control, the creature was gone, and he had not seen it since.

Now, several days later, the town still lay largely underwater, and there was still no sign of the water receding. Of course, the rain that had fallen steadily for months stopped only the day before, and Tal could not reasonably expect the waters to recede for many days—if indeed the rain stayed away. Spring

Rise, which normally signaled the coming of the rainy season, had ironically marked the end of the storm, and he and everyone else hoped it was truly the end.

"Five days, Garin," Tal said.

Garin nodded.

"Two days since we found the last living person out here," Tal added, almost to himself. "Maybe I'm just wasting our time."

"There's not much else for two old men like us to be doing," Garin answered. "We might as well spend our days doing something rooted in hope. There is enough despair among the townspeople as it is. When we stop coming out here, when we stop searching, then they'll have to accept that no one else is ever coming back with us."

It was Tal's turn to nod. In the distance, he scanned rooftops protruding above the water. "Was there anything else we could have done, Garin?"

"When?"

"To evacuate those who wouldn't leave."

"I don't think so. You told them what they should have already known, that the flood was going to come and that their homes were not likely to survive. They denied the truth of what you were saying long before we came around to their homes and actually said it."

"They wouldn't leave," Tal added, "and now most of them are buried here. The houses they thought would be their havens are now their tombs."

The men rowed on, drawing closer to the rooftops, with no sign of life. As they passed through a cluster of these taller buildings, Tal signaled to Garin to start turning the boat around. "Let's head back out through the southern parts of town."

Garin swung the front of the skiff around so that the prow was pointed almost due west. It seemed to Tal that Garin's even strokes accelerated as they started back. He couldn't say that he minded. They'd spent almost every waking hour of this day in the boat, and his own aching body longed for rest.

There it was again, coming from their left, farther south than they could see. The skiff glided through the water.

"Garin, did you hear that?"

"Maybe, but it was faint."

"Yes, but if we both heard it, it must be something."

Without needing to be told, Garin swung the skiff south. They pushed deeper into the flood zone, toward the south road that led out of Peris Mil to the ferry, perhaps. They were headed in the direction of the sound, what might be a waste of time brought on by wishful thinking, or perhaps a miracle beyond all hope.

Every few strokes Garin paused. He held the oars still above the water, and they both listened while the boat glided. For several minutes they proceeded this way, but they heard nothing. "Do you think we've come too far, Garin?" Tal asked, feeling anxious that there might be someone out here, someone nearby, but as lost to them as though he or she were leagues away.

"I don't know," Garin answered, pausing in his stroke again, "it may be."

They listened. From somewhere off to their right there came a slight splash. They turned and peered west of their position. A second small splash reached them across the water, then they heard someone cough and gasp.

"There is someone," Tal called excitedly, leaning so far to the right that he almost fell out when Garin swung the boat around vigorously. They were soon gliding in the direction of the sounds, and in the distance Tal saw movement.

As they drew nearer, Tal was better able to pick out the pieces of the scene. A small figure, what he eventually came to realize was a boy, was struggling to climb up out of the water onto a large table floating upside down. On one end, two gracefully curved legs protruded upward. The boy was struggling mightily to get onto the table, in part because one of his hands was clasping a large, soaking-wet sack.

The child, perhaps ten or eleven, managed to get up just in time to see the men approaching. His eyes grew wide with wonder, perhaps not willing to acknowledge at first what he was seeing.

"Are you all right, lad?" Tal called out to him.

"You're real?" the boy responded.

"Yes, of course we are," Tal answered, trying to sound soothing and welcoming.

"I dreamed I was rescued last night," the boy said, "and the night before, but each time I woke up all alone. Am I going to wake up now?"

"No," Tal said as they drew up alongside the table. "You aren't going to wake up now."

He reached over and took the boy's free hand. "We really are here, and we're going to take you to land."

"Land?" the boy said, his eyes growing wider. "There's land?"

"Yes," Tal said, settling the boy and the sack to which he was still so desperately clinging in the bottom of the boat. "It isn't so very far. We'll be there in less than an hour."

At this the boy began to cry, first, with little sobs and tears running down his face. Then, as Tal took his head and cradled it gently, the tears began to really come. The sobs echoed across the water, and Tal shook with the boy's violent shuddering.

"It's all right," Tal whispered. "You're all right now. The nightmare is over. You're safe."

The boy's sobs slowed for a moment. He opened his mouth to speak, but he couldn't regain control of his voice.

"Don't worry about it now, son," Tal said gently. "You can tell me later."

"My mom and dad," the boy gasped, and then the sobs came even harder.

Tal let the boy bury his face against his tunic, and most of the rest of the way back, the boy cried and clung to him.

As they drew nearer to dry land, the number of houses and buildings that remained upright of course increased. They rowed past these buildings through the streets like they were canals, seeking the place where the water ended and the land began. By this point, the boy had stopped crying, though he remained curled up against the grandfatherly figure who held him.

"We're almost there," Tal said at last, breaking the long silence. "What's your name, son?"

"Peran," the boy replied.

"What are you clinging to so tightly, Peran?" Tal asked, pointing down to the sack lying at the bottom of the boat. The smell coming from the sack was pungent, but Tal had left it alone.

Peran lifted the sack and handed it to Tal, looking almost ashamed. "It was all I had to eat. I, well, I didn't know what else to do."

Tal opened the sack and a waft of spoiled cheese greeted him. He almost gagged but controlled himself, peering in at the soggy remains of the moldy cheeses that had kept Peran alive.

"You did what you needed to do, Peran," Tal said, closing the sack hurriedly. "Fortunately, though, you won't be needing this anymore," he said, heaving the sack over his shoulder and out into the water.

They both watched the sack hit, begin to fill with water, and partially sink as it floated away

"How old are you, Peran?" Tal asked.

"Eleven."

"How long were you on that table?"

"Since the waters came."

"The whole time?"

"Yes, sir," the boy answered.

"Well, Peran," Tal replied, looking the boy steadily in the eyes. "Tonight you must thank Allfather for your life, for surely only a miracle could have kept you alive for five days and nights out there."

"Yes, sir," the boy said again.

"Where were you when the waters came?"

"Outside our house."

"And where is"—Tal corrected himself—"where was your house?"

"Between Peris Mil and the Kellisor Sea."

"What?" Tal exclaimed. "Where exactly?"

"We live halfway between the northwestern corner of Peris Mil and the southern shores of the Kellisor Sea," Peran answered, looking uncertainly at his rescuer.

"My boy, you've floated for days and for leagues upon a table that was for you as seaworthy as the largest of ships. I can hardly imagine your voyage, but I am very glad that we found you."

Garin added, "You must be quite a gifted sailor, my boy. You can be my first mate any time."

Then, for the first time since they'd found him, Peran smiled. He sat less timidly in the front of the skiff, and when they reached at last a place where the boat ran aground, he hopped out and helped the men pull it well up from the water's edge.

"Food isn't exactly plentiful these days," Tal started as they began walking slowly. Peran's initial exuberance had given way to some shaky strides. His body had long been tossed by the waves, and his legs had to remember how to walk. "Still," he continued, "I think we can afford to be a little extravagant with you tonight, Peran. What do you think?"

"I'm very hungry, sir," Peran said, hesitantly.

"I guess you are."

By this point a handful of people had seen the two men and Peran coming their way. Their conversation stopped as they realized what they were seeing. They started to run excitedly toward the threesome, and Peran drew closer to Tal. "Sir, what is your name?" he asked, looking up into Tal's kindly face.

"My name is Tal Kuvarin."

"Thank you for saving me, Master Kuvarin."

"You are most welcome."

They were surrounded now, and Tal ended up telling Peran's story several times. Even when he finished, word continued to spread. He could hear men and women telling those newly drawn to the excitement what was going on. Peran was instantly a celebrity, and soon a whole handful of women had taken him under their many wings. Tal smiled and waved as they led the boy off to feed him and find him some suitable clothes.

He turned to Garin. "Rooted in hope, you said. We are fortunate that hopefulness was not a prerequisite for our success. I had given up hope entirely and despaired of finding anyone at all."

"Me too."

"Let us remember this lesson, Garin," Tal said, "should other things seem as hopeless."

Garin nodded. "We will remind each other."

"Yes, now let's find some food. Hope is hungry work."

They strode away through the buildings surrounding the edge of the water. These structures untouched by the floodwaters were few and full to bursting with refugees. Tal and Garin walked past them all and out past the edge of town. Tents, as many as could be salvaged, including many from the Kuvarin estate a couple leagues west of Peris Mil, had been erected to shelter the rest of the refugees. They had been full to bursting too, but with the end of the rain, some now slept outside, helping to alleviate the crowding. Again Tal Kuvarin found himself silently praying that the rain would stay away for a good long while.

Eventually, they found not only a small dinner for themselves but a relatively comfortable seat on a pair of rocks some distance from the nearest tent. Though they had been alone most of the day, neither man craved to be part of the crowd. For Tal Kuvarin, eldest Novaana of the region and in many ways the leader of this disparate crowd, some distance from the others was necessary to have any peace and quiet at the end of a long day. It would be easier for Tal to spend more time among the others if only the meeting scheduled for the following morning wasn't weighing so heavily upon him.

"What's on your mind, Tal?" Garin asked.

"Tomorrow morning."

"No use worrying about that until you have to," Garin said.

"I know." Tal sighed, but with a smile. Garin knew him well, very well indeed. "It isn't really what will be said at the meeting that is bothering me, but the spirit. If we can hold together, even if we can't agree, it'll be all right."

Garin looked at him soberly. "And the likelihood of that?"

Tal shrugged. "Not very likely, I suppose."

"No," Garin answered, "not very."

Tal stretched, feeling the small of his back with his hands. His years seemed to come upon him all of a sudden. His bad hand hung almost useless at his side, and his good hand ached from overuse. "I'm too old for days like these, Garin. If only they had come upon us in my youth. Then I'd have been ready for the challenge."

"Perhaps, Tal, but no one asked us if we were ready, did they?"

"No, they didn't."

"We're not young anymore, and the battles of the young are not for us anymore. We just need to do what our limited strength and wisdom allows."

"Indeed, and the rest we leave not just to the young but to Allfather," Tal answered. "The insoluble tasks of this age are, as always, in His hands and His alone."

"Very true," Garin said, standing and stretching. "Well sir, it is time for this old man to get some sleep. A full day of rowing takes its toll."

"I'm sorry I'm not of more help."

"Don't be silly, Tal," Garin answered, "I'm not complaining. Just ready for sleep is all."

"Of course, Garin. Thanks for your tireless efforts. Peran really has you to thank for his life."

"He was fortunate, as were we."

"Maybe we'll be fortunate tomorrow."

"Maybe." Garin smiled, patted Tal on the shoulder, and turned away.

The sky was growing dark, and Tal remained behind for a few moments. He looked up into the night sky, reflecting on the absence of rain. He wished he had some idea what was going on. So much rain for so long, then the wall crumbles, the city floods, and the rain goes away. Then there was the dark creature looming above the impending flood, and the armies of Malek unleashed upon Kirthanin from the Mountain. So much all around them, and yet there had been no word of Malek's movements for weeks. They were cut off completely from any knowledge of the wider world, cut off and blind. Perhaps the end of all things wasn't far away. Maybe he would live to see the prophecies come true.

His heart sank. That was, at its root, a hopeful thought, but this seemed even further out of reach than Peran's deliverance. It was more likely by far that his days would end in darkness, with Malek on the throne of Avalione. The day would come, Tal believed, when Allfather would liberate Kirthanin from its curse and from Malek, but there was no guarantee that day would come soon. For all he knew, the land would groan under Malek's rule for years and years to come.

Tal Kuvarin watched the sun rising in the east. He never slept late any more, even if his day was empty, though of course this one wasn't. In the silent hours, the stillness before dawn, he always found himself alone with his thoughts while the world around him slept.

Fourth Watch was drawing to a close and First Hour was coming, the start of a new day, though it almost certainly would bear the marks of the same old arguments. Ever since the townspeople of Peris Mil had scrambled up the wet streets to these heights and watched their homes being washed away, the differences had emerged. The same people voicing their same concerns, over and over. They sometimes chose different words or a different approach, but always their message was the same. He could save them all a lot of time by having them come to the tent of meeting and sit while he summarized briefly what each had come to say.

He smiled at the thought. He could concisely cover it all in perhaps half an hour. He could do away with the dramatic flourishes and emotional appeals. He could avoid the petty disputes and endless vying for the chance to be the center of attention. He could deal as fairly as possible with all the alternatives and state clearly and plainly the pros and cons.

He checked himself there. He wasn't without opinion in these matters, so it was perhaps wishful thinking to believe he could be equanimous. His convictions shaded his ability to moderate fairly. He sighed as the happy image slipped away. There was nothing for it but to let each man or woman speak for themselves and hope for some voluntary restraint.

Before too many people began to stir, he appropriated a meager breakfast and started up the road leading from the town to the tent they'd been using for their meetings. Even though the breakfast was meager, he couldn't help but wonder if he wouldn't soon be looking back at these days as times of plenty. So much food had been ruined by the flood. He personally owned multiple warehouses by the river that had contained stores of food stockpiled from the previous autumn. As the rain had continued unabated, the town council rationed its food supplies in case the spring harvests were effected. As autumn became winter, it was increasingly evident that there might not be a spring harvest at all. Now much of that stockpile had been washed away, and even with the sudden end to the rain, their hope for a spring harvest had not returned.

As he passed through to the outskirts of the makeshift community, he saw Garin waiting by the side of the road, rubbing the sleep from his eyes. His stocky friend's curly black and grey hair was unkempt and his beard as scraggly as a bramble bush. Tal could tell as he approached that Garin, by far the heavier sleeper, had struggled to be up to meet him this morning. This was no surprise, as Garin had rowed almost without break all the previous day, and even his powerful arms must have ached by the time they returned. At least the meeting would afford him a time of physical rest, even if it was more unpleasant than the skiff in other ways.

"Good morning, Garin."

"Tal," Garin answered, stroking his beard. "I thought you were an early riser. I've been waiting here for ages."

"Sure," Tal laughed. "By *ages* of course you mean at most a quarter of an hour, right?"

"That's ages at this hour of the morning."

Tal laughed. "My apologies, friend. I see the error of my ways."

"Good," Garin said with mock gruffness. "Now let's get on with it."

"Indeed, let's."

They headed off along the sloppy road. Tal wondered how much time would need to pass without rain before the saturated ground could dry. Would it ever be dry again? As they walked, water seemed to ooze up from the mud as if the pressure from their footsteps forced the earth to yield some of its watery store.

Aside from the squishing of their feet, they moved on together in quietness through the cold morning. One of the things Tal most appreciated about Garin was his economy with words. Tal was not, at least in his own estimation, given to excessive discourse, but Garin was generally a man of only occasional expression. It wasn't for lack of ability, for Garin could be eloquent when he chose to be, he just didn't choose to be very often.

Eventually they reached the tent of meeting. The benches and chairs scattered within were haphazardly arranged and bare. It would not be so quiet for long. Tal walked in and took a seat on one of the empty chairs.

"The calm before the storm," Garin said as he pulled up a nearby bench and lay down upon it, closing his eyes.

"Yes, but where will the storm blow us, I wonder?" Tal answered, but only half out loud. Garin didn't answer and in a matter of moments, he was snoring happily away.

As others arrived, not all that much later, a few decided to move the meeting out into the open space just beyond the tent. Without rain to plague them, some reasoned, why not? Besides, with the tent between them and the road, they at least had the illusion of privacy even if they lacked the real thing.

When most of the expected group had assembled, a quiet fell upon them. Tal surveyed the three to four dozen men and women. They were what remained of the town council, along with other prominent citizens who had asserted their intention to be part of whatever decision-making process would govern their next move. Whatever their reason for being there, Tal could sense in many of them, in their eyes and in their body language, the same thing. They were all afraid, and after all they had been through and lost and might even now be facing, they had reason to fear. This wasn't going to be easy or pleasant.

Tal opened the meeting and moderated, and as he could have predicted, two basic options were pressed over and over, though from different angles and with slightly different details. There was of course the faction that wanted to stay. These were perhaps more unified than the faction that wanted to go, but not by a whole lot. Some who wanted to stay thought that they needed only to wait for the waters to go down and then rebuild the town exactly as it had been exactly where it had been, but others thought this predicament contained a larger lesson about being too close to the river and hoped to raise Peris Mil anew here, a safe distance from the water. Supply wagons could run with regularity down to the water's edge, to the docks and wharfs, minimizing the inconvenience. Peris Mil would then be flood-proof, a town born of the river but a safe distance from it, a town that could reach out via the river to the whole land, but a town beyond the river's reach.

Of course, those who wanted to go thought both of these ideas were equally ludicrous. They believed that the whole rebuilding faction was living either too far in the future, in a world where Malek had already been defeated and cast down, or too far in the past, in a world where Malek had not yet come forth. For surely, they argued, any sensible person would see that to simply remain and rebuild was to ignore reality. Malek had come forth. Word of his passage through the Erefen Marshes southward had come some time ago. Refugees had come from Werthanin across the Kellisor Sea to Peris Mil. Rumors had come as well not long ago that dragons had been seen overhead and that mighty armies were passing northward on the eastern side of the Barunaan. How then could anyone speak of staying? How could anyone speak of rebuilding and life as it had been? They were caught blind beside the river and below the Kellisor. Their doom could come upon them in a moment where they were, and they would not have anywhere to go or any plan to resist.

Furthermore, some of them had seen the dark creature that Tal had seen. They had seen their destroyer, and though they did not come out and say it explicitly, Tal could see it in their eyes. They didn't want to stay so close to where the monster had been. They didn't want to face the damage the receding waters would reveal. They didn't want to face the losses and the ghosts. They didn't want to carry the fear of the thing, the nameless terror that must haunt their dreams as it did Kuvarin's.

But this was as far as this faction agreed, for though they could each articulate the need to go, they could not agree about where to go. Some argued that they should go west, as far from the river as possible. The river was a trap, a barrier they couldn't cross. They should find a quiet place far away from this waterway, as far from the center of Kirthanin as possible, a place where Malek wouldn't even think to look. Others said they should go southwest and find refuge in the large and spacious grasslands of Suthanin. Rumor had it Malek had already passed and perhaps would not pass through again. Even if he did, it was a place affording many avenues of retreat. If trouble came, they could evade it from there. Still others called upon them not to forsake the river altogether. The river was what they all knew. The river could still be their friend, especially as the waters might now begin to recede. After all, if the land wasn't going to yield its harvest, the river still might. They could feed their children from the river. Could the muddy and trampled centerlands of Suthanin do that?

All told, the conversation was the endless argument that Tal had feared. Every man or woman advocated his own vision, again and again, hammering away at the same points and ignoring the counterpoints of his neighbor. By now it was midday and Tal could see no end to the bickering.

He raised his hand to stop a developing squabble. The two men primarily involved gradually quieted down, as did the supporting parties. "Good citizens of Peris Mil," Tal said gently. "I wonder if I might say a few words? Until now I have been content to watch and to listen, but I can see plainly, as I'm sure you all can as well, that consensus is unlikely to come today. Allow me, if you will, to tell you where I am on these questions and then to encourage you all to agree to let it go for today, to go and think on what you have heard here. Consider carefully and thoughtfully the objections of your brothers and sisters, and come back with a spirit more open to real fruitful dialog. Will you hear me?"

"We will," several of the men and women said, and most of the others nodded and waited.

"I am seventy-four years old," Tal began, "and I cannot stop any of you from leaving if it is your will to leave. But, as for me, I think we should stay. I not only think we should stay, I think we should stay together. Whatever we decide, I would exhort you all to embrace the importance of staying together. We are Peris Mil. The buildings are destroyed and washed away, but the buildings were not Peris Mil. The Mound has likely been leveled by the flood, but even the Mound was not Peris Mil. We are the town. If we break, then Peris Mil breaks.

"Some of you have rightly pointed out that we are blind here and could be trapped. But isn't it also true that, lacking clear and certain information on where Malek might be, we are blind wherever we go? We could flee right into his path if we choose our next step poorly.

"My point is not that there might not be better alternatives to staying put, but that we don't know what they are. Should we go west? How do we know what we will find? Refugees came to us from Werthanin, bringing word of devastation stretching across the breadth of that land. How do we know the west coast of Suthanin has survived? And even if the scourge of Malek has left it untouched, what of the floodwaters? If the Barunaan did this to us, what have the ocean waters done to the coast?

"And what of the centerlands? Having been trampled, what food can they offer? What shelter? If their only advantage is that they are a place easy to flee, why go in the first place? As for heading south along the river, what does this do but take us from what little solid shelter we now have? If we are in danger of being trapped by the river here, will we not also be in danger of being trapped by the river there? If the river affords our greatest hope for food, what could be better than to stay here where our knowledge of the river is greatest?

"I realize some of you feel strongly the urge to go away. I understand that. I too saw the creature that ripped our flood-wall to pieces. I too still feel the chill and the fear that he caused inside me. I both long and dread for the waters to go down, to see the town I love and what has become of it. I feel the urge to avert my eyes from its destruction, but I also feel the urge to rebuild it.

"I ask you to stay, at least for now. Perhaps Allfather will show us clearly at some point that it is time to go, but until that time, I think we should be patient and seek His leading."

"Allfather has abandoned us."

"Where was He when the flood came?"

"Enough!" Tal shouted over the few who had objected. "There will be no more disparaging of Allfather, not while I have breath in my body and strength to stop it. Don't be fools! Allfather owes us nothing and has granted us long years of peace in this place. Will you now turn on him because we have experienced the sorrow that entered this world when Allfather's wise and just commands were disobeyed? Whether Malek triumphs for a day or for a thousand years, never doubt that Allfather is in control and is working out His purpose for this world. You would do well to be found faithful, to be about the business day by day that has been laid before you."

No one spoke. Tal glared around the gathering, feeling anger boil within him. As a younger man he might have dealt with them more gently, but the older he grew, he seemed to have less and less patience for any suggestion that Allfather didn't know His own business better than his creatures did.

The gathering did not last much longer. Most acknowledged, some begrudgingly, the need to "think about things" a little more, and while no definite time was set for a follow-up meeting, it was acknowledged that they needed one. And so the chairs and benches were gradually returned to the tent, and the people began to disperse.

"You kept pretty quiet," Tal said, turning to Garin in the now empty tent.

"You were doing fine," Garin answered. "Besides, we weren't really suffering from any want of opinions. I thought most every possibility was discussed, don't you?"

"Yes, and then some," Tal laughed.

A movement in the distance caught his eye, and both Tal and Garin turned to see a figure on horseback approaching not from the east, from Peris Mil, but from the west. The lone figure was riding hard along the road, drawing closer.

The two men strode out of the tent and down toward the road. "Do you see more coming behind?" Tal said, straining to look more closely.

"There's only one."

"That's strange," Tal said, "riding alone in open country in days like these."

"Yes."

"Did we send anyone to my estate recently?"

"No."

"Well, maybe someone went out for a ride this morning before we came to the meeting and is just now coming back."

"It's possible, I suppose."

Tal could see now that the rider was a man with white hair. He couldn't make out any features of his face yet, but the white hair was unmistakable.

"At least he doesn't look too ferocious," Tal added.

"No, not so much, but then again, look at us. We may not be much to look at, but we have some fight left in us I'd say."

"True, very true."

The rider was now not far, and he was drawing his horse to a halt having seen the two of them waiting beside the road. Tal started walking toward the man.

"Hello there," Tal called out.

"Do you not know me, Tal?" the man replied, dropping from his horse and stepping forward.

"Monias?" Tal asked, realizing suddenly why the man looked so familiar.

Monias stepped forward and threw his arms around Tal. "It is good to be here at last."

3

NOT TURNING BACK

"ELSORA IS DEAD."

Monias Andira and Tal Kuvarin walked together along the road, headed toward the makeshift settlement on the outskirts of Peris Mil. Garin had hurried in ahead to find a comfortable place for Monias to rest, but Tal stopped at Monias's words. "What?"

"Yes, she's returned to her maker."

Despite the self-control, Tal read the grief in his old friend's eyes. He should have seen it earlier. He had noticed something lying close behind the smile of greeting, but he hadn't recognized it for what it was. "Monias, I'm so sorry for your loss. In days like these, it is a hard burden to bear."

"These days aside," Monias answered, "I cannot conceive of any time when this burden could be lighter. I had thought that after Joraiem, any grief would be light by comparison, but this is not so. It is as if this blow opens the old wound and makes a new wound all of its own, leaving me with the pain of both."

Tal nodded slowly as he started moving again. He walked silently beside his friend, trusting that his presence more than his words might console. He had known loss in his time, and images of Larinda passed before him as he walked. In those days, those who loved him best said least, knowing that words fall hollow when the heart is ripped open and left raw. He would take his cue from Monias, who would speak of what he wished when he was ready.

"It was shortly after the celebration of the New Year," Monias said not long after. "That night, on Midwinter, she danced and smiled. It was so long since I had seen her that happy. For a brief moment, though, despite the storm and gloom and dark times we are living in, she pushed aside her maternal pains and she was Elsora again. She was the golden-haired girl I first met in Sulare, standing in the bright noonday of the Summerland with sunshine and laughter sparkling upon her face. It was glorious. She was glorious.

"By noon the following day, the fever had come upon her and her condition quickly deteriorated. She grew weak and pale, and despite the suddenness of it all, I knew she was slipping from me. I knew she was going where I could not follow. She died that night, during Second Watch.

"Near the end, she was conscious and mostly lucid for a time, and she asked me to call the children in. She insisted. I didn't know how to tell her they were far from home, so she asked for each of them by name. She asked for Brenim, for Kyril, and also for Joraiem. She seemed at the end quite unaware that she had sewn Joraiem's burial shroud herself, and I did not try to remind her."

Monias turned to Tal. "Was it wrong of me, Tal? To let her believe that Joraiem was alive and well? To let her believe her children were on their way when they had no knowledge of her sickness?"

"Monias," Tal said gently, "she was feverish and near death, she wouldn't have understood even had you tried to correct her."

Monias didn't say any more about it, but he seemed to Tal a little more relaxed, even relieved. "We buried her the next day, and as I watched the muddy earth take her in, I knew I couldn't stay in Dal Harat. I knew I would have to go. My children are out here somewhere, along with my grandchildren, my son-in-law, and my daughter-in-law. The world is on the verge of being swallowed in darkness, but I will face my own end and the end of this world, if it is coming, with my family if I can."

"Do you know where to look for them?"

"Evrim and Brenim were serving under Aljeron Balinor in the war with Fel Edorath, but I don't know where they are now. I know Malek's advance pushed the Werthanim army out to sea and southward, but what has become of them I do not know. I suspect Kyril and her girls were in Amaan Sul, likely with Wylla and Benjiah, so that is where I am headed. Wylla is almost certain to be in Amaan Sul still, making it the one fixed point that I can navigate by. I will start there if I can make it and decide what to do next depending on what I learn when I arrive."

Tal realized that the flooded Barunaan to the east and the Kellisor Sea to the north stood as seemingly insurmountable barriers to Monias, for even if the waters could be crossed in their current state, who would venture out as long as that creature lurked within? He kept quiet, though, knowing that this was not the time for that discussion. "How is Dal Harat? I mean, from what you say, it sounds like the village came through Malek's crossing of the Erefen Marshes unscathed."

"Not unscathed, but yes, Dal Harat came through."

"What happened?"

"The main body of Malek's army passed well to our east, but some of the outlying homes and farms were terrorized by

Black Wolves. Twelve people were killed, and much was plundered by men on horseback who swooped in after the wolves.

"The wolves were one thing, Tal, but to know that men, flesh and blood like you and me, were raiding on behalf of Malek and his minions—it was terrible. I tell you now, Tal, this remnant of the Nolthanim that fights with Malek must be accursed by Allfather. The Black Wolves and Malekim are little more than senseless beasts, if indeed they be any more, but men should know better."

"Men have followed Malek since his first rebellion, Monias. Their continued allegiance does not surprise me."

"Nor me," Monias answered, "but when I saw it personally, it enraged me. We should be enraged that men would serve Malek like faithful pets. The Nolthanim are traitors of old, and I can only hope that they will reap what they have sown."

"They may yet," Tal said. They approached the outlying tents, and Tal asked, cautiously, "Monias, you're very important to Dal Harat and its council. As much as you long to see your family, is it possible that your duty in these days lies more with Dal Harat than with them?"

Monias gazed straight ahead, but after a moment he looked up and placed his hand on Tal's shoulder. "You are a good friend to be willing to ask such a question. Even so, I do not think leaving Dal Harat was a mistake. I do not think myself so remarkable as to be indispensable to Dal Harat or any other place. There are many leaders there, though some have yet to understand it. At any rate, Tal, I'm sixty-nine years old. They weren't going to have me around forever. They might as well start learning to live without me, and I might as well spend what time and strength that is left to me with those who matter most. I have been over all these things many times in my mind. I am going to my children."

They could see on the horizon the many tents teeming with people. It was after midday now, and still the rain stayed away. Tal looked at Monias and nodded. "I know you well enough to know that you would have considered your people before you left. As a friend, but also as a member of the Assembly who often feels the weight of his responsibility and influence as you do, I had to ask, just in case. It is good to see you here, my friend. Let us find you some lunch and a place to rest."

"I would be most grateful," Monias said.

Monias sat, enjoying the feeling of being out of the saddle and surprisingly also enjoying the sight and sound of people. As he quietly observed the citizens of Peris Mil going about their business, trying still to make sense of the flood that leveled their homes, he felt a deep thirst inside being satisfied.

After Elsora's death, the people of Dal Harat, long his friends and neighbors, had sought to come around him and console him. He had allowed as many gestures as he thought he could bear, not because he needed any, but because he knew they did. What he most wanted was to be left alone to grieve, to stand in stillness before his house in the dark and feel the empty ache. He wanted to feel that unmitigated deep wound inside his heart without disturbance, for it was in those moments that he felt closest to the woman he had loved most.

When he had settled his affairs in Dal Harat, saying publicly that he did not know when he would be coming back, he prepared to leave. As he saddled his horse to go, he contemplated the long ride before him through rain and muck, for the roads were already terrible by that point and there was no sign of relief in the stormy skies. He found the thought of prolonged and solitary misery to be just the thing he desired. And yet, even as he allowed himself to wallow in his grief and sadness on the road, he hungered for the warmth of human contact, for the solidity of human touch, and the strange comfort of community. Now that he sat here, a broken man among a broken people, he knew that wherever his road took him and whatever he might find at the end of it, it was right and good to come here first.

Garin appeared, carrying a pair of plates and followed by Tal. Garin had changed little since the last time Monias had been to Peris Mil, though that was more than twenty-five years ago. The man had more grey in his hair and beard, yes, but he was still surprisingly lithe and agile for a man of his sturdy build. His very stature seemed to embody dependability, and Monias almost envied Tal for the many years he had relied on this man's constant aid and support.

Garin handed him one of the plates and sat down opposite him, as did Tal. "Thank you, Garin," Monias said.

"My pleasure."

Monias savored his lunch, not only because it was hot and had been prepared by the hands of another, but because he knew that in these days of turmoil, the survivors must undoubtedly be concerned over provisions.

"How is the morale of the people?" Monias asked as he set his plate on the ground.

"About what you would expect," Tal answered. "The initial wave of resilience, of defiance against the river for its intrusion, is beginning to wear down. Beneath their determination is the very real fear of what comes next. We've lost buildings and lives to the river before of course, but never on this scale. The magnitude of the devastation, the destruction, and the difficulty of any path forward, whatever it might be, has begun to sink in for all but the youngest children."

"And what has been decided about the path forward?" Monias inquired. "Where does Peris Mil go from here?"

"An excellent question," Tal answered, quickly glancing at Garin.

"Ah, I see," Monias said. "There is no need to say more. I know the difficulty of finding consensus in the much smaller world of Dal Harat. I can only imagine the debates that rage here."

"You really don't want to," Tal said, smirking. "Imagine the debates, that is. Spare yourself the agony."

Monias nodded. "So the people are divided, and it isn't too hard to imagine the possible alternatives. What do you think of them, Tal? Having just been presented with Peris Mil's predicament, I can see good arguments pushing in very different directions. What is your more considered opinion?"

Tal prepared to answer when a voice interrupted their peaceful conversation. "Master Kuvarin, Master Kuvarin!" Then a young boy ran into their midst.

"Peran," Tal said. "Good to see you, my boy."

The boy bounced happily with a large, half-eaten carrot in his hand. Monias looked at the tousled blond hair and thought of another little boy with bounce in his step and a smile always beaming. He looked down at his feet. Everything reminded him of Elsora or Joraiem these days. There didn't seem to be any hiding from them, no matter where he went, for they went everywhere with him.

"Did you have a good night?" Tal asked the boy.

"I did," Peran answered. "I slept in a real bed, and that was great. Out on the raft, I never really did sleep very well. I mean, I would fall asleep all right, but water would wash up over me every so often and wake me up, or sometimes I would roll off the table."

The boy's face grew sober, and for a moment he trembled, like he might cry again, but he composed himself. "The first time I fell off, it was night and dark and I couldn't see anything and I was so scared. I woke up in the water and didn't know where I was or how I'd gotten there. When I finally realized what had happened, the table had floated away from me far enough that I couldn't see it. I thought I was going to drown, but I swam around and around as best as I could and my hand struck the table in the dark. I climbed back up and lay shivering all night, too scared to sleep. After that, I tried not to sleep at night any more, though sometimes I still did."

Tal reached over and put his hand on Peran's shoulder. "Try not to think of that now. You're safe here on land with us, and you don't have to worry about the river or the table any more."

Peran nodded.

"Have you had your fill of food last night and today?"

"Oh yes," Peran said, his spirits reviving. "I've had bread and soup and all kinds of vegetables. It's been really good."

With that he bit off a big chunk of carrot and was crunching away when a pair of women came up behind Peran.

"There you are, Peran," one of them said, reaching down to take the boy's free hand. "Let's not bother Master Kuvarin any more right now."

"Oh, he's no bother, Riana," Tal said, but the woman just smiled and started to lead the boy away as though Tal hadn't said a thing.

"Goodbye, Peran," Tal called after them.

"Goodbye!" the boy called back.

"Come and see me again."

"I will," the boy's voice faded as they disappeared from sight.

Tal briefly shared with Monias the story of Peran's rescue, and when he was through Monias said, "The boy is a testament to your persistence, Tal."

"No, he is a testament to Allfather's goodness," Tal answered. "Even here, amid the wreckage of our town, our hopes and our lives, Allfather is good."

Monias smiled, tears welling in his eyes, "Yes, He is good."

For a little while no more was said, but after some time, Monias spoke at last. "Now, Tal, the subject we've been carefully avoiding needs to be brought up. How can I get across this flooded river here so I can continue on my journey?"

Tal was quiet and Garin asked, "You're headed to Amaan Sul?"

"Yes."

"That means more than crossing the Barunaan."

"I know."

Neither Garin nor Tal answered right away, and though Monias looked steadily from one to the other, they were both reticent to return his gaze.

"You think the way is impassable?" Monias asked.

"Likely enough," Tal said, looking at Monias at last. "Listen, Monias, we are old friends, you and I. I wouldn't say this if I didn't think it was true, but I think you should reconsider your plans, at least for the time being."

"Why?" Monias asked. "You just told me how you two have been out on the floodwaters several times since the river burst its bonds, why do you think I couldn't get across?"

"It isn't just a matter of getting across," Garin said. "Though that might prove trickier than you think. We've ventured out over what used to be Peris Mil, but we haven't tried to pass into the heart of the river, where the current even when not in flood stage is not for the faint of heart. Not that you are, Monias," Garin quickly added.

"What I'm saying is that crossing the river will be hard work, and beyond it lies a lot of unknowns. The quickest way under normal conditions would be to work your way upriver to the Kellisor Sea, and skirt the coast to the mouth of the Kalamin. That's no small journey, even in good weather, and who knows what all this rain has done to the Kellisor. Strange stories have come south since this storm began. If you can't cross the Kellisor, you'll have to drag your boat across land all the way to the Kalamin, which again would be very difficult, and at the end of your trek you'd almost certainly be faced with another river crossing as difficult as this one."

"I'm aware the journey will be hard," Monias said.

"I don't think you realize how hard," Garin replied, "and if you don't want to throw your life away, you should wait until the water goes down."

"I don't have time to wait," Monias said, his voice rising with emotion. "Time is slipping away, I can feel it. My time, the world's time. Can't you feel it, Tal? Malek is stretching forth his hand to take what he has long desired. There may not be time to wait for the waters to go down, if they are even going to be allowed to go down. I want to see my children and grandchildren before I die, and I will go with or without your help."

"There is something else," Tal said at last.

"What?"

"A creature out of a nightmare, large and dark and strong enough to rip to pieces our great floodwall. I saw him in the Barunaan the day the flood swallowed the city, and though I haven't seen him since, he may still be in the river. Taking the boat out into the remains of the city is one thing, for the water is so shallow there, but the body of the river is another story. The water is deep and wide and you could survive the river only to face him, and him you would not survive."

Monias looked at Tal and Garin, and this time both returned his stare. "Some abomination of Malek's?"

"No doubt."

Monias shook his head, "Even so, I must go on. I haven't come all this way to turn back to Dal Harat. I will not end my days waiting for news to reach me of my children's death or Kirthanin's subjugation. Though I may fail to reach the other side, I will set out across the Barunaan. Can I have use of a boat? I know many were lost in the flood, but I am compelled to ask."

Tal nodded. "You may have a boat."

"Thank you," Monias said. "I'll just get what direction from you I can tonight, and in the morning I'll head out."

"I'll go with you," Garin said, and Tal looked at him, surprised.

For a moment Monias seemed to ponder this offer. "You won't make the journey on your own," Garin said, "and though my coming won't guarantee safe passage, you'll have a better chance."

Tal was forced to agree. "Yes," he said at last, sadly. "You are right. You should go. In days like these, we have to do what is put before us to do. Monias is called to a long and difficult journey. My task is to hold Peris Mil together until we figure out what to do next. Monias needs you more than I do. You saw that before I did, but you are right. You must go with him and help."

"Garin, I appreciate the offer, but—"

"Monias," Tal said, reaching over to put his hand on Monias's arm. "Take him. Garin has been my strength and my right hand for years. If the river can be crossed and the Kellisor navigated, he will get you through. My task will require patience and wisdom more than strength, and while Garin has plenty of both, mine is a burden I would bear for the most part alone, either way. I'll be all right."

Monias looked back to Garin, "Are you sure?"

Garin stroked his bushy beard. "I'm sure. I haven't been abroad in years. It's time I traveled some again."

Monias laughed. "A holiday is it?"

"Why not? If we can avoid being swallowed up by the Barunaan, the Kellisor, and the Kalamin; if we can avoid being eaten by the great brute that tore down our floodwall; if we can avoid being captured by Malek's armies, which are rumored to be east of the Barunaan, then we might have an enjoyable trip."

"Let us hope so," Monias said. "I want to see my family again."

Monias sat by the fire. He had traveled alone and in rain most of the way from Dal Harat to Peris Mil. All that way, he had not enjoyed the comfort of a warming fire. He had tried once on his first night on the road. He had not expected to be successful and wasn't. There was no fuel at hand that was not thoroughly soaked, and even if there had been, he doubted a fledgling fire would last long on nights like those.

Now, though, he sat beside not only a fire, but a good one. The people of Peris Mil had possessed the foresight to move vast quantities of firewood into several outlying barns. Though most of those stores had been consumed during the previous few months, more wood was being moved into the storage spaces in the hopes that they would dry quickly enough to be of use when the current stash was used up.

He scooted back a little bit. In his excitement to be warming himself by a fire, he had settled perhaps a bit too close. The heat, at first welcome and pleasant, was now raging a bit too hot. He felt his face cool as he pulled back, and the pleasantness of the fire was restored. *I'll probably get cold here when the fire begins to wane,* he mused, thinking not for the first time in his many years of the difficulty of finding and maintaining real comfort anywhere in life.

Tal approached and took a seat nearby. Most of the afternoon and early evening Monias had rested (in fact he had even slept for a while in dryness—a blessing as welcome as this fire) as his host attended to the affairs of his beleaguered people. For weeks he had been alone with his own plight, but now that he was here, his eyes were being slowly lifted above his own grief to the sorrows of the wider world. So many people displaced by this flood, and yet Monias knew that this was but a foretaste of the displacement and devastation that Malek intended to bring to Kirthanin.

"Is this the future prefigured, Tal?" Monias asked, looking from the crackling fire to his friend's face, where the light of the flames danced with the shadows of the darkness.

"What do you mean?" Tal asked.

"All of this, the storm and flood, this displacement, disruption, devastation, and division. Is it but the beginning of the end of life as we have known it, as Allfather from the beginning of time intended it?"

"We have never known life as Allfather intended it, Monias. Not since the First Age has any seen the world as it was meant to be."

"I know that, Tal, but we have all lived in relative peace. We have all hoped for a day when the world would be restored. Is it not for us to see? Are the days of darkness coming, when Allfather will allow the full measure of Malek's hate and malice to spread unchecked?"

Tal shrugged. "It may be as you say. Who can know? The prophets spoke long ago of Malek's three attempts to conquer Kirthanin. They also spoke of Malek's ultimate defeat. None knows how much time must transpire after the one before the other will come to pass. Malek may fall tomorrow and restoration come just as quickly thereafter. Of course, he may not. He may reign a thousand years and cover the land with darkness even darker than these clouds, but he cannot reign forever. That is, when I am pressed, all that I know for sure about it."

"Yes, and in the end," Monias concurred, "I suppose it is all we were really meant to know, for it is all we truly need to know. But there are times, Tal, there are times when I really wish I knew more."

"Me too," Tal nodded.

Monias looked up at the dark sky. "It's nice that the rain stopped, but I'd sure like to see a clear sky again. I miss the stars. I miss the sun and the moon. I miss . . . " He faltered. "I miss Elsora, Tal, and I miss Joraiem. It's been so long."

"I remember him, you know," Tal said softly.

"Yes?" Monias said, turning toward him. "Tell me."

"I remember the day he showed up here in Peris Mil, on his way to Sulare. It was quite a memorable day, I can tell you.

Garin had just killed a Black Wolf near my house west of town, not far from where Joraiem had sheltered for the night, though of course I didn't know it was Joraiem at the time. All I knew was that Garin had seen a traveler, a young man, sleeping under one of my hedges.

"Well, Garin came to me in town that morning with the Black Wolf and showed it to me. I'd never seen one with my own eyes. I was fascinated. Then, later that day, into my warehouse walks Joraiem, the son of my old friend Monias, and what does he tell me? He tells me that a Black Wolf had been recently killed near Dal Harat."

"That's right, not long before Joraiem set out," Monias nodded. "In fact, we had more than one around, and a Malekim as well."

"I remember," Tal answered. "I couldn't believe it. I thought maybe the time of Malek's coming was near."

"We wondered that as well."

"Yes, but the trouble seemed to pass with the coming of summer and the years went by without more sightings, so eventually it was more or less forgotten. Until this year, of course, when Malek really did come forth."

"Yes."

"That autumn and winter I waited for Joraiem's return. I'd made him promise to stay with me on the way back. Young Balinor and Pedrone Someris's daughter arrived in town on an unusually warm and sunny day for Winter Rise. It was just before the weather really turned cold, and I remember thinking how glorious the day was. One of my stewards came running down to the waterfront with news that the heir to the Enthanin throne was in Peris Mil with several other young Novaana, returning from Sulare. When he added that one of them was dead, a sudden fear stabbed my heart. I'm so sorry, Monias. He was such a delightful young man."

"He was, Tal. From his earliest years he really was a delight. My younger son, Brenim, well, he was a bit more difficult, but Joraiem was usually pretty compliant. That doesn't mean he didn't have his days, but I guess all children do."

"They do indeed."

"There were two things that Joraiem was really good at from an early age: using his bow and arrows, and running. Running was as natural to Joraiem as it is to a hare or a horse. He ran, ran, ran. Everywhere he went when he was a little boy, he ran. If he was moving at all he was running. I never saw such life, such energy. And shooting, Tal, you wouldn't believe how good the boy was. He had an amazing eye, steady hands and flawless technique. By the time he was ten or eleven years old, he was better than I was. He didn't realize just how good he was at first, but by the time he was of age, he knew he was a gifted bowman. They tell me that in one of their battles, before Joraiem was murdered, he helped a dragon fight two Vulsutyrim. They also say his shooting helped keep them alive when they were in Nal Gildoroth on the Forbidden Isle. I can almost imagine it."

Here Monias faltered again, looking down at the ground between him and the fire. "Neither his speed nor his marksmanship could save him, though, from the cowardly malice of his enemy. I just don't understand it, Tal. I understand that we live in an imperfect world and that sometimes our children die young, but for a boy with so much promise to die in such a senseless way, I just don't understand.

"I didn't even get a chance to see him with his wife. I didn't have the opportunity to welcome Joraiem and Wylla to Dal Harat properly, to have a wedding feast worthy of the occasion. Instead I met his bride as she was mourning his death. And my grandson, Tal, he never knew his father, and Joraiem never had the pleasure I had three times over, to take his newborn in his arms and feel the soft warm flesh of his own child.

How we would have laughed, father and grandfather together, when Benjiah was born. How we would have loved to talk together as Benjiah grew, so like and yet in some ways so unlike his father.

"Tal, he was beautiful. He was beautiful, and I miss him. I still do. After seventeen years I miss him like he left for the Summerland yesterday. He was taken away too soon. I've never understood how Allfather could let that happen. And now, with Elsora gone and the world crumbling to dust, his death seems but the beginning of the end. He is lost, and it is likely enough all things will soon be lost with him."

"All is not lost, Monias," Tal answered. "It may feel like that sometimes, but all is not lost. Whatever Malek may do, you still have two children, three grandchildren, a son-in-law and daughter-in-law out there somewhere. When the morning comes, go with Garin and seek them out. If the world comes apart, you can face the end together, and if Allfather delivers us, you can rejoice together in hope. Either way, you have served Dal Harat well for a lifetime. Go in peace, now, and bless your family."

"Thank you, Tal," Monias said, wiping tears from his eyes. "I ask your forgiveness for my gloominess and for dumping my troubles in your lap when you and all Peris Mil have had enough trouble of your own."

"Nonsense, Monias. I have lost a wife in my time, and now I have seen my city flattened by a flood. I know which hurts more. You have nothing to apologize for, and there is nothing to forgive."

"I say it again, Tal, thank you. You have been a true friend."

"I wish I could do more."

"You are doing enough. You are sending Garin with me and losing your right hand. Don't think I don't understand your sacrifice."

"Losing Garin will be hard, but as I said before, in days like these, hard things must be done and sacrifices must be made."

"All the same," Monias answered, "I am grateful."

"Well, I'm glad he will be of service. Though he would stay and help if I asked him, I think he would rather face the flooded river and the dangerous journey than the seemingly irreconcilable differences of the townspeople. In fact, it is probably good that you are leaving tomorrow. If you'd come along next week or the week after, I might have been forced to go with you as well."

"You'd be welcome. If I've served Dal Harat sufficiently, then surely you've paid your dues in Peris Mil."

"Yes, but my family isn't out there." His arm swept in an arc, taking in the shadows. "What's left of it is right here. And besides, Dal Harat isn't in turmoil, or it might have been harder for you to go. No, here is where I need to be, for better or for worse."

Tal stood and stretched. The fire was still burning strong, but it had gone down somewhat, and as Monias had predicted, he was starting to feel a little cold. "Well," Tal added, "tomorrow will be here soon enough. Sleep well tonight and enjoy what little comfort we can provide."

"I will, Tal," Monias answered. "Good night."

"Good night. I will see you off in the morning."

Their parting the following morning was brief but emotional. Monias thanked Tal again and waited in the small but durable skiff they would take across the Barunaan while Tal and Garin said their farewells. The two men embraced, and Monias did not hear what passed between them, nor did he wish to.

They did not tarry long, for it was Garin's hope to make the crossing by nightfall, and the journey to the far side of Peris Mil alone would take them many hours. He didn't want to be battling the river as darkness fell, even if finding dry land on the far side might be too much to ask.

For Garin, the passage through the flooded-out town might have been familiar by now, but it was both fascinating and horrifying for Monias. It was fascinating to think that even now, some of the buildings of the town still stood, their proud rooftops peeking up above the waters. It was fascinating to think that underneath them wasn't some muddy riverbed or sandy ocean bottom, but streets and the streetlamps that once illuminated them.

It was horrifying, too, to think that the river could unleash such power. He had known all his life, of course, that water could crack open a stone or cut a channel in the earth, but destroy a town the size of Peris Mil? Roll over it and sweep it clean of life and light? He scooped up a handful of water and cupped it in his hands, letting it seep between his fingers. So delicate a thing, and yet so mighty.

The hours passed, and midday came and went. Garin spoke little and Monias honored his silence. Garin did almost all the rowing, though Monias convinced him now and then to hand over the oars, even if only briefly. After all, Monias argued, he would likely be of little help to Garin on the Barunaan itself. The least he could do was spell Garin in the relatively calm waters over Peris Mil.

Just past midday, Monias caught his first glimpse of what remained of the floodwall. A long ridge rose along the horizon, though lengthy breaks were visible here and there where the wall had given way. Where the floodwall still stood, it towered over them the closer they drew. Garin drew up alongside it in one long, solid stretch and reached out to steady the boat by taking hold of the rugged rock wall.

"We'll wait and rest here for a little while," Garin said. "I want to take a break before we have a go at the crossing. This is as safe a place as any."

"Whatever you think is best," Monias replied, and he sat still as the large man pulled in the oars and stretched out to rest. The boat bobbed up against the wall every so often, and Monias could tell it was slowly drifting southward, but not at any great rate. He imagined that just a few strong strokes from Garin would make up any distance lost during the man's brief reprieve. Less than an hour later, they were on the move again and, finding a hole in the floodwall, Garin pulled the skiff through.

Immediately the downstream pull of the Barunaan flung them southward as the skiff began to spin somewhat. Garin pulled to maintain control over the little craft. Slowly, he managed to pull the skiff out from the floodwall, where they were in somewhat serious danger of being dashed none too gently against the solid stone by the swirling current.

Progress out into the middle of the Barunaan was hard, and Monias maintained a tight grip on the side of the boat. At times the pull of the current was such that the upstream side of the boat was literally tilted downward toward the water's surface, and there were moments when Monias feared the skiff would be flipped.

Garin proved masterful, though, at keeping them not only upright, but moving across the rushing waters. Span by span, they made their way away from the floodwall, now fading in the distance. As the afternoon became evening, Monias began to see that they would likely be all right. The water's pull wasn't so strong any more, and from this and from other factors, Monias concluded the worst was behind them. They were likely not far from the somewhat placid waters of the flood zone on the eastern side of the Barunaan.

What Monias suspected Garin confirmed by pulling the oars in and sitting back, groaning as he stretched.

"All right there?" Monias asked.

"I ache all over," was Garin's simple reply.

"You did well," Monias said. "We are alive, and the worst of the Barunaan is behind us."

"We are alive," Garin concurred. "As for the worst of the Barunaan being behind us, we shall see. The journey northward to the Kellisor Sea will be long and arduous."

And it was. For the better part of a week they traveled, from dawn to dusk, skirting the banks of the Barunaan. No matter what they did, though, they didn't sleep much by night, and their weariness grew. When they would go ashore, uneasiness over the possibility of being discovered by the enemy prevented them from really resting, but if they didn't, the narrow confines of the skiff made their bodies ache no matter how they contorted themselves.

Their early days on the river were quiet, but a total silence fell upon them as they slowly slid, stroke by stroke, closer to the Kellisor. They rose in silence, rowed in silence, ate and drank in silence, even signaled to one another in silence when they saw something of interest. The rhythmic sound of the oars rising and falling was often all they heard, league after league.

On the seventh day, they saw the place where the Barunaan opened out onto the Kellisor Sea. Monias thought as he looked upon it that he had never seen anything more beautiful. If they had made it this far, they could make it just a little farther. Perhaps he would soon be on solid ground again, but this time in Enthanin, and on his way to Amaan Sul.

Just as this thought occurred to him, a sight unlike anything he had ever seen appeared in the distance, and Garin stopped rowing at exactly that same moment. Across the mouth of the Barunaan a great dark shadow moved, sliding from east to west. Monias could make out an enormous head, terrible and majestic at the same time, gliding across the surface of the water, with an immense body trailing behind. The creature's wake—waves of impressive size—moved at substantial speed in the otherwise calm waters.

Monias caught his breath. For a moment, he couldn't tell if the creature was moving across the mouth of the river or turning into it, and Monias glanced around, confirming what he knew already. They were far from any refuge, and if it turned downriver they were doomed.

Fortunately it did not, eventually disappearing into the sea. Monias turned back to Garin and broke the silence that had ruled them for days. "I take it that was the creature Tal mentioned?"

Garin nodded. "Yes, that was it."

Monias peered north to the Kellisor, which no longer seemed quite as inviting. The creature hadn't turned into the river, but it was up there. Either they were going to have to try to slip past it or go ashore and take their chances on land. Neither option appealed to Monias.

My children are out there. One way or another, I have to reach Amaan Sul.

4

REBORN

"IT CAN'T BE."

"Not so. It can be, and it is."

Aljeron stood, his body trembling, though not from the cold in the air or the snow sliding down his leg inside his worn boots. "Valzaan?"

"In the flesh."

"But how?"

"Ah, now that is the question, isn't it?" Valzaan smiled and stood beside the fire, his long white hair even wilder and more unkempt than Aljeron had remembered. He wore a solid green cloak, but his hands were empty, the trademark wooden staff with the carved windhover at the top having passed on to Benjiah.

"Come, my friends and fellow sojourners in this barren wilderness," Valzaan said. "You are well met indeed."

He extended his arms, and Aljeron and Koshti, Saegan and Evrim all made their way to him. The three men embraced him as Koshti moved excitedly in and out of their tight-knit group.

"You are not alone," Valzaan said after a moment, appearing to look past them in the direction of Erigan, who wasn't far behind, and Synoki, who was hanging back a bit.

"No," Aljeron said, looking over his shoulder. "Sarneth's son, Erigan, has journeyed here with us, as has Synoki. You remember Synoki, don't you, Valzaan? The shipwrecked sailor?"

For a moment Valzaan said nothing, but eventually he acknowledged Aljeron's words. "I do remember." Valzaan turned his attention back to those nearest him as he again settled in by the fire. "Please. The snow has stopped falling—a happy change in the weather, I think we would all agree—but it is still cold and my fire is waiting. Sit and warm yourself, for you have reached the foot of Harak Andunin at last."

"Yes, we have," Aljeron answered, settling in across from Valzaan, "but again I ask how? How are you here? I saw, we all saw, you cast into the sea. I thought you were lost."

"Lost?" Valzaan said, as though the word needed to be said with reverence. "I was lost indeed, and more than lost. Cheimontyr, the Bringer of Storms, sought to destroy me, and when the lightning bolt struck me, I thought I was destroyed. I thought I was unmade. But I was neither destroyed nor unmade—I was reborn."

Aljeron leaned in, as did the others, waiting for Valzaan to continue. Erigan had settled down in the snow beside the fire, as had Synoki, and quiet reigned over the small group huddled for warmth.

"Since we should probably wait until morning to begin our journey up the mountain, there is time now for my story tonight, if you will hear it."

"We will hear it," Aljeron answered for them all, "and gladly."

"Then listen," Valzaan said, "and though I may wax on and on as old prophets and storytellers are wont to do, hear not of my own might or power, but of the grandeur of Him who made us all.

"As I stood on the beach with the waves of the sea behind me, I felt my strength waning. Having wielded Allfather's power to bewilder the enemy with the sand, I was too weary to escape to safety myself. My situation was grave. Even so, a strange and sudden sense of peace passed over me as Cheimontyr prepared to strike. It was the hand of Allfather, and I knew at that moment that, whatever happened to me, I had done exactly what I needed to by helping all of you, and especially Benjiah, to escape. I knew that even if this was my end, the world remained under the watchful care of Allfather.

"Cheimontyr raised his monstrous hands, and the ball of lightning flashed out from them and hurtled toward me. Even though blind, I was overwhelmed by the bright and searing light that seemed to penetrate the dark places within me. I felt the incredible heat swallow me up, and then I was struck, lifted off my feet and hurled backward above the waves and out over the sea. The impact of the blow drove the wind from my chest, and I thought that surely I would never breathe again.

"My body ached as I flew backward through the air. Each drop of rain stabbed my face and hands and seemed to tear at my flesh as I soared, not seeming to lose momentum or altitude at all. I was unable to concentrate sufficiently to search for a windhover, and Allfather granted me no vision of myself as I flew.

"Then, after a long time in the air, I felt myself begin to descend. I braced myself for the impact, which was every bit as violent as I had imagined. My head and neck snapped forward as I hit the water on my back, which now hurt more than my chest had ached when I was first struck.

"Some relief followed, though, as my rate of descent through the water gradually slowed and the spinning of my head came to an end. Down and down I sank, no strength in my arms or legs to even try to fight what seemed to be more than gravity. Rather, it was the irresistible pull of some larger outside force. It felt as though I fell forever, and though I could see nothing of the watery world around me, images of the immensity and darkness of the great deep swirled in my mind, whether put there by Allfather or pulled from my own imagination, I could not say.

"It occurred to me that I might not be in the ocean at all, but dead and sinking into the oblivion of the grave. What I had taken to be the impact of my body striking the surface of the water could have been my transition out of this world into the next, and my gradual and irresistible descent could signify something very different than my entrance into the ocean deep.

"This thought stayed with me until I struck the sandy bottom of the ocean, which was cold and gritty and real. I knew then that I wasn't in oblivion, but where I was and how I wasn't dead, I could not explain. I lay on the ocean bottom and slipped into darkness.

"I woke some time later and realized only after a time where I was. I remained upon the ocean floor, my body nestled somewhat into the densely packed sand. My body still ached from the blow I'd received from Cheimontyr and from where I'd struck the surface of the ocean, but I was alive, and I began to think that I had been allowed to descend to this place that I might find healing and rest. Little did I know that my trial had just begun.

"As I began to stir, struggling to sit up, I sensed a massive form glide over me. I knew what it was, for I had been in its presence before and had visions of it thereafter. In my visions, a voice had named the creature Kumatin, and it is a creature unlike any I have ever seen, truly immense in size and strength. It is a terrible presence, a cold darkness that haunts the waters of this world. It is the culmination of our enemy's creative powers, a nightmarish shadow in the deep. Some of you who sit here beside this fire have seen it before, for I first encountered it on the Forbidden Isle, deep below the city of Nal Gildoroth."

"The creature in the water," Aljeron said.

"Yes, but it was even then only a newborn, its full size and strength not yet realized."

"And it was swimming right above you?" Saegan said, incredulous.

"It was. Whether it had been lurking off the coast of Werthanin as I battled Cheimontyr and thus saw me hurled out to sea, or whether it had some special sense that alerted it of my presence, it came to devour me.

"I was nearly despondent, for I felt drained beyond measure and weary beyond hope. And yet I did not despair, for in my visions I had foreseen this struggle, though its outcome had been shielded from me. I had foreseen myself exchanging blow for blow with this terrible creature, and I rose to my feet, calling inwardly for Allfather to strengthen and guide me in the battle that was to come.

"Strengthen and guide me He did, for the might and power of the Kumatin was directed against me in full. The power of Allfather flowed through me. Despite my weariness, I was light and nimble on my feet. I sensed the creature's blows before they came and blocked or dodged them. I absorbed blows from his great claws and massive tail, and I struck him in return with power as great as any I ever wielded on land. Though I no longer bore my staff, I was not hindered in my fight, for Allfather's strength empowered me.

"I seized my adversary by his tail and flung him several hundred spans across the ocean floor. He flew back, tumbling over and over, kicking up a cloud of sand that swirled in the water like a dust storm in an arid land. I pursued him, and again we grappled. He struck back viciously, driving me backward step by step to the place where we had started.

"Twice more we repeated this pattern. After the third time, my enemy struck me with his hardest blow yet, and I crumpled to my knees. The blow staggered me, but I wasn't broken. I rose to my feet again, and when the Kumatin saw that I was not destroyed he cried out with rage. It was the first time he had made a sound, and it struck my ears like a hammer striking rock. It was high and piercing. Even now, so long after, I can hear it echoing in my head, but I can't describe it fully. Suffice it to say it was almost as painful as the blow he had just dealt me, and I covered my ears with my hands and dropped once more to my knees.

"The Kumatin came at me again, but despite my vulnerable position, I was ready for him. I rose, quick as lightning, and struck him squarely in his monstrous face. I felt his scaly hide shudder under the blow, and the creature reeled. Then suddenly Allfather granted me a vision of the spectacle. I saw the swirling sands all around us, stretching upward and outward for leagues, like a great storm arising from the ocean floor. I saw myself, standing right there at the center of the storm, on my feet and unconquered. And then I saw my enemy, gliding away from me toward land.

"I saw my enemy flee and collapsed once more to the ocean floor. Again my body lay nestled in the cold sand. Again I felt aching all over and weariness beyond measure. Again I closed my eyes and felt consciousness slip away. Surely this time, I thought, this is the sleep of death, for I am undone.

"But again I awoke. Allfather was not finished with me yet. Though the quiet waters of the ocean deep seemed as good a place as any to leave this body of flesh and bone behind, such was not to be, at least not for me. I once more became aware of a great shadow passing overhead."

"Not again!" Evrim exclaimed.

"Surely not," Aljeron echoed. "Having faced Cheimontyr and then this other already, this Kumatin, there can't be more."

"The great shadow above me was not my enemy," Valzaan continued. "I could feel the difference immediately. My enemy had fled and not returned. No, this was the Leviathan, the great fish and master of the ocean."

"The Leviathan?" Saegan said, his voice echoing the incredulity on the faces of the others. "Surely the Leviathan is a myth."

"Truly," Synoki sneered, "I've sailed with many a superstitious crew, but I've never found any that took the ancient tales of the great fish seriously. They are stories told to frighten cabin boys."

"Believe what you will," Valzaan answered without a moment's pause, "I tell you the Leviathan came to me there where I lay in the sand. The dragon of the seas, master of the waters, he swooped down to where I lay and took my body entire inside his mouth, with room in there for twenty more men beside."

"He swallowed you?" Evrim's eyes bulged.

"No, but he kept me in his mouth as I might keep a seed that I had found in a piece of fruit but did not want to swallow."

"What was it like, inside his mouth?" Aljeron asked.

"It was many things, I suppose, but if you really want to know what it was most of all, it was safe. I felt the hand of Allfather upon me there as clearly as anywhere I've been, protecting me through this long-forgotten creature, one of His most glorious creations.

"Upward he swam. I could feel his great body rise. It was only then that I understood just how far down I had descended, for our ascent took ages. With each passing moment I hungered more and more to reach the surface of the water and feel the wind upon my face.

"Then the mouth of the great fish opened and gently he expelled me. I floated out from him and felt the cold sea air on my face and hands. The Leviathan was already gone, submerged and sinking fast as he returned to the darkness of the great deep.

"I opened my mouth and breathed. Air filled my lungs like life itself filling me anew. It was then that I knew I was reborn. I had survived the Bringer of Storm's blow, and yet I had not survived. I was Valzaan, and yet I was not Valzaan. All that had transpired—the long descent, the battle in the dark and mystical deep, and the strange and wondrous ascent—they were all part of my rebirth. Twice before in my life I have undergone what you might call a transformation, though they were both long ago and their stories are not for today, but this was different. This was something that even my ancient years had never known. This was something altogether new, and as I floated there upon the ocean's surface I marveled afresh at the strange and wondrous power and plan of Allfather.

"I was not left to wonder long, for I sensed a windhover circling in the sky. He called with a strange cry and soon an entire flock of Merrion, white as snow with brilliant streaks of blue blurred by their motion, dove toward me from the sky. They took hold of my garments and lifted me out of the water. I sank down as their beaks strained to lift my soggy cloak with me inside it, but they were enough for the task and soon I rose high above the ocean waters and began to fly north and east across the Bay of Thalasee.

"For leagues they flew, never seeming to grow tired of me, their burden. Their wings beat rhythmically together, and I felt the beauty of their grace and power. They had not the majesty of a dragon, but I rested as comfortably in their grip as ever a man reclined within a garrion of old.

"After a time, they began to descend with me, and eventually they set me down gently upon solid ground. Very solid, in fact, for it was not a beach, but the smooth and unmistakable feel of paving stone. I summoned the will to look through the eyes of the windhover that had flown above this flock of Merrion all the way with me, and there I saw the place where I had been deposited. I knew it right away for I had been there before, though not for many years. It was the ancient city of Avram Gol."

"Avram Gol!" Aljeron said.

"I don't understand," Evrim added. "We were there. Were you there before or after us?"

"Right before," Valzaan answered. "Had I to do it over again, I might have waited there for you, but I had no certainty which way you were headed. What's more, when I searched the heavens for a windhover to give me a bearing upon you, what I found wasn't you at all, but a Vulsutyrim headed from Werthanin toward the border of Nolthanin. I had survived Cheimontyr and the Kumatin and been raised from the great deep, but I had no great desire to be drawn into another battle. I had to decide what to do and where to go.

"I decided fairly quickly to head to Harak Andunin. I realized that the Merrion had brought me north for a reason. I knew Aljeron and possibly more would be headed here, and what's more, I knew Benjiah was headed south with the rest. The time had come to entrust them to his care, for I could sense his time approaching sooner than even I had thought. In the end, it seemed to me that Kirthanin would best be served if I could aid Aljeron in his task upon his arrival here, for if Sulmandir indeed lies within Harak Andunin alive, his return to us now could well decide the war.

"And so here I have come. I have traveled the northern waste and like you battled the relentless snows to arrive, just two short days ago."

"Even so, it is remarkable," Aljeron said. "You have crossed Nolthanin alone. We were seven men, two Great Bear and Koshti, and we almost didn't survive the journey."

"In part because a traitor was in our midst," Saegan all but growled, turning his head slightly in Synoki's direction without looking at him.

"A traitor?" Valzaan asked, though his tone betrayed neither worry nor surprise.

Aljeron briefly relayed the events of their journey, including the Red Ravens, the Vulsutyrim, the snow serpent, and Cinjan's attempt on his life. Valzaan asked a few questions here and there, but mostly he just listened and nodded as Aljeron spoke.

"Your way has been perilous indeed," Valzaan said when Aljeron was finished at last. "You have all sacrificed much, even if Evrim's sacrifice was the most painful."

"We did what we needed to do to get here," Evrim said.

"And here you have come," Valzaan said. "Which brings us out of the past and into the present, at the foot of Harak Andunin. In the morning, some or all of us need to begin our ascent of this mountain, and we must talk further about this later. For now, though, it is high time we made good use of this fire and ate!"

Dinner turned out to be a more pleasant proposition than anything Aljeron and the others had experienced in quite some time. To be sure, the absence of precipitation had a lot to do with it. The snow that had been falling steadily had indeed come to an end. Aljeron thought about how hard it would be for someone who had never lived through anything like this storm to understand just how good it felt to stand outside and look up to the sky and not feel rain or snow upon his face. It was like being able to breathe freely again after being sick, when every breath is a celebration of wellness. Aljeron vowed never to take for granted the blessing of dryness again.

And yet, the change in the weather did not fully explain the pleasantness that marked the meal. The real cause was Valzaan, though Aljeron did not realize this at first. The presence of the prophet changed everything. When he had been blown out to sea, much of their hope had been blown out to sea with him.

But again, Aljeron's happiness wasn't that simple. It was more than simply joy at Valzaan's return. It was more than the deep feeling of rejoicing at the sight of their ally in the fight. Aljeron realized that a lot of it had to do simply with having another friend and companion present. Those who remained had come so far through so much together, but their shared trials hadn't exactly drawn them closer in bonds of camaraderie. Aljeron remembered how close he had felt to Joraiem and Caan and the other Novaana after their voyage to the Forbidden Isle. In that case their shared trials had tied them together with deep and lasting connections.

Aljeron realized as this thought occurred to him that it wasn't entirely true. He had felt the bonds of friendship grow and seen the closeness in himself and others, but Rulalin's treacherous act had proved that this experience hadn't been universal. Things were broken apart during that journey as well as bound together.

Even with that exception, however, that experience more than seventeen years before had made lifelong friends of a disparate band of people, people who had been friendly before but true friends after. This journey and these trials had been different. This group of sojourners had grown league by league almost more distant from each other. They generally woke in silence, traveled in silence, and went to bed in silence. They were imploding upon themselves. As their small party dwindled with each new death and loss, they seemed to drift further and further apart. Evrim and Saegan were still his friends, but the ease between him and them was diminished. At some point, the struggle and tension of their outer journey might very well have altered for good their inner connections. As Arintol, Karras, and Tornan had fallen, and as the suspicions dividing Cinjan and Synoki from the rest deepened, each day became more and more laborious. Even with Cinjan exposed and disposed of, the burden did not lift. It was too late. The damage was done. What's more, though they had no certain evidence to prove it, Aljeron and the others suspected Synoki wasn't being entirely forthright. It was certainly possible that Cinjan had been holding some threat or another over Synoki's head, but Synoki's story did not ring true.

And so they kept going, limping along at half their strength, Evrim's struggle to adapt to life with one arm a visible portrayal of the journey's very real toll. Silence continued to reign in their midst, and they continued to drift apart.

But now, Valzaan was here. The longer they talked with the prophet, the more Aljeron felt he could see what Valzaan meant when he said he was himself but not himself. Indeed, he was Valzaan as Aljeron remembered him, and he was not. He was not lighthearted, exactly, but he seemed somehow more merry. His voice still carried the same authority and command it had always carried, but it was softer. Aljeron could feel in himself something changing as a result, and he could see it in the others. Saegan and Evrim were responding to it as well. They seemed more at ease, and Koshti, lounging at his feet, also showed signs of being more at ease than he had been in a long time. Even Erigan, never talkative and always sober in his words, seemed almost visibly more relaxed.

Synoki, though, was as withdrawn as he had been since Cinjan's death. He was quiet as always and stayed just a little way off. Aljeron watched him at times to see if he could read an emotion that might explain his odd behavior, but he found Synoki as inscrutable as ever. That much at least hadn't changed.

Aljeron tried to let most of his thoughts about their journey and about Synoki go. They enjoyed a fine dinner of two hares Valzaan had trapped before they arrived. How a blind prophet could secure such a dinner in a place where Aljeron and a few other very good hunters had failed for days on end, he had no idea and frankly, he didn't care. It was a fine evening, cold but dry, and they were eating well-roasted meat around a warm fire. What's more, he realized it must have been at least the first day of Spring Rise by now, which meant warmer weather would come sooner or later.

It was dark by the time they had finished eating, and they remained close to the fire. Aljeron was pleasantly full and enjoying the heat upon his face. He had no desire to go anywhere or do anything. So much time walking and riding, wading and burrowing through snowdrifts that went on for hundreds of spans—he'd had enough. He didn't even want to think about beginning the climb of Harak Andunin in the morning.

"Valzaan?" Saegan asked.

"Yes?"

"Out in the middle of nowhere, on the Andunin Plateau, we found something curious. There was a great Water Stone, unlike any I've ever seen before, simply enormous. On top of it was a marker bearing a sort of message—"

"Left by the Nolthanim at the end of the First Age," Valzaan finished. "Yes, I know, I have seen it."

"Well," Saegan said hesitantly, as though looking for the right way to ask his question. "I guess I'm wondering what you make of it. To me, it seems pretty obvious that they knew they were doing wrong and were leaving a sort of apology for posterity. But if they knew they were doing wrong, why did they do it in the first place?"

"It is not a simple question," Valzaan said, rubbing his hands together before the fire. "Who can speak for every man among them? Perhaps there is no one answer that accounts for them all. I would say that Andunin followed Malek because he was afraid of what Malek could do to him if he did not, but also because deep down inside him, Malek created a desire for the thing he had promised. Andunin wanted a crown. He wanted it for himself and for his son. He didn't get it in the end, and he might have known by the time he marched away with Malek that he wasn't going to. He went anyway, perhaps by that point feeling trapped by his commitment.

"As for the other captains of the Nolthanim, I cannot say what their reasoning was. The monument suggests they all felt Andunin's fear. They were all afraid of Malek's wrath and what it would do if it was directed against Nolthanin."

"But surely, Valzaan," Saegan continued, "they knew that Malek was rebelling against Allfather. Surely they knew Allfather and the rest of the Twelve wouldn't allow Malek to simply destroy them."

"I don't know what they knew. Malek had other Titans on his side. That part of his threat was real. How were mortal men in Nolthanin to know how many would side with Malek and how many would not?"

"Still," Saegan persisted, "they knew it was wrong. We know that we may not have strength to win this war we are currently fighting, but we won't join Malek just to save our lives and homes. We won't do it, because we know it is wrong."

"You live in a different age. You have the benefit of seeing and hopefully learning from the mistakes of those who have gone before you. Don't misunderstand me, Saegan. Fundamentally you are correct. They were wrong. They should not have followed the Master of the Forge. In this you are most certainly right.

"However, do not presume that had you found yourself in Andunin's shoes you would have done better than he did. You may have, but how can you know? You have no wife and son and cannot understand what it is to fear for their survival or hope for their glory. You live in a world where Malek's evil is evident and any suggestion that his purposes are in keeping with Allfather's is preposterous. You cannot understand the trust that was implicit between the Twelve and the world of men.

"What I'm saying, Saegan, is that you should leave the judgment of Andunin and the Nolthanim to Allfather. He is just and knows the hearts of all. It may be that not all Nolthanim embraced Malek's call, and though they follow him still, I suspect that it is not entirely a matter of love and devotion that keep them serving at his command."

The talk of Malek and the Nolthanim brought back images for Aljeron of the great army that marched behind Cheimontyr up to the ruined walls of Zul Arnoth. Not for the first time, he wondered if Shalin Bel was now but a burned-out ruin, an empty shell. The speed with which they had been pursued suggested that perhaps Malek had not lingered long there, but Aljeron had seen the destructive power of the Vulsutyrim in Zul Arnoth. They would not have needed much time.

His thoughts quickly moved to what Malek and his army might even then be doing. Aljeron wondered how Caan and the others were holding out. "Valzaan," he said, "Have you seen any visions of the war? Do you know how things are going?"

"I have and I do," Valzaan answered, turning from the fire to Aljeron. "That is a slight change of topic. I should make sure that the first matter is concluded before I address the second."

"I'm sorry," Aljeron said, meaning to continue before Valzaan cut him off.

"There is no need to apologize, I simply wanted to give Saegan a chance to finish what we had begun."

Saegan shrugged. "I don't mind talking about how the war is going. I'd like to know myself. As for Andunin and the Nolthanim, you're right. I don't know what I would have done if I were in their shoes. I'll never know, I guess. The memorial we saw has been bothering me, that's all."

Valzaan nodded. "It is enough to be responsible for your own choices. There is no need to worry about the choices of another. As for the memorial, I don't know what more to say. You could call it a confession if you like, but it was for them what they named it, a witness—a witness to the fact that they were in a desperate place and were uneasy about where they were going.

"As for what is going on in Suthanin," the prophet continued, "there are many ways to answer that question. The simplest answer would be to say that the battle for Suthanin has been abandoned."

"What?" Aljeron asked, shocked.

"Yes, it is true, I have seen the evacuation of thousands of men and Great Bear across the Kalamin into Enthanin."

"Great Bear?" Erigan asked, joining the conversation for the first time.

"Yes," Valzaan replied. "And from what I have seen, I believe that among their number are Great Bear from Taralin and Elnin. More than that I cannot say for sure. There are limits to what I understand even when the images are clear. Still, I can safely say that Great Bear by the thousands made the crossing with soldiers from Werthanin, Suthanin, and Enthanin as well."

"And yet they were retreating," Aljeron said, half musing to himself. "Can you explain this?"

"I can give you a glimpse of the pieces given to me. I have seen many ships beached along the shores of Suthanin.

I have seen an army of Great Bear emerge from Taralin to join the surviving Werthanim. I have seen Cimaris Rul besieged by the waters of the Southern Ocean. I have seen the beacon fires of a Dragon Tower burning with Benjiah beside them, and dragons coming to the light of their fire. All this I have seen."

The others stared at him. For Aljeron, images of Great Bear and dragons, cities and Dragon Towers swirled in his head.

"But the real story," Valzaan continued, his voice growing excited, "was the crossing of the Kalamin by the Kirthanim armies and how it came about.

"Malek's hosts had been pursuing them steadily, and as they began to evacuate across the river, despite the great number of ships they had, there weren't nearly enough to get across quickly. A good many if not a majority would have been caught and slaughtered there if not for Benjiah. Alone, and without aid, he walked out into the space between the Kalamin and Malek's approaching army. The vision Allfather showed me of that event was truly remarkable. I have long been a prophet of Allfather, but the power Benjiah wielded then was unlike any I have seen by another. He raised the earth and held back the entirety of Malek's host. Even Cheimontyr was powerless to counter so long as Benjiah wielded Allfather's power.

"I tell you this," Valzaan continued, growing more and more animated, "from what I saw, the prophecy has been confirmed without doubt. The 'child who was born to lead' has been revealed, and even Cheimontyr must realize that he has an equal among his enemy."

"You speak in riddles, prophet," Synoki said with an unexpected coldness.

"What place do children have in the battles and the affairs of men?"

Valzaan turned to Synoki and answered. "Ordinary children have no place in war, though Malek has brought this war to more than enough children. This child, though, was born for this."

Synoki watched the prophet for a moment and then shrugged. "Believe what you will. Children born to do signs and wonders are as believable to me as the return of the dragons he is supposed to have summoned at the Dragon Tower. I'll believe it when I see it with my own eyes."

For a moment there was quiet in the small group. Aljeron felt a strange chill sweep through him, and he watched Synoki and Valzaan and felt, or seemed to feel, a strange struggle of will of sorts between the two men.

"Wanderer," Valzaan said after a moment, his impassive face and empty eyes trained steadily on Synoki, "you are again far from home. The timing of your return is most interesting. When we have done what we have come to do, you and I will have more to say. For tonight, though, we should plan on getting some sleep. The climb before us will not be easy."

"Is that all the news you have then of the south?" Aljeron asked. "If Benjiah wields such power and dragons have returned, why are Caan and the others still in retreat?"

"Because the foe aligned against them is also great. While there are many men and Great Bear, there are still only a few dragons, and the power that Benjiah wields is not his own, nor does he control it fully any more than I do."

"Then despite Benjiah's heroics, Suthanin is lost. Only Enthanin remains."

"All the more reason we need to be successful here."

"But we don't even know if Sulmandir is alive," Saegan said.

"We shall see," Valzaan answered.

"We shall see," Aljeron replied. "And if he is, what will we say? How shall we address the Father of Dragons?"

"If you have the opportunity to speak to Sulmandir, you would be wise to be concise and to the point. Don't mince words. State your case and be done. He will not be persuaded by rhetoric. He will do as he sees fit."

"Maybe I'm missing something," Evrim said. "Valzaan, you've already said that there were dragons with Caan and the others as they retreated up the Barunaan. If they couldn't turn back Malek's host, what will Sulmandir be able to do, even if he is still alive? A dragon is a dragon, right?"

"Yes and no," Valzaan said. "Sulmandir isn't just any dragon, he is *the* dragon. The Golden Dragon, the great father of all dragons. If he comes, then they will all come. However many are left and wherever they may be, they will answer his summons. I do not discount the power of Sulmandir alone, for he is mighty indeed. Only the Titans among all living creatures were mightier than he, but getting Sulmandir means chiefly, for our purposes, getting all of his children, and that could change this war in a hurry."

Quiet fell upon them, and Aljeron looked over the tops of the nearby trees and surveyed the mountain, Harak Andunin, rising above them in the darkness. It was an ominous object in which to place his hope, but it was what he had come all this way to see. In the morning, they would begin their climb, and soon their questions would be answered, for better or for worse.

5

IN MOTION

THE FOLLOWING MORNING was crisp and cold. Aljeron sat up and stretched. Beside him, Koshti also stirred and lifted his head to see what Aljeron was doing. The air was cold in a different way, and for a moment Aljeron couldn't place the difference. Then he realized what it was. The air was dry.

He rubbed his hands along his arms and mumbled to himself about the cold. The snow had stopped falling, and for that he was glad, but already he hungered for something more. Spring Rise had come, and he desired warmth. He had no idea how long it normally took spring weather to come this far north, if it came at all, but he hoped it wasn't long.

The light of early dawn illuminated the other sleeping figures, and he looked around at his companions. They seemed so small next to Harak Andunin and the task before them. He'd never been a big fan of swimming or climbing. He was much more comfortable on solid, level ground, whether on foot or on horseback. He figured, though, that if he'd managed the voyage to the Forbidden Isle, he would be able to cope with this ascent.

The rest of the camp began to stir, and soon all were awake and reasonably alert. "Should I build a fire for breakfast?" Aljeron asked Valzaan.

"No, we will eat it cold and be on our way. I don't want to spend any more time than necessary on the face of Harak Andunin. We will begin the climb as soon as possible and make the most of the light of day."

The remnant of sleepiness as much as the solemnity of the task helped to create a silence that felt like reverie to Aljeron. He wanted to say something that would bring back the collegiality of the previous evening. He couldn't think of anything, though, and he thought that maybe the silence was best left unbroken. He looked at Evrim, kneeling in the snow and doing the best he could to gather his things with his single arm. Even if Aljeron didn't know what to say to the rest of them, there were things that should be said to Evrim, even if they had all been said before and he knew how Evrim would respond.

He walked over and knelt down beside him. "Can I help?"

"No, I'm all right."

"I know we've been over this before, but now that we're here, now that we've found Valzaan, well, I wondered if that might change your decision."

"How?"

"Well, I thought that maybe part of your reasoning for going was a sense of responsibility to me or to the task, so perhaps knowing that Valzaan is going with us might change things."

"No, not for me it doesn't. I'm going up, Aljeron."

Aljeron hesitated. They stood on delicate ground, but Evrim was too good a friend for him to keep silence. "Look,

Evrim, I don't know how carefully you've looked at Harak An-dunin, but this is no hill. This is going to be a serious climb. I don't know how far up the entrance to Sulmandir's gyre might be, but this is going to be hard."

"Valzaan's going, isn't he?"

"So?"

"Well, he's a lot older than me and blind besides."

"Sure, but Evrim, you know that he has ways of compensating for his lack of eyesight. He has advantages."

"Aljeron," Evrim said, frustration evident in his voice and body language as he leaned back in the snow, "I've been over this with you. I didn't come all this way to sit at the bottom of the mountain while you and the others go up to the top. I'm not going to do it."

"I'm not going up," Synoki said from not far away.

Aljeron hadn't been as quiet in starting this conversation as he might have been, but it was too late now, however, and he noticed Valzaan, Erigan, and Saegan also looking at Synoki.

"When I was a young man," Synoki said, "I could handle myself all right in the rigging of a ship. I could go up and down with relative agility. I'm not a young man any more and this is not the rigging of a ship. I came along to help guide and because, as I've already explained, I was forced to serve as Cinjan's accomplice. This is as far as I go."

"The rest of us are going," Valzaan said. "What do you propose, wanderer? Will you remain here, or do you desire to be set loose to make your way alone across the Nolthanin waste, back toward your now abandoned home, Cimaris Rul?"

"I'll stay here and tend the horses," Synoki said. "How long do you think you'll be gone?"

Valzaan shrugged. "Depending on how far we must go and whether we make good time, we might be able to get there in two days, perhaps three, and get back down in a similar time. The question is how long it will take once we're there."

"So, leave me a week's worth of food, and I'll wait here for your return."

"So be it, no one need come who would prefer to stay below. Is Synoki remaining behind alone?"

No one said anything, and all stood with pack in hand, looking ready for the ascent.

"Aljeron, what about Koshti?"

"He will not be left behind. If we find a place impassable to him, he will wait there for our return, but it would be the first time I have gone somewhere that he could not follow."

"Very well," Valzaan said.

"Erigan," Aljeron said, turning and looking at the Great Bear. "You have come so far with us. You don't need to come up if the climb would be difficult."

"You are gracious, Master Balinor," Erigan said, his voice gentle and deep as always but with a hint of something like humor in it. "However, I will gladly come. You need not worry for me. Great Bear are not afraid of the mountains and are able climbers. Koshti and I will be fine. If the progress of our fellowship up the mountain is slowed, it is unlikely we will be the reason why."

"If we are decided," Valzaan said, "we should get under way. There will be time to talk further and to rest when darkness falls and we are well up the mountain."

Aljeron took up his gear. He cradled his sword in his hand. Any thought he might have had about leaving Daaltaran below was gone. He couldn't imagine what Synoki might do with it. He strapped it on tightly even as he watched Erigan rest his great wooden staff beneath a tree. *Synoki probably couldn't even lift that*, Aljeron thought. *It will be safe enough until our return.*

They started through the trees in the direction of the foot of Harak Andunin, and Aljeron put his hand on Evrim's shoulder.

"I said what I said because we almost lost you once on this trip, and I don't want to run the risk unnecessarily of losing you again."

"I know," Evrim said, and Aljeron could see there was no bitterness there.

"Let me ask you one more thing, and if you say no, I will let it be. If you will not stay down for your own safety, would you consider staying behind to keep an eye on Synoki? Likely enough he's telling the truth that the climb would be too much for him. I wouldn't want to try to do this with only one good leg. Even so, my gut still tells me he's not to be trusted. I don't like leaving him behind alone."

"What do you think he'll do?"

"I don't know. I just don't like it."

"I don't like it either, but I don't think there's much trouble he can get into while we're gone. Not here anyway, and I don't think he's going anywhere. Where would he go? Out into the waste, alone?"

"Like I said, I don't know. Maybe I'm just being paranoid. I'd feel better knowing you were keeping an eye on him though."

Evrim glanced back at Synoki, a short distance behind. He turned back to Aljeron. "You know I'm not a coward, Aljeron."

"Of course you aren't."

"Well, I don't want to be left down here with him. He doesn't frighten me so long as I'm awake and alert, but I can't stay awake for a week. With all of you gone and even Koshti going as far up Harak Andunin as possible, I'd be asleep and alone at some point. I'm not going to do that."

Aljeron nodded. "I understand. Think no more about it. He will not come up and must be left behind. That is all there is to it."

They made steady progress all morning and into the early afternoon. The lower slopes were not as formidable up close as they appeared from a distance. The climbers' muscles, after wading through snow a span deep or more for weeks upon weeks, seemed almost to be relieved by this change of use. All of them, even Evrim, made good speed.

The farther up they went, the more frequent difficult patches became, however. The difficulty was usually dependent upon three factors. In some places, there were lots of loose rocks and stones, and these slowed their progress because everyone had to tread cautiously. As Erigan had intimated on the ground, only he and Koshti seemed able to maintain a constant speed, even across these portions.

The second factor that affected their climb was ice. Snow lay upon the mountainside in uneven drifts, but the real danger lay in the possibility that underneath the snow was rock covered with ice. The icy patches visible to the naked eye were usually circumvented with ease, but when they faced snow as far as they could see, then their footsteps and forward progress were slowed indeed, as they could not know with any certainty what the next step might bring.

The third factor was the presence, periodically, of rough and uneven fissures. Some were very thin, no more than a hand across, and these were easily stepped over and left behind. The group encountered two, though, that were far wider and deeper than that, gaping scars in the rough mountainside. The first of these they had been forced to follow some distance before finding a place where they could traverse it, and even then it had been a frighteningly large step for the men. The second was not so wide, but the steep slope on the uphill side had made the crossing even more difficult.

Aljeron kept close to Evrim all the way, and with the exception of the two crevices, his friend did not struggle any more than anyone else. Aljeron lifted his eyes to gaze up the mountain, where the peak noticeably narrowed and seemed also to stretch upward more steeply. There, Aljeron thought, more than steady footwork would be required. There is where Evrim would struggle, but that was probably a matter for tomorrow.

They were making good time now and had been for a while. The slope was steep but the ground wasn't icy and the stones weren't loose. Koshti led the way, his orange and black fur a stark contrast against both the white of the snow and the grey of the clouds and rocks.

Aljeron, who had felt pretty good most of the day, was beginning to feel fatigue set in. The up and down motion and the strange mixture of trying to move quickly while also stepping carefully was taking its toll. He would be glad of a rest when night fell, but from the look of the sky, that would not be for a few hours yet.

Koshti had stopped up ahead, and Aljeron could not at first see why. As he drew nearer, though, the reason became evident. Another fissure ran right across their path.

"Another one," Saegan said as they all came up and stood side by side along its downhill edge.

"Too wide to cross here," Aljeron added.

"Well," Valzaan said quickly, wasting no time, "let's follow it uphill if it is cutting across our path in a diagonal trajectory like the last two. Is it?"

"It is," Aljeron answered. "It moves slightly uphill on our right. Do you want to put your hand on my shoulder as we go like you did last time?"

"Yes," Valzaan answered wearily, or at least his voice seemed weary to Aljeron. "It is at moments like this that I miss the more practical applications of my old staff."

They started uphill along the edge of the fissure, moving as quickly as the terrain allowed. This one was the widest they had seen, and how deep it was Aljeron could not imagine. He peered down into the darkness but saw nothing to indicate its extent.

For a long time they kept along the crevice, and it seemed only to widen. That did not encourage Aljeron, and he began to wonder if it wouldn't be wise to head back the other way. While they would have to backtrack quite a distance and ultimately drop below the point where they had begun, it seemed prudent if there wasn't going to be a way across the chasm in this direction.

But, before he could voice his suggestion, the fissure began to narrow again, and before long it was no wider than when they first encountered it. As they went farther, it grew even narrower. They came at last to a place where it was small enough to jump across.

"As long as the crevice continues to narrow, should we go a little farther just to make sure the crossing is safe?" Aljeron asked.

"Yes," Valzaan answered, "but not too far. We need to make better use of our time by heading more directly uphill while we still can, while daylight and the degree of incline allow it."

They continued along the downhill edge of the fissure, but Evrim did not let the conversation revert to its former quietness. "Valzaan, all this movement left and right around the mountain has made me wonder, how will we know that we haven't passed Sulmandir's gyre by being on the wrong side of Harak Andunin?"

"We won't miss it. I saw the entrance to the gyre through the eyes of a windhover three days ago. I know that it is higher than this, so we need not be concerned about what side of the mountain we are on until tomorrow. What's more, I know that the entrance faces north."

"And what side are we on now?"

"Look away from the mountain," Valzaan answered, "and tell me what you see."

Aljeron paused with Evrim and Saegan and peered outward from the mountain. His focus had been so completely directed at the mountain itself that he realized as he looked away that he hadn't done so since very early in the morning.

The first thing he was struck by was just how high and how far they had already come. The ground lay far below them, far below indeed. As he looked out to the horizon, he saw a sea of white snow, occasionally interrupted by patches of stark brown where barren trees jutted up, or even more occasional patches of green, where evergreens grew in clusters both large and small.

"I see snow as far as the eye can see," Evrim said.

"In every direction?"

Aljeron swept his eyes across the horizon from side to side and nodded involuntarily as Evrim said, "Yes, in every direction."

"Then we aren't on the north face, which is good. We will need to pass the night here, and I'd rather pass it on the south face myself. Tomorrow, we will gradually work our way around to the north side, and there you will see in the distance the blue and grey waters of the Great Northern Sea, and you will know that we are on the right side of Harak Andunin."

They came to a halt and Koshti leapt easily across the fissure, now no more than half a span wide. The men also stepped across it, Valzaan in the middle with Saegan on one side and Aljeron on the other to help steady him. Last of all came Erigan, the self-appointed guardian of the rear.

As Valzaan desired, they turned straight uphill to make all possible haste. The terrain, Aljeron thought, was not too bad, if a little slick from a thin veneer of ice. It would have been nothing that morning, when they had first started out, but now that the muscles in his legs burned as they made their final push, he realized he would have to be careful lest he misstep here out of weariness.

Even as that warning flashed through his head, he saw Evrim slip, land awkwardly, and begin to slide and roll with alarming speed down the mountainside. His hand flailed about, trying to grab hold of something, but it closed successfully upon nothing.

Aljeron started immediately down after him, and in his hurry he felt his own feet slip. Soon he too was on his back and rolling out of control down the mountainside.

The short, quick slide was a blur, and the next thing he knew, the ground dropped away entirely and his body was swinging downward in a very different trajectory. His feet struck something solid, and at that moment he realized what had happened. Somehow his legs and lower body had slipped into the fissure they had just crossed, and now his feet were sliding down the interior wall of the downhill side. He pressed with all his strength and, hitting the slightest of ledges inside the fissure, his downward progress stopped.

He had only a moment to look up before his view was eclipsed by the great brown fur of Erigan, who took hold of him with both great paws and quickly removed him from the fissure, setting him down gently on the uphill side. He shook his head in a bit of the daze and looked at Evrim, who had come to a rest mercifully beside the fissure and not in it. Koshti was quickly at his side, his great furry face nuzzled against Aljeron's own as his warm wet tongue began to lick the gash that a stone had given Aljeron square on his chin.

"Are you two all right?" Saegan asked as he came up to them a moment later.

"A little bruised and cut," Aljeron asked, downplaying the painful beating his body had just taken, "but other than that, just fine."

"Evrim?"

Evrim looked up at Saegan and nodded.

"Good," Valzaan said, approaching most slowly of all, his voice even but full of concern. "Perhaps I was wrong to push us so far. Should we stop here for the night?"

"I don't want to sleep by this crevice," Evrim came straight back. "Let's have another go. I just lost my balance. I'll be more careful this time."

"All right," Valzaan said. "Let's go on."

As they prepared to go, Aljeron put his arm on Evrim's shoulders. "That was quite a tumble," he said, smiling.

"Sorry, Aljeron. I know you only fell because you were trying to help me."

"Don't worry about it. Let's just put some distance between ourselves and this place, all right?"

"Fine with me."

They kept going, for almost another hour, without further incident. When they finally did stop, darkness had fallen, but they had found the closest thing to a level ledge they had passed in quite some time. It wasn't truly level, but lying with their feet downhill, none of them felt like he would roll. They ate quietly and quickly, and no one tried to prolong the day further as their weary bodies sank into sleep.

Aljeron was awake long before dawn. Sleep had been hard to come by. If it was cold at sea level, it was positively freezing up here. Even wearing all his warmest clothes, he felt naked and exposed before the howling, cold wind. This was not what he had been dreaming of down below when he had longed for spring. What little sleep he got he got in the early evening, for by the middle of Second Watch he was fully awake and shivering. He doubted he was the only one awake, but he didn't want to waste the energy it would take to talk, and the shivering in his lips probably precluded the possibility his words would be intelligible anyway.

When dawn eventually graced the southern face of Harak Andunin, they were all up and preparing to go on immediately. From the weariness in their eyes and on their faces, Aljeron could tell he wasn't the only one who'd passed a near sleepless night.

He stepped over to Evrim. "Hey, I had some time to think last night. I didn't sleep so well."

"Me neither."

"It's only going to get steeper, Evrim. Here you don't have to worry about Synoki. You could wait for us."

"No way. I'm going up to that gyre if only to get out of this cold. Besides, you guys could miss me on the way down."

"We could figure out a way to make sure we don't."

"Aljeron, I'm not staying here. I've come this far, I'm going to go the rest of the way."

"We almost lost you."

"But you didn't." Aljeron sighed. "Look, Aljeron, I need to do this. I need to reach the top. I would be able to do this if I hadn't lost my arm, and I need to do it now to prove to myself that I'm still me."

"Of course you're still you, Evrim, but you've changed. It's all right to acknowledge that, to acknowledge your limits."

"When I've reached them, I'll acknowledge them."

Monias looked over the edge of the boat. Below them in the water were the strange and surreal images that he had seen many times in their journey. The jagged and barren branches of large bushes and small trees wavered ever so slightly with the movement of the waters. Sometimes, when Monias and Garin were near the shore like they were now, he could feel the tops of these branches scraping against the keel of their skiff.

He looked past Garin at the land. Yes, he had seen sights like this many times in their journey up the Barunaan and along the edge of the Kellisor, but the shore ahead was not Suthanin but Enthanin. They had successfully crossed the mouth of the Kalamin River and before long, they would be on dry land, safe and on the last leg of their journey to Amaan Sul.

Garin stopped rowing and Monias felt the almost indistinguishable shift of him tensing. Ever so slightly, Garin turned his head. Monias started to do likewise, but Garin grabbed the front of Monias's cloak with a firm grasp and, leaping from the side of the boat, pulled Monias into the water with him.

As all this was happening, Monias saw the shadow of a great black hand descending rapidly toward the skiff. Beyond the hand rose the enormous creature they had seen in the Kellisor Sea. In the brief moment before Garin pulled Monias into the water and the whole sight disappeared, he caught the merest of glimpses of a great, probing eye, looking down at them from so astonishing a height that Monias was awed even as he slipped beneath the surface.

Monias was underwater completely, and his eyes, still open, were gazing up at the bottom of their boat. Even underwater the sound of the boat splintering into pieces was dramatic. The broken pieces radiated outward in waves and the massive hand pushed downward through the water, ripping branches from the trees that Monias had just moments before been admiring. Fortunately for Monias, Garin had a good grip and had been pulling constantly since they struck the water. The creature's hands missed Monias by the slimmest of margins.

It is to no avail, Monias thought. *We will run out of air and have to surface eventually. He will see us. We will be killed, and all we have overcome will be for naught.*

The great hand rose from the water, and Monias, now no longer a spectator in his own rescue, flipped onto his stomach and tried to keep up with Garin as he swam away from the wreckage. It was easier said than done. His heavy winter cloak was soaked and weighed him down. His arms and legs felt like they'd been tied down with wet blankets, and the little amount of air he had been able to gasp before striking the surface of the water was all but gone. His lungs were already on fire, and he knew that his need for air would soon override all other desires, including the desire to get beyond this creature's reach.

Garin, who had let go of the cloak when Monias reoriented himself, was outdistancing Monias by a good bit. Monias saw the kicking feet through the churning water and knew he'd never be able to catch up before returning to the surface. With no power to go on, he had nowhere to go but up. Kicking hard he rose far enough to stick his head out of the water and gasp.

As his eyes refocused in the world of air, he half expected to see the great dark clawlike hand reaching down to crush him, but there was none. In fact, the creature, though still towering close by, didn't seem to be aware of Monias at all. Thinking at first he should take advantage of this good fortune to swallow a deep breath and get on his way, Monias saw why the creature's attention had strayed.

High in the air, far, far higher than the creature's head even, a gliding golden form sailed across the grey sky. It was this golden form that captured the creature's attention.

Monias looked over his shoulder and saw Garin's head, now above the surface of the water, but retreating stroke by stroke farther away from him and closer to the shore, which Monias estimated to be perhaps twenty-five spans away. Monias likewise began to swim as fast as he could toward the shore. If the dragon—for though Monias in all his years had never seen one, he could not but believe that was exactly what he had seen—if the dragon passed on and the creature's attention returned to the water, Monias would surely be lost.

It seemed to take forever to reach water shallow enough for Monias to stand, but he did. He stumbled the few spans that remained onto dry land and collapsed on hands and knees.

"Are you all right?" Garin whispered.

Monias lifted his head and nodded at Garin, who motioned with his finger on his lips for Monias to stay quiet. Garin pointed out over the water. The great creature still stood there, his frame just as impressive from this distance. His powerful arms hung by his side and his back was to the men. Monias searched the sky for some sign of the dragon, but there was none.

Monias looked back at Garin, who motioned for him to follow. Half crawling, they scurried across the muddy bank, moving inland as quickly as possible. After several minutes they reached a small cluster of bushes and ducked behind them. Looking back, they saw the great creature disappearing beneath the surface of the Kellisor Sea. Where it was now headed, Monias could not have said.

When the creature disappeared, Monias felt as though he could breathe again. Hope, like the first rays of daylight, began to spread over him. Whatever had just happened and no matter how close it had been, he was ashore in Enthanin. With the Barunaan and Kellisor behind them, the worst of their journey—he hoped—was over.

Wylla stood under the high stone arch of the entrance to the royal residence. She gazed out into the large open courtyard that lay between it and the gate that opened into the city. She looked not so much at the courtyard as at the grey clouds, which stretched across the horizon. She looked up at these clouds and smiled. There had been a time when a sight such as this would have dampened her spirits rather than cheered her, but not at present. The sky was grey, yes, but more importantly, it was still dry. For more than a week now, it had been dry. There were even a few places on the smooth paving stones where the standing water had begun to recede, not that they didn't still appear like reservoirs.

The hope she had initially refused to allow to take root inside of her returned. Maybe the storm was over. Maybe the rain was really gone. The sky had not lightened in the slightest, so this hope might not be entirely logical, but she didn't care. She couldn't suppress the thought any longer, and she didn't want to.

"Hello there," a voice called from behind her, and she turned to see Kyril and Karalin smiling at her from the front hall of the palace.

"Would you like to walk awhile outside?" Kyril continued. "We're headed out now ourselves."

"Where are you off to?"

"Only just outside. We weren't thinking of leaving the palace grounds, actually. All we wanted was to walk outside, out in the fresh air."

"Since there's no rain to worry about," Karalin added.

"Yes, since there's no rain."

"Sure," Wylla replied. "I will gladly come celebrate the rainlessness of the afternoon with you."

Together the three walked out into the courtyard, heading toward the large circular fountain that in warmer weather would spray water high into the late-afternoon sky. They couldn't get there directly, as one of the large pools of standing water lay directly between them and it, but by winding their way carefully through the courtyard, they eventually found themselves standing beside the low wall that contained the fountain pool.

Despite the absence of rain, the water inside the pool came right up to the edge of the low wall. In fact, as Wylla looked down upon it, it seemed that the water actually rose above the side of the wall and curved slightly down at the rim. She reached down with her finger and poked ever so lightly at the curve. The surface tension was broken and a small stream of water rushed across the top of the stone wall and down into the courtyard.

"It's strange," Karalin said, "but the absence of rain makes me think of spring."

"Why is that strange?" Kyril asked.

"Because spring is usually so wet here. Usually the spring rains begin, and then the evidence of spring begins to creep over the land. The smell of spring seeps out of the earth and wafts across the land in the breeze. But this year there wasn't the barest hint of spring in all that rain. Now, though, now that it's gone, I can almost begin to sense it coming at last."

"I hope you're right," Wylla said, turning to look at her friends. "And I hope that spring brings with it a blue sky. That's all we're lacking."

"That would be great," Kyril concurred.

"Imagine that spring, real spring were here," Wylla said suddenly, excited. "What would you do?"

"Real spring?"

"Yes, warm weather and clear blue skies with the occasional high white cloud drifting lazily across the horizon. What would you do?"

"Well . . . " Kyril thought for a moment. "I'd have to find my spring clothing and change, but after I had, I'd grab Halina and Roslin I guess, and go walking out in the city. The palace is lovely, but it has been too long since we've wandered the streets of Amaan Sul for hours, exploring. I know they'd love it."

"Can you smell the marketplace? The bread and cakes, the fresh vegetables lining the stalls?" Wylla inhaled as though she could smell them even now.

"It all sounds lovely." Karalin smiled. "But you'd need to watch out for jugglers."

The other women looked at her for a moment and then laughed, recalling the excited story Roslin had told about a journey into the city and her incident with the jugglers.

"And yet," Wylla said after a moment, "How fortunate for me that her adventure brought me Yorek."

"Fortunate indeed," Karalin agreed.

"And you, Karalin? What would you do?" Wylla asked.

"Me? Oh, I think I'd just slip out through the outer gate into the fields and lie down in the grass. That is, if the ground was dry too."

"As long as we're dreaming, why not?"

"Then yes, I'd lie down in the grass with the warm sun beating down on my face. It would be great to feel warmth on my face, not the flickering or unbearable warmth of a fire, but the steady and constant warmth of the sun riding slowly across the sky. I'd nestle right in so I could feel the soft stalks tickle my neck and poke my scalp. I'd lie there and close my eyes and dream about happy things, warm and soft and pleasant things."

"Ooh," Wylla said, a tingle running down her skin. "That does sound good. You almost make it seem real."

"Yes, I think I could join you. Forget my expedition into the city, and forget Halina and Roslin. We'd like some peace and quiet in the grass, wouldn't we?"

The others laughed, and after a moment Wylla continued. "It makes me think about being young, before I was queen. Lying in the grass without a care or worry in the world."

The laughter died away, and Wylla, aware that she had almost broken the lovely spell that enchanted them, asked them another question in hopes that she might lure it back. "What is your favorite spring memory?"

"You mean specifics? Or a favorite spring pastime, like Karalin's vision of lying in the grass?"

"Specific memory. When you think of happy spring days or nights, what comes to mind first?"

"That's easy," Kyril answered.

"What?"

She blushed. "Let's hear Karalin's first."

"All right," Karalin said, closing her eyes and clasping her hands before her. Soon enough a smile crossed her face.

"The gardens of Sulare," she said at last. She opened her eyes and looked at Wylla. "Walking in them, smelling them. Looking in from them at the immense fountain of the Great Hall bathed in light from the open roof. I have no memory like it."

"A good memory," Wylla murmured. "And now yours, Kyril. Whatever it is, you can't keep it to yourself anymore."

"All right," Kyril said. "My favorite spring memory is of Evrim proposing to me on a moonlit night in Dal Harat. We were walking through the town, going nowhere in particular, and he suddenly stopped and stepped in front of me and took me by the arms. I looked into his eyes and knew what he was going to say before he even said it. I threw my arms around him and said yes before he even asked. Poor Evrim, it took him a few minutes to recover, but when he did, he kissed me for the first time and held me tight, and I couldn't have been happier."

"That's a good memory too," Wylla added.

"Yes," Kyril said, the smile slipping from her face. "I have no better memory since before news reached Dal Harat that Joraiem was dead, since before the world fell apart and collapsed all around us."

"My favorite spring memory," Wylla said as if Kyril hadn't added this last part, "is from the same spring as both of yours. Imagine that, when asked for our favorite memory of spring, we all go back to precisely the same year. My favorite memory is not from Sulare, though, but from the road to Sulare. It is the day I first saw Joraiem, coming toward me through the snow trees. My heart leapt as he approached. I could barely breathe. I didn't know exactly where in Kirthanin I was, but I knew I was home."

Kyril reached out and stroked Wylla's back. Tears suddenly formed in Wylla's eyes and rolled down her cheeks. "Here I go," she said, wiping them away, "ruining a perfectly good rainless day by crying."

"Don't worry about it," Kyril said softly. "You haven't ruined anything."

"Joy and sadness," Wylla said, "so often tied together, and always with memories of him."

"I know."

"Let's head back inside," Wylla said, and the others nodded. They stepped away from the low fountain wall and worked their way back across the courtyard.

"Your Majesty?"

Wylla was watching the latest trick that Roslin and Halina had mastered in their ongoing attempts to juggle when Yorek summoned her from Kyril's spacious guest quarters. "Yes?"

"A messenger," Yorek said, almost breathlessly, as though he'd run up the stairs. "From the river."

Wylla said nothing but started on ahead of him, heading back down the long narrow hallway to the main stair. The messenger waited patiently at the entrance to the Great Hall, his riding gloves in hand.

"You've come from the Kalamin?" Wylla asked.

"Yes, Your Majesty."

"From Merias?"

"Yes," the man replied.

"Well?"

"Thousands of soldiers from Werthanin and Suthanin, as well as Your Majesty's own soldiers, have crossed the river into Enthanin. Along with them have come Great Bear in large numbers as well as a few dragons."

"Dragons!" Wylla exclaimed, a distant memory flashing before her mind's eye of Eliandir leaping into the sky and circling in ever widening arcs as he rose high above the Great Hall of Sulare. "What happened, was there a battle?"

"Not exactly," the man replied, hesitantly. "The captains of the army were afraid that our forces would be trapped by the river. Apparently, a great sea creature has been unleashed upon the land through Kirthanin's flooded rivers. The soldiers who retreated up the Barunaan ahead of Malek's forces all had stories of it, and though it was only in the distance, I saw glimpses of him myself, Your Majesty. So we crossed, before we could be caught."

"I see," Wylla said, wondering what this creature might be and feeling much of the growing elation of the past week slip away. The rain had stopped, not because something had gone wrong with the enemy, but because its purpose had been accomplished.

"I am sent," the man continued, "to tell Your Majesty that the hosts of Kirthanin are even now on their way to Amaan Sul. In the next couple days, they should be arriving, the soonest probably less than a day behind me."

A hundred thoughts raced through Wylla's head. Lodging. Food. Siege. They swirled out of control, but a single, dominant thought emerged above them all. "Benjiah?" she said out loud, almost without realizing she had. She turned to the man. "My son, the heir to the throne, was he among those who crossed the river?"

The messenger looked uneasy. "I have no news of him. He was among those who passed through Elnin Wood, but I had no personal knowledge of his crossing when I was dispatched. There was much confusion, but he may have been among those still on the south side of the river when Merias sent me."

"I see," Wylla said. "Thank you."

Wylla summoned a steward to take care of the messenger, then walked with Yorek to her private parlor. "What do we do, Yorek?"

"What we can. They will be here before we are ready for them. We need to just accept that and do what we're able to."

Wylla nodded but said nothing further as they reached the door to the parlor. She halted, taking the handle in her hand but not opening it.

"Your Majesty?"

"Yes," Wylla said quietly.

"No news isn't necessarily bad news," Yorek said gently.

"I know," Wylla said, offering a faint smile. She opened the door and they passed inside.

The evening wore on and Synoki reined in the horse he rode. It had been Aljeron's and was the best of the lot. He had not been able to ride as fast as he would have liked, in large measure because it was harder than he had expected, leading the other horses south with him. The mountain was now but a distant form rising high into the sky behind him in the north. Tomorrow, after he had set the horses free to roam the Nolthanin waste, he would make better time. Making better time was important, for now that he knew Joraiem's son was the child of the prophecy, there was no time to lose. What he had sought in his long sojourn northward he did not find, but what he had found would be of use. It would be of use indeed when he could find and rejoin Cheimontyr, Farimaal, and the others, but first there was a long journey ahead of him.

A WARNING

RULALIN DROPPED FROM his saddle. He looked back over his shoulder at the camp in the distance. There was no evidence of pursuit, and he felt relief wash over him. He assumed that a certain amount of freedom came with his promotion to the position of a captain of the Nolthanim, but he still didn't really know how much. During the three days since he noticed this tree at some distance from the camp, he'd thought often about coming out to it, but it had taken him until today to actually do it. Though it was within sight of camp, he still felt strange taking the liberty to ride out here unaccompanied.

He turned back to the tree. It was no wonder of nature, not at all, just a lone, leafless tree standing stark and bare against the dismal backdrop of the grey sky and endless plain. Even so he walked over to the trunk, tied his horse to it and felt the rough bark with his fingers. He couldn't explain what had drawn him to it, really, but he had very much wanted to come. Now that he was here, he felt a little silly.

Again he looked over his shoulder. No pursuit, just the distant camp. Turning back around, he looked up at the low-hanging branch just a hand or two above his head. Impulsively he reached up and grabbed it with both hands, and almost before he knew what he had done, he swung himself up into the tree.

He looked down at the ground and felt strangely giddy. He had not been up in a tree since he was a boy, and probably a young boy at that. In a moment, images of trees in and around Fel Edorath that he had climbed flashed before him. One tree in particular grew just inside the false eastern gate that in his youth had been a symbol of the city's defiance of Malek, but the memory of it now mocked him. The tree, though, was majestic, spreading its limbs out and up, the top of which stood a span or so above the gate. From an early age he had practiced climbing that tree, at least since he'd been tall enough to haul himself up into its lower limbs. Once, and only once, he had climbed high enough to see over the wall.

The view from the top of that tree had been spectacular. Looking out over the imposing gate at the vast open spaces beyond had filled the young and wide-eyed Rulalin with wonder. He had been struck with the largeness of the world. Yes, he'd been outside the walls many times, but the view on those occasions was never like this.

That particular excursion to the top of the tree had ended badly. After a long time of resting in the crook of two of the uppermost branches still big enough to support him, he'd made the considerable mistake of looking downward, straight downward. The ground was alarmingly far away. Despite having remained perfectly still the whole time he'd been in his seat, he started to wobble. Instantly he clasped the trunk of the tree and turned inward, holding on for dear life.

A long time he remained there, unwilling to move and unwilling to call out for help. Eventually, he forced himself to look up and out again, and after a while, the trembling stopped. Slowly, one cautious move after another, he worked his way down the tree. Once on solid ground, he swore to himself he'd never go that high again, and he hadn't.

Now he looked down at the ground, so close he could drop from the branch and barely feel the impact. Suddenly he regretted never going back up to the top of that tree. He should have gone back the next day and the day after that. He should have gone back every day until the fear was gone, but he hadn't. He'd missed his chance.

You can't ever go back.

The words passed through his mind, but he didn't really know if they were chronologically or geographically connected to his memory, though either explanation was probably equally true. What was done was done, and what was left behind was left behind.

He looked out through the jagged branches scarring the grey sky. The wind was still cool, but the sharp, wintry bite was not as strong. In fact, it seemed to him noticeably more bearable, though not being soaked could have had something to do with that perception. He leaned back against the tree trunk and closed his eyes. He'd have to go back, and soon, but for the moment, the rest and reprieve were nice.

When he dropped down from the tree at last, it was with reluctance that he climbed up into the saddle again. He hadn't known what he was looking for when he had decided to come, and he still wasn't sure exactly what he'd found. Even so, he didn't regret coming. Anything that could take him back to life before the war, life before he was in hiding, life before Sulare—

anything that could do that was worthwhile. He turned from the tree and spurred his horse back toward the present.

At the outskirts of the camp he dismounted and handed his horse over to be groomed. He found himself hurrying back to his tent and so consciously slowed to a mere stroll. As his tent came into view, he smiled to himself, because he had neither been stopped nor accosted by anyone. No one had taken any notice of his departure at all.

Rounding the corner, the smile slipped from his face. Standing at the entrance to his tent was Tashmiren. The impudent peacock was preening, running his hands through his long flowing hair and adjusting the ridiculously ornate pendant so that the chain wasn't twisted upon his chest.

Rulalin hadn't yet been seen so he stepped to the side of the tent and grumbled under his breath. "What's he here for?"

He had seen relatively little of Tashmiren since the promotion. Rulalin's advancement had no doubt limited Tashmiren's ability to have fun at his expense, making it much less worth Tashmiren's while to come round at all. This was perfectly all right with Rulalin. Seeing him here, waiting before the tent, wearing his characteristic expression of annoyance, reminded Rulalin just how much he despised the man.

He toyed momentarily with the idea of walking away again, but he didn't. Tashmiren might be there with an important message, and if he was, Rulalin's protracted absence could raise questions. About what exactly, Rulalin didn't know, but he didn't want to find out. No, sooner or later he'd have to get this over with, so it had just as well be sooner.

He walked around the tent and toward Tashmiren, doing his best to look indifferent and unconcerned. Tashmiren looked up at him and the sour look didn't change in the slightest.

"About time you showed up," Tashmiren said.

AWAKE

"I come and go as I please," Rulalin said, hoping he didn't sound as defensive as he felt.

"Maybe, but it is never wise to keep Farimaal waiting, whatever your other business might be."

"Farimaal?" Rulalin said, his veneer of confidence cracking. His body tensed. It didn't seem possible. In the whole time they'd been camped here by the Kalamin, the previous hour was the only time he'd been unaccounted for. He had not seen or been sent for by Farimaal in all of that time. That such a summons should come now of all times would have been laughable, if it wasn't so unfortunate.

"Yes, Farimaal, and he doesn't like to be kept waiting."

"How could I know he'd send for me?" Rulalin snapped. "I'm no longer a prisoner, Tashmiren. I don't just sit around in my tent all day."

Tashmiren shrugged, evidently enjoying Rulalin's discomfort. "That's as it may be, but Farimaal's expectations are more important than the apparent reasonableness of your position."

Rulalin couldn't help shifting where he stood so he could look out over the camp in the direction of Farimaal's quarters. He turned back to Tashmiren reluctantly. "What does he want?"

"What he wanted when he first sent for you an hour ago, I don't know, but I can imagine what he wants now." Tashmiren smirked and with evident delight added, "You just can't ever seem to get things right, can you?"

"Shut up, lackey," Rulalin fairly hissed, scowling. As soon as the words had escaped his lips, he regretted them. It was too late to take them back, though, so he didn't bother trying to hide the contempt that prompted them.

Rage boiled on Tashmiren's face and in his eyes. "You're a tool in Malek's hand, and a fool besides. When you've served your purpose, I'll exact payment for your insult."

Rulalin stepped closer to Tashmiren, returning the hateful glare in his eyes with equal intensity. "Not likely. You'll exact nothing from me. I don't have anything to fear from you, unless you plan to come for your payment while I sleep."

Tashmiren said nothing but stood there gazing spitefully at Rulalin. After a moment, he stepped around him and walked away.

Rulalin watched him go, then, cursing his luck, started off toward Farimaal's quarters.

Even in his distracted state, Rulalin noticed an unusual amount of activity in the camp. Men were scurrying to and fro, many carrying things and moving in small clusters. He wondered if they had finished their project at last and if the time was upon them to cross the Kalamin.

Normally, the thought of crossing the Kalamin River and proceeding on to Amaan Sul would have produced a strange sensation in his stomach, the result of high anxiety and extreme anticipation mixed. Now, though, with the image of an angry Farimaal looming in the back of his mind, Rulalin felt nothing of the sort. All of his plans for what would take place when they crossed the river and marched to the capital city of Enthanin depended first and foremost upon his being in the good graces of Malek, which meant being in the good graces of Farimaal.

Since Benjiah had been placed under his care, he had heard nothing from Farimaal nor seen him. In all the activity going on between the camp and the river, he had never been called upon to help, observe, or participate in any way. He was left to assume that other than watching over the prisoner, he had no real duty during this lull. So, the summons from Farimaal and the increased activity suggested that the time to move was near, for he could think of no other reason he would suddenly be needed by the high commander of the Nolthanim.

A pair of young Nolthanim soldiers squatted by the door to Farimaal's tent, eating a loaf of bread between them. They ripped off hunks and swallowed them hungrily, as though they were starving. They looked up at Rulalin as he approached and then nodded toward the door when they recognized him. The idea that he was becoming known among the soldiers of the Nolthanim had been comforting before this, but their recognition of him today seemed a dubious distinction. Neither man moved as Rulalin pulled back the flap and stepped through.

The interior of the tent was as bare as always. A pair of torches, which seemed always to burn steadily but dimly, stood on either side of the entrance as he passed through, and by their light he saw Farimaal standing not far away. The lean, grizzled man wore a simple linen tunic of thin cloth and short sleeves. Rulalin shivered just looking at it. He couldn't imagine, even with the slight improvement in the weather, how cold Farimaal must be, but the man did not shiver or shake. Indeed, in his right hand was a long, dark blade, held almost perfectly flat and perfectly still. Farimaal was gazing at it as Rulalin stepped into the tent. The sight of Farimaal holding a sword, something he'd not seen in some time, kept him rooted in the spot. Instinctively, his hand sought the handle of his own blade.

"This is not meant for you," Farimaal said without moving or looking in his direction. "Keep your hand away from your sword if you would keep it that way."

Rulalin's hand dropped to his side. Still, Farimaal did not move. He did not speak. Rulalin shifted his feet, nervously, keenly aware that sweat was running down his side under his heavy cloak. Maybe that light tunic wasn't such a bad idea after all.

"I am sorry I wasn't at my tent to receive your messenger immediately, commander," Rulalin began, but a raised hand from Farimaal silenced him. The high commander turned away, sheathing his blade in one quick, fluid motion. Then he walked over to the slight wooden chair that sat upon the smallest of platforms, which raised the chair just half a hand off the ground.

"Our advance guard crosses the Kalamin tonight," Farimaal said as he settled into his seat. "That means you will cross tonight."

"Yes, sir," Rulalin said, the nervousness fading a bit. He could read no change in Farimaal from his other visits to this place. Familiarity had not led to comfort with Farimaal, exactly, but at least the uneasiness was not as great as it once had been.

"You have hopes, do you not, for what lies on the other side of this river?" Farimaal asked, hesitating just slightly enough before the word *hopes* to emphasize it clearly, even alarmingly.

"Yes, sir," Rulalin said. "I do."

Farimaal looked into Rulalin's eyes and for a long moment, the man surveyed him silently. There was something there that Rulalin hadn't noticed before, a flicker of something distant but also real and alive. It seemed to Rulalin almost as if Farimaal was looking through him, as though seeing a vision of something long ago. Whatever it was, it passed, and Farimaal looked down at his lap again before continuing the conversation.

"She is the Queen of the Enthanim?" Farimaal asked.

"Yes."

"Her name is Wylla Someris?"

"Yes."

"You killed her husband?"

"Yes."

Farimaal looked up at him again but said nothing further about the murder. "The boy, Benjiah, is her son?"

It was all Rulalin could do to keep his mouth from dropping open. He hadn't spoken the boy's name to anyone other than Soran, and he was sure Soran hadn't repeated this information.

He had thought they were the only two who knew exactly who Benjiah was. How Farimaal knew, he had no idea. He doubted Benjiah had volunteered the information, unless Malek had questioned the boy with some supernatural power and compelled him to reveal it.

"Yes, he is her only son," Rulalin said at last, realizing that Farimaal's question remained unanswered. There was no purpose not telling the truth. If Farimaal knew the boy's identity and name, he would likely know more. Rulalin's words couldn't save Benjiah if he was slated to die, but with a lie he just might join the boy.

"He will continue under your supervision," Farimaal said, then added, "But take care. His life and yours are tied together. We are keeping him alive for one reason and one reason only. The sight of the queen's son, captive and in a cage, will be a sign to those who resist us of their future. Regardless of what wonder he may have worked while using that staff the old man once carried, no talisman or relic will save him now. And in the end, when Enthanin has surrendered to avoid his fate, we will execute him in public so that all may see that being a boy and a prince and even a miracle worker are nothing if you stand against Malek. Keep him safe and alive for that day, or you will stand beside him at his execution. Understood?"

"Yes."

"As for his mother, if she resists us, we will also kill her," Farimaal said. "You know that, don't you?"

Rulalin swallowed. Despite his urge to argue for her, he controlled the impulse. The time might come for pleading, but it wasn't time yet. "If you decide when the time comes that she must die, then she will."

"She will not need to die, though, if you succeed in your job. If you deliver her to me, and her city with her, then you may have her as your reward, as you desire."

"Yes, sir," Rulalin said, Wylla's face appearing momentarily before him in the darkness.

"Do well in this, our last campaign, Captain Tarasir," Farimaal said, standing up and stepping off the platform. "And I will give you both of your wishes. I will give you Someris, and I will give you an inheritance among the Nolthanim when we go home again at last."

"Yes, sir. Thank you, sir."

"You may go." Farimaal turned back to his seat, and not waiting for anything else, Rulalin quickly stepped out of the tent.

For a while Rulalin wandered aimlessly, in a daze. Men and Malekim rushed all around him, going here and there with direction and purpose as he drifted in and out of them haphazardly. He had aggrandized his importance to Farimaal and to Malek's mission and overestimated his power to save Wylla. After all these leagues and all he had done to get here, she seemed even now to be fading from view and receding beyond his reach. If she resisted, as surely she would, she would die.

He stopped where he was. The world around him snapped back into focus. He looked around to see where he was and started back through the camp in the direction of his tent. He was being sent across the Kalamin tonight, and he would be among the first to reach Amaan Sul. He must direct all his creative abilities and all his energies every step of the way from this spot to the gates of Amaan Sul toward figuring out exactly how he could dissuade Wylla from defending the city. To this end, Benjiah's capture would undoubtedly be the key, but he must figure out exactly how best to use the boy's imprisonment to achieve his goal.

As he neared his tent, or at least the spot where it had been, he found Soran squatting on the ground in front of the now empty space. His lieutenant looked up from the ground at Rulalin's momentary hesitation and look of uncertainty. "They took it."

"Took it?"

"The tent. I got here a short while ago and they were packing it up. You just missed it. I think we're on the move," Soran said, smiling slightly at his understatement.

"Yes, we're to cross the Kalamin tonight," Rulalin answered.

"So I gathered." Soran peered more intently at Rulalin as though just realizing that all of Rulalin's strange reactions were not the result of his missing tent. "What is it?"

Rulalin looked at Soran, wondering for a moment what to say or not say. In the end he sighed and sat down beside him. "I'm weary, that's all."

"I hate to tell you, Rulalin, but we've been camped in one place with essentially nothing to do for more than a week. We're as rested as we're going to be."

"I know. I didn't mean physically."

Soran didn't say anything, so Rulalin continued. "All this way, I've kidded myself that I went to Malek to save Fel Edorath. It's not true."

"No?"

"No," Rulalin replied. "Truth be told, I didn't even go to him to save myself, though I know that's probably what Aljeron and all the others believe."

Again Soran didn't say anything, and Rulalin looked at him. He understood at that moment that even Soran had been operating under that assumption. He nodded with the realization. "No, believe it or not, Soran, I didn't even go to the Mountain for me, or at least, not primarily for me. I went to Malek to save her, Wylla Someris, and she's somewhere out there on the other side of this river."

"So, here you go then. Finish what you started."

"I will, if I can, but her life hangs in the balance."

"How so?"

"Farimaal just told me as much."

"He did?'

"He said that Benjiah is to be used as an example of what happens to those who resist Malek. He is being kept alive to be used in the conquest of Enthanin, perhaps as leverage for surrender and certainly as a symbol. Wylla, as queen, will likely also play the role of symbol if she fights back."

"Do you think she'll fight?"

"Yes."

"Are you being sent to the city as Malek's envoy?"

"Yes."

"You'll try to talk her into surrendering?

"Of course."

"Can you?"

"I don't know," Rulalin said, shaking his head. "That's just the thing. Having come all this way, all for this moment, I thought that I would have some idea of what to say when I saw her again at last. But now, now that the moment is almost upon me, I still don't know."

"Surely the boy will be key. She may be a queen, but she's a mother first. She will surrender for sure if she thinks the boy's life is at stake."

"Perhaps," Rulalin said, "But there is peril in that road. If she believes Benjiah's situation is such that nothing will save him, she may not surrender at all. I will have to be careful how I walk that line. Indeed, I'll have to be careful with the whole task. I have, shall we say, a credibility problem with her."

"Yes."

"Well," Rulalin said after a moment. "There are still many leagues between us and Amaan Sul. I have some time to figure out what I will do. What's important, Soran, what's most important, is the fact that this is the last campaign. We march to war together one last time. Whatever happens, it will be settled in Enthanin, and it will be settled soon."

"You may be right."

"I know I am, Soran. What remains of the Werthanim resistance, and a large part of the Suthanim, lies ahead of us in Enthanin. If we win this battle, the strength of Kirthanin will be broken. When Enthanin falls, Kirthanin falls, whatever the specifics may be. This will all be over before we know it."

"By the Mountain, Rulalin," Soran said, responding eagerly to his words. "May it be even so. It is good to hear you so confident."

"I am confident, for Valzaan has been blown into the sea and Benjiah is a captive here among us. Unless yet another surprise prophet or the like waits among our enemy to wield supernatural power against us, it seems likely our enemy will not hold out long. Whatever happens, though, I am not going back to Fel Edorath."

"What?"

"I'm not going back."

"Why?"

"Because whatever lies ahead, I can never go back. If I fail to secure Wylla's life, then my own life will mean nothing. I will plunge myself into battle and into blood until I fall, and I will count it the happiest day I have seen in many a year. If I succeed in saving her, then I will keep her safe until all is over and then go to Nolthanin. I will take her as far away from everything and everyone else as I can, and I will spend the rest of my days trying to earn her forgiveness for the happiness I stole from her."

"But what about Fel Edorath?"

"You will go back, Soran, and you will put the pieces back together, as best as you are able, so long as Malek allows it."

"But I will need help."

"Of course you will, as would I if I were going, but you are already a leader of men, Soran. You will need help, but you will not need my help. You are ready to do this work without me, and Fel Edorath deserves a new start without a Tarasir to mess things up."

"Rulalin, you're being ridiculous. There's no reason you couldn't go back, with or without Wylla."

"I'm not going back, Soran, ever. There really is nothing to discuss and nothing more to say. That's all there is to it. I knew when I passed the gates as we left that I would not be back, but I haven't said so because I haven't let myself admit it until now. But I know. I know this as surely as I know anything. What's done is done, and what is left behind is left behind."

Rulalin stood, then reached down to help Soran to his feet. "Look, we are crossing the river tonight and presumably heading immediately northward toward the city. Go, put your things together and meet me by Benjiah's cage. It is time I tried talking to him again."

Benjiah adjusted himself in the cage, trying to find a comfortable position. The small space was cramped but adequate, so that up until the morning a few days before, when the soldiers brought the chains in which he was now bound, he had been comfortable most of the time. Afterward, when his feet were chained together with perhaps a couple hands of loose chain between them, and when his hands were likewise bound, finding comfortable positions on the hard wooden floor became increasingly difficult. Some positions were no longer manageable at all because the chains constrained him, and finding variety for his body was nearly impossible. Other achievable positions could not be maintained for long, because they required him to lie with certain lengths of chain underneath the weight of his body and over time the hard links bruised his soft flesh. He groaned, thinking that he would almost rather be soaking wet and sleeping in mud than sleepless in these chains.

The thought of all those days in the rain now inevitably took him back to the same thing. All thoughts of water, from the lukewarm water left in a pitcher in his cage each morning to last him through the day, to the rains of the previous months, to the images of the ocean, the Barunaan, and the Kalamin—all of them led his mind to the explosive force of the erupting water in his dream. The dream was a mystery. The progression of images was always predictable and clear, up until the explosion of water that ended it. He could see everything else, and indeed, sight was the dominant sense through all of it. But after the water, he could not so much see the sequence of events as hear and feel it, as a sound like the rending of stone and the earth itself shattered the quiet of the moment. Water sprayed and covered him, lifting his body upward as the swell continued to grow. In his waking moments, he pictured himself like a ship upon the ocean, tossed to and fro by a seething and tumultuous mass of water.

His reflections on his dreams were interrupted by the sight of Rulalin Tarasir making his way toward the cage. Benjiah realized something serious must be on his mind, because in the week since he'd been moved out here, Rulalin had not come to speak to him once. He was always circling in the distance, much like a wolf might circle its prey before leaping upon it. Today he was not circling, and the safe distance he had previously maintained was rapidly disappearing.

Rulalin stopped a few feet shy of the cage and looked in at him. Benjiah did not avoid his gaze but returned it calmly. "I hope the chains are not too uncomfortable," Rulalin started. "I argued against them, but in this one thing, my authority over you was overruled."

Benjiah did not reply. Keeping quiet had unnerved Rulalin the last time, and Benjiah thought he would see how the same approach worked this time.

"I saw you before, you know. Before you were brought into the camp. I even saw you before the battles along the Barunaan on the way north from Cimaris Rul."

Benjiah shifted his feet, and the chains scraped along the wooden floor. He thought he knew what Rulalin was talking about, but he couldn't see where Rulalin might be going with it.

"It was in a dream, some time ago. I guess it wasn't a really long time ago, but it feels almost like a lifetime ago. In the dream I was at home, in Fel Edorath, and the city was empty. I dreamed that I stood at the western gate of the city and you stood outside." Rulalin hesitated, seeming to study him for possible reactions. "It was very strange. You asked me to come out, to leave the city behind, but I didn't, and then you turned away."

Benjiah almost opened his mouth to speak, but he controlled the urge and kept quiet. Rulalin didn't continue and for a long time stood looking out at the camp. After a while, he turned back to Benjiah and said, "I never thought we'd meet in real life."

There was great sadness in Rulalin's face, and for a moment, Benjiah almost felt compassion for him, but the feeling was short-lived. Rulalin recovered from his momentary lapse and regained his composure. When he spoke again it was less familiar and with a clearer tone of authority. "Benjiah, do you understand who I am?"

"Of course," Benjiah said almost involuntarily. He was immediately disappointed for having spoken, but almost as quickly as the feeling came it passed. He felt instead a strange assurance that talking to Rulalin was all right, even necessary.

"I didn't hate your father, Benjiah. Not that you care one way or the other, I realize that. I don't expect you to understand why I did what I did or to hate me less for it. I did, however, want you to know, though in one sense, I guess it doesn't really matter anymore."

Rulalin hesitated, and Benjiah waited, silent this time not because it was some sort of strategy, but because he didn't know what to say. After a moment, Rulalin went on. "What might matter, Benjiah, is that I want to save your mother's life."

The words hung in the air before Benjiah, sharp and clear and almost visible. They came like a slap in the face, drawing his focus from the lifelong yearning he'd always had to know his father to the more immediate situation. It had of course occurred to him that this great host was perched on the border of Enthanin and that out there beyond the Kalamin, the hosts of Kirthanin now included his mother and home, but Rulalin's words put the stark reality of her immediate danger bluntly before him.

"Saving her, Benjiah," Rulalin continued, "may depend on you. They know you are her son. How they found out I don't know. I thought that I was the only one who knew, me and my lieutenant anyway, but I have found out tonight that they know. You must cooperate, whatever may lie ahead. You must do as you're told. It is not just your life at stake."

"What are they planning?" Benjiah asked impulsively, knowing that Rulalin almost certainly couldn't tell him. "What are they going to do to her?"

"Hopefully nothing, but that will depend to some extent on her," Rulalin answered. He stepped closer to the cage and took two of the slats in his hands. "Benjiah, do you think there is any chance she would just surrender?"

"None."

"Look, I know that's the reflex response. No surrender, under any circumstances. I need you to think, though. Is there anything, anything at all that might induce her to lay down her arms and save her own life?"

Benjiah just shook his head. He knew his mother well enough to know that she was almost incapable of entertaining that idea.

"Then, it is as I suspected. You may be the only hope I have, which is exactly why you can't do anything foolish. You have to stay alive so I can save her." Rulalin had never raised his voice at any point, but now it grew positively soft, like a whisper. "That's one thing we have in common, you and I, the desire to save her."

A strange wave of images washed over Benjiah, and he saw them in rapid succession. He saw his arms outstretched above his head, chained to two massive poles. He saw a vast assembly. He saw an ominous grey sky pierced by intermittent rays of sunshine. He saw Rulalin and a man he had never seen before with a knife, but Benjiah saw evil and hatred in his face.

"You want to save my mother?" Benjiah asked as the images faded.

"Yes."

"You should worry more about saving yourself."

"What?"

"The dream you mentioned a few moments ago. It was a chance offered to you to be free. This is your second."

"What are you talking about?" Rulalin asked, letting go of the slats and moving back a step.

"You know very well what I'm talking about. I am in this wooden cage, but the prison you're in is worse, far worse. I appeared to you in that dream to offer you a way out, but you wouldn't take it. I am offering it again. Your time draws near, but there is still time to be free. Will you not avail yourself of it? Will you not renounce what you have done and choose even now to serve your true master? It is not too late."

Rulalin stood, his face pale, with confusion in his eyes. Benjiah sat still, watching him. After a moment, Rulalin turned and walked away through the camp.

Benjiah watched him go, saying nothing. *A second time you refuse. You will have one more chance, but only one more.*

7

RETURN

"GARIN," MONIAS SAID. "Look at that."

Garin turned and looked in the direction Monias was pointing. Houses and farms were increasingly remote this far north and east of Garring Pul, but the men still had not come across one that was occupied. That was one reason why Monias had halted when he saw movement beyond the house.

"A horse?" Garin said after a moment.

"That's what it looks like."

"Let's go see."

They turned out of their course, now making for the small farm. *Maybe here, at last, there will be someone to speak to, some sign of life.* Monias thought of Garring Pul as they made their way across the wet grass. The southwestern portion of the town had been badly damaged and partially flooded. The rising tide of the Kellisor had been devastating, though admittedly not as comprehensively as it had been at Peris Mil. That's one reason why it was so surprising to find the northeastern parts, not underwater and still largely intact, abandoned.

They were a blow, the empty buildings and deserted streets, in many ways far more demoralizing than finding part of the town underwater. They had hoped to find horses, or some other form of help, to aid the remainder of their journey to Amaan Sul. They had at a minimum hoped for news. What was going on in Enthanin? Had Malek's hosts come yet? Were they on their way?

But there was no one to ask and no signs to read. Whatever had happened here, it did not appear that there had been violence. It seemed rather that the population had simply packed up and left. Monias imagined they had not debated for long about where, for unlike the predicament that Peris Mil found itself in, the recourse for Garring Pul seemed obvious. Garin agreed with him that if the exodus had been peaceful and voluntary, the people of Garring Pul had undoubtedly left for Amaan Sul. After watching the encroaching waves destroy part of their town, the distant strength of their capital must have beckoned them to safety. That a tide far more frightening and ultimately far more destructive might even then have been rolling toward Amaan Sul probably did not occur to the shopkeepers and merchants and their families, who sought only a place of refuge from their more immediate troubles.

Monias could see it. He could see the people from Garring Pul and the surrounding countryside with packs on their backs walking toward the great city. He could see them streaming through the great gates, refugees looking to their mighty capital for a place to ride out the storm. And yet, the capital itself was likely to be the locus of the storm when it truly came. If Amaan Sul could not withstand it, he feared for what might be.

The farmhouse loomed before them. Hope that it might be occupied faded as Monias noticed the front door, left slightly open, bouncing back and forth in the stiff evening breeze. He thought about calling out, but thinking about the possible animal that had drawn them this way, he thought better of it. If there were no people here to claim it, then the horse might reasonably be requisitioned for their journey. He didn't want to spook the creature.

"Looks like no one's home," Monias said to Garin as they walked around the side of the house.

"Looks like it."

Around back they saw the horse. He was saddled, as though for riding, but he was untethered and seemed uneasy as they appeared in his peripheral vision. Monias looked him over. He was tan and midsized, with a white blotch between his eyes. He had probably never been much of a horse, but he looked lean and unkempt and no doubt even less spectacular than he normally was.

Garin started forward, but Monias took his arm. "Let me."

He walked slowly, smiling warmly as though the horse could read his expression. He took his time, and the horse sidestepped nervously but didn't run away. When at last he reached it, Monias held out his hand and allowed the horse to smell him and be filled with his scent.

"Nothing to fear from me," Monias whispered gently, trying to sound reassuring. The horse did not shy away, and Monias patted the horse's head and rubbed the side of his neck.

Garin came up beside him and the horse reacted, but he allowed Monias to calm him and then allowed Garin to stroke him on the other side.

"I wonder what his story is?" Monias mused out loud.

"Who knows? Somehow separated from his owner, he has probably come home."

"Should we take him?"

"Of course. It will be good for us and good for him. I wouldn't expect someone to come back here for him, and chances are his owner is heading where we are, or maybe he's already there. Not to mention that we need him."

Monias nodded. "You're right. It just feels strange, taking a horse that is not my own, but the situation warrants it, I think. In times of war, sometimes exceptions must be made."

"It is almost dark," Garin said. "We'll stay here tonight. In the morning we'll make an early start."

They did make an early start, and, though they agreed in theory to take turns riding the horse, in practice Garin only took the saddle twice that whole day and both times for less than an hour. The rest of the day he jogged beside the trotting horse with Monias marveling at his endurance. The man was thick and heavyset, and Monias would never have imagined he could keep going so. Still, Monias had come to see over the course of their journey together that Garin had astonishing willpower. Monias believed that if running all the way to Amaan Sul was what would have to be done, Garin would do it.

Monias of course suggested frequently that Garin rest and ride, but Garin generally refused and Monias did not press the issue. Though he had been tired of riding by the time he reached Peris Mil, it was hard to leave his horse behind. He was not a young man anymore, and as uncomfortable as too many hours and too many days on a horse's back might be, too many leagues on foot would be just as wearying and even more time consuming. While he wanted Garin to get rest on the horse, he knew that with Garin running and him riding, they were making their best time. The more that Garin rode— and as the days went by the man would almost certainly need to ride more—the slower they would go.

Images of Garring Pul returned again unbidden. Monias didn't know why the memory of the town was so disturbing, but this time he thought also of Dal Harat. He pictured it empty and deserted. *Will all Kirthanin look like this if Malek wins all?* Monias shuddered. He'd spent more time than he probably should have imagining what would happen to the world if Malek was successful and seized dominion. It was possible that he would, of course. Monias believed the prophecies that all things would be made new one day, when the Mountain would be cleansed and Malek would be destroyed, but there was no guarantee that Malek wouldn't rule for a while before that day came. There was also no guarantee that Monias or his children or even his grandchildren would live to see it.

So the questions remained. Would Malek destroy the great cities of Kirthanin, pulling down their walls and toppling their towers? Would he be content to simply rule over them? Perhaps he would build cities of his own, monuments to his conquest and might. More important than the cities themselves, what of their inhabitants? Would Malek kill them or subjugate them, and which would be worse? Would Malekim and Black Wolves and perhaps even other beasts be used to terrorize and control them? Perhaps the whole world would become a waste like Nolthanin, a desolate land full of death and decay.

Suddenly Monias saw an image in his head of Agia Muldonai, the Holy Mountain. It was blighted and dark, and the blight and the darkness radiated outward from it like a disease, spreading in concentric circles until all of Kirthanin was ugly and ruined and even the waters of the sea withdrew from its shores as though to touch it was to be defiled.

The sea. Perhaps the sea is our hope. He grew excited. Maybe, just maybe, a remnant of the Kirthanim could escape this place by ship. Maybe they could find refuge in an island or some distant shore unknown to any living creature. It was counterintuitive, he knew, to look to the sea for deliverance, especially after the sea had brought so much destruction to the coastal regions of the world. But it might be that they had no other choice. It might be that the only place they could go to escape from Malek's reach was the sea and whatever might be beyond it.

Of course there might be nothing, but dying in the search might be better than what remained for them here. The excitement in Monias began to diminish. Not only might they die in the search, but Malek might well follow them, even there. It suddenly seemed to be extraordinarily naïve to think that Malek could be evaded in such a way. Was it not an illusion, that there was any place where they could flee that Malek could not follow? Had Malek not guided his followers across the Southern Ocean to the Forbidden Isle? Did that not suggest that Malek was well aware of the world beyond Kirthanin's shores, whatever it might or might not consist of? Monias sighed. It was unlikely that anyone would escape Malek until Malek was dead and gone.

Garin ran out a little ahead of the horse, which Monias had taken to calling Merrill for reasons not entirely clear even to himself. Monias halted and dropped from Merrill's back and walked up beside Garin, who stooped over the vegetation.

"What do you see?"

"Look."

Monias peered at the grass and saw hoof marks, many of them. "Horses have been here."

"Widen your gaze," Garin said, straightening and sweeping his arm across the plain in front of them.

Monias looked again and, not being experienced at such things, didn't see anything in particular at first, but eventually he began to understand. An enormous swath of the plain in front of him betrayed signs of many feet. "Thousands of people have been here. The refugees of Garring Pul?"

Garin shook his head. "No, I don't think so. We would have seen tracks like these before now if it was them. These come from the south more directly, from the Kalamin, and they are fresh. Three or four days old at most."

"So, if not the refugees from Garring Pul," Monias said, "Then surely it must be one of the two armies."

"Yes," Garin said, "but which one? There are tracks here that are neither from men or horses. They could be from Great Bear. They could be from Malekim. I can't tell which. There is too much confusion in the grass."

"The tracks are headed toward Amaan Sul?"

"Yes."

"And you think that whoever made them are only a few days ahead?"

"Yes."

"Then we are behind them all or between them," Monias said. "Either way, we will need to be careful."

The great southern gates of Amaan Sul rose before them, and Pedraal felt inside the indescribable comfort of home. He remembered visiting this field as a little boy with Wylla and Pedraan and their parents. Reaching the gate from the inside he had rushed outward into the open grassland. It was only when he turned around to look back at his family that he realized just how large and impressive the gates to the city were. Today, it was not their size and strength that comforted him, for he had seen the power of their enemies unleashed too many times to imagine that there was hope in the walls or gates, but even so, their familiarity did bring comfort, for he had passed through Gyrin and battle and beyond and returned home again, safe.

"It's good to be back," Pedraal said to Pedraan.

"Yes," Pedraan answered.

"We've traveled a long way, I know," Pedraal added, "but it seems like an age since we rode out. We were so concerned about Gyrin, and yet we all passed through safely. Little did we know that Valzaan would fall and Benjiah be taken."

"If you'd told me that only two of us would return from this journey," Pedraan answered, "I would have sworn it would be Valzaan and Benjiah."

"I know. But, in the end, they were both beyond our aid."

"So now what do we do?"

"What do you mean?"

"I mean," Pedraan continued, "We promised Wylla to see Benjiah home safely, and not only have we failed to bring him with us, we've lost him to the enemy. What are we going to do?"

"We're going to tell her the truth," Pedraal replied. "We'll tell her how Benjiah defeated the Grendolai and how he laid himself down to save our army as it crossed the Kalamin, and we'll help her to grieve his loss. That's what we'll do."

Pedraan sighed. "It's hard to admit that though we rode from here half a year ago expecting to be Benjiah's guardians during the journey, it was Benjiah who protected us."

"I know," Pedraal said again.

They walked through the gates but stopped when a voice called their names from behind. They turned to see Mindarin and Aelwyn riding up. It was Mindarin who had called out to them.

"Mindarin, Aelwyn," Pedraal said, looking at the sisters. He thought he should probably add something more welcoming, since they were about to enter the city he called his home, but he could think of nothing to say.

"Are you headed to the palace to see Wylla?" Mindarin asked.

"Yes."

"Would you take us with you? I have not seen Wylla since before the war began in Werthanin, and though I'm sure I would see her eventually, I would like to go with you. It's strange, but so much of what we've been through takes me back to our adventures in Sulare and beyond. I find myself craving for us all to be together."

"All?" Pedraan asked, looking levelly at Mindarin.

"Well," Mindarin blushed, "Not all of us. Those who are still alive and able to be together."

"Meaning those who are actually fighting against Malek," Pedraan answered.

"Yes," Mindarin said sharply, "Meaning those who journeyed with us and are actually here in the city, working toward the same purpose and fighting to achieve the same ends. Of course that's who I meant."

"Pedraan," Pedraal said, putting his hand on his brother's big arm and stopping him from speaking further. "Enough. Mindarin, you are welcome to come with us, and I'm sure that Wylla will be happy to see you. Aelwyn, you're welcome to come too, I didn't mean to leave you out."

"I understand," Aelwyn answered, trying like Pedraal to sound calm and conciliatory.

"I must ask, though," Pedraal continued, "that you be sensitive to the situation. Wylla may not know that Benjiah has been taken, and if she is to hear that news for the first time today, she should hear it from us."

"Of course," Mindarin answered. "We will help to comfort her if we can, but it is certainly your duty and your right to inform her."

As the twins started off into the city, Mindarin leaned across her horse to Aelwyn and whispered. "Not that they'll do it right, mind you. I wouldn't trust those two with a serious message of any kind, let alone something like this. Come on, Aelwyn, Wylla will need to talk to women who have been along for all this before it's over."

Pedraal and Pedraan waved and responded to many of the people of Amaan Sul who knew and recognized them, even if the brothers did not know precisely to whom they were responding. Word of the army's approach spread rapidly throughout the city, and though men and Great Bear had been funneling in through the great gates for almost a day now, the excitement in the air was palpable. A great army, far larger than any the men and women of Amaan Sul could have imagined, had come. All hoped, of course, that safety had come with them.

Though some sought to engage Pedraal and Pedraan in conversation, the twins kept moving, and any who were left behind in this way understood that the high captains of the city were needed at the palace. Mindarin and Aelwyn followed on horseback, drinking in the sights and smells of Amaan Sul. It had been so long since they had encountered the comfort and stability of a city inhabited and structurally intact. For both of them, the almost giddy reception they were receiving brought back to mind the images of the people of Shalin Bel streaming out into the countryside. In a matter of days, the teeming city had been emptied and dispersed, and since that time they had known only the harsh realities of the road—endless rain, cold, and marching. Now hopes of warmth, dryness, and perhaps even luxury grew within them.

The entrance to the palace grounds was within view when the thundering hooves of a rider came up from behind them. All four turned to see who was riding so hard. It was Brenim, his eyes focused upon them all with intensity as he drew up to a halt.

"Brenim, greetings," Pedraal said as the younger man dropped from his horse onto the street.

"Sorry to startle you, Pedraal, but I was trying to catch up to you before you reached the palace and I took a wrong turn somewhere back there. I've only been here once before."

"It's all right, Brenim. What is it?"

"Kyril and my nieces are up there, and I'd like to be with you when you bring word of our journey. I know," Brenim said, haltingly, "that the queen's attention will be absorbed with Benjiah's capture, and properly so, but I should be there to comfort Kyril, as Evrim's absence from our number will be hard for her."

"Of course," Pedraal said, "You are welcome. We bear much hard news, though the attitude of the people in the streets would not suggest it."

"They revel like a victory has already been won," Mindarin said.

"They have found in us the first small shred of hope they've had in ages, and they cannot be expected to understand the full measure of the wrath that will be directed against them here," Pedraan answered.

"No, indeed they cannot," Mindarin replied, "nor did I expect it. I was marveling at the hope they have. It has been a long time since I've had any myself. I almost couldn't recognize it."

Pedraal surveyed his brother and friends. "The news we bring is bleak enough as it is. I would ask you all to keep such thoughts to yourselves until Caan comes tonight for the Council of War. There will be time, then, for an honest and straightforward assessment of where we are and what we think is coming. We've had league after league to contemplate the terrible forces directed against us. The people here, the queen included, can only have the barest sketch of it. They must know the truth, the full truth, but we must be merciful as we divulge it. It is too overwhelming to swallow all at once, and I must insist that we do our best to maintain morale until then, no matter how we personally feel."

With that, Pedraal started into the courtyard, followed by the others. They were seen by stewards long before they reached the front entrance, and by the time they had handed over their horses and stepped inside, Wylla, Yorek, Karalin, Kyril, and her girls, among others, were all there waiting.

"Uncle Brenim," Roslin began, running to him and throwing her arms around him. "It is so good to see you after so many years. Mom said I shouldn't monopolize the conversation and

I'm not going to but I can't help talking because it's so great to see you and I'm really, really happy to see you and . . . "

"Roslin," Kyril said quietly, coming up behind her and putting her hand on her shoulder. "That's enough, dear."

Roslin looked up at Brenim and he smiled. He followed her and Kyril back to where Halina stood shyly, beaming. He let go of Roslin and hugged Halina too.

For a moment after Roslin was contained, there was an awkward silence, but it was short-lived as people all over the large foyer crossed the stone floors to hug and be hugged. Wylla embraced Pedraal as Pedraan found Karalin. Kyril and Brenim embraced after he greeted Halina. Words of greeting were spoken and tears of relief appeared on many cheeks. Wylla briefly introduced Yorek to Pedraal and Pedraan, promising further information later, and then the queen of Enthanin turned her attention to Mindarin.

"Mindarin," she said softly, crossing the space between them. "Forgive me for my rudeness in not welcoming you sooner."

"There is nothing to forgive, Your Majesty," Mindarin replied meekly.

"I am Wylla to you, Mindarin," Wylla answered, embracing her friend. "It has been a long time."

"Yes, a long time." Mindarin stepped back and motioned Aelwyn forward. "Wylla, this is my sister, Aelwyn."

"Welcome, Aelwyn," Wylla said smiling. "You are welcome in Amaan Sul. You have come a very long and hard way."

"Thank you, Your Majesty."

"You must also call me Wylla," Wylla said, smiling at Aelwyn, then placing her arm around her, she added, "We both know Mindarin wouldn't let you live it down if I made you call me Your Majesty while she didn't have to, so please don't."

Aelwyn laughed and thanked her, and Wylla surveyed them all. "We are glad to have you here, each of you, and I can see by your faces"—she paused for a moment—"and by the absences, that there is news to tell, but not here. Let us go and be seated where it is more comfortable."

"Taken," Wylla murmured. "By Malek's army."

Wylla said the words out loud, but the reality they described seemed no more real. She'd listened silently to the tale that was told of Valzaan's fall, Aljeron's quest, the Kirathanim's flight and Benjiah's capture, and now a sinking despair washed over her.

"Yes, sister," Pedraal said. "He is taken."

"Then he is dead."

"We don't know that," Pedraal said, but Wylla was on her feet and moving toward the door.

"You are all welcome to whatever you need," she said as she opened the door to the hallway, "I have matters to attend to that require my attention."

With that she disappeared from their midst, and after hesitating for a moment at the door, Pedraal disappeared after her.

Once inside her room, all pretense of strength or control slipped away, and Wylla fell to the floor. She opened her mouth to cry but no sound came, and her body hurt with a deep, piercing pain. Then the flood burst and she wept and sobbed as her body shook uncontrollably. She had told herself over and over that Benjiah was in Valzaan's care, which was as good as being in Allfather's care, but her son was at best captured and at worst dead. She had told herself that Allfather wouldn't take her son as He had taken her husband, but she cursed herself bitterly for this senseless and forlorn hope. Why had she believed such folly? Why should Benjiah be safe if Joraiem had not been? What did it matter if Valzaan believed Benjiah was a child of prophecy? He had believed that about Joraiem and had been wrong. She had been a fool to let him leave. Now he was lost, and she was lost with him.

"You took Joraiem," she called out to the empty room, "and I survived that. But not this! Not this! Anything but this!"

The knock on the door was light but persistent. "Not now!" she called out angrily.

"Wylla, it's me, Pedraal."

"I said not now!"

The door opened. She had not thought to lock it. No one had ever come in when she'd refused entrance, at least not since she had become queen of Enthanin. "Don't you listen?" she said bitterly.

"I do, which is why I came in. I can hear that you need someone to share this grief. I may not be the best person, but I won't leave you alone with it."

Pedraal crossed to where she sat upon the floor and knelt down beside her. "Sister, I'm so sorry."

Wylla grabbed Pedraal and pulled him tight. She began again to sob and for a long while cried until her body ached from the violence of it. When she had calmed somewhat, she wiped her eyes and looked at Pedraal. "He came so far. Just a little farther and he would have been home."

"I know."

"I don't understand. He was supposed to be important to Allfather's plan."

"He has been. He killed the Grendolai, summoned the dragons, and single-handedly delivered a large portion of our army. He has saved the lives of thousands, and if we survive this war, perhaps it will be thanks to him."

"But he's lost."

"Wylla, it's my fault," Pedraal said at last, tears in his eyes. "I promised you I'd bring him back. I promised, but I couldn't . . . "

Wylla took Pedraal's face in her hands and leaned in, kissing his forehead. After a moment of holding him, she added. "My brother, I know you did everything humanly possible. Don't blame yourself. I sent him forth in Valzaan's care, in Allfather's care. His blood is not upon your head. It is upon theirs."

"Perhaps his blood has not yet been spilt."

"Perhaps, but even if not, what hope is there for him now? What hope if alone and captured in the midst of Malek's host?"

"I don't know."

"No, of course not, because there isn't any. First Joraiem, and now apparently both Valzaan and Benjiah. It would seem a dangerous business to serve Allfather as his prophet."

Not long after Pedraal had slipped out of the room after Wylla, Pedraan had managed to slip out with Karalin as the others had left for food or to go to their newly prepared rooms. Taking her by the hand, he led her through the great hall and out to the courtyard by the back gate.

"Come with me up to the wall?" he asked as they stepped into the fading light of the early evening.

"Wherever you'd like to go," Karalin said as she followed.

They passed across the courtyard and into the corner tower with the spiral stair that led up to the broad wall. There they walked along the top, and Pedraan noticed for the first time the small encampment of soldiers outside the northern gate. "What's all this?" he asked as they looked out over the northern grasslands.

"We were attacked after you left."

"Attacked!"

"Yes, by Black Wolves and Malekim and men. We were fortunate, and though they breached the gate, we were able to hold them off. You should have seen Wylla that night, Pedraan. She was every inch a queen."

Pedraan looked at Karalin's face, and reaching over, took the wisp of hair that the wind had blown down between her eyes and pulled it back for her. "I thought I'd never see you again. I thought I'd die somewhere out there, a long way from here. It never occurred to me that I might survive and you might not."

"But I did, and so did you," Karalin replied. Pedraan stepped closer.

"Yes, I survived."

"And now you've come home again," Karalin let herself be swallowed by his enormous arms. She felt safe and secure as she had never known.

"I was so worried I'd never see you again," Pedraan whispered as he squeezed her tightly.

"I knew you'd be back."

Pedraan leaned back and looked down. "You knew? How did you know?"

"Well, I guess I didn't know, but I believed. I believed, and it looks like my faith was well placed."

"Well it is good to be back."

"It is very good to have you back," Karalin answered. She looked up into his eyes. "Is it all right, Pedraan, to feel so happy when we're surrounded by so much misery?"

"You mean Wylla?"

"Yes, but also Kyril. All day the hope that Benjiah and Evrim would be here by supper has been in everything they've said and done even though they didn't talk about it directly. I think they were afraid to give their hopes a voice lest it prove, as it now has, ill-founded. And now they're somewhere in the palace, overwhelmed with worry and grief, and here I am with you back safely and in my arms. Is it fair to be happy?"

"I don't know about fair, but maybe that's not the question."

"All right, is it the act of a friend, then? Knowing the tears of their hearts? Having cried a few of my own while you were away and I was missing you? Is it an insult to them to rejoice in every fiber of my being at seeing you, to be wrapped in delight as I am wrapped in your arms?"

Pedraan in answer pulled her tighter. "Karalin, the burdens they bear could not be made lighter if you pretended to be heavy-hearted. The sadness they feel could not be made happier if you feigned misery. You cannot take away the pain they feel by denying the joy that is in you. So rejoice!"

"But shouldn't I go to them? To grieve with them?"

"Yes, probably, and I'm not saying you should be insensitive and throw your gladness in their faces, but when you are alone with me, and when we feel the joy we have so long desired, then don't be ashamed of it. At times like these, we need all the joy we can get."

"I agree."

They stood for a little while, then Karalin stepped back. "I should probably go find your sister."

"All right, but one thing first."

"Yes?" Karalin said, smiling as she looked up at him.

"I told you that I'd marry you when I got back, and I meant it."

"I'm glad you did, and so did I."

"Well, the council will have heavy matters before it tonight, and looking to the defense of Amaan Sul is likely to fall to Pedraal and me. So I'm not sure how soon we'll be able to schedule the ceremony. I didn't foresee my return with Malek right behind me."

Karalin put her arms around Pedraan. "You are back, and that is what's important. I have waited for your return, and I can wait just a little longer, until the time is right."

"I love you, Karalin."

"And I love you."

Pedraan bent down and kissed her, and the touch of her lips was even more like coming home than passing through the gates of Amaan Sul. He slid his big, rough hand down her arm and took her small, delicate hand, and led her back along the wall, down the stairs, and into the palace.

8

FATHER OF DRAGONS

THE HORSE SNORTED loudly as it exhaled, his breath snaking out of his flared nostrils. It was a mist, dissipating as it spread, a thin vapor escaping into the chilly morning air of the Nolthanin waste. Synoki looked down at the creature with a blank gaze that spoke neither of frustration nor surprise. The creature writhed and twisted one last time, then was still, its wide, staring eyes the clearest indication to any onlooker that the beast was dead.

Synoki gazed out toward the mountains in the distance. Not far south of where he stood, the Tajira Mountains swung east, inward, from his perspective. The horse had taken him almost all the way, but he couldn't really have expected it to do more than it had. It ran for two days and nights without rest, and at a speed the poor animal had probably not known it was capable of. To be sure, the remarkable pace was due to power the creature did not understand, power that was killing it with every step, but the animal's death didn't matter. What mattered was that it had served its purpose. What mattered was that it had taken Synoki over a week's journey in the space of two days, and now he had crossed the Surnok River and passed into the relatively easy terrain of the flatlands.

Even so, he was still a long way from the Zaros Mountains and beyond them, Enthanin. That was where he needed to get, and quickly. The child of prophecy had been revealed at last.

If he experienced a flicker of anger, or frustration, or annoyance, or any self-recrimination for coming all this way only to find out the answer to the riddle was far to the south, it passed quickly. Synoki did not brood on the past, for it was gone without possibility of return. There was only today and what needed to be done now.

In the distance, movement attracted his attention, and he turned from the towering skyline of the mountains to the flatter horizon farther south. At first he thought he must have been imagining it, but after a moment he saw it again. There could be no denying it, a small band was running his direction. He stepped away from the horse and started off across the plain to meet them.

It took longer than he expected for them to meet, but he didn't mind. He'd been in the saddle without a rest since leaving the foot of Agia Muldonai, and though the same power that had kept the horse going also sustained him, he was glad now to be stretching his legs. His bad leg hurt, of course, but then it always hurt. Even in his dreams it hurt. It ached and throbbed, always. He was never free of it. The rest of him, though, inwardly rejoiced at the walk.

"You have come in good time," Synoki said to the three Vulsutyrim who had stopped before him and now stood, panting, trying to catch their breath.

"We have run as we were commanded, with only the shortest of breaks for water and rest, by day and by night."

"You have done well, Amontyr, but I am afraid there can be no rest for you yet. We must head immediately south. I have business to attend to there."

Without a word, Amontyr nodded and reached down, taking Synoki in his immense hands and setting him upon his shoulder. If Synoki had been Amontyr, he would have used his position of authority to direct one of the other giants to take the first shift carrying him, but that wasn't the way of the Vulsutyrim. He supposed it didn't really matter, since they would need to cover many leagues, and all of them would get their fill of carrying him. Of that there was no doubt.

Aljeron reached down and took Evrim's outstretched hand. With a heave he lifted him up onto the solid ground at the mouth of the gyre. It had been hard going there at the end, but they were here now, all of them.

Evrim smiled at Aljeron, then both men turned and looked out from the wide opening in the side of the mountain. Shimmering in the distance was the water of the Great Northern Sea.

"It's beautiful," Evrim said.

"The water?"

"The view." Evrim reached up and leaned against Aljeron. "For a while there, I really didn't think I'd make it."

"But you did."

"I did, and it's beautiful."

Saegan scrambled up and joined them, the last of their number to reach the entrance to the gyre. Valzaan, Erigan, and Koshti, his long lean body pacing at the entrance to the gyre, were already there, waiting.

"Well," Valzaan said as they were assembled. "It took a little longer than we expected, but we're here, all of us."

"All of us," Evrim echoed him, laughing.

"Not much longer than expected," Aljeron added. "I'm sure none of us wanted to spend a second night on the mountainside, but we all knew it would be difficult to get here before sunset."

"True," Valzaan answered. "And though I have felt keenly the press to get here, it seems fair to say that Sulmandir, should he wait within, cares not for the timing of our coming, one day more or less."

With that, they all turned slowly from the exterior world and examined the entrance to the gyre. The opening was indeed very large. Aljeron had only encountered a dragon once, many years before on the Forbidden Isle, but his memory of Eliandir suggested that the entrance was more than large enough for a dragon to pass through, even if Sulmandir was a good bit larger than his sons.

What struck him, though, was not the size of the opening but the smoothness of the stone, both underfoot and overhead, as well as on either side. The entrance to the gyre seemed to Aljeron almost like the gateway to another world.

"It's remarkable," Saegan said, voicing what Aljeron felt. "Standing here, in the heights, so far above the earth, looking at this fantastic doorway to a place of legend and myth."

"It is indeed a wonder, but no myth," Valzaan answered. "You are looking at one of the truly ancient places of the world."

"You mean it is older than the end of the Second Age, when Sulmandir came here after his fight with Vulsutyr?" Aljeron asked.

"Oh, it is far older than that," Valzaan said, turning toward Aljeron. "This is not a gyre, this is *the* gyre. Allfather carved this gyre out of the rock of the mountain, long before it became known as Harak Andunin. It was here that Allfather breathed life into the Father of Dragons, giving birth to the first creature of Kirthanin aside from the Twelve whom he had already created and installed in Avalione.

"Yes, indeed," Valzaan continued, stepping forward under the great arch. "Allfather hollowed this gyre with His own hands and fashioned it to be the perfect resting place for the lords of the air. There is a scent here that smells like Avalione, like the Holy Mountain itself."

Aljeron looked from the entrance to the prophet, his white hair jutting out from his ancient head. A shiver ran through his body as he thought that he was standing at the entrance to the birthplace of the mightiest creature to ever roam Kirthanin, save only the Titans. "It is the thumbprint of Allfather," Valzaan continued, almost in a whisper. "That feeling you had, Saegan, is not as strange as it may first sound. This is a doorway of sorts, and it does lead to a place now lost to us. It does seem an entirely different reality, a far older and greater reality than myth and legend."

"And we're going in," Evrim whispered.

"We are going in," Valzaan said.

The chill returned and Aljeron shivered. He had walked the empty streets of Nal Gildoroth on the Forbidden Isle and felt the awe of that ancient place, but the awe he felt now was of a different kind. He had felt awe at the scale of the city, the sheer size and shape of the place, as well as awe at the thought of a time when giants had roamed its streets. This place, though, was even older than that one, and the hand that had carved it even more powerful than the hands of those who had erected Nal Gildoroth. He was about to go deeper into the past than any man had ever been.

"What if, after all this," Saegan began, breaking the silence, "what if Sulmandir's not here? Or worse, what if he's dead? What then?"

"What then?" Valzaan answered. "Then we'll know. We'll have our answer, and we'll come back here and go down. We'll go down and start the long journey south while we try to figure out where to look next for aid in this great war. But for now, the question on our minds shouldn't be, 'What if Sulmandir isn't here?' The question should be, 'What if he is?'"

What then? What if the Golden Dragon is indeed alive and well and dwelling within? Have you thought of that? You're about to enter the gyre of the Father of Dragons. You are about to set foot where no man has gone before, and I suggest that you should not do so lightly. Sulmandir, if he is alive, could kill all of us in an instant. He could destroy us completely, without difficulty, only to find out later, if at all, that we had come in peace and as friends. Again, I say to you all, tread lightly and follow my lead. Where we are going, I have not gone before, and it is with respect and great care that I go now. Keep quiet, and keep close."

With that, the prophet turned toward the great dark opening and, stepping forward a few paces, was lost in the shadows.

Valzaan did not remain lost in the shadows long, for a moment after he left the half-light of the gyre's entrance, a small sphere of light appeared above his cupped hand. It hovered there a finger's width above his skin, glowing brightly enough that they could make out not only Valzaan but the sloping stone of the tunnel. The light seemed to Aljeron, not like the light of a fire or burning torch, but like a handful of sunlight held by the force of the prophet's will. As they proceeded and the darkness closed around them, the light in Valzaan's hand seemed to change, appearing now like the light of a falling star in the distance, a small twinkling comet guiding them forward.

As they walked, the ground began to slope up, and Aljeron was surprised.

"We're going up," he said out loud.

"We are," Evrim answered, echoing Aljeron's surprise.

"I just assumed that once we reached the gyre's entrance," Aljeron continued, "if anything, we'd go down. It never occurred to me that the inner chamber would be uphill."

"Me too," Saegan said from behind him.

"It is the nature of a dragon to want to be as high as he can be," Valzaan said. "All gyres are built in the crown of the mountain they are in, that is, the place still big enough to house them without weakening the exterior wall. The only thing that dragons crave as much as height is dryness. For obvious reasons, a gyre with an entrance above it would be much more vulnerable to water from rain and snowmelt."

"I see," Aljeron said.

"If dragons don't like the water," Evrim said, "then it's a good thing the rain and snow have finally stopped. Otherwise we might have had a hard time convincing Sulmandir to come forth."

"We still might," Valzaan replied, not breaking stride as he moved steadily inward and upward. "Though, the difficulty, if we have it, will have nothing to do with the weather. Dragons like dry gyres because they don't want to sleep in pools of water any more than we do. That doesn't mean they won't fly in storms or that they are ineffective in the rain. Far from it."

"What will be our greatest challenge in convincing Sulmandir to come out?" Saegan asked.

"Dragons do what dragons want to do," Valzaan said.

"It's disheartening to think that even if Sulmandir is here and alive, we could still end up heading back to Enthanin without anything to show for our quest," Aljeron said.

"It's possible," Valzaan said, "but you're getting ahead of yourself. I am hopeful that Sulmandir can be convinced to come, otherwise I would not have sent you here. In fact, it is precisely for this task that I have come, instead of lending my aid further south. Sulmandir may need coaxing, and while you might have been successful without me, you are more likely to succeed with me."

The slope grew steeper, and for a moment the party stopped. The smooth stone inclined to such a degree that it was hard to keep their footing. Koshti darted out in front of

Valzaan, his padded feet falling soft and sure as he scrambled up ahead of them. Next, Erigan with his powerful legs bolted up the incline and likewise disappeared in the darkness.

"It levels out somewhat after just a little bit," Erigan's deep voice came down from above them in a whisper, and a great paw reached down into the radius of Valzaan's light.

"Saegan," Aljeron said, "go first."

Saegan reached up and took hold of Erigan's paw and was soon hoisted up into the darkness. The paw reached down again, and soon Evrim and Valzaan had likewise been lifted away. One last time, Erigan reached down, and Aljeron took hold of the warm furry arm and held tight as Erigan lifted him off the ground as easily as a cat might lift her kitten.

The smooth floor indeed leveled out somewhat, but that was not the only change. The walls had receded on every side. Even behind them, on the other side of the great opening through which they had emerged, there was no wall close enough for Aljeron to see it. He felt the chill of nervousness and excitement as it occurred to him that this might be it, the very interior of the gyre of Sulmandir, the Father of Dragons.

Valzaan's light had dimmed, whether by the prophet's choice or by some greater power that had ordained darkness for this place, Aljeron didn't know. He knew instinctively not to move or speak, and he stood frozen by reverence for this place and its mighty inhabitant, whether he still lived or no.

He felt a brush of fur against his leg, and looked down to see Koshti rubbing up against him. His battle brother stopped there, Aljeron's leg braced against the firmness of Koshti's ribs. Aljeron could sense not fear, but perhaps apprehension. In all the years they'd been together, and in all their adventures through Nal Gildoroth and beyond, their battles with men and Malekim, Aljeron couldn't remember Koshti ever seeming afraid. He wanted to stoop beside the tiger and soothe him, but he didn't dare move so much. He reached down with his hand and stroked softly and ever so slowly his plush fur.

All the hair on Aljeron's arms and legs and neck was standing on end. They'd only been here a moment, but his nerves were taut and sensitive to every movement, however slight, of his companions, all clustered tightly in the dark. Even Erigan, who in all their journey had always seemed undaunted, seemed to apprehend the otherness of the place.

This is a place of wonder and awe, ancient and holy. I'm not worthy of this place. I don't belong here.

Valzaan raised his hands above his head, and the small ball of light raised with them. "Sulmandir," the prophet spoke into the surrounding darkness. "Father of Dragons, awake!"

Aljeron gulped and blinked, but nothing happened. The darkness remained unchanged. His eyes detected no movement and his ears detected no sound. A cold chill washed over him in the darkness. *He is dead. He is not here. He is gone forever. We have come in vain. We have wasted our strength and our time. We will go back with nothing to show for our ordeal and with no aid. We will go back to face an enemy we cannot defeat, and we will fall—*

Again he was silenced by Valzaan's words, but this time they were more sung than spoken, a soft but audible lyric somewhere between a chant and a song that seemed to search the darkness.

Sulmandir,
Golden Father,
Ancient Protector,
Clothed in light and
Royal splendor,
Awake

Sulmandir,
Your uneasy dreams
Now leave behind,

Raise your head and
Rouse your heart,
Awake

Sulmandir,
Stretch out your arms,
Open your eyes,
See the light that
Bids you arise,
Awake

Sulmandir,
Rejoin the world
Left long ago,
Come back now and
Feel the wind blow,
Awake

Sulmandir,
Lord of the clouds,
Leap from this place,
Soar on high with
Glory and grace,
Awake

Sulmandir,
Vulsutyr's sons
Roam Kirthanin,
Malek's creatures
Ravage the land,
Awake

Sulmandir,
The Time is come

For shedding blood,
Restore the peace,
Bring back the sun,
Awake

As soon as the sound of his words had faded from Aljeron's ears, two great eyes opened in the darkness, and two golden beams of light emanated from them, filling the gyre with an ethereal glow. The light that streamed from those eyes swept across the dark chamber until they came to rest upon Valzaan and the others, and the great golden eyes fixed steadily upon them. As they did, Aljeron felt himself transfixed by the marvelous light, unable to move or think, mesmerized. The light was glorious, beautiful and wonderful beyond words.

"Erevir?" A voice both deep and terrible, both splendid and awe-inspiring, spoke. The voice was majestic and filled the gyre like the rumble of thunder echoing through clouds, like the rumble of the Water Stones thrust above the earth by the explosion of waters in the deep. Aljeron trembled at the sound of that voice, and though there was no threat in it, he feared for his life. The mighty speaker spoke with authority like nothing or no one Aljeron had ever imagined.

"Is it you, Erevir? Have you come after all these years to rouse me from my slumber and call me from my sleep?"

"Erevir's time passed with the Second Age," Valzaan said in reply. Aljeron didn't know how the prophet could muster the courage and strength to answer. "I am Valzaan, and I have served as a prophet of Allfather since the seventh year after Vulsutyr's fall, since the seventh year of the Third Age."

"Why have you come, Prophet?" Sulmandir replied, the great golden eyes still fixed upon them all. "And why have you brought these with you, this Great Bear, this tiger and these men?"

Aljeron thought he detected a slight shift in tone as Sulmandir said this last bit about men, but it was hard to tell. The deep and commanding voice of the dragon sounded disdainful from first to last. He remembered Valzaan's words upon the Forbidden Isle about Eliandir, so many years ago. Dragons always sound like dragons. They are never soft, and their words are never gentle. They are always dignified and majestic, and the air of dragon-ness that had seemed like gruffness in Eliandir was magnified a hundred-fold in Sulmandir.

"We have come because Malek has come forth. For almost a thousand years he has lain in wait in a labyrinth of caves and tunnels built far beneath Agia Muldonai. Now he has come as prophecy foretold, seeking as he has ever done to take Kirthanin for himself and cover the world in darkness. He has unleashed the full might of his hosts, men and Black Wolves, Malekim and Vulsutyrim, as well as a new enemy, a great monster of the sea called Kumatin, all directed against what strength remains in the races of men and Great Bear. He has entrusted much of his power to Cheimontyr, the heir of Vulsutyr and captain of the Vulsutyrim, and Cheimontyr has summoned a storm without equal in our history to flood the world and cover large parts of it with water. This Kumatin has come inland and roams the rivers of Kirthanin and the Kellisor Sea at will.

"We have come because the combined strength of men and Great Bear is not enough. A few dragons have come to our aid, but we need all! We need the Father of Dragons and all of his children to roam the skies and bring to bear their might and power in this great war. We need you, Sulmandir, for you alone can summon the remaining dragons to our aid. You alone can rally your sons so that one last time, the free peoples of Kirthanin—dragons, Great Bear, and men—may stand together."

Valzaan finished and there was silence. The great golden eyes remained focused upon them and Aljeron waited breathlessly.

A W A K E

"You have come in vain, Prophet. I am through involving myself and my sons in the affairs of men."

Sulmandir's words rumbled around the gyre and inside Aljeron's head. There was no hesitation that might be construed as misgiving about the pronouncement. No sense that perhaps reason and persuasion might shift the dragon's opinion. Aljeron heard only finality in the echoes.

Despair washed over him like he hadn't felt in months. When news of Malek's coming from the Mountain had reached him in Fel Edorath, he was taken aback, even afraid. When he'd seen Cheimontyr summon lightning from the heavens at Zul Arnoth and when the giant had cast Valzaan into the sea, he felt that fear deepen and grow. The long trek across Nolthanin had on the one hand deepened this gloom and on the other hand had fed the smallest fire of hope in his heart. He felt that small flame flicker and go out, finally extinguished.

"You are the Father of Dragons," Valzaan was saying as Aljeron's mind gradually refocused. "We need you. You are essential to this war."

"Has Kirthanin not done fine without me for almost a thousand years? Have not generations come and gone? Have not myriads of men and Great Bear been born, lived, and died since last I flew above the clouds and kept watch over them? The seasons have cycled over and over, always the same. Spring turns to summer and summer fades into fall. Winter spreads out its hands and swallows the earth and holds it tightly until spring breaks its grip and it all begins again. So it has been and so it will be. The sun rises. The sun sets. These things you speak of have nothing to do with me."

"All this time we have endured only because Malek was gathering himself, slowly preparing for his third and final assault, that he might come with overwhelming might to claim Kirthanin. While the seasons may continue to cycle and days may continue to come and go, they may very well do so without men and Great Bear alive to enjoy them, unless you bring your aid and the aid of your children."

There was a pause this time, and Aljeron could not tell in the dark if the pause indicated thoughtfulness or the resolve of a mind made up, closed like stone and impervious to any plea. Valzaan perhaps felt the uncertainty of the silence as well, for after a moment, he continued.

"Sulmandir," Valzaan continued. "At least consider aiding us against Cheimontyr, who spreads fear and destruction as wantonly as his father. You turned the tide of the last war against Malek by killing Vulsutyr. You can turn the tide in this one by striking down his son."

Again the pause, and Aljeron felt the agony of the long, silent moment.

"I have no love for Vulsutyr's sons, for they killed many of my own, but they are no longer my concern."

"Sulmandir!" Valzaan fairly shouted, though Aljeron could tell it was excitement and not anger that moved him. He hoped the dragon could also tell the difference. "You can do what we cannot! You can kill this accursed fiend who plagues our land like a disease. You can deliver the world, not just for men and Great Bear but for all of Allfather's creatures, from the insects that scurry to and fro across the face of the earth to the birds that soar high in the skies. You can help us rid the world of Malek once and for all, so that even your own children can come forth again and taste the joy of light and rejoin the land of the living. Will you not come?"

"No."

If Aljeron thought he had ached with despair before, he was positively crushed now. He had felt Valzaan's impassioned plea working on his own heart and felt certainty rising within him that the answer would be yes. He saw just for a moment a blue sky filled with golden wings and majestic dragons riding upon the wind. He tasted just for a moment a gasp of hope.

"Sulmandir," Valzaan began again, this time without the passion but with a new tone of authority. He no longer sounded like a supplicant before a king, but rather like a king upon his throne. "I no longer address you as a man among men. Now I speak as the mouth of Allfather, His prophet and spokesman in Kirthanin. As such, in the name of Allfather, I bid you rise. I call you to come forth!"

Again there was silence. It was awful. Aljeron wanted to collapse under the weight of it. Valzaan's words reverberated with authority that almost compelled Aljeron to move toward the prophet. But the two great dragon eyes neither blinked nor moved, and Aljeron detected neither sound nor motion from anyone.

A moment later, though, the great golden eyes rose higher off the ground, much higher in fact. A sound like echoing thunder rumbled through the gyre, and Aljeron realized that Sulmandir had risen to his feet and was moving toward them. At the same moment, it occurred to Aljeron that Sulmandir might be coming to kill them. Perhaps time and his wound had so hardened his heart against the world of men that he would kill in order to avoid having to be involved. Perhaps he didn't believe Valzaan's claim to speak for Allfather. After all, he hadn't seemed to know who Valzaan was when the prophet had first spoken.

Meanwhile, the glowing orb held up by Valzaan glowed brighter as Sulmandir approached, but it was glowing brighter asymmetrically. It wasn't that the orb was now illuminating a wider and wider radius, but it was illuminating a larger and larger section of the space between them and Sulmandir. Perhaps Valzaan was directing it to do so out of the same thought and fear that had just occurred to Aljeron. Or, perhaps it had nothing to do with Valzaan's will at all. Perhaps there was something inherent in the Golden Dragon himself that drew the rays of light from the orb, like a lone tree in a plain will draw lightning.

All of this took place very quickly, as it did not take long for Sulmandir to traverse the gyre. He stepped within the glow of the orb and at the same moment obscured it and was illuminated by it. The glow seemed to come from him now, though Aljeron realized it probably only seemed to be so, for no doubt the light of the orb was simply reflected in such a way as to make the Golden Dragon appear to be the source.

"Prophet," Sulmandir said, his great head swooping down to hover before Valzaan. It must have been a full span higher off the ground than Valzaan, but having come down from such a great height, it appeared to Aljeron to be unnervingly close. "I will come with you to the entrance to my gyre and look once more upon the outer world."

"Good," Valzaan replied, not bothering to hide the relief and joy in his voice. "Go on ahead of us, and we will follow."

They stepped aside, and the mighty dragon passed. Aljeron watched as Sulmandir descended the great slope in a single stride and continued downward toward the distant entrance. They quickly scrambled down after him, and when they reached the opening, Aljeron marveled at what he saw.

Sulmandir's great silhouette, framed by the grey but still more penetrating light of the outer world, cast an enormous shadow. The great dragon did not completely fill the entrance to the gyre, but then again his wings were folded at his side as he overlooked the world from the mountain where he'd been created.

Aljeron could not imagine what it must have been like for Sulmandir to stand there, if indeed he had been hidden away all these years. What would it be like to look out over land and sea after almost a thousand years of darkness? Surely human eyes would go blind, to be unused for so long and then opened again to the light of day. If the transition from darkness to light bothered

Sulmandir, though, it wasn't evident. The dragon showed no signs of pain or agitation, at least none that Aljeron could see.

Valzaan led the small party to Sulmandir's right until they came to rest at last beside him. Aljeron looked up at the great silent dragon, remembering what it had been like to look up at Eliandir. He could also see now the difference between Eliandir's golden hue and Sulmandir's. While Eliandir had appeared almost completely gold except for in a few places, Sulmandir's gold was comprehensive. From his great taloned feet to his wide, staring eyes, there was no hint of anything but gold, glinting anew in the light of Kirthanin day.

"What is it that you want from me?" Sulmandir said without moving or looking down.

"I want you to summon your children. Call them forth from their gyres in the mountains of the world. Summon them all, red, green, and blue. Muster the combined might and strength of the dragons and go to war with us. Let us fight—men, Great Bear, and dragons together, one last time. That is what Allfather desires. That is what I ask."

"Our strength is not what it was. Many of my sons fell when the Master of the Forge came forth the last time."

"I know, but we must fight with the strength we have."

"Even if I come, we may fall."

"If we fall," Valzaan said, "we fall. So be it, but let us fall doing all that we can to wrest this world from Malek's tyrannical grip. Since he first led Andunin into treachery and betrayal, the world has lived under the shadow of its past and future. It is time to free it from this shadow, his shadow, if we can. If we cannot, then Allfather will deliver Kirthanin somehow, in another way perhaps, or in another time. That we cannot know, nor do we need to know in order to do what we must."

"It would be good to see the world cleansed at last," Sulmandir said, his deep voice for the first time almost wistful.

"Yes," Valzaan said.

"Once and for all."

"Once and for all."

Sulmandir shifted slightly so that he could look down on the assembled group. As he did so, Aljeron had a clearer view of his belly. He almost gasped as he saw the long and jagged scar that ran almost the length of it. That must be the injury inflicted by Vulsutyr's flaming sword. Instinctively, Aljeron lifted his hand and traced his own scars running the length of his cheek.

The scar was the only blemish that Aljeron could see, for above, below, and all around the mark the golden scales shimmered in the light, a dazzling armor covering Sulmandir's body. Aljeron felt the urge to step up to the great leg of the dragon, to reach out and feel the smooth scales for himself, but he resisted the urge with such effort that he actually stepped backward.

"I will do as you ask, but my sons are spread all over the world. To summon them all, even for me, will take time."

"I understand," Valzaan answered, "but that is where we must begin."

"What will you do?" the dragon asked.

"We will head south to Enthanin."

"It is a long way on foot, and I have no garrion in which to take you."

"We know, and we wouldn't ask you to, not yet anyway. What is needed now is not so much our return as yours. We have horses at the foot of the mountain, and we'll take them south while you are away. By the time you have gathered your sons, you will have seen, no doubt, where the storm of battle is brewing. Return when you are able, find us, and then we will decide what to do next."

Sulmandir's great golden eyes looked them over. "You are a strange company, man and beast, prophet and Great Bear."

"We are indeed," Valzaan said, laughter in his voice. "These are strange times."

Sulmandir looked back out over the land toward the Great Northern Sea. Suddenly, his wings unfolded above them, and his right wing extended above their heads and drew all of their gazes upward. "It will feel good to fly again, to soar above the clouds and feel the sunlight on my scales. It has been very long. I will spy out land as I go about my errand, and I will bring word of what is transpiring in the wider world when I return."

"Good," Valzaan answered. "I am more encouraged than I have been in many a year. We may not be enough to stop Malek and Cheimontyr, but we will give them a battle."

Sulmandir's wings pulsed, sending a strong breeze down in their faces. "We will do more than that," his deep majestic voice answered. "We will give them a war."

9

THINGS LOST AND
THINGS LONGED FOR

RULALIN PRESSED ON, knowing without needing to turn
around that a vast column of Malek's hosts stretched out behind
them all the way to the Kalamin and beyond. Thinking of the
river brought back the awesome and terrible image of the Kumatin, his great black form an immense shadow in the gloom as
it glided through the water during the crossing. He knew the
beast was supposed to be on his side, his friend and ally in
Malek's cause, but everything in him reacted to the creature with
fear and revulsion. The Kumatin was the very epitome of a creature of nightmare, the dark beast that haunted every young boy's
dreams. How was he then to make peace with this hideous thing
under the great flat ferry that shuttled him across the swollen waters? Dry land could not come soon enough, and once there he
couldn't put enough leagues between himself and the river

quickly enough. He didn't survey the great host following him until far beyond the river, and now he struggled to put the memory of the thing from his mind.

Fortunately for Rulalin, setting foot on Enthanin's soil again had a most profound effect upon him. Despite the saturating greyness and gloom, a renewed sense of the beauty and preciousness of life overcame him. He found himself hardly able to contain his excitement as he thought back upon his first journey here a quarter of a century before, and he wasn't even sure that he should contain it. It bubbled up inside him and spilled out in random smiles and laughs, to the point that he sent Soran to scout out the front of the column in hope of regaining composure privately. For the better part of his life, ever since he first saw Wylla in Amaan Sul, Enthanin had been for him enchanted territory.

He found in his memory that the adolescent Wylla he first met in Enthanin and the older Wylla he spent time with in Sulare were somewhat interchangeable. It gave him pause to recall an evening at the palace in Amaan Sul, when he realized that the Wylla he envisioned there in the moonlight was the Wylla of Sulare, an older, more mature Wylla whom he'd never seen in Amaan Sul. It made him wonder how many of his "memories" were fabrications in full or in part. Even so, he knew that the elegant beauty, regal carriage, and gentle spirit she had always possessed was real, and the love he felt for Wylla was also real. It didn't matter if his mind sometimes mixed the two experiences, as they both held the most cherished memories of his life—and the most painful.

He slipped back into the world of memory, as he had already several times since crossing the river. He recalled the city of Amaan Sul on a busy market day. The day was sunny but cool, for he remembered drawing his cloak tight around him as Wylla led him wandering through the crowd and a maze of streets from shop to shop.

Rulalin had never been quite comfortable outside the palace walls. This was due in part to the fact that he quite treasured the private setting and the quiet times he had with Wylla there. It was also due in part to his discomfort in busy settings that were unfamiliar. Fel Edorath was a big city, if not as big as Amaan Sul, but it was known to Rulalin and therefore comfortable. Amaan Sul, with its grand architecture and teeming streets, left him ill at ease.

Only his desire to be with Wylla had induced him to say yes to her invitations to walk with her in the city. He had been surprised the first time to find just how busy and active life outside the palace was. He had thought that the official state of mourning the city was observing would mean dark, plain attire and a generally sober approach to life. Perhaps it had meant so immediately upon the death of King Pedrone, but by the time Rulalin had arrived with his father, this was not the case. Life seemed to be going on as usual for most of the citizens of Amaan Sul, though a certain sadness appeared in their eyes when they would see and recognize his guide. Rulalin could not tell if the people of Amaan Sul had been very fond of Pedrone, but it seemed clear that they cared for his daughter and grieved for her loss.

On this particular venture out of the palace, Wylla had led him from stall to stall and shop to shop in the market. What exactly she was looking for, if she was looking for anything concrete and tangible at all, he never discovered. All he remembered was that they had ended up in a small, out-of-the-way baker's shop down a relatively quiet street. Inside, she introduced him to the elderly man who owned it. The man was unusually tall, perhaps two spans and a hand, with wisps of white hair lying to and fro upon his mostly bald head.

"This is Madrus," Wylla said happily. "The best baker in all of Amaan Sul."

"Hello," Rulalin said shyly.

"And this is Rulalin Tarasir, visiting from Fel Edorath with his father," Wylla explained to Madrus.

"Good morning, Master Tarasir," Madrus said kindly before turning to Wylla. "If only more people shared your enthusiasm for my goods, princess. I'm afraid I'm not the baker I once was."

"That's ridiculous," Wylla said. "Let's let Rulalin here be the judge. Give him one of my favorites."

The elderly baker stepped into the back of his shop, and Rulalin turned to Wylla. "Your favorite what?"

"You'll see." Wylla grinned.

Madrus reappeared, carrying a great round plate with two large pastries. Rulalin had no idea what was in them, but he took one with a smile and a thank you and bit into it. Inside the light, fluffy pastry was a mixture of sliced fruit and a sweet, sugary cream. It was marvelous.

"This is really good," Rulalin said after swallowing. He looked at Wylla, who had also taken a bite and had a small splotch of cream on her cheek. Rulalin checked his own cheek for any similar residue and found a small dab.

Wylla laughed as he blushed, cleaning it off, and then she cleaned off her own face as well. "It is impossible to bite into one of Madrus's pastries without making a mess of yourself— your shirt or cloak if not your face. That's one of the reasons they're so good. They're chock full. You don't have to eat half through one like you have to with some bakers' pastries to get to the good stuff."

Madrus refused to let Rulalin pay for the pastries, despite his valiant and repeated attempts to do so, and in the end they were sent out from the shop with another one apiece, which they ate as they continued to walk through the city. The sugar loosened Rulalin up, and as they walked, he grew more talkative and laughed more easily. When at last they finished their pastries, he licked his fingers clean and turned to Wylla. "Those were really good. Thanks for taking me there."

"You're welcome," Wylla replied, her smile slipping suddenly. She recovered, however, and managed to replace it with a somewhat reduced version.

"What is it?" Rulalin asked, somewhat baffled by the flickering sadness that had momentarily appeared in her eyes.

"Oh," Wylla started, "it's just that my father used to take me to Madrus's shop when I was a little girl."

Even now, as Rulalin looked back through the years at Wylla's face, he could see the deep sorrow in her eyes. The sadness welled up from time to time. Some places, some topics, some things predictably evoked the response, while other places, other topics and other things quite unexpectedly took her deep down inside to that place as well. He had spent a great deal of time trying to understand so that he could console her, though he had never felt very successful.

He looked back over his shoulder now at the trio of Malekim in the distance, each holding the long pole that connected them to the great wagon they pulled. They tugged and strained, step by step, pulling both the wagon and the wooden cage it held. He could make out the hands holding two of the wooden slats in the front and the arms that led back into the shadowy interior of the cage.

Rulalin had once wept for Wylla and her grief. Now he was the source of it. Could anything he might say or do change that? Could delivering Benjiah into her hand, if he was able, could even that do it?

He turned back around. He knew that it couldn't, at least not at first. He could not expect Wylla to greet him with warmth and gratitude the minute he showed up with Benjiah in a cage. He would have to earn the response he desired, the forgiveness that he needed. Perhaps he would be able to show his devotion to her over time, and perhaps then she might, possibly, learn to live with what he offered.

When Rulalin saw Soran approaching, he felt relief. Sometimes, he had come to recognize over the long years, he needed rescuing from his own obsessive self.

"What news?" Rulalin asked, expecting none.

"The front of the column is bigger than both of us expected. I had to go about half a league to really find the front."

"Really?" Rulalin said, not especially surprised.

"Yes, and as expected, there are men on horseback leading the way. I'm sure there are Black Wolves scouting ahead of them, but I didn't think it wise to go much farther."

"No, you were right to come back," Rulalin concurred. "Are there many Malekim ahead of us?"

"Yes, actually. There is a solid contingent on foot, none of them burdened with wagons or supplies. That part of the column seems entirely behind us, intermingled with the Nolthanim under your command."

"I see," Rulalin said. He really was seeing nothing new. He had guessed already that the men under his command wouldn't really be at the front of the column as it advanced on Amaan Sul. Whatever he was trusted with at this point, he would never be trusted with that. He hadn't expected to be. He was here to be ready at hand when the city was reached so as to be an ambassador to those within.

Soran fell in beside him and they rode together again. They had come a long way, Rulalin thought, but he suspected that it would not be long now before their paths parted, for one reason or another.

"It won't be long now," Soran said, seeming at first to read his mind. "We're on our way to Amaan Sul, where hopefully this whole affair will be brought to conclusion."

"It just might be."

"I, for one, am ready for it," Soran said.

"Are you?" Rulalin said, looking over at his young friend. "You have found your niche in war. Do you not fear what peace may bring?"

"I have proved myself in war, and now I will have a chance to prove myself in peace."

"Even if the peace is imposed by Malek and followed by Malek's ascension to Avalione?"

"I have served Malek loyally. I trust that he will reward me even as you hope he will reward you, and I trust that I will have further opportunity to serve."

Rulalin nodded. He would pursue the matter no further. Both of them were weary of war. Both of them longed for peace. He also knew, however, that the peace he craved for was deeper and more elusive than that which Soran spoke of. It was a kind of peace, he feared, that could not be regained once lost.

Monias looked up at the thick bank of grey clouds. Though he had despised the constant rain, the cloudy skies that still dominated the sky day after day mirrored his mood and were strangely comforting. He remembered a time when every day was different, when sunshine and blue skies with thick white clouds or thin wispy clouds or no clouds at all were just as possible as this impenetrable greyness, but it seemed to him so very long ago now.

"How are you feeling?" Garin asked, looking down from where he was standing above Monias.

"Better, but I need just a moment more." Monias lay flat on his back. There was no denying any longer that he was old, not that he ever really had. His back just couldn't take life in the saddle from dawn until dusk without rest or pause anymore. "How much farther do you think the city is?"

"Maybe a day," Garin said, stroking his thick black and grey beard, "but I'm not really sure. I've only been there once before, and that was long ago. How about you? Have you been to Amaan Sul?"

"Yes, three times actually. Once when I was only a teenager, and twice in the decade before the war between Shalin Bel and Fel Edorath began. I know I ought to be clearer on how far away we are, but I find there are so many things that once were clear but are now hazy, or at least hazier than they used to be."

"Don't worry about it," Garin said. "Our pace is as good as we can manage, and that has nothing to do with how far off the city is. We'll be there when we get there."

"Maybe when we do get there, I can rest," Monias said, closing his eyes. "Rest would be good."

"Maybe we can, but we should get there first. There's something on the breeze today that I don't like. We shouldn't linger."

"All right," Monias said, "Help me up."

Garin reached down and took Monias's outstretched hand and helped him to his feet. Monias's bones in his back cracked as he straightened up and his knee popped. He winced. "It's a frustrating thing to grow old, Garin. I didn't feel old before Elsora passed, but age seems to have caught up with me."

Garin nodded, "Sometimes those we love keep us young."

"True," Monias answered, stretching out a moment, more to avoid getting back on the horse than to seek any physical benefit. "When you start to wonder if you've lived too long, that's a bad sign."

"You are not yet seventy, Monias," Garin said, addressing the Novaana by his personal name rather than *Master Andira*, which was rare. "You have many good years still in you."

"Maybe I do, Garin," Monias replied. "Whether I do or don't, though, I can say this: All I really long for now is to see my children again. I want to hug them again, one more time. I want to feel their skin against my face and know them as my own. My hopes are really no higher than that, my desires no greater."

"Perhaps you will soon be able to—"

Garin's words broke off. His head turned slightly, and he stared past Monias into the broad open plain. Monias turned to look but could see nothing.

"Mount up," Garin said. "Something is following us. We need to go, now."

Monias did as he was told. He was soon back on the horse, and they were on their way, the horse trotting quickly with Garin running beside it, looking back over his shoulder every so often. They had already covered much ground this way, but before now they had not been running from anyone or anything.

They did not go far before Garin motioned to Monias to stop. He ran to the horse and hastily untied the small axe that was bundled together with their provisions and other items they had foraged from abandoned farmhouses. "Keep going," Garin said, looking up at Monias. There was no panic in his eyes, but the glint of intensity was unmistakable. Garin's words slipped almost breathlessly out of his mouth. "I will catch up to you if I can."

Monias, who still couldn't see anything behind them, replied, "Garin, what's going on?"

"There's a Black Wolf, or Wolves, following. We can't outrun them. I'll try to buy you some time."

"I won't leave you."

"You can't help me by staying unless you're carrying a weapon I'm unaware of."

Monias's bow, brought all the way from Dal Harat, had been lost when the sea monster smashed their skiff to pieces in the Kellisor Sea. He had nothing and knew Garin was right.

He could not help. Even so, he didn't like the thought of riding alone across the big, grassy plain any more than he liked the idea of leaving his companion in trouble.

"I'm still not going," Monias began, but he didn't finish his thought, for he spotted the fast-moving black form in the distance. "There it is!"

Garin had already seen the Black Wolf and was moving away from Monias. Monias felt his pulse quicken, and fear washed over him. He had come so far and was so close. It couldn't end like this. He watched Garin continue out from him, axe in hand. It struck Monias that though Garin was the hunted, he didn't move like it. Quite the opposite, he moved stealthily, like a hunter circling his quarry.

The Black Wolf was closing the distance quickly now, his powerful body majestic and terrifying as it flew across the open land. Garin was no longer moving but had stopped and seemed to be bracing for the Black Wolf's leap. Suddenly the creature sprang, and in the moment that it did, it seemed to Monias that Garin must certainly be overpowered and destroyed.

But something happened that Monias could not believe, not while it was happening or even thereafter when he replayed the scene in his mind. Garin dropped to one knee so that the wolf's trajectory was a little high, and like lightning, Garin's big, thick left hand shot out and grabbed the wolf under his jaws, sinking his hand into the thick fur around his throat. A muffled yelp escaped the wolf's mouth as his forward motion was slowed by the powerful hand. In a flash, Garin buried the axe deep in the wolf's neck, and the beast fell dying and spewing blood upon Garin's shoulder. Garin struck twice more so that the head was severed completely, rose, and ran back to the place where Monias waited, open-mouthed.

"You killed him," Monias said with a mixture of disbelief and surprise.

"Yes."

"I mean, it wasn't that I didn't think you could, but just like that. So simply, so matter-of-factly."

"We need to keep going. He's a scout, but he's probably not the only scout around."

Garin wiped the blood off the axe and tied it back up in the bundle. They were soon on their way again, Monias riding and the strange, reserved, deadly man running beside him.

As the day wore on, the adrenaline from the episode passed and weariness returned, weariness and the almost endless supply of daydreams and memories. They had come and gone unbidden all the way from Dal Harat to Peris Mil while he traveled alone. They persisted even as Garin traveled with him. They continued even now, so soon after their exciting encounter and Garin's remarkable feat. Memories of Elsora, young and smiling with her golden hair hanging low upon her shoulders. Elsora, standing in the door to their house in Dal Harat, holding Joraiem in her arms. Joraiem, the small, beautiful boy with golden hair of his own. The images came and went, shadows of things lost. There was only Kyril and Brenim now, though he knew even as he thought it that this wasn't so. There were also Kyril's girls and Evrim, who was like a son now as well. And there were Wylla and Benjiah, who though less familiar and more distant were nevertheless precious to him.

Malek could have the dead world when he had ruined Kirthanin, Monias thought bitterly, when he had destroyed all that was good and beautiful and killed all those whom he loved.

The road that departed from the great eastern gate of Amaan Sul wound through a series of rolling hills that on a bright summer's morning must have been beautiful, Aelwyn thought. She had found it helpful during the seemingly endless days of their interminable journey to pass the time by imagining the terrain through which they were traveling in happier times. She'd start by trying to picture the stretches of beach or grassland or forest with a bright blue sky overhead and a round, golden sun shimmering above the horizon and shining down benevolently upon them. She'd try to blot out of the picture the pools of standing water that were everywhere, and then she'd try to envision blossoms on the trees or flowers in the fields, adding splotches of welcome color to the all-too-drab world that now surrounded her.

As a process, it was easier to do in some places than others. She'd found the high bridge over the Barunaan harder to transform into a warm and inviting place than Cimaris Rul itself. She expected this had as much to do with her own state of mind as it did with the particular place, though she didn't want to rule out the possibility that those two things were connected. At any rate, these hills felt quite warm and inviting, despite the great disappointment of being back in the saddle and on the move again.

"By the Mountain," Mindarin said from her place beside her sister. "I can't believe I ever liked riding a horse."

Mindarin was leaning forward awkwardly, trying to massage her posterior where too many days in the saddle had brought considerable discomfort. Though Aelwyn likewise ached, she didn't think she could bring herself to address the problem in such an undignified way, though if they spent too much more time traveling in this manner, she might well consider it.

But how much more time could they spend? They had traveled as far south as Kirthanin allowed, and then they had come north and east all the way to Amaan Sul. Now they were on their way north and east again, and beyond their new destination there was only the sea and Nolthanin, both equally unreasonable options for further retreat. Surely their long road would have to end soon, for better or for worse.

"Oh, this just isn't to be borne," Mindarin said, sitting back down in her saddle with disgust on her face. "We were supposed to be going to Amaan Sul. We were supposed to be staying there, taking our stand there. Nobody mentioned anything about just passing through."

"That's because we didn't know what we'd find when we got there," Caan said, riding up alongside them with Gilion at his side. Aelwyn was surprised to see him appear beside them like that, though she knew she shouldn't be. He'd passed down the column from the front not more than a couple hours earlier, so it stood to reason that eventually he'd need to head back up. If Mindarin was fazed by Caan's sudden appearance, it didn't show.

"And what did we find, Caan?" Mindarin asked. "A lovely city, surrounded by a great big wall. Sounds to me like the ideal place to get a little rest before facing our enemy in the field."

"Yes, a lovely city teeming with its own population, plus refugees from all over Kirthanin who have fled there to find protection. The city was already strained by its extra population. It was not prepared to support all the soldiers and Great Bear who arrived with us, not to mention the additional refugees we brought from the south."

"All right, so why not do what we've done anyway, namely send the civilians north to the foothills of the Zaros Mountains? Then we could have prepared for siege and stayed behind in the city. Why'd we send them off and then leave ourselves?"

"Because it was the right decision," Gilion said. "The food supplies of the city, already dangerously low, were insufficient for a siege. That's the main reason. Beyond that, Tol Emuna has the best natural fortifications in Kirthanin. It's not as large as Amaan Sul, and so defending its walls won't unnecessarily tax our forces. It's just the better option."

"Then why didn't someone say so a couple hundred leagues ago?" Mindarin grumbled. "It wouldn't be so hard to keep going if we'd known that was the plan all along. I could have been preparing myself for this instead of dreaming of sleeping in a bed and spending a whole day in one place."

"Tol Emuna was not part of our discussion, Mindarin, our public discussion, at least," Caan said, "because Gilion and I had hoped it wouldn't come to this."

"Why not, if it is so obviously better?"

"It is better given the untenable situation we found ourselves in at Amaan Sul. We would have preferred to face the enemy in Amaan Sul, where avenues of retreat were available should our defense of the city go poorly. From Zul Arnoth we could drop back to Shalin Bel. From Shalin Bel we could head to Col Marena. From Amaan Sul we could always retreat in a number of directions, one of them being to Tol Emuna, but from Tol Emuna there is nowhere to go. It is the end of the line. In Tol Emuna we will stand or fall."

"And what makes Tol Emuna so much stronger than Amaan Sul?" Aelwyn asked.

"Tol Emuna is a city carved out of a great mountain of rock. It is hard to envision if you haven't been there, but the city is nestled in the crook of a great arc of a mountainous rock, some hundred spans high all the way around and easily as thick. There is only one gate, and it is carved out of the solid rock wall that rings the southwestern side of the city, which is only half the size of the ridge that protects it in the back but is still fifty spans high and five to ten spans thick.

"The land around the city is hard and desolate. No grass grows there, only a tough sort of sage brush that is as hardy as the land itself. There would be little or nothing surrounding the city to sustain the besiegers. The people of Tol Emuna are likewise hardy, as tough as the rock that protects their homes. If we are going to have to endure a siege, there could be no better place. They will do what must be done, whatever it might require of them."

"Saegan is from Tol Emuna," Aelwyn said, half to herself.

"He is," Caan answered.

"That explains a lot."

"That it does." Caan smiled.

"Caan," Mindarin said, her voice soft, even though no one else rode close to them. "I am going to ask you a question, and I don't want you to tell me anything but the truth, the full truth. Is Tol Emuna strong enough to stand against the Bringer of Storms? I've heard about what happened at Zul Arnoth, and I've seen him on the battlefield since, and, well, it is unnerving."

"I don't know, Mindarin." Caan sighed. "But if there are walls anywhere in Kirthanin that are strong enough to withstand him, they're in Tol Emuna."

"Caan?" Aelwyn asked.

"Yes?"

"Will the people of Amaan Sul and the other refugees be all right?"

"I think so. Malek's scouts will be able to see that a large group of people have gone north toward the Zaros Mountains, and they'll know that another large group has left by the road headed to Tol Emuna. If they are any good at all, they'll figure out pretty quickly that the group headed to Tol Emuna includes the soldiers and Great Bear, and they'll follow us. Their goal is to destroy all resistance to Malek's rule, and that means destroying us, not the civilians."

"And if we fall? If Tol Emuna doesn't stand?"

Caan looked at Aelwyn, sadness in his eyes. "If Tol Emuna falls, Aelwyn, Kirthanin falls."

Caan and Gilion rode on, and Mindarin and Aelwyn stayed side by side. All Caan's talk about the great stone walls of Tol Emuna and the strong hardy people, it had all done little but bring Aljeron to Aelwyn's mind. She thought of him now, standing on the rooftop garden where she'd run into him the previous autumn in Shalin Bel. He stood there, his masculine, rough appearance an odd contrast to the delicate beauty of the blossoms and flowers. He stood there looking out over his city, so strong, so assured, so sad.

How she'd wanted to take his sadness away. She would have reached out and plunged her hand into his heart to extract it if she could. She would have gladly taken it upon herself if she could have borne it for him. Of course she could not, and at the time, Aljeron had not even been aware of how she felt about him, so she'd been forced to conceal it, or at least try to. His mind had long been focused on only one thing, and it hadn't been her.

She wondered about the focus of his mind now. On the one hand, she certainly hoped he held memory of her close to his heart during the time they had been parted, but she hoped he hadn't held it so close he couldn't focus on what was necessary. She hoped he could hold onto memory of her in some deep place that wouldn't affect his reactions and decisions in the deadly Nolthanin waste.

"What are you thinking about, little sister?" Mindarin asked. "You're looking all starry over there."

Aelwyn blushed. When she did, Mindarin softened immediately. "Oh," she said. "Don't blush, Sister. There's no shame in that."

Aelwyn, encouraged by her sister's compassion, spoke. "He comes increasingly to mind, unbidden."

"Well, Sister," Mindarin said. "It's good to know that a crisis and the probable end of the world can't slow you down. When we stop dreaming of things and a time more lovely and desirable and beautiful than this one, then we've lost."

"Will I ever see him again?" Aelwyn said, not really asking.

"I hope so."

Aelwyn pictured him riding toward her in the distance, like she had a million times during the long days on the road. "So do I."

"I'm sure that wherever he is, he's dreaming of you. In a way, as long as he is, as long as you hold onto his memory and he holds onto yours, you can't really be separated, not completely anyway."

Wylla stood at the great eastern gate of Amaan Sul, facing the eastern road and the stiff breeze that blew off the plains and whipped her long cloak about her. The great emptying of her city had been remarkably organized and efficient but still had taken more than two full days. Now, at last, it was over, and both the column of soldiers and Great Bear and the caravan of refugees had disappeared from view.

Even so, she was not thinking of them. Standing here, at this gate, had brought back a memory that hadn't come to her in years. There had been a day, when Benjiah was only about nine, ten at the most, and they had been out in the city all morning. Wylla had promised him that when they were finished with her business, she'd bring him here to the eastern gate to play. Her father, when he had the eastern gate replaced, asked the engineers to construct a great arch over the top of it. This arch was a favorite plaything of young climbers. The inside of the city wall was laced with stones of varying sizes that were perfect handholds and footholds for little hands and feet. Once a child scrambled up to the top of the wall beside the arch, the arch itself, which was a full span wide, became a perfect little bridge on which to play, though many a mother had all but fainted the first time she'd seen her loved one scurrying across it.

Wylla had lost that battle with Benjiah already, and she no longer tried to deny him opportunities to play upon the arch, though she did limit the number of days she was free to take him. Further, she tried not to come without one or both of her brothers, who would shadow Benjiah from the ground in case a misstep led to a fall. On this particular day, both Pedraal and

Pedraan had been free, and so she'd been more than happy to take Benjiah to the arch. It would silence, if only for a short time, his insistent pleas that they go there.

Unfortunately, several unexpected events had put her behind schedule, and they had only just come into view of the eastern gate when a steward from the palace brought word that the chief steward had sent for them. Normally, Wylla would have left Benjiah with Pedraal and Pedraan and gone back on her own, but on this particular day, Master Carlian, a Novaana of the Assembly, was visiting from Kel Imlaris with his family, and it would have been improper for Wylla to receive them formally without Benjiah in attendance.

Predictably, this was not well received. Being within view of the gate and the arch, Benjiah argued most strenuously that a few minutes couldn't hurt. Wylla, aware that this was in part her fault, since she'd made a promise she could no longer keep, turned the emotions within her outward and dealt severely with Benjiah. After the tongue-lashing she gave him, Benjiah sullenly and silently fell into line and returned with her to the palace. He changed and attended the formal reception for Master Carlian and his family and said exactly what was required of him and no more. To his mother, he said nothing at all. She went to his room at his bedtime, but she found the light out already and Benjiah insistent on keeping his silence. He kept his back turned to her at all times, no matter how she moved around his bed to face him.

She went from there to her own room, where tears, not for the first time, nor the last, were her only companion in her sorrow. She felt on most days like she was competent to rule Enthanin, but she felt competent to raise Benjiah well far less often.

The day after the incident she had been busy. No doubt she made herself busier than she really was just so she could avoid Benjiah and the pain that came from facing his disapproval.

When the end of the day came, she realized she had successfully navigated the whole day without seeing him at all.

When she retired to her room, though, she found a token from him on her pillow. There she found a parchment on which he had drawn a picture. When he was younger, he often drew for her on days when she was too busy to spend time with him, as a means of reaching out to her. It had been more than a year since he had done it last, maybe even two, and just seeing the parchment lying there moved her. When she took it up in her hand though, the tears began to flow in earnest, and she sat down on the edge of her bed and sobbed.

The picture was simple. The high walls of Amaan Sul were unmistakable, as was the arch of the eastern gate. Underneath it were three people. In the middle was a golden-haired boy, smiling. Wylla had seen enough of Benjiah's drawings to know this was how Benjiah saw himself. Next to Benjiah in the picture was a woman with long, raven hair, which was her, and on the other side was a tall, stately man with golden hair just like Benjiah's. Benjiah had never drawn a picture of his father before, but there could be no doubt that this was exactly who Benjiah meant it to be. The man in the picture was supposed to be Joraiem, and looking at the happy threesome, Wylla wept more deeply than she had wept in years.

The voice just behind Wylla snapped her back to the present day, and she wiped away the tears rolling down her cheek before she turned to face her counselor.

"I'm sorry, Yorek, what did you say?"

Yorek, seeing the tears despite Wylla's efforts to hide them, stepped up to her and put his arm around her. He did not ask what was wrong or offer words of comfort; he merely hugged her close.

After a moment Wylla stepped back, looked up at Yorek, and smiled. "Thanks, Yorek. I'm sorry about that."

"Don't apologize to me, Your Majesty," Yorek replied. "You have done nothing wrong. It strikes me, especially these days with all that's going on in the world, that tears are far less out of place than dry eyes. We should all probably cry more often than we do."

Wylla hugged him again. "Good old Yorek," she said into the thick cloak that he wore. "I don't know what I would have done if Allfather hadn't brought you back to me. He knew this storm was coming. He knew I'd need you. He brought you to me."

"He may have," Yorek replied quietly.

"Not *may*. He did. A bird stole your juggling ball? Could it be any more obvious? The story was ridiculous then, and it still is. There is no doubt. You were meant to be summoned to the palace, and so you were."

Hooves pounded in the distance, and Wylla looked up and found at last the sight she'd been waiting for. Two riders were approaching quickly. *They're back at last.*

"Well?" she said as Pedraal and Pedraan drew up and dismounted.

"Well," Pedraal replied, "so far, so good. The column is moving well. Everything is going smoothly, at least for now."

"And Captain Merias?"

Pedraan laughed. "No change there. He will do his duty and do it well. There's no question about it, but he isn't happy."

"No, he certainly isn't." Pedraal added. "He keeps looking southeast over his shoulder, wistfully."

"Still," Pedraan said, "he understands why he and his company are going with the refugees. He can see the need for leadership among them. It's just that he'd rather be on his way to Tol Emuna with the rest of the army."

"He may be glad he isn't, soon enough," Wylla said. "If Tol Emuna falls, then he may well be the only captain of Amaan Sul left alive in all Kirthanin."

"A fair point," Pedraan answered, "but if Tol Emuna falls, then he may survive a little while, only to have the war come to him eventually. If Tol Emuna falls, he'll fall too, and that's undoubtedly part of the reason he wants to be there. His fate hangs in the balance as much as anyone's, but he won't have a chance to play a part in determining what comes to pass."

"Even so," Wylla replied, "if things go badly, he'll have more time than the rest of us, and some time is better than none."

Pedraal looked closely at his sister. "Another fair point, Sister. So I ask you, will you not reconsider your plan?"

"I will not."

"Wylla—"

"We've had this discussion, and we will not have it again. It's as likely the two of you are riding to your doom as it is that I am riding to mine. Let's say goodbye as planned and be on our way."

"Farewell, Sister," Pedraal said as he hugged Wylla tightly.

"Farewell, Pedraal."

"Farewell, Sister," Pedraan said when it was his turn.

"Farewell, Pedraan."

Once upon his horse, Pedraal called down to Yorek. "Take care of her."

"I'll do my best."

"Allfather's mercy be with you, Wylla, until we meet again," Pedraal said. "So be it?"

"So may it be," Wylla replied, emotion breaking into her voice at last. "Keep safe, my brothers!"

The twins turned their horses around and were soon galloping along the eastern road toward Tol Emuna and the main contingency of the army. Wylla stood at the gate, gazing out after them.

"Your Majesty?"

"Yes, Yorek," Wylla said turning away. "I'm ready."

"To the palace?"

"Yes, but quickly. We should be on our way too."

"You know, they are almost certainly on their way here. Even though they will quickly realize the city is empty, they will undoubtedly search it and find us when they do. There is no need to go anywhere. They will come to you."

"Perhaps not."

"You still want to go?"

Wylla looked up at him. "Yes, we will go. It is time to see my son again."

10

A WARRIOR
ONCE MORE

ALJERON DREW DAALTARAN and with a vicious stroke angrily chopped several branches out of a nearby bush.

"He's gone all right," Evrim said, sighing. "Along with the horses."

"If he were here I'd end his miserable life," Aljeron said bitterly. "I should have cut him down after Koshti killed Cinjan, then left them to rot together."

"You didn't know."

"I did know, Evrim," Aljeron said, looking at his friend and touching his chest with his free hand. "In here, I did."

"Well, there's nothing we can do about it now, except tell Valzaan when he gets down."

Sulmandir had brought Aljeron and Evrim, Koshti and Erigan, all down from his gyre in the crown of Harak Andunin. It had taken two trips, bringing them down in the talons of his forelegs, and it would take one more to deliver Valzaan and Saegan, for whom they were now waiting. They did not need to wait long, for soon the majestic golden form descended gracefully, alighting on the field of white snow near the other four.

"The horses are gone," Aljeron said, the bitterness of the words a vile taste in his mouth, "as is the traitor, Synoki."

"I know," Valzaan said. "Sulmandir told us."

Erigan walked over to the tree where he had left his staff and reclaimed it. Valzaan stood silently, as though surveying the empty clearing where they had left Synoki and their horses. Koshti padded back and forth lightly, almost on the very surface of the snow, no doubt happy to be back at sea level once more.

"It is as I feared, Valzaan," Aljeron said, speaking into the silence. "Synoki is a servant of the enemy. He has betrayed us."

"So it would seem," Valzaan said.

"We all suspected him," Evrim said. "Why didn't we do something when we had the chance?"

"What would you have done?" Valzaan asked. "Kill him on the strength of your suspicion alone?"

"Tie him up, maybe."

"Which might well have killed him. Three days we've been gone. He could have died from exposure."

"We could have forced him to come with us. I made it up with one arm. He could have made it, deformed leg and all."

"Perhaps," Valzaan said, "but the bottom line is that we didn't know then what we know now. Now we must deal with the situation as we have found it."

"It seems to me there's not much we can do," Aljeron said. "He has three days' head start. There's no way we could overtake him on foot."

"No, but a dragon could," Saegan said, looking to Sulmandir.

Several heads turned to face the dragon, who had not yet departed. He looked down at them, listening.

"What is most important for Sulmandir to do now is still to be decided," Valzaan said evenly. "But both of you are correct. Synoki is for now beyond our reach, but he is likely not beyond Sulmandir's.

"The question that troubles me most about this disappearance and needs first consideration is, why now? If Synoki was a servant of Malek's all along, why would he travel so many leagues across such difficult terrain, only to flee now? According to your story, his companion Cinjan tried to kill Aljeron some time ago but failed. If that was their mission, it is still unrealized. Why would he go now?"

"Maybe he left because he could," Aljeron said. "Maybe he knew the mission had failed and that he wouldn't get another chance because we are wary of him, so he grabbed the opportunity to flee when it came."

"Perhaps," Valzaan replied, "But Synoki's master, his true master, is not very forgiving of those who fail him. I don't know that he would leave without fulfilling his purpose here, even if he knew his life to be in danger."

There was silence again. Valzaan shook his head after a moment. "I can't see it. I was blinded to his true loyalties, though like you, I had my suspicions, and now I can't see what he could have wanted here."

"He knew why we'd come," Evrim said. "Perhaps he was afraid of Sulmandir."

"I just don't know," Valzaan said, then looked up. "Whatever his true purpose, we can't delay making our decision about what to do now. We must decide on our own course of action, and Sulmandir's role is all the more important for this unexpected change of events."

"Because you have lost your steeds, I could locate a garrion to take you south," Sulmandir said, his voice resounding in the open air only a little less impressively than it had in the gyre.

"You could," Valzaan said, "though I had hoped you would be free to set out to gather your children. It will take you time to cover the length and breadth of the land and gather them, and it is their aid that Kirthanin needs most of all."

"And now we have a third possibility," Aljeron said. "Hunting and killing Synoki, though I would like the privilege of doing so myself."

Valzaan shook his head. "Even with Synoki's unfortunate disappearance, I think we should stick to the original plan. Sulmandir should not delay, either to seek our revenge or to find transport to replace our lost steeds. Who knows how long it would take just to find a garrion, or how far he would have to fly for it? No, I think that Sulmandir should go and begin the process of waking and summoning his children. He can return to us when he is able, or send one of his sons with a garrion to aid our journey south."

"So Synoki just gets away?" Evrim said, almost angrily.

"If I spy him on my way south, he will not escape me," Sulmandir said, and there were no further objections to the plan.

"It is decided then," Valzaan said to Sulmandir. "Fly with all haste and muster your children. The might of the dragons is essential to our hopes."

"I will go, and I will return with news and help as I may."

Sulmandir leapt off the ground, and circling over them in ever-widening arcs, rose higher and higher off the ground. In a moment, when he was far, far above them, he took off south and faded from view, a brilliant gold speck against a great grey sky.

Amontyr motioned for silence. The other Vulsutyrim who were talking stopped immediately, and Synoki looked up at Amontyr, who was now pointing up through the branches.

From where he was sitting, Synoki did not have a good view of the sky, and he slid closer to Amontyr. Amontyr pointed again, and all four heads followed the outstretched finger and surveyed the northern sky.

At first, Synoki could not see what had attracted Amontyr's attention, but in a moment he did. Way up high was a golden shimmer as bright and clear as it was distant and small. Against the greyness that dominated the skies, there could be no mistaking it once he had seen it. It grew only larger and clearer as it drew closer. It was a dragon.

As it flew overhead, Synoki realized that it was not a dragon; it was *the* dragon. He had seen the sons of Sulmandir in flight and knew how to differentiate the red and the green and the blue. This was none of the above. The pure gold and grandeur of the creature in flight confirmed what he had feared: The quest to Harak Andunin had been successful. The Father of Dragons had been awakened.

Following Amontyr's lead, they all moved back under the trees as Sulmandir approached the area directly overhead. They remained deathly quiet and still. It was fortuitous that the dragon's coming coincided with the break the Vulsutyrim had decided to take beneath the shelter of the trees—a habit long ingrained in those who moved about in Kirthanin only at night or carefully under cover by day. Indeed, it was very fortuitous, but if Sulmandir detected movement and decided to investigate, the shelter from prying eyes would likely prove less successful against the directed might of the dragon. In a large and expansive wood they might hope to take refuge far enough within so as to lose him, but in this small cluster of trees, there would be no where to go but back out into the open, and there they would be in real trouble. So Synoki held his breath and waited, even as the other three held theirs and waited also.

When there had been neither movement nor sound from the world above them for a long time, Amontyr crept out to the edge of the trees and peered into the sky. He saw nothing. Venturing further, he drew his long, curved blade and stepped out into a place of full exposure. Still, there was nothing from above. Eventually, he sheathed his sword and returned to their hiding place under the trees.

"He has passed by," Amontyr said.

"Are you sure?" Synoki asked.

"As sure as I can be. We can stay longer if you desire."

"No," Synoki growled. "His coming means we must hurry all the more. Curse him! We must go faster!"

Amontyr motioned to one of the other Vulsutyrim, who took Synoki up in his powerful arms. "We will go as fast as we are able."

"You will indeed," Synoki sneered, "or you will be sorry."

With that, they were all up, out, and on their way.

Wylla could not remember the last time she'd been outside Amaan Sul. Of course she'd been outside the walls, out among the soldiers so long encamped just north of the palace, but that hardly counted. Now she was riding with Yorek beside her, feeling the wind in her face and trying not to think about just what exactly she was getting herself into.

"Your Majesty," Yorek called.

"Yes," she slowed so they could speak more readily.

"Ahead, just there," Yorek pointed in the distance.

She looked and saw immediately what he indicated. It appeared to be two figures, one mounted and one on foot, headed roughly in their direction.

"Malek's scouts?" Wylla asked.

"Possible, but unlikely."

"Why?"

"One is on foot. Scouts would almost certainly be mounted, both of them."

"Who are they then?" Wylla wondered out loud. "More refugees?"

"Possible, but until we know, be careful."

"I'll be as careful as I can be, but we aren't armed. That was part of the whole approaching-the-enemy-under-the-banner-of-the-city idea."

"I know, but we are both on horses, and if flight is necessary, we should be able to evade them."

Yorek and Wylla came to a complete stop. The figures in the distance had clearly seen them and were now headed directly for them, the horse at a steady trot and the man jogging beside it matching the horse's pace. Wylla stroked the neck of her mount and whispered into her ear, as much to keep herself calm and steady as to reassure the horse. Inside Amaan Sul's walls she was queen of Enthanin; out here she was just another traveler.

As the two drew nearer, it became clear that the man on the horse was elderly, Yorek's age or older, and the bushy bearded man on foot, while younger, was not young. She felt relieved. For some reason, though not entirely logical, she felt safer seeing the men were older.

It occurred to her, as she looked from the man on foot back to the man on horseback, that he looked familiar, very familiar. For a moment she tried to place him—a former steward of the palace, a member of Amaan Sul's council, a trader . . . then it hit her. She dropped from her horse and ran across the plain toward him.

"Your Majesty!" Yorek called out, stunned by this strange turn of events.

"Monias!" Wylla called out.

Both the horse and the man beside the horse had come to a halt, and Monias was dismounting, carefully. Wylla saw him grimace as he stepped from the horse.

"Are you all right?" she said, reaching out for him.

Monias turned to her and welcomed her embrace with a warm smile. "All the aches and pains of age in the world can't make me anything but all right now that I see it's you, Daughter."

For a long moment Wylla held on to Monias. *Daughter.* He had called her that from the very first. She had arrived in Dal Harat in the winter snows, with the horse that bore his son's body, but she had been greeted as a member of the family and treated as such ever since. From the grief they had shared at Joraiem's death to the joy of Benjiah's birth, she had always been Daughter to both Monias and Elsora.

She stepped back. There were tears in Monias's eyes. She looked from him to Garin and back again. "Monias? Where's Elsora? What brings you here, so far from Dal Harat?"

"She's dead, Wylla."

"Oh, Monias," Wylla said, feeling the tears rise inside her too as she embraced him again. "I'm so sorry."

"Forty-four years we had together," Monias said as he let go of her and took her by the hands, "but I find now that it passed like a dream that comes in the night and is gone by morning. It is too soon."

"I'm sorry."

"I know, and I shouldn't complain to you, of all people, about losing my beloved too soon. You know about that better than most."

"I do," Wylla nodded, squeezing Monias's hands tenderly.

Soon, both Garin and Yorek had been introduced and all four stood together on the plain. Wylla returned to the second of her original questions. "What brings you both here, so far from home?"

"I realized that with Elsora gone, all that I have in this world is here, in Enthanin. At least, what I knew last was that Kyril was here with you, as were my grandchildren. I assume that if Brenim and Evrim still draw breath, they are with Aljeron Balinor's army, wherever that may be. So, I set out to find you, that I might face the end of this war and possibly this world with those I love."

"Ah," Wylla said, looking to Yorek.

"What is it?" Monias looked from Wylla to Yorek, and then confusion appeared in his eyes as he looked beyond them at the empty plain. "What's going on Wylla? Why are you out here? Where are you going?"

"There is much going on here that needs explanation, but now probably isn't the time. I will tell you quickly what I know, and that will have to suffice until you are able to get more answers from those you seek. All right?"

"Yes," Monias said. The agitation she had seen in Monias and felt in his hands, which she still held, was passing.

"Kyril has been with me, as you said, with Halina and Roslin. They are all well. So also is Brenim."

"Thanks be to Allfather," Monias said, relief visible in his whole body as he said it. Garin patted him on his back, and Monias smiled at his traveling companion. "That's great news, Wylla."

The rest of Wylla's news wasn't as great. It was disappointing for Monias to hear that his family was not just ahead in Amaan Sul as he had hoped, but on the road to Tol Emuna. What's more, as Wylla caught him up on Evrim and the action in the west, the news that Valzaan had fallen before the enemy and was lost struck him like a physical blow.

"Lost," Monias whispered. "Allfather's prophet, cast into the sea. Who then will lead us in these dark days? He has been our guide in times of trouble from the dawn of the Third Age. We are like sheep without a shepherd."

Wylla looked at her father-in-law and saw the despair in his eyes. She felt the hopelessness in his voice, and she could not keep silence. "We were not left entirely without aid, for Valzaan himself identified another prophet of Allfather's before he died."

"A new prophet?"

"Yes, and from what I have been told, he has done great wonders in Allfather's service, though but a boy in both years and understanding of his call."

"Who is this new prophet?"

"Benjiah."

Monias stepped back from her, and his body trembled. "My grandson is a prophet?"

"Yes," Wylla answered, steadily, "as was his father before him."

Monias reached out sideways, for Garin, who caught his arm and steadied him, his eyes searching Wylla's face. He rubbed his forehead with his free hand and closed his eyes. "I am sorry," he murmured. "I am not as strong as I once was. I must sit."

He stooped down and sat in the grass. Garin took a water-skin off of the horse Monias had been riding and offered the older man a drink, which he accepted gladly, gulping down large mouthfuls of water.

"I am sorry, Monias," Wylla said, "not to have told you sooner. I had planned to, but I never figured out the how. I always wondered if it would be a comfort or not. Trying to reconcile what happened to Joraiem with who he was gave me more questions than answers. I didn't want you and Elsora burdened too. It was wrong of me to keep it from you. He was your son, and you had a right to know."

Monias looked up at her, calmly. "Never mind now, Daughter. You did what you thought was best. I will not hold it against you."

"Thank you."

"But what of Benjiah? You have not numbered him either among those who went north into Nolthanin or among those who are marching to Tol Emuna."

"I have not, because he is not in either place. With power wielded from Allfather he held back Malek's hosts at the Kalamin River so others might cross safely, but he was captured as a result."

"Captured! By Malek?" Monias struggled to his feet again and looked back over his shoulder in the direction from which they had come. He turned back around and stepped up to Wylla and took her hands in his again and gazed deeply into her face. "I understand now. We have embarked upon the same mission, you and I. I will come with you."

"No, Monias, you will keep going."

"Why?"

"Because your son and daughter and granddaughters are just ahead, on the road to Tol Emuna. You should finish the journey you have begun and see and hold them before the end comes."

"But you are also my daughter, and Benjiah is my grandson."

"I know, and I appreciate what you are offering, but I don't even know if he is still alive. What's more, even if he is, I don't know if I will be allowed to see him. If all goes well for you, you will catch the column on the road or at least reach Tol Emuna before Malek. You have come so far already to turn aside from your mission. Go to your children."

"All right, Wylla," Monias said quietly, hugging her once more.

"Your Majesty?" Yorek said after a moment.

Wylla turned to him in answer.

"May I suggest giving Monias and Garin my horse? They have much farther to go than we do, and their chances of outrunning Malek's scouts will be greatly increased if they are both mounted."

"Yes," Wylla said instantly, "I insist. You must take it."

"But daughter," Monias said, "Though you don't have far to go, your horse is your protection. What will you do if you come upon wolves?"

"We can share my horse," Wylla said, stubbornly. "If we are beset by wolves, our chances are not much worse than they already were. I knew when I left Amaan Sul that I was likely headed to my death. Giving up a horse doesn't greatly increase the odds of that, but it can greatly speed your own mission. I am a queen without a throne, no longer able to do any good for anybody. Let me do this one thing. Let me give one last gift."

Monias bowed low before her. "Your Majesty is most gracious, and we will gladly accept this gift."

"Monias, you need not bow to me, not before, not now, not ever."

"Perhaps I need not, but it is an honor, my daughter."

"We should not belabor the parting," Garin said matter-of-factly, taking the reins of Yorek's mount from Yorek's outstretched hand. "If you come upon wolves first, try to outrun them in the direction you are already heading. They will expect you to run from them, not past them. If you can get to human scouts on horseback, you may live. Do you have a plan?"

"Yes," Wylla said. "We have a large banner of the city. We had hoped to approach them under truce as though common messengers from Amaan Sul. Once taken captive, I had hoped to speak to someone in authority about seeing Benjiah."

"It's possible they'd spare you as emissaries, if you live long enough to come upon a human scout."

Garin and Monias both mounted, and Wylla stood beside Monias' horse and looked up at him. "I am so glad to have seen you. You have lost a son and know why I must do what I am doing."

"I have. May Allfather watch over you and grant you your desire. May you find Benjiah alive and hold him in your arms again."

"And may you find Brenim, Kyril and the girls and have the same joy."

Just as Monias and Garin prepared to ride, Garin pointed up into the sky and cried, "Dragon!"

All four heads turned up and there, far, far above them was a small but clearly visible golden, gliding form, headed east at a remarkable speed.

"If only we could move like that," Monias said in wonder as the golden form hurried away as quickly as it had come. "Farewell, Daughter. Perhaps we will meet again."

"Perhaps, Monias. If not in this life, then we shall meet again when Allfather makes all things new, and we will sit down to supper together, you and Elsora, Joraiem and me, at last."

"At last. I would like that very much." Monias smiled. "If you do find Benjiah, tell him his grandfather loves him."

"I will. Farewell."

"Farewell, Daughter."

Monias and Garin turned away from Wylla and Yorek and rode off into the east. Wylla turned to Yorek. "It's strange, Yorek. I am happy to have seen Monias and Garin, of course, but I am a little unnerved."

"Unnerved?"

"Yes, I had reconciled myself to the seemingly inescapable fact that the next face I saw would either belong to a Black Wolf, a Malekim, or an enemy soldier. I was certain of it. And now that my certainty has proven uncertain, even if in a positive way, I am unnerved."

Yorek smiled. "You are a human being, Your Majesty, and we never like to be wrong, do we?"

"No, especially when we're so far wrong about something we were so certain of."

"Perhaps, Your Majesty, in addition to being unnerved, you should be hopeful. After all, you have been equally certain that you are riding to your death, and that if Benjiah isn't dead already, he soon will be. Perhaps you will be equally mistaken about that."

"I see your point, but that is like assuming one remarkable turn of fortune means all your turns will be equally remarkable, but that is a dangerous and misguided assumption. Yorek, I'm too afraid to hope. I am bracing for the worst, namely, that I'll live long enough to come to Malek's camp and find Benjiah dead. But even bracing for it, I don't believe I'll be able to survive if it comes to that. If I set my hope on finding him alive, and I don't, well, I don't want to think about it. Hope can keep you alive. I know that. I've experienced it firsthand, but when hope fails, it can destroy you."

Synoki's thoughts returned to this barren terrain. They were approaching the foothills of the Zaros Mountains, and even though the flat desolation had given way to slightly more interesting ground, the change in scenery gave Synoki no joy, for it only represented a less direct road and a slower pace.

At least he had saved them a few hours by overriding Amontyr's suggestion that they move south under the cover of the woods. Ever since sighting the dragon, all three Vulsutyrim had been behaving like the skies were swarming with them. Caution was one thing, but losing valuable time weaving in and out of trees when they could run faster and cover more distance out in the open, well, it wasn't to be tolerated. Time was what mattered, and they would just have to risk the exposure.

Amontyr came to an abrupt halt and knelt, and the Vulsutyrim carrying Synoki likewise stopped and knelt. All three grew instantly quiet, and Synoki understood enough of their ways to likewise refrain from movement and speech.

The slightest glint of golden light was all it took, and Amontyr was back on his feet, running with renewed vigor, not south as he had been but directly east toward the trees some hundred and fifty spans away. Synoki could hear the Vulsutyrim carrying him panting as he ran as fast as his weary legs would go across the uneven ground. Synoki searched the sky, and it took a moment, but he found the dragon at last. He could tell right away the creature was descending in a great, swooping arc. It had spotted them.

The Vulsutyrim below Sulmandir broke to their left and were running for the wood. He was not concerned, though, since he could gauge the speed at which they were running and knew they wouldn't be able to reach the trees before he would be upon them.

The Vulsutyrim apparently realized this too, because they broke off in different directions as he came at them just a few spans above the ground. As flame erupted from his mouth they each dove to the ground, even the one carrying the man. They evaded his flame, but Sulmandir had achieved his objective, and all three were pinned down at a distance from any cover, at least for the moment.

He wheeled back upon the giants more quickly than they probably expected. One of the Vulsutyrim had risen to his feet already, but he had not drawn his weapon, no doubt thinking there would be time. The giant's look of surprise and fear were written clearly in his face as Sulmandir fell upon him. He managed to pull his long, curved sword completely from its sheath, but Sulmandir struck his arm so forcefully with his powerful front claw that the sword flew several spans away and Sulmandir heard the bone in the giant's arm crack, his shoulder shattered by the reverberation of the blow.

Expecting the other two to be upon him in a moment, Sulmandir made quick work of this Vulsutyrim, ripping him open from the neck to the waist in one, swift, mortal stroke. The giant sank to his knees, his eyes empty, then toppled sideways, falling like a heavy stone.

Sulmandir whirled, tail lashing in all directions, prepared to defend against any attack, but no attack was coming. The other Vulsutyrim had abandoned their brother and were racing toward the wood. Sulmandir roared with rage, and the sound shot across the empty plain. He leapt into the sky and flew after them.

The one carrying the man had set him down, and both giants had blades drawn as he approached. They would not be caught by surprise as the first one had and would stick together now. He would need to be careful. He still remembered the flaming pain of Vulsutyr's sword. The Vulsutyrim were his enemy, but they were strong and smart and not to be treated lightly.

Three times he made passes by air, trying to separate one from the other just far enough to take them one at a time, but they were agile and quick and managed to evade his passes without being separated. The man they had been protecting disappeared into the wood, but he might still be retrieved if Sulmandir could but finish the giants who were his transport. He wouldn't get terribly far in this rough terrain on his own.

As the Father of Dragons wheeled above the trees after his third pass, however, an eruption of power ripped the tops off of several trees and struck Sulmandir so hard in the side that he tumbled twenty or thirty spans in the air before hitting the ground on his side. A little dazed and winded, he nevertheless pulled himself up immediately, though his legs were weak and wobbly. The giants weren't coming for him though. They had availed themselves of the opportunity to head for the forest, and Sulmandir's eyes caught sight of them just as they took cover.

What had struck him? Sulmandir felt as though he'd been hit in the chest by a boulder, but he had seen nothing but air when the treetops had been ripped off their trunks. Could the limping man have been responsible? Did they have an unseen ally or allies of some sort under the cover of the wood?

He leapt into the air and soared toward the edge of the wood, spewing a steady stream of fire. Half a dozen trees burst into flame and sent thick black smoke billowing up into the air. He knew the smoke would further hinder his ability to see what was happening in the trees, but he could not be too cautious, since he didn't know what he was dealing with. With his forelegs he ripped the smoking trees out of the ground, roots and all, and tossed them a dozen spans to either side. He roared as he ripped up more trees, these not even burning, tossing them like twigs to either side as he tore deeper into the wood.

Amontyr remained crouched where he was. The roar of the dragon and the cracking of the uprooted trees had ceased some time ago, but he knew the patience of dragons on the hunt. He would not make a foolish mistake. They had retreated steadily and stealthily, deeper and deeper into the wood, and now they were in a dense, dark thicket that provided them with a heavy canopy of leaves to shield them from penetrating eyes.

Nirotyr was crouched beside him, still holding his unconscious burden. They had found him that way when they'd slipped into the wood, exhausted and passed out upon the forest floor.

When darkness finally came in full, hours later, Amontyr tapped Nirotyr on the shoulder, and they moved out, weaving quickly through the trees in the darkness. For a long time they ran in silence, until Amontyr finally gave the sign to halt and rest.

"Is he awake?" Amontyr whispered.

"He stirred for a moment as we ran, but I think he was soon out again."

"I will carry him now."

There was a silent transfer in the darkness, then both drank deeply from a cold stream running through the wood before preparing to move out again.

"Have you seen anything like that from him before?" Nirotyr asked as he looked at the pale, sweating face of the man draped across Amontyr's shoulder.

"Not for a long time," Amontyr replied. "Come on."

11

UNEXPECTED
MEETINGS

SULMANDIR LANDED in front of the small fellowship of travelers, who were surprised not only by his unexpected reappearance so soon after his departure, but also by the blood still dripping from the talons of his front right claw.

"Welcome, Sulmandir," Valzaan said. "I cannot imagine you have been able to summon your sons already, so I must conclude something else has driven you. You are bloodied from battle. What news?"

"The news I came to bring is not connected to the blood, though of that I will also speak," Sulmandir replied. "There is a great host of men, Vulsutyrim, and Malek's creatures moving toward Amaan Sul from the Kalamin River."

"They have crossed the river already then," Aljeron said, disappointment and perhaps a bit of despair evident in his voice.

"This I have already seen," Valzaan replied.

The heads of Aljeron, Saegan, and Evrim all turned to the prophet. "You knew this?" Aljeron asked.

"Why didn't you tell us?" Evrim added.

"I only saw the movement of Malek's hosts by windhover this morning, shortly before setting out. I was unable to survey our defenses at the city before the time came to set out, and at that point, my attention was focused on more immediate things. I decided to wait to speak of the enemy's movement until I knew more of our own situation."

"Yes," Evrim said, "but you knew we thought Malek's host was stranded at the river. You could have told us what you knew."

"I am a prophet of Allfather, Evrim Minluan, and unless directed otherwise by Allfather, which I was not, I am at liberty to decide when I do or do not tell what I know and have seen. Is that clear?"

"Yes, Valzaan," Evrim replied rather sheepishly. "I'm sorry."

"Good, now remember what you've learned," Valzaan said, returning his attention to the dragon. "You spoke of Malek's hosts on the move. What have you seen of the Kirthanim and Great Bear, of Amaan Sul's preparedness for the coming battle?"

"Amaan Sul is empty," Sulmandir said. "At least it was empty as far as I could see."

"Empty!" the men said more or less together.

"Indeed. Two great companies have left the city by the eastern gate. The first, consisting mainly of women, children, and the elderly, is moving toward the Zaros Mountains, though they are a week or more away from arriving, at the pace they are maintaining. The other, comprised mainly of men and Great Bear, is moving east, it seems to me, toward Tol Emuna."

"Tol Emuna," Valzaan said. "Then they have decided Amaan Sul is indefensible, else they would not abandon it."

"Tol Emuna has the strongest natural defenses of any city in Kirthanin," Saegan said. "It's people are tough and strong. It is a wise decision."

"That shall be seen in due time," Valzaan said. "The problem all this poses for us, then, is that we are headed toward the wrong city."

"That is why I have returned," Sulmandir said. "If it is still your desire to go directly to your friends, you are going the wrong way."

"If we keep heading south on the western side of the Tajira Mountains, we will be forced eventually even farther west," Valzaan said, musing out loud. "The only way to take a more direct path would be to cross the Tajira Mountains here and cut across the eastern portion of Nolthanin."

"So our choices are either to cross two mountain ranges and go directly, or to do a long march south and west out of the way," Aljeron said, the disappointment and despair definitely audible in his voice now.

"Unless . . . " Valzaan said, lifting his head to Sulmandir. "Have you come to assist us?"

"I can."

"Three trips across the Tajira Mountains will take some time and further delay your mission."

"Yes, but all things considered, it is best. You cannot hope to make useful progress until you have crossed the mountains, and the crossing without my aid would be difficult. The Tajira Mountains are far higher and harsher than the Zaros Mountains." Sulmandir paused, his deep voice growing even deeper. "And there is another reason it would be wise."

"What reason?" Valzaan inquired.

"I have seen the man you said deserted you, heading south with three Vulsutyrim."

"Three giants!" Aljeron responded.

"How far south?" Valzaan asked.

"Many leagues. They have moved at great speed. I engaged them on my return from Enthanin and killed one of Vulsutyr's sons, but the other two and the man escaped into a wood. The man wielded great power. He is more important to Malek than you realize. He is no ordinary man."

"Synoki?"

"Wielded power?"

"How can it be?"

Valzaan waited until the others grew quiet before speaking. "If Synoki was in the company of Vulsutyrim and wielding power, then you must be right, Sulmandir, but I am perplexed. If Malek has bestowed power on him, as on Cheimontyr, why could I not see or sense it? Why has Allfather masked this from me?"

To this question no one offered an answer, and silence hung heavy upon them for a few moments. For the first time since hearing Sulmandir's voice in his gyre and seeing his majestic form in the daylight, Aljeron felt the despair wash back over him. He had not realized until that moment just how much he relished the hope Sulmandir's waking had brought. Now the darkness seemed even darker, having returned. He stooped, head in hands. Never in his adult life had he felt so close to breaking.

Koshti's warm breath tickled his face as he nuzzled Aljeron's cold cheeks with his warm nose. He looked up at his battle brother trying to console him the only way he knew how. Reaching out, he took Koshti by the scruff of his neck and rubbed him affectionately. Taking heart, he stood again and waited.

Valzaan, seemingly oblivious to the fact anyone had moved at all, seemed to be alone with his thoughts. All of them, including Sulmandir, waited in deference to him, and the moments stretched on as the prophet contemplated their next move.

"Well," he said at last. "Synoki is beyond us now. He is more important to Malek than we thought, and he knows who Benjiah is."

The others groaned, recalling their conversation with Valzaan upon first finding him by the fire, before ascending Harak Andunin. "I would send you to seek him and kill him, Sulmandir," Valzaan continued, "but that would delay your mission even further, and not knowing how much power Malek has bequeathed him, it could be dangerous to you. We must go forward with our plan and trust Allfather. Sulmandir, we will accept your offer of transport across the Tajira Mountains."

By the time Saegan and Valzaan joined the others on the eastern side of the Tajira Mountains, Aljeron had a good fire going to welcome them in from the cold night air. Attempts to secure a welcoming meal had been less successful. Despite his hopes that the eastern side of the Tajira Mountains might be more abundant with respect to game, Aljeron had only a single, white-and-grey flecked hare to show for his efforts. What there was of the rabbit was roasting now over the fire, but Aljeron realized it would do little more than stir the appetites of the gathered men. It certainly wouldn't satisfy the hunger they felt to feast as they all had before in better times in faraway places. Even so, Valzaan and Saegan received their appointed portion with all due gratitude and more, and the small company sat in the glow of the fire and ate.

"We should get some sleep," Valzaan said at last. "We will need to run with speed and strength tomorrow, for though Sulmandir has taken us a distance, we still have a long way to go."

"I just want to know one thing," Aljeron said. "Was he Malek's servant when we found him on the island?"

"Of course he was," Saegan said. "That's probably how he came to be there in the first place."

"But he fought with us. I remember him crushing a wolf's head with that hammer he carried away from the forge below the city."

"The hammer," Valzaan said, turning to Aljeron. "Maybe that's it. Perhaps the hammer is the link between Synoki and Malek's power."

"You think the hammer had power inside it?" Aljeron asked.

"I don't know," Valzaan said. "Certainly the hammer has always been the sign of the Master of the Forge. A hammer seems to be the link between Cheimontyr and his master, even the source of power received from him. Still, I was thinking along different lines, that perhaps the power granted Synoki was a reward of some type for retrieving the hammer from the island."

"So after we rescued the women, we just let Synoki walk away, carrying some important artifact to the Mountain to give to his master?" Saegan asked.

"Perhaps," Valzaan said, then he shrugged and shook his head. "It is all just fumbling in the dark. I don't have any clarity about Synoki, and I never have. It has always been as though a fog was wrapped around him, keeping me from seeing him as he truly is. From the beginning, I had my suspicions, but I had no proof before now of what we have all feared."

"But if he has some sort of power," Evrim said, "Why didn't he just strike us all down? Why didn't he kill us long ago?"

"Exactly," Aljeron said.

"The power of our enemy is not limitless." Much to their surprise, Erigan spoke this. "My father always told me from my earliest days that our enemy is not omnipotent. His power has limits, and so does he. We do not know how much power has been granted this Synoki, or for what purpose, nor do we know whether he has access to more once it is exhausted."

"Erigan is right," Valzaan said. "It is important that you all understand the nature of such things. I have at times wielded great power from Allfather, but such power was never stored

AWAKE

within myself. It was always as though I was granted a link to a great reservoir of supernatural strength, but, even then, my access has never been limitless, for such would overwhelm and destroy me. For my own protection, the amounts I have wielded have always been but fractions of the whole."

"Are you saying Synoki might be linked to Malek in some way, drawing upon Malek's power in time of need?" Saegan asked.

"No, not necessarily. Malek's power, though great, is not like Allfather's. What supernatural power he wields was given to him in the moment of his creation at the dawn of the First Age. He controls whether it is used for good or ill, but it was not originally his. His power, then, unlike the power of Allfather that I have felt and wielded, is limited, as Erigan suggests. Malek cannot just bequeath great powers to whomever he chooses, one after the other, for every gift of power leaves him a little weaker. Surely the creation of the Grendolai, Malekim, Black Wolves, and Kumatin all required a portion of his power. Cheimontyr wields some as well, and now we see that even Synoki has been so empowered. It could be though, that Synoki used it only because his life was in imminent peril from Sulmandir. It could be that had any one of you tried to execute Synoki, you would have received the blow that knocked Sulmandir from the air. What he survived, you might not have. Perhaps, after all, it was Allfather's mercy that stayed your hands when you wanted to kill him."

"Or maybe it was Synoki's power, manipulating our wills to act, or really, to keep us from acting," Saegan grumbled.

"We don't know, and for now, we should not let our questions keep us from doing what we must, which is sleep."

Despite Valzaan's words, Aljeron did not find sleep easy. He lay in the dark, images of Synoki from almost eighteen years ago on the Forbidden Isle, as well as from more recently, flashing through his head. Who was he, and how had he twice insinuated himself into their business unawares? Aljeron was angry at having allowed it, angry and confused.

Morning came all too quickly, and Aljeron's body groaned as he forced himself to rise from the ground.

"Is there any point?" he grumbled as he stood. "We can't possibly reach Tol Emuna before Malek's army gets there."

"No, it isn't likely, but we can try," Valzaan replied. "Come, all of you, circle around me."

The three men, Koshti, and Erigan all drew closer. The prophet had his hands outstretched. "Take my hands, and make sure you are all connected to me, directly or indirectly."

Aljeron reached out and took Valzaan's hand, and with his other hand, he reached down and took hold of Koshti's fur. Evrim placed his hand on Aljeron's shoulder, and Saegan and Erigan connected to Valzaan through his other hand. "Now, I have spoken to you all about the power of Allfather. He has granted my prayer that you might feel and know what it is that I mean. I have also prayed that we might receive strength to run far and fast, without growing weary. He has answered."

Aljeron was suddenly aware of warmth and light inside him. It didn't necessarily seem to start in the hand that held onto Valzaan and then spread, it was suddenly just there. Despair and dismay slipped away. He felt renewed, strong and hopeful. Suddenly he realized that what he wanted, wanted most in all the world, was to run, to feel the wind in his face. He looked around him at the others and saw that he was not alone. In a moment the circle was broken and all of them were moving through the grey light of dawn, running south, strong and fast.

Three days and nights they ran, stopping only for short breaks by day for food and water and for a short sleep each night. Though he knew he was running farther and faster than he'd ever run before, Aljeron never felt tired, and stopping was almost a sorrow, an unwanted interruption to an experience of sheer joy. Each night as he lay down beside Koshti, he felt sure he would not sleep, but each night sleep came immediately. When he woke each morning, long before first light, he knew that he had slept soundly, and he would rise ready to run once more.

The days were growing longer. Signs of spring were starting to show themselves, even in the plains beyond the eastern foothills of the Tajira Mountains. The brown land was turning green, at least in part. Tough, scraggly plants were beginning to emerge, and Aljeron marveled at their durability. Pummeled for weeks by rain and snow, their roots somehow managed to survive, buried deep in the nourishing soil and waiting for their chance, waiting for a cessation of the deluge and for the warming sun to shine upon them.

It was growing warmer. He could feel the shift in the weather. He had wondered at first if it wasn't the residual effect of feeling his body strangely warmed when receiving Allfather's gift of strength, speed, and endurance, but Valzaan confirmed that the weather was indeed changing.

"Take heart," Valzaan had said on the first day as they were paused, drinking from a steady stream coming down into the plain from the foothills. "Let the change of seasons be a reminder of Allfather's providence. Since the creation of the world, spring has always followed winter, regardless of the storms that have billowed and buffeted the land in autumn and in winter. Dark days lie behind, and darker days may lie ahead, but Kirthanin's great spring will come, and Allfather will make all things new. That, He has promised. That is our great hope. Now let us run again and feel His tender hand upon us!"

And they had run, on and on, league after league. On the third day, Valzaan had led them at last away from the Mountains.

"I have not traveled north of the Zaros Mountains and Saladar River and east of the Tajira Mountains since the dawn of the Third Age, but I have scouted the area ahead through the eyes of several windhovers, and there is a pass between the mountains and a great wood to our east, and beyond that is the Saladar River. Ordinarily the Saladar is no larger than a swift stream, but after the rain and snow that has pounded Kirthanin, it is now much more than that. The river flows south and east to the sea, a few days north of the Zaros Mountains. I recommend we follow the course of the river all the way, seeking to cross over at the delta, swimming it if we have to, then heading by coast to the Zaros Mountains. Once beyond them, in Enthanin, we can approach Tol Emuna from the northwest, the opposite direction that Malek and his hosts will be taking."

"We will follow you where you lead," Aljeron had answered for all of them, and they set off across the open land, gradually leaving the peaks of the Tajira Mountains behind.

By evening that day, the mountains were a silhouette in the distance and the expansive wood loomed so close that scattered trees on its edge were only twenty or thirty spans to their east. The trees were tall and majestic, but Aljeron took note of the buds beginning to open all along the boughs. He ran beside Evrim and pointed. "See, if spring is coming here, so far north, what do you think home must be like?"

"I don't know," Evrim said. He turned to Aljeron, smiling. "But it's nice to remember what it has been like in springs past."

They came upon a beautiful glade surrounded by a handful of the great trees. A small lake in the middle held water that was clear and smooth on the surface like glass. Each of them stopped at the water's edge, not only because it was in their way, but because it was beautiful.

"Can we stop for a drink?" Evrim asked Valzaan.

"We may indeed, but we should hurry on before night-fall comes."

They each stooped to drink, and the water was cool and refreshing. Aljeron rose to his feet first, as Koshti and the others drank on. After so many days in bleak surroundings, this spot was a true oasis: sprinklings of green grass and plants around the edge of the lake, tall beautiful trees reflected in the water and ringing it like sentries, and the lake itself, not the swollen dirty waters of a flood, but the expansive spread of a small pool transformed by inconceivable quantities of rain.

Koshti's head shot up and his body straightened and tensed. "What is it, Koshti?" Aljeron asked, drawing Daaltaran instinctively.

"We're not alone," Erigan answered, stepping back from the lake and turning to survey their surroundings as he quickly drew his massive staff. They were all alert now, weapons drawn and forming a tight circle by the water's edge.

"Steady, everyone," Valzaan said. "Until we know what's going on, just be steady."

Aljeron peered around him in the fading light, and though he could see nothing at first, eventually hundreds of shapes emerged. Around the lake in all directions, like a noose tightening slowly, they came closer. As the forms of men with spears became clearer in the dusk, so also did the incredible sight of animals mingling freely among them.

They were leopards, white with dark spots, moving in with the circle of men. Koshti was still tense, straining toward the closest men and leopards.

"Steady, Koshti," Aljeron said. "Stay with me."

As the men on their side of the lake drew closer, Aljeron clasped Daaltaran tightly. They were so many, lean and clothed in rough garb, each man holding long slender spears, like javelins. What's more, they were wearing what appeared to be small, tight-fitting masks. The masks were dark brown, a striking contrast to the pale whiteness of their blanched skin, and covered their faces from their eyes to the top of their mouths.

"Their hair is red," Evrim whispered to Aljeron.

"Yes, deep, dark red," Aljeron replied, maintaining a firm grip on Daaltaran. "Strange."

"And there's a leopard for every man," Evrim whispered, wonder in his voice. "Or almost every man."

"They are battle brothers," Valzaan said, tilting his head slightly toward Aljeron. "Can you feel the bonds, Aljeron?"

Even as Valzaan asked, Aljeron did. He could sense the connections. That's what Koshti had sensed, not only the approach of living things, but the approach of battle brothers like him.

"I told you once that bonds like yours and Koshti's were not always as rare as they are now," Valzaan said. "I just didn't expect to find so many more examples, and here of all places."

"That's all very well," Evrim said, "But what do we do?"

"Do? We hope they can be reasoned with, that's what we do."

Valzaan stepped forward, slowly, and immediately the advancing men raised their spears as the leopards at their feet ran forward, encircling Valzaan without attacking him.

"We greet you in the name of Allfather," Valzaan said, appearing unfazed by the pack of swarming leopards and men with spears.

"Allfather? The Master-Maker?" said one of the men in a mask, lowering his spear to his side as he stepped forward beyond the others. "Impossible. You are Blade-Bearers. You are servants of the Forge-Foe, and your life is thereby forfeit."

Wylla dipped her hands in the waters of one of the large lower pools of the fountain. The Great Hall of Sulare was just as she remembered it. The sun shone brightly through the opening in the roof above the fountain, and the great, open stone-paved room extended in all directions. The familiar sight of the great tapestries upon the walls telling the stories of Kirthanin brought a smile to her face.

She looked at Joraiem beside her, and her smile widened. He was looking down at her, beaming.

"What's gotten into you?" she asked.

He shrugged his shoulders and laughed. "I don't know."

"Really?"

"You, I guess," he said, leaning his forehead down gently on hers and closing his eyes. "It's nice to just sit here with you. Peaceful."

"Yes," Wylla agreed, turning around so she could lean her head on his chest. "Relaxing."

She leaned back and closed her eyes.

When she opened them again, she was no longer in the Great Hall. Rather, she was in one of the small, open-style, cottage-like houses they had stayed in while at Sulare. The massive window flaps were propped open on all four sides of the house, and a warm sea breeze blew in off the ocean.

She sat up and yawned. For some reason, she felt very sore. Maybe Caan had worked them too hard the day before, or perhaps she and the girls had spent too much time swimming in the Southern Ocean. Whatever they'd done, it had made her legs ache, and she rubbed them firmly with her hands, trying to soothe the tired and protesting muscles.

Stepping out of the house, she saw the sun low on the horizon. It was early, and she was beginning to feel confused. She looked around. There was no one else here. Where were the other girls? Why was she all alone? Where was Joraiem?

If it was early, Joraiem was probably on the beach, running.

She tensed. *The beach.* She ran to the wide avenue that cut a broad swath all the way from the Great Hall to the waters of the ocean. At the avenue, she turned toward the beach, hiked up her long dress above her knees, and ran even harder.

The sand was warm and soft beneath her feet, but the pleasure of feeling it sift between her toes was no match for the frustration of it slowing her down. She cursed it as she struggled to maintain a good pace, running westward along the shore. She made her way down to the wet, packed portion and ran where her feet didn't sink quite so far.

The waves were crashing to her left, and the water shattered into thin sheets that glided up and washed her feet, swirling around her heel and toes. She looked up ahead along the beach and could see nothing. Where was he?

Let him be all right. Her inaudible cry of desperation echoed in her brain. *What if I'm too late?*

He was there, in the dry sand, midway between the trees and the waves. He was kneeling in the sand, head bowed, hair hanging disheveled around his shoulders.

"Joraiem!" she shouted as she ran toward him. The dry sand stuck in clods to her feet and every step felt heavier and heavier. She almost stumbled and fell, but she caught herself and pressed forward. She'd closed half the distance, maybe more. Just a few steps. She'd be there.

She dropped down just behind him, taking his arms in her hands, firmly but gently.

"Joraiem?" she asked, fear and hesitation striking her. She leaned forward and peered over his shoulder.

His hands were pressed against his stomach, blood caked to the stiff fingers and bloody cloak. She sobbed. *Too late.*

Wylla turned to look at his face, but his blond hair obscured it. Reaching up, she felt the softness of his hair. She used to love to feel his hair between her fingertips as he lay in the grass, head in her lap. For a moment she could see him there, eyes closed but happy in the sun. Reaching down, she brushed the hair back and gasped.

Benjiah.

Wylla opened her eyes to see Yorek leaning over her in the darkness, eyes full of worry. "Yorek?"

"Your Majesty?"

"How long have we been stopped?"

"Not long."

As awareness returned, Wylla was keenly aware of the ropes that bit into the flesh of her wrists. She had been a captive before, bound and guarded, and the memory was dark and evil. Now she was a captive again, and this time she had even sought it out. *I must be mad.*

She sat up and looked around. The Nolthanim riders and scouts were only a few spans away in the darkness, obviously preparing their horses to ride again. She wondered if they'd let her ride this time, but she didn't really think they would. When they dragged her to her feet, they'd tie her bound hands by a rope several spans long to the saddle of one of the riders, and she would again spend her day running to keep up with the trotting horse.

Her legs ached just thinking about it. All day yesterday, she and Yorek ran this way, following the riders after their capture. They explained that they had been sent from the queen of Enthanin herself with an important message for the enemy's commander. Little had been said. They were instantly bound and tied to the horses, and off south they had gone.

She looked over at Yorek, crouching in the grass. "Did you sleep?"

"Not really."

"You should have. You'll be tired."

"I'm already tired," Yorek smiled.

"Be serious. I need you with me," Wylla said. "I don't think I can face this alone."

"You don't have to," Yorek answered, compassion in his eyes.

"I'm afraid."

"So am I."

"I'm afraid for Benjiah."

"I know. Just hold on a little longer. We're almost there."

"Do you think so?"

"Yes, I heard some of their conversation a little while ago."

"Good," Wylla said, feeling some relief. Whatever was coming, at least it was coming soon.

Rulalin was sipping water from a cup, sitting on the wooden bench that served as the centerpiece of his camp while on the move. The sun was down and darkness had fallen, but at least these days lighting a fire wasn't impossible, and a small fire burned between him and Soran, who lay on his side in the grass.

They weren't talking at the moment, and they hadn't been most of the evening. They were tired from the day's ride, and beyond that, as each league brought them closer to Amaan Sul, Rulalin could feel the heaviness of his task. He had left Fel Edorath and gone to the Mountain for her. He'd traveled the length and breadth of Kirthanin for her. If he couldn't make her see reason, his choices would all prove to have been for naught.

Rulalin stood at the sound of hooves from the north and peered through the darkness to see who was coming. Two riders slowed to a halt before the fire, and the first of them dropped to the ground.

"Captain Tarasir?"

"Yes," Rulalin said to the young rider.

"We have two prisoners from Amaan Sul."

"You've been all the way to Amaan Sul?" Rulalin asked, incredulous. Soran rose quickly to his feet.

"No, they were outside the city, riding together, both of them on one horse. They said they had a message from the queen of Enthanin."

Rulalin nodded. The words were still sinking in. Messengers from Wylla. Bringing terms of surrender perhaps?

"Two messengers on one horse?" Soran asked, puzzled. "That doesn't sound like an embassy from a queen."

"Yes," the rider said. "It seemed strange to us. They bore a large banner of the city. It seemed to be good work, perhaps of royal quality, otherwise we wouldn't have believed them at all. As it is, we weren't sure whether to trust them or not, so we've brought them to you."

"Good," Rulalin said. "Where are they?"

"They're on foot, not far behind us. Should I have them brought to you, or should we seek Captain Farimaal?"

"Since I am entrusted with negotiating with the city, bring them to me," Rulalin said. "If they are who they say they are, and if I decide that they need to be sent on to Captain Farimaal, you may escort them there."

The rider nodded, remounted his horse, and rode back through the darkness with his companion.

"Prisoners," Soran said, coming around the fire to Rulalin.

"Yes," Rulalin said, "but are they really messengers?"

Soran shrugged. "Even if they aren't, it is good news for us."

"Do you think?"

"Sure. If they're from the city, they'll certainly be able to answer some basic questions, especially if they left after the arrival of the army."

"Perhaps."

"At the least, we should be able to get a good feel for the morale of the Enthanim. I don't know why they headed south if they knew we were coming, but I bet they wish they were somewhere else now."

"No doubt," Rulalin said, his attention focused on the darkness beyond the light of his fire. "If they aren't wishing it yet, they will."

The two stood in silence, shoulder to shoulder. Eventually, the sound of horses announced the captives. Rulalin wondered if taking a seat on his bench would appear more authoritative to the prisoners, but in the end he decided to remain where he was. He would receive them standing, with Soran at his side.

Half a dozen horses appeared this time, and trailing behind them were the two captives, stumbling along on foot, hands bound and connected by a rope to a single horse that brought up the rear. He could see, even at this distance in the dark, that one of them was an old man. What Wylla was thinking sending a man with creaking bones and wrinkled skin as a messenger to Malek, he couldn't imagine. What Wylla was thinking sending a messenger at all was baffling. He wasn't sure that he could convince her to accept an embassy, let alone terms of surrender, but if she wasn't seeking them, why send a messenger?

The prisoner beside the old man was bent over, head down, taking deep breaths. Rulalin couldn't be sure, but this one appeared to be a woman. A woman and an old man? Maybe Wylla knew messengers sent to Malek would not return, and so she had sent her servants, not wanting to spare any soldiers. Again, it didn't sound like Wylla. Rulalin had always seen her as the type of queen who would go into danger herself before sending anyone else into it.

Rulalin tensed. He peered closer. Long dark hair, and definitely a woman. It could be. She straightened. The cup of water in his hand dropped to the ground.

After all this time.

ARISE

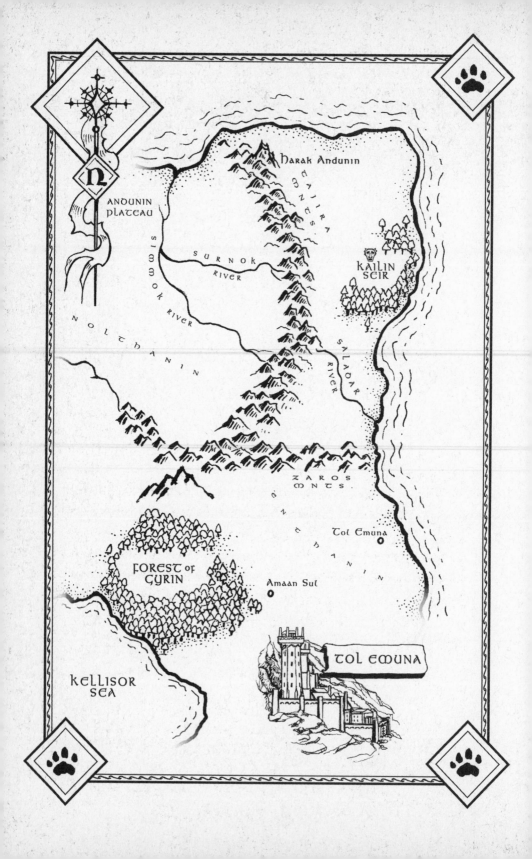

ANDUNIN
PLATEAU

Harak Andunin

KAILIN
SEIR

SURNOK
RIVER

SALADAR
RIVER

ZAROS
MNTS.

Tol Emuna

FOREST OF
CYRIN

Amaan Sul

KELLISOR
SEA

TOL EMUNA

SECOND CHANCES

BEFORE HE COULD STOP HIMSELF, Rulalin was walking away. Soran, befuddled by Rulalin's behavior, hurried after.

"Rulalin," Soran called.

Rulalin didn't stop. Instead, he continued away from Wylla and the older man. Though Rulalin had recognized her, she hadn't yet looked at him, though possibly she could have noticed his retreating figure in the dark. Surely she couldn't have known it was him. He hoped not, at any rate. Seeing a Nolthanim soldier, he approached and pulled him aside.

"Soldier," Rulalin said, "find some others and put up my tent."

"Your tent?" the soldier said, looking confused.

"Yes, my tent."

"But, you told us not to bother about it—"

"I know what I told you," Rulalin said. "I've changed my mind. Prisoners from Amaan Sul have been brought to the camp, and I will receive them in my tent. Hurry. Every moment you delay prolongs your sleep."

The soldier moved off through the darkness to find help for his task, and before Rulalin could move from that spot, Soran grabbed him by the shoulder. "What is going on?"

Rulalin turned to Soran, burning with a fiery intensity that he hadn't possessed since the war with Shalin Bel was at its height. Soran let go of Rulalin's shoulder and stepped back.

"Rulalin," he continued, his voice softer, betraying his bewilderment. "You've got to tell me what's happening here."

"I just want to receive the prisoners in my tent."

Soran frowned. "You were perfectly content to receive them over there just a moment ago. What's changed?"

Rulalin looked at Soran's quizzical look. Soran at least could be trusted with what apparently only Rulalin knew. "It's her, Soran."

"What do you mean *her*?" Soran started, but whatever he'd been about to add, he never said. He caught himself as realization dawned on him. "Her? You mean—"

"Shh." Rulalin hushed him and stepped in very close, looking around to make sure no one else was near. A handful of men in the distance were rolling out Rulalin's tent. "I don't think anyone but the two of us know who she is. For now at least, I want to keep it that way."

Soran searched Rulalin's face. "I'm not sure how wise that is. This is big news."

"I know, but that's how I want it."

Soran shook his head. "How sure are you of your favored position? If you're found out, it could go ill with you. If things go ill with you, they'll go ill with me."

"I've been given discretion in dealing with the enemy. Specifically, I've been given discretion to negotiate with Amaan Sul, and that is exactly what I'm going to do."

"Farimaal might not see it quite that way."

"Let me worry about when and how to tell him. For now, we keep her identity a secret. All right?"

"All right," Soran said reluctantly. "So what are you going to do?"

"Receive her," Rulalin said, looking at the men busy at work. "As soon as my tent is ready."

Rulalin looked back toward Wylla. He couldn't see her, but a Nolthanim soldier was approaching them.

"Sir?"

"Yes?" Rulalin said, as though he didn't understand the hesitation in the soldier's question.

"The prisoners from Amaan Sul?"

"What about them?" Rulalin said, trying to strike a balance between sounding authoritative and mildly inconvenienced, as though the soldier should know exactly what was expected of him in this situation already.

"We thought you were going to speak with them tonight?"

"I am. As you can see," Rulalin said, pointing through the darkness at the men working to assemble his tent. "My tent is almost ready. I think our messengers will be more suitably impressed by their need to capitulate to our demands if they are received by a captain of the Nolthanim in his quarters rather than in an open camp as though I were but a common soldier."

The soldier looked at the tent going up, and Rulalin could see he wasn't entirely convinced that Rulalin wasn't speaking utter foolishness. He didn't question Rulalin's rationale, however, and that was the important thing. *Let him think what he likes.*

"What should we do with them in the meantime?"

"Do what you've been doing," Rulalin retorted. "Look after them and keep them bound. I'll send someone for them when I'm ready."

"Yes, sir," the soldier said. He turned and retreated through the darkness.

"You might want to try to relax a bit," Soran said when the soldier was out of earshot. "You seem a little irritable."

Rulalin looked at him, scowling. "Good thinking."

Rulalin took a closer look at where his tent was going up, and realized the misfortune of it. He started walking toward the tent, then continued past the soldiers as though they weren't even there. A few spans beyond them, he stopped. Benjiah's cage was there in the distance, as he had feared.

"It has to be moved," he said, turning to Soran. "I can't run the risk of her seeing him before she sees me."

"Do you want me to take care of it?" Soran asked.

Rulalin looked at him, grateful. "Yes, would you?"

"Sure, just give me a few minutes to round up some help. Where would you like him?"

"Just far enough away that she can't possibly see him before she's brought to my tent. Not too far though."

"All right," Soran said. "I'll take care of it."

"Thanks," Rulalin said, and he watched as Soran headed off.

His tent was taking shape, and Rulalin felt the immensity of what was happening. In just a few moments, Wylla Someris, queen of Enthanin, to whom he had given his heart so long ago that he could not now remember a time when it had not belonged to her, would be brought to his tent. She would be brought. She would enter, and he would see her again, face to face.

The lamps were lit and the sparse furniture that traveled with him was in place. Two wooden chairs were on the far side of the small wooden table, in case Wylla and her companion were to sit. Water and food had been placed on the table as he requested. He would welcome her. He would offer food and water. He would receive her graciously. She would not, he realized, be glad to see him. He couldn't expect that, not yet at any rate, whatever might come later, even much later, but he

248   ARISE

would still be gracious, no matter what she might say or do. He'd always known that would be crucial to any hope he had that, over time, she might soften toward him.

Soran appeared through the flaps. "You all right?" he asked.

"Fine," Rulalin said, trying to sound like it. "Benjiah?"

"He's fifty spans past any possibility of being seen, unless she has better eyes than a falcon. The only way she'll see him tonight is if she's taken to him."

"Good," Rulalin said as Soran poured himself a cup of cold water and sat down in one of the wooden chairs on Rulalin's side of the table. Rulalin stood looking at the flaps of the tent wondering, now that Soran had mentioned it, if Wylla would be taken to him. She would want to see him, of course, as soon as she found out he was alive. Rulalin felt divided about whether to allow it as an act of good will and generosity, or to withhold it as an incentive for cooperation or coercion, should it become necessary.

It also dawned on him, and he felt foolish for not realizing it sooner, that seeing Benjiah might well be the main reason for her unexpected appearance. He had been so focused on the mere fact that she was here, in the flesh, that he had not yet stopped to think about why. Why was she so far from the walls of her city and the soldiers of her army? The Nolthanim soldiers had spoken of her as a messenger, and until this moment he had assumed subconsciously that this was the truth, even if Wylla had deceived the scouts about her real identity. Now, though, he realized even that might be a deception. She might be here with no message at all, with no purpose at all save to see Benjiah.

But why? What could she hope to achieve? Surely she must know that now she was a prisoner and captive just as much as Benjiah. Surely she must know she was taking an enormous gamble with her own life.

Perhaps she was counting on using her claim as a messenger to get her out of the camp and back to Amaan Sul safely. Maybe she was just there to gather information with her own two eyes. After all, she couldn't know that Benjiah was there or even still alive. Obviously, Benjiah was not among those who had crossed the Kalamin.

Voices approached the tent. Rulalin was frustrated that he still could not see why Wylla had come. He had expected to go to her, trapped behind her walls and awaiting the appearance of Malek's mighty host. That was the scenario he had envisioned over and over. Now she had come to him, unexpectedly, and he felt somehow at a disadvantage.

The flaps of the tent opened.

Later that night, the moment that followed played again and again in Rulalin's head. Yes, he had recognized Wylla from a distance, but when she walked into his tent behind the Nolthanim soldier, she was as close to him as she had been when last he'd seen her, in the Great Hall of Sulare, hundreds of leagues away and a lifetime ago. It would not be true to say that she had not changed. She was older and the cares and concerns of the Enthanim were evident in her eyes and face. And yet, it seemed to Rulalin that none of these things could touch the heart of her beauty, that warm familiarity and winsome delight that was Wylla Someris. These elements of Wylla were beyond the reach of time. She had aged and would continue to, but she would always be herself and thus beautiful.

The actions and reactions that followed her entrance into the tent transpired in a remarkably small amount of time. As Wylla stepped through the flaps, she was obscured from Rulalin in part by the soldier who had come in first. As Wylla made room for her grey-haired companion, Rulalin felt his heart quicken at the sight of her beautiful face, and she turned to face him.

Everything was nearly lost in the moment. The sudden and dramatic shift in Wylla's countenance would have raised alarms and questions in any even remotely alert observer, but the soldier who had escorted them was turned to Wylla's companion and missed the change. Even so, Rulalin was momentarily paralyzed by Wylla's reaction.

Knowing that Wylla would not be happy to see him was one thing. Seeing her reaction to him was quite another. Rulalin had expected anger, even hatred, but what he saw was worse. There were elements of those things, yes, but they were mixed with something deeper, something Rulalin could not quite put his finger on. Was it fear? Terror of what would happen now that she had been placed in Rulalin's hands? He had expected her to hate him, but her fear struck him like a blow to his face. He could never harm Wylla. That was as close to bedrock truth as it came. That she so evidently believed he could was a surprise, and before that moment, inconceivable.

Had Rulalin reeled from that surprise for a second longer than he did, things would have gone badly. But he recovered his wits just enough to raise his hand just enough to motion to Wylla to be careful, a hint she quickly understood. With admirable self-control, she pulled the emotion that had sprung to her face from it, though Rulalin could see the steely look of determination was artificial and strained.

Before Wylla's companion could notice anything awry, he spoke into the silence. "These are the prisoners?"

"Yes, sir," the Nolthanim soldier said, turning away from them to Rulalin.

Rulalin looked from the young man to Wylla, concentrating on looking determined and dispassionate. "You are from Amaan Sul?"

"We are," Wylla said, playing along.

"You are messengers?"

"We are."

Rulalin turned back to the young soldier. "Thank you. You may go now."

The soldier bowed slightly, then turned and disappeared through the flaps into the night. There was silence in the tent. Rulalin stood behind the table, and Soran sat beside him. Wylla stood where she had stopped, a span or so inside the tent, with the old man beside her. If her companion was surprised by the quiet stalemate, he didn't show it. He stood, waiting patiently beside his queen.

"Have a seat," Rulalin said at last, motioning to the chairs on the other side of the table.

"I'd prefer to stand," Wylla said.

Rulalin studied her. He knew she must be weary. Tied behind a horse and on her feet for who knew how long, her body must have ached. He also knew Wylla, and he didn't challenge her.

"Suit yourself," he said, taking his own seat. His knees were shaking, and sitting down was an immense relief.

He reached over and poured himself some water, then motioned to the spread of food and drink. "Please, help yourself."

Wylla looked for a moment like she would refuse this as well, but she held her tongue and simply said, "Thank you."

She walked to the table and poured water for her companion and herself, and then she held the plate to him so he could take some food. Having served him, she served herself, and both ate hungrily. All the while, Rulalin watched her dignified and graceful movements, even in the face of her captor and enemy, adoring her silently.

"Will you sit now?"

Wylla looked at her companion, who showed no visible reaction to the question, then turned back to him. "Yes."

They both sat. Scarcely in her seat, Wylla turned to her companion, "Yorek, this is Rulalin Tarasir, who killed my husband."

The man named Yorek looked at Rulalin, for the first time betraying emotion in his presence. To Rulalin's surprise, that emotion appeared to be, more than anything else, sadness.

"You'll have to forgive me," Wylla said, looking at Soran. "I don't know your name and so can't introduce myself properly. I'm Wylla Someris, Queen of Enthanin."

"I'm Soran—"

"My loyal friend, assistant, and fellow Werthanim."

"—and I know who you are," Soran finished.

"Ah," Wylla replied, looking from Soran back to Rulalin. "You knew I was in the camp."

"I saw you arrive," Rulalin said.

"It was you who walked away."

"Yes."

"And your soldiers? They know who I am?"

"No one knows but us."

"Why did you not give me away just now?"

"Why did you not tell my men when they captured you who you were?"

"That is my affair."

"It's mine now," Rulalin replied.

Wylla was looking intently at Rulalin, and he could see that whatever emotion he had seen before, loathing and anger had gained the upper hand now. He felt relieved. This, he had expected.

She was wavering, he knew, with the decision to cooperate or not. He could see that part of her wanted to be as difficult as she could, but by now she realized that she had been entrusted to Rulalin. Whatever she was there to do, antagonizing him was not going to help her.

"I thought it safest to be taken as a simple messenger," she said at last. "I needed to be delivered to a person of authority."

"And so you have been," Rulalin said.

"I see." Wylla looked at him for a moment, as though debating whether to go on, but at last she did. "And how does a soldier of Fel Edorath come to be a person of authority among the hosts of Malek?"

"I have been rewarded for service and valor in battle," Rulalin said, his voice betraying the bitter irony he felt.

"Service and valor?"

"Yes."

"What happened? Despite what you did, I never saw you as a traitor. A coward and a murderer, yes, but not a traitor."

Rulalin motioned to Soran to sit back. "I bear Malek no love, but I have my reasons for what I have done."

"Reasons," Wylla said disdainfully.

"Wylla, you have not yet explained why seeing someone in authority was important to you."

Wylla looked long and hard at Rulalin. She seemed to be examining him, and for his part, Rulalin tried to return the look with calmness and equanimity. She folded her hands together in her lap. "For whatever reason, Allfather has led me here to your tent, so I will be plain. I need your help."

"My help?"

"Yes. I need information concerning my son, Benjiah." Wylla's voice faltered as she pronounced Benjiah's name, but she finished with pride, looking steadily into Rulalin's eyes.

"Ah," Rulalin said. "What information do you seek?"

"Any," Wylla replied, leaning forward, her calm facade showing cracks of emotion. "And all. Is he alive?"

"He is alive."

Wylla's head bowed momentarily, and when she raised it a moment later, he could see the relief that his words had brought. He was glad. The man called Yorek rested his hand on Wylla's knee, stroking it soothingly.

"He is alive," she said, echoing Rulalin's own words.

"Yes."

"May I see him?" she asked, looking almost pleadingly at him, the anger and loathing having given way to a driving maternal desire.

"Perhaps it is time for us to speak alone. There are things that should be said about Benjiah and about the decisions I have made."

Wylla looked at Yorek, but the older man did not speak.

"I can assure you," Rulalin said, "you will be safe."

"You will forgive me if I am slow to accept your assurance," Wylla said sharply, looking back to him.

She leaned in close to Yorek. "This is why we've come. Whatever happens, I will see our mission through to its end."

Yorek bowed in acknowledgement, then rose from his seat.

"Soran will step outside the tent with you," Rulalin said, motioning to Soran to take the man out. "I doubt we will be long."

Soran rose and walked around the table to escort the old man out. The flaps opened, giving Rulalin a glimpse of some soldiers standing a short distance off, no doubt awaiting word on the interview. The flaps closed again, and he was alone with Wylla.

Again, there was silence in the tent. Wylla sat quietly, watching Rulalin, waiting. Rulalin, having imagined this moment hundreds of times, thought he should have figured out by now what to say, but he could think of nothing. He took a deep breath, opened his mouth, and trusted that words would come.

"We can't really speak of the present, let alone the future, without speaking first of the past. I'm sorry, Wylla, for everything. I've wanted to tell you that for a very long time."

He could see that his apology took her off guard. There was uncertainty in her countenance toward him for the first time since she'd been brought into his tent.

"Why did you do it?" she asked, but the bitterness and anger were still there. Her eyes upon him made him uneasy, and he looked down at the table, where his fingers were tracing the curves in the woodgrain.

"I don't know anymore," Rulalin said, shrugging. "It was like I couldn't see anything else. All I knew was that I'd lost you, and I couldn't bear the thought of knowing you were out there with somebody else."

"Joraiem trusted you. He wanted to be your friend."

"I know. I knew it was a mistake, the biggest mistake of my life, long before I stopped for sleep that day I fled Sulare."

"You ruined my life that day."

"I ruined both our lives that day."

He looked up. Wylla was still peering across the table at him. "I don't feel sorry for you."

"I'm not asking you to. I just wanted you to know that I'm sorry for what I did, for the pain I've caused you, and that I would undo it if I could."

"But you can't, so your words are hollow." Wylla sat back in her seat, and her eyes dropped from his face. When she spoke again, there was resignation if not despair in her voice. "Where is all this going?"

Rulalin stood and turned away from the table, away from Wylla. "I went to the Mountain to save my own life, that's true. I won't deny it. But, saving my own life was not the only reason I went. It wasn't even the main reason I went. I went to the Mountain to save your life, for it is more precious to me than my own."

"What?" Wylla asked, incredulous.

"It's true," Rulalin said, turning back around.

"How will helping Malek help me?" Wylla started, angrily. "You've helped him sweep across Werthanin and Suthanin, and now you've brought him to my doorstep. That's your idea of help?"

"For years before I went to the Mountain, Malek had been soliciting my help. A messenger came repeatedly to me with offers of aid in Fel Edorath's war against Aljeron, if I would pledge loyalty to Malek. These offers I refused. In fact, I almost found comfort in the thought that when Malek came forth, I would be among the first to die. That is, until I realized that Malek's coming would also mean your death. I decided then, that having done what I had done, I owed you everything. I decided that I would do whatever it took to save you. So when the messenger returned, I accepted the offer, went to the Mountain, and pledged my loyalty. Now I have come to Enthanin to offer you your life."

"You have the authority to offer me my life?"

"I have requested permission to settle among the Nolthanim after the war. Malek has pledged their ancient homeland to them. They will live there, men ruled by men, under Malek's ultimate rule, of course, but largely independent."

Rulalin stepped back to the table and sat down. He was growing excited, and he leaned forward in his seat. "You can come too, Wylla. I have sought permission to take you to Nolthanin. All you have to do is cooperate."

"Cooperate?"

"Yes. Surrender the city and Enthanin," Rulalin answered. "It is the prudent course anyway. There is nothing you can do, Wylla. Malek's hosts are vast and the creatures he has unleashed, they wield power beyond my imagination. The future if you resist is fearful. Why fight and die when you can live?"

Wylla started to shake her head. "You've come all this way, thinking I'd abandon my city to go to Nolthanin with you?"

"You will be doing your people a favor. They will live rather than die in a vain and pointless war."

Wylla pushed back her chair and rose to her feet, drawing herself up as a storm of indignation swirled in her eyes. "I would rather die by Malek's own hand, a gruesome and bloody death, then surrender my people and my city, and I will never go anywhere willingly with you."

Rulalin rose as well, his hands outstretched, palms toward Wylla, trying to encourage her to calm down and lower her voice. "I understand," he said. "I don't blame you for reacting this way, for being angry. You don't have to decide now."

"I'll never accept this offer."

"I hear you, but you don't have to decide now. Just don't do anything foolish while you're in our custody. Think about it."

Wylla glared. After a moment, though, the anger dissipated and the pleading look she had earlier returned. She leaned toward him over the table and whispered. "You would save me?"

"Yes."

"Save my son."

Rulalin looked down as Wylla continued. "Save him, Rulalin, and you will save me."

"His fate is in not my hands."

Wylla reached out her hand as though to place it on Rulalin's arm, but she stopped short and withdrew it. "Please," she said, "he's all I have left. He's everything to me."

"You don't understand," Rulalin said, looking up at her. "I am his jailor, but his fate is not in my hands."

"You are his jailor?" she asked, excitement growing in her voice. "Is he nearby? May I see him?"

Rulalin hesitated a moment, then answered. "Yes, you may see him."

Benjiah lay on his back, looking up at an angle through the slats behind his head. The sky was dark as always. He had loved to peer up at the stars on cold clear nights at home, and he wondered now if he would ever see the heavenly lights again.

He couldn't get back to sleep. He'd been sleeping soundly when the soldiers had come and, for no apparent reason, lifted and moved his cage. They dispersed into the darkness of the camp, and he found himself once more alone.

Although he was weary, he wasn't sure he wanted to go back to sleep. He had dreamt of the two poles again. He could almost feel the ropes in the dream, cutting into his wrists. His arms were stretched and exhausted as he tried to hold himself up so that they wouldn't be wrenched from their sockets. Before him, as far as he could see, a vast assembly looked on.

Even though he was awake now, the images were so real they made him tremble. This new dream had been haunting him with eerie regularity, and he found it increasingly difficult to shut the image out of his mind while awake.

He closed his eyes and the image was there still. *Allfather, I don't want to be in this cage anymore. I don't want to be tied to those poles. I want to be free. Grant me just a fraction of the power you granted me in the dragon tower before the Grendolai, just a fraction of the power you granted me at the Kalamin River. Grant it, and I will be free.*

He lay, waiting for something, anything, for direction and guidance, for the feeling of light and heat inside of him that had accompanied these other manifestations of Allfather's hand. He waited, hoping for power to flow through him, but it did not come. He had made this basic request many times since his capture, but no response had come, and it seemed now all too likely that it would never come.

"I am forsaken," he whispered, the words slipping from his lips into the starless sky.

You are not forsaken. You are mine. I have brought you to this very place, and in this place you will serve me. Fear not. Though the way ahead will be hard, you are not alone, and you never have been.

Benjiah opened his eyes as the sound of the voice inside his head disappeared. He blinked and stared back up into the sky. It was not the reply he had sought, but it was a reply.

He heard the sound of footsteps approaching, and leaning up on his elbows, he saw a man and woman approaching. They were already close enough that he could not see their faces, obscured from his eyes by the cage. He was surprised to see the woman. He had not seen any among the Nolthanim, and he couldn't imagine why he would see one now, here in advance of the main contingency of Malek's hosts. The man stopped several spans away, and the woman continued toward the cage alone.

As she came up beside it, she stooped to look in. He peered up at the face beyond the slats and knew it instantly. He sat up. "Mother?"

"My son," the trembling voice came back, and her slender arm reached out for him between the slats.

He sat up and moved close enough to her that her hand could feel his face, and there was immeasurable comfort in her fingertips. He looked at her looking at him, tears running down her cheeks. He wondered if he had somehow fallen asleep again, or if Allfather was sending comfort in the guise of his mother in some passing vision that would disappear in a moment.

He blinked, but she was still there, her hand now sweeping away the hair that hung down over his eyes.

"I don't understand," he started. "What are you doing here?"

"I came to find you," she replied.

"But you must be a captive now, too."

"I am."

Benjiah's heart sank. He had imagined his mother, like the rest of Enthanin, still some leagues away and safe, but she was not safe. She was here, and if she was here, then Rulalin must know.

"You have seen him already," he said.

"Yes. I was brought here from his tent."

"Be careful."

"Be careful of what?"

"Of him."

"I will, of course, but why do you say it?"

"I'm not sure, but something is at work deep inside him, and I can't figure it out. He seems intent one moment to convince me that he is my friend and I should hope for survival. At other times, it seems equally clear that I am but a tool he will wield so long as I am useful."

"I'll be careful," Wylla assured him.

"Good, because it is you that he wants."

"So he says."

"He's told you?"

"Yes, essentially. He promises to preserve my life, so long as I turn over Enthanin to Malek."

"Which of course you won't do."

Wylla looked at her son, trying to smile encouragement. "Of course not. Even for you, Benjiah, I could not."

"Good."

"Though you know he may be our best chance of saving you."

"Then perhaps I am better off not being saved."

"Don't give up. I've come to save you if I can."

Benjiah took his mother's hand. "I think I am beyond your reach, or anyone's. I am Allfather's prophet, Mother. If you didn't believe it when I left, believe it now. I know it beyond question."

"I know."

"I must do what He calls me to do."

"What are you saying?"

"Only that my life is no longer my own. I am His, and He has brought me to this place for a reason."

Wylla bowed her head at this, but she didn't contradict him. "Don't worry about me," he continued. "He will not let harm come to me before my time."

"He didn't save your father."

"No," Benjiah replied, "and I can't offer you any assurances that my service will not cost my life, but I must serve."

The man approached now, and Benjiah knew without needing to see him more clearly that it was Rulalin. He paused momentarily beside the guard, then continued on his way toward the cage.

"He's coming."

"He said I'd have only a few moments," Wylla said, clasping Benjiah's hand tightly. Her tears, which had stopped for a short time, flowed freely once more.

"What will happen to you?" Benjiah asked.

"I don't know," she said as if she didn't care.

"It is time to go," Rulalin said.

"Can you not spare me another moment?"

"Not tonight."

"When can I see him again?" Wylla asked, all the while not moving or taking her eyes off Benjiah.

"That will depend."

"On what?"

"On many things. For now though, we must go."

Wylla pressed her forehead against the slats of the cage and whispered to her son. "Be strong, my son. I have desired nothing more than to see you again, and Allfather has granted my request. He may be pleased to do more even than this."

"He may."

"Sleep well," she said as she rose to go.

"I will." He crawled up close to the slats where she had but recently been. It seemed to him he could feel the warmth of her flesh against them.

"Mother!" he called after her.

She stopped and turned.

"I love you."

"I know," she answered him, "and I love you. Always."

2

THE KALIN SEIR

VALZAAN STOOD OPPOSITE the tall, strong man in the brown mask who had stepped out from the others. The failing light of day was almost completely gone. Aljeron looked at the prophet, who stood with head erect and body alert. Though he hadn't followed everything the man had just said, he understood the man thought they deserved to die. He hoped Valzaan would be able to tap into Allfather's power, or whatever he did, because it seemed pretty clear to him that the man had brought enough of his friends along to follow through on his threat.

However, if Valzaan was on the verge of a remarkable display of power, he didn't show it. For a long moment, he simply faced the masked man. The apparent leader, for his part, seemed to be waiting for some word from them. A part of Aljeron, the part that had led the army of Shalin Bel for the last seven years, urged him to respond to the man's enigmatic statement, but he restrained himself. What was unknown or obscure to him might well be known to Valzaan.

"Blade-Bearers?" Valzaan said after a moment, indicating that the confusion Aljeron felt was shared.

The man with the mask pointed his long, wooden spear unmistakably toward Daaltaran in Aljeron's hand. "You are Blade-Bearers," he repeated. "You carry that which is forbidden. You are servants of the Forge-Foe."

"I am Valzaan, prophet of Allfather, and I serve no one but Him."

"You lie," the man said, stepping closer and brandishing his wooden spear more forcefully. "True servants of the Master-Maker would not carry the forbidden, ever, for any reason. You are spies of the Forge-Foe."

"You speak of Malek."

The man in the mask fairly snarled at the mention of Malek's proper name, as did many of the others. Still, he did not say anything, and Valzaan continued.

"The Master of the Forge is not my master. He is the fallen Titan, the great enemy of Allfather, and I have opposed him all my life, as do these who are with me." With that, Valzaan motioned to the rest of his fellowship, taking them all in, from the men to Koshti to the Great Bear, with the sweep of his hand. "In addition to my word, I offer as evidence of my true allegiance our friend Erigan, a Great Bear. Never, since the world was founded, has one of the Great Bear served Malek."

"Not willingly, perhaps," the man replied.

"Not ever."

The man looked at Erigan, standing tall a couple spans to Valzaan's right. He murmured to one of the men behind him, who jogged toward a cluster of men some twenty spans away. "Do not move from this spot or show aggression of any kind. We will confer together to decide what to do with you."

ARISE

"We will await your return, and I trust our compliance will also speak to our allegiance."

"Your compliance will speak to your lack of foolishness, perhaps, but not to your allegiance," the man replied. He joined the small assembly waiting for him.

"If we're going to wait awhile," Evrim said quietly, "do you think they'd mind if we sat down? I'm tired."

"I wouldn't think so," Valzaan replied. "Who knows how long this will take?"

With that, Valzaan settled upon the ground, and the red-haired men nearest them didn't stir. The rest of them sat as well, save only Erigan, who remained where he was, and Koshti, who stood beside Aljeron, eyes trained on the nearby men. He wasn't growling or showing obvious signs of hostility, but Aljeron could sense that his battle brother was on edge.

"What do you think is going on here?" Aljeron asked Valzaan as the four men sat huddled close.

"I don't know."

"Do you have no idea who these people are?" Evrim asked.

"None."

"At least they seem to be aligned against Malek," Saegan said.

"Which is great," Evrim added, "except they seem to think we are in his service, which isn't so great."

"Yes," Valzaan mused, "apparently the swords we carry have marked us as servants of the enemy. Very interesting."

"And all these snow leopards," Aljeron said, scanning the host of sleek white cats, spotted with black patches of varying sizes and shapes. "I've never met anyone else with the bond, and suddenly here I am, surrounded by people with it."

"Yes," Valzaan agreed, "it is wondrous and odd all at the same time. It will be fascinating to hear their story, if we can keep them from executing us."

There was no laughter at Valzaan's grim joke, and as the small group that had been convening moved in their direction, spears in hand, the four men stood. Regardless of what they appeared to think about his sword, Aljeron wasn't about to set Daaltaran down. It was his only defense.

Several bowmen stepped to the fore of the larger group with arrows nocked and trained upon them. Valzaan's party was covered with two or three dozen arrows, and Aljeron had no doubt that any aggressive movement on their part would go ill for them.

Among the small group of perhaps eight to ten archers were an equal number of snow leopards, who now came forward and circled Koshti, who regarded their approach with suspicion. As they surrounded him, he turned around and around, agitated, but they made no hostile movements and Koshti did not interfere with their examination. At long last, the man who had served as spokesman before spoke again, this time addressing not Valzaan or the group as a whole, but Aljeron.

"The tiger is your battle brother?" the man asked.

"Yes, he is," Aljeron answered.

The men murmured among themselves, and the leopards, as though in reaction to this answer, drew back among them. "We sensed the bond," the spokesman continued, "and we admit that we don't know how you could be a servant of Malek and also have a battle brother. The bond is sacred, symbolic of the harmony that once existed between men and all of the Master-Maker's creation. How you could maintain the union while having forsaken your Creator, we can't imagine."

"I have not forsaken my Creator," Aljeron answered simply.

"Yet you are a Blade-Bearer."

"I have slain many servants of our common enemy with this blade."

"You cannot defeat the enemy by using his weapon. Are all men south of the Mountain Blade-Bearers?"

"Not all."

"But many?"

"Many."

"We do not understand, but we will not pursue it further at the moment." He turned to address them all. "We find sufficient evidence to believe you may not be servants of the Forge-Foe, enough to grant you your lives, for now. We will hear more of what you have to say at a later point. For now you are our captives, however, and you should be warned that if we find you have deceived us in any way, your deaths will be swift. Do you understand?"

"We do," Valzaan replied.

"Then you will sheath your weapons and come with us. Tonight we will camp not far away, and we will move on at first light."

The circle of men in masks began to reform into a small column of some hundred and fifty men and leopards, and soon they were marching away from the glade.

When they camped that night, few words were spoken among the captive men, who had run long and hard for days and were now disheartened at this turn of events, disappointed by their delay as much as the reason for it. The night passed uneasily for Aljeron, who did not sleep well and who rose in the morning feeling both poorly rested and ill-prepared for the new day.

As he looked around himself in the light of morning, Aljeron was struck by the uniformity of their captors' appearance. Though he supposed he shouldn't have been surprised, he was. All wore rough clothes of brown or grey. All carried a spear or bow. All had pale white skin that matched the snowy landscape. All had deep, dark red hair. All walked beside a snow leopard. All wore masks.

Not all were men. Aljeron realized as they moved on, that women, though a minority, were also armed and freely intermingled with the men. The women he could see walked as surely and carried their weapons as confidently as the men. Aljeron found himself thinking of Bryar astride her horse, battle-tested and as determined as any man. He had no doubt that if she were here, she would share a kindred spirit with these who were in fact as much their captors as the men.

They moved out in silence, and Aljeron noted that they were headed generally in the right direction. Whatever might come of this, if they found themselves free and disentangled from this wild group, at least they would be a little closer to the Zaros Mountains and Enthanin.

Of their hosts they knew nothing, for Aljeron, like the others, deferred to Valzaan as their representative, and so far the prophet had asked nothing. Perhaps he sensed something that suggested it would be better to wait; Aljeron didn't know. Of the man who represented their hosts, however, they had learned a little. His name was Naran, and he walked beside Valzaan on the way.

For a league or more, Naran was content to walk in silence, as was the prophet. The others were not so silent, and the sound of conversation could be heard all around them. The morning air was crisp and cool, but it was noticeably warmer than the day before. The snow was more slushy than it had been. This sign of the coming spring heartened Aljeron, though their present circumstances prevented him from too much celebration.

Naran eventually broke the silence, asking without looking at them, "If you are indeed servants of the Master-Maker and not the Forge-Foe, though you carry that which is forbidden, why do you travel in the Curse-Country? Men of the southern lands no longer come here and have not for long years."

Valzaan did not answer immediately, and Aljeron wondered if the prophet was weighing whether to tell Naran the truth. "We came here across many leagues, through the great storm, all the way from the shores of the Bay of Thalasee at the southern edge of the Great Northern Sea in the west to the northernmost reaches of the Tajira Mountains."

"What did you seek there?"

"We sought Harak Andunin."

Naran stopped, his face twisted as though in anguish and pain. Valzaan stopped with him and so did the others. The men and women behind them slowed but went around, though Aljeron noticed a reasonable contingent stop just beyond them and wait.

"You went to Harak Andunin?" he labored over the last word, but said it clearly enough in the end. "Why there?"

"Malek, or the Forge-Foe as you call him, has come forward from the Mountain where long he lay in hiding. He has come forth to conquer Kirthanin and claim this world for his own."

"The third war?" Naran asked as he started walking again, as did the rest of them.

"Yes," Valzaan said. "You speak as though you expected it."

"From the earliest days, it has been foretold."

"I see," Valzaan said, considering. "Have some from among you prophesied of what is to come, or have men from the south come with word of this?"

"Men of the south never come here. A few, a very few, have traveled in the Curse-Country since it was abandoned long ago, but we never speak or reveal ourselves to them."

"But you revealed yourselves to us," Aljeron said.

"We did, but you were nearer the border of our wood than any man has been in a thousand years, and you were not an isolated man who would be no threat to anyone. You had to be confronted. We had no choice. But come, we have wandered from the point. How is the coming of the Forge-Foe a reason to seek Harak Andunin? It is a symbol of our shame and bears the name of the Blade-Binder, who tied our ancestors to the Forge-Foe and led us to death and exile."

"Ancestors?" Valzaan asked, a hint of wonder in his voice, which was strange for Aljeron to hear. "You are saying that you are Nolthanim?"

"We do not acknowledge that name. We are the Kalin Seir."

"The language of the Mountain," Valzaan answered. "Sons of truth."

"Yes, or 'true sons' as we would call ourselves. So why Harak Andunin?"

"We traveled to Harak Andunin as representatives of the men and Great Bear of Kirthanin, seeking aid in our time of need."

"Aid? What aid can come from there?"

"Harak Andunin is the ancient home of Sulmandir, the Father of Dragons. It was our hope to find him and in doing so solicit his aid and the aid of all of his children."

"Sulmandir?" Naran said, wonder overflowing in his voice. "You mean *the* Sun-Soarer, father of all Sun-Soarers?"

"Yes," Valzaan agreed, "Sulmandir is the Father of Dragons."

If Naran had shown signs of life or excitement during any part of their discussion before this, it paled in comparison to his reaction now. He jogged through the moving column and disappeared momentarily from their sight.

"He's not the best of guards," Saegan said wryly.

"Getting away would still be difficult," Evrim said, looking from side to side as though scouting out the possibility.

"Very, and we're not going to try," Valzaan added. "We have not stumbled upon these Kalin Seir, or perhaps I should say they have not stumbled upon us, by accident. We have been brought here for a reason, and we're not going anywhere until we figure out what it is."

"Do you think they're really Nolthanim, or descendants of them at least, or whatever?" Aljeron said, not sure how to ask his question.

ARISE

"I have no reason to doubt their testimony," Valzaan answered, "and no better explanation for their sudden appearance."

"Amazing," Aljeron replied. "What in the world have they been doing for two thousand years?"

"Perhaps we'll find out," Valzaan said, and at that moment, they noticed Naran returning with several of the others.

Naran spoke excitedly as they approached. "I have summarized for the others what you have said, and perhaps at a later point we can go back over it for them so they can ask questions if they have any. For now, though, confirm what you spoke of last. You came north into the Curse-Country in the hopes of finding the Sun-Soarer."

"We did. Our mission was to ascend to his gyre in Harak Andunin and, if we found him, induce him to come forward."

There was excited chatter among the men, and Naran, who had of course expected that reply, asked, "And? Did you find him?"

"We did," Valzaan answered. "And he has gone forth to summon his sons."

More excited babble. As it died down, Naran continued. "You say that you are a prophet of the Master-Maker, do you not?"

"I do, and I am."

"Do you know us?"

"I admit it. I do not."

"The Kalin Seir do not go south of the Zaros Mountains, and as I explained to you, we have successfully hidden ourselves from all eyes for two thousand years. I only asked because I know that the Master-Maker can show what can't be seen."

"He can, but He has not shown me anything concerning the Kalin Seir."

"Then I will tell you, and perhaps when you have heard our story you will understand what your coming and your words mean to us. This is the story of the Kalin Seir as my father told me, and as his father told him, as it has been passed on from generation to generation in my family.

"Andunin's proposal that we follow the Forge-Foe in his war against the Twelve caused much anguish. Many were conflicted, as indeed Andunin himself was, over what course of action should be taken. In the end, though, the decision to take up arms and go to war with Andunin as our captain was agreed upon. A vow was taken by the leaders of all the clans of Nolthanin upon the tip of his spear, Ruun Harak, and that is how he came to be known among us as the Blade-Binder. Few liked it, but most agreed to do it. Some, however, were absolutely unwilling to join that war, no matter what the cost of refusal might be. They went along with the rest until the summons came to meet on the plateau and assemble for war, at which point they fled from their homes and crossed the Tajira Mountains to come here. They were few in number, no more than a hundred and fifty, and they knew that Andunin and the Forge-Foe would come for them eventually if their war in the south went successfully. They never came back, and those that had fled were left to create for themselves a new life.

"There was much debate about what to do. Some said that they should return to their homes. These argued that we had done nothing wrong, for we had refused to follow the Blade-Binder and Forge-Foe. Others argued that we could not go back, that we could never go back. They believed the land was defiled. It had been defiled by the forging of weapons and blades. It had been defiled by the oath. It had been defiled by our collective capitulation to the will of the Traitor-Titan.

"The Master-Maker sent a vision to one of their leaders that the land was indeed cursed and would remain so until the Fountain should flow again and the springs in the great deep bring cleansing to the land. There were at that point but two options: stay in hiding here in the wild, east of the Tajira

Mountains and north of Enthanin, or head south across the mountains and settle among the rest of the Kirthanim.

"At first, almost all of the faithful remnant of the Nolthanim were in favor of heading south, but as preparations for the migration began, opinion among the people began to change. We came to realize that though we had not followed the Forge-Foe into battle, we bore a great shame. All the clans of the Nolthanim had sworn upon the blade tip. We were all oath-sworn, even if we had not kept it. Our brothers and sisters, moreover, had indeed fought for the Traitor-Titan, and they had killed many, soaking the ground with their blood. Their shame was our shame, and their guilt was our guilt.

"And yet, mixed with that shame was a pride, pride that though we were oath-sworn and though our brothers and sisters had betrayed the Master-Maker, we ourselves were as faithful as we knew how to be. We adopted our name, Kalin Seir, to distance ourselves from the Blade-Binder and the Nolthanim who had followed him, but we did not want to cut ourselves off entirely from our ancestry, which would be a disgrace to our fathers and their fathers before them who did not deserve to be disowned.

"We grew afraid of two things. We feared that perhaps the men of the south would hold against us the sins of our brothers, and that we would be branded and labeled among them. We also feared that to escape our own shame, we would become completely assimilated and the true heritage of the north would be lost.

"So, the decision was made to stay. The Kalin Seir would neither return to their homes nor flee south. The early years were difficult. The winters in this part of Kirthanin are brutal, and without established houses and towns, we struggled to keep our name alive. Our numbers dwindled, and some believed that we would not make it.

"But, the Master-Maker is merciful, and eventually we learned how to survive. We constructed our homes deep in the forest, so that we would be invisible to any eyes but our own. Our losses diminished, and eventually we began to grow in number until the peril of extinction passed.

"It was also in those early days that Allfather again raised up a prophet, who foretold the day when the Kalin Seir would have a chance to redeem themselves for the failure of their brothers. That same prophet foretold that the Forge-Foe would twice more come from the Mountain, and that the third time the Kalin Seir would have an opportunity to oppose him.

"This same prophet spoke of a sign whereby we would recognize the right day and opportunity. He said that the Sun-Soarers would return to Nolthanin, and specifically that the Sun-Soarer would come to the Kalin Seir. So, you can see why your claim to have journeyed to Harak Andunin to find the Sun-Soarer provoked such excitement. Every child of the Kalin Seir has been taught to look for that day when he would return, and now you say that you have found him."

"Yes," Valzaan replied, "we did find him."

"And he has come forth into the world again."

"He has." Valzaan said as they continued to walk beside Naran and the others. Aljeron looked at the snow leopards walking among them. He didn't know how numerous these Kalin Seir were, nor how effective they would be in battle against Malekim and giants without swords, but help was help.

Valzaan must have been thinking along similar lines. "We are headed to Enthanin, to rejoin the war already in progress against Malek and the hosts he has led forth from the Mountain. This would be a most opportune time for the Kalin Seir to display their honor and show Kirthanin that true sons of Allfather still live in the north."

Naran did not need to consult the others with him to answer. "That may be, but you are not the sign, nor will your word on the matter of the Sun-Soarer's return suffice. We will need the sign itself. If what you say is true, the day may be close when the Kalin Seir march to war, but not until the Sun-Soarer comes."

"If that is the sign Allfather promised," Valzaan said, "then that is the sign you must wait for. I would not induce you to leave before your time."

"Naran," Aljeron asked, daring to insert himself into the conversation.

"Yes?" The masked man turned to look at him.

"Have the Kalin Seir always been battle brothers with snow leopards?"

"Yes, as far back as any of our stories go. The first Kalin Seir were bonded, and as that first remnant of men learned to survive and prosper here, so did the remnant of the snow leopards that came with them. We see the continuance of the bond among us as a sign that the Master-Maker remains pleased with our desire and our attempts to be faithful to Him. Are there many with the bond in the south?"

"No," Aljeron answered. "I've never known anyone else with it."

"No one?" Naran asked, amazed.

"Not one."

The men beside Naran murmured at this, but Naran was careful with his response. "The ways of the Master-Maker are His own, and He deals with the lives and fates of men as He pleases. I would have said that being Blade-Bearers had cost them the ability to have the bond, but you are a Blade-Bearer and you have a battle brother. I have no explanation."

"And the masks," Valzaan said, "do they also go back as far as you remember?"

"Yes," Naran replied. "The Kalin Seir have worn masks since the second or third generation. They are symbolic of our shame, a visible reminder of who we are."

"Will you remove them when you have fought Malek in the third war?"

"If we are successful. If the Forge-Foe is defeated and the curse lifted, we will remove them. We will take them off gladly, and when the Fountain opens again, we will also go home to our ancestral lands and rebuild what has long since been destroyed."

"You say if," Valzaan replied. "Did none of your prophets indicate if your war against Malek would be successful?"

"No. No prophet of ours has ever spoken of the outcome of the third war, only that it would come, as would the Sun-Soarer, and that then we would have our opportunity to fight. The focus of the prophecy has always been on our chance to choose honor in battle. Victory or defeat is a secondary matter."

"And your weapons?" Valzaan asked.

"Yes?"

"You don't make weapons with metal because of the blades that Malek made for Andunin?"

"And because Andunin seduced our brothers with them, and because we swore the oath to serve the Traitor-Titan upon the blade tip of Ruun Harak."

"Are you not afraid to go to war against your enemy when he has weapons of metal and you have only weapons of wood?" Saegan asked.

"Watch," Naran said, pausing to take a wooden spear in hand. He gripped it, surveyed the wooded area beside them, and hurled it on a straight line some twenty spans into the trunk of a small tree.

Naran led them to the tree and pulled out the spear. Aljeron took it in his hand and felt the small hole it had made in the tree and then the point of the spear. It was not as heavy as metal, but it was sharp and solid. The end was blackened a bit, as though heat or fire had somehow been used to harden it, though how fire could harden wood without burning it, Aljeron could not guess.

"I could have a demonstration arranged for you with one of our bowmen, but I trust that you will take my word for it when I tell you that every Kalin Seir trains with both bow and arrow from the age when they are old enough to hold them. Every man and woman and most of the children could kill you from thirty or forty spans away, even without that which is forbidden."

"I will take your word for it," Saegan said, nodding to Naran.

"Come," Naran said, leading them back to the rear of the small column, for it had passed them by. "We will enter the wood soon, and there you will need to pay attention and keep up. An hour or so more, and then you will be where no man except the Kalin Seir has ever been."

The way through the wood was difficult. For Aljeron, who had followed Great Bear along their secret ways, it was a striking contrast. The way through Lindan had been hard to follow for one not privy to the secret of the path, but the path itself had been wide and spacious. The Kalin Seir's way wound through narrow confines, often slipping under and around densely overgrown thorns and other tough and unpleasant plans. All kinds of gnarled vines dangled around them, and it seemed clear to Aljeron that the ground of this place must be cursed indeed to have produced such nasty plant-life. Despite the coolness of the air, the confines made Aljeron sweat, and he wiped his brow with his sleeve to keep the perspiration from rolling into his eyes.

"Glad I'm not the only one," Evrim said, and Aljeron turned to see the sweat trickling down his friend's face.

"Unhappy terrain, isn't it?" Aljeron replied.

"Very."

Aljeron looked back at Erigan, squeezing along the path. Though much too large to move along without rubbing against the vines and thorns, he didn't seem especially miserable to

Aljeron, who wondered if his forest upbringing made Erigan impervious to the irritation he and the other men felt when they brushed up against the hanging obstacles. He rubbed the sweat away again. He was growing weary and would maybe ask Erigan later. For now it was enough just to keep going, one foot after the other, deeper and deeper into this wild place.

Eventually the long, narrow, and winding way ended in an open place filled with several long, low houses, and trees some three and four spans tall that formed a dense canopy. Some distance away was a reasonable-sized clearing where there were no houses, only grass and bushes below the dense grey sky.

Moving in and out of the scattered village were men and women dressed just like the Kalin Seir who had brought them there. All wore masks and rough clothing of brown or grey. All had pale skin and dark-red hair, and the population of snow leopards seemed every bit as large as the population of men and women. Many stopped what they were doing when Naran led Aljeron and the others through their midst. Hundreds of pairs of eyes gazed at them through those masks, watching them as they eventually entered one of the long, low houses.

Inside was a rough wooden table on a flat dirt floor, a couple of chairs, and not much else. Naran stood in the doorway. "For my part, I believe your story, so I apologize for this. But as I have said, for the time being you are our prisoners, and you must be kept under guard. I will meet with the elders and see what will be done with you now. They will likely want to speak to you themselves, so make yourselves as comfortable as you can. I don't know what exactly comes next."

"We understand," Valzaan said. "Do not trouble yourself over us. You are only doing what you must."

Naran nodded and turned away, closing the door. There were a few small square windows high in the walls, and as soon as Naran left, Valzaan rose and walked to one of these. Opening the shutter, he stepped back, and immediately a King Falcon fluttered inside.

While Aljeron and the others stared in amazement, the majestic bird perched on Valzaan's wrist, and the prophet whispered in his ear. Then, just as suddenly as it had arrived, it leapt off of Valzaan's arm and exited through the window. Valzaan reached up, grabbed the shutter, and closed the window.

"Joraiem said he saw you talking to a windhover on the Forbidden Isle," Aljeron said, "and I wasn't sure he really had when he told me, not until Eliandir came, at least."

"I hope you've sent for similar aid this time," Saegan added.

"Even better. I've sent for Sulmandir himself."

"The Sun-Soarer?" Aljeron said, half laughing at what appeared to be the slightest of smirks on Valzaan's face. "Have you had a word from Allfather that it is time to fulfill the prophecy of the Kalin Seir?"

"Not as such," Valzaan answered. "I had planned from the moment we were taken captive to send for help when I could. Having heard the prophecy, though, I believe the sooner that help comes, the better. Surely it couldn't hurt to give our hosts a little nudge in the right direction?"

"Seriously, Valzaan," Evrim said. "Are you sure that's all right? I mean, isn't it kind of interfering with things?"

"Interfering?" Valzaan said. "How do you think prophecies come to pass? Allfather ordains things, but the actions of human agents and Great Bear and dragons are usually what bring them to fruition. It is a great mystery, to be sure. Even as Allfather guides the events of history, He uses the likes of people like you and me to bring about His plan. I may have just set in motion the agency by which Sulmandir will be brought to this distant location, and his coming may be seen by the

Kalin Seir as the fulfillment of Allfather's prophecy, but that doesn't mean this wasn't exactly what Allfather intended from the beginning."

"Let's hope he comes quickly, then," Aljeron said.

"Let's hope so indeed."

The elders came later that evening as Naran had predicted, and the interview did not take long. They spoke to Valzaan mostly, perhaps because he had proclaimed himself a prophet of Allfather, perhaps because he was not a Blade-Bearer like the rest. When they had finished with their questions, they took their leave, saying nothing about the group's future as prisoners.

Despite the potential danger of their situation, held captive and surrounded by a host of unknown allegiance, Aljeron had little interest in staying awake and keeping watch. Despite the aid they had received from Allfather in running beyond all ordinary mortal limitations, his body was exhausted. The dirt floor was far from luxurious, but it was flat and dry and free of snow. No sooner had he and Koshti lain down, when he heard the breathing of his battle brother become relaxed. He listened to the easy rhythm and soon fell asleep.

The next morning he rose with the others when the door to the long narrow house was opened. A small procession of men and women walked in, crossed the room to the lone wooden table, and set down an array of trays bearing pitchers and cups, bowls and plates. The deposit having been made, the small troupe exited the room with as much purpose and as few words as they had entered.

Having eaten very little the previous day, Aljeron was hungry and soon rose from where he lay. So did the others, and when they crowded around the table, they found a whole assortment of foods, some recognizable and others not so much. The bread was easily identifiable as bread by sight and by touch, but the taste was peculiar and to Aljeron, not very appetizing. There were some other items, including vegetables, meat, and cheese, and of these, only the meat was agreeable to him, and what he really liked about it was the spice that had been used to flavor it.

"Interesting fare," he murmured after he'd sampled little bits of it all.

"An acquired taste, no doubt," Saegan replied.

"I'd rather not stay long enough to acquire it," Aljeron grunted, looking down at Koshti, who didn't seem put off at all and was happily devouring a large chunk of the unknown meat.

"Me neither," Evrim agreed, setting a half-eaten hunk of bread down on his plate and lowering it to the ground.

"We should be grateful they are feeding us at all," Valzaan said. "I take it as an indication that they don't mean to execute us today."

"Unless it is intended as a final meal," Saegan offered.

"Doubtful. Though we are held as prisoners, we are being treated as guests. It is, I believe, a good sign."

There was some discussion of this theory but no chance to verify it, for they were left alone most of the morning. When the hour for lunch came, a smaller group of Kalin Seir returned, replenishing the water from the pitchers and checking to see that sufficient food remained from the morning for the midday meal. There was plenty, so most of them left without further interaction, save two of the female Kalin Seir who stopped at the doorway.

One of them, tall and lean with long, thick braids, stooped down and peered at Koshti through her mask with dark blue eyes.

"You are bonded with this tiger?" she asked Aljeron. Her voice was deep for a woman's, but not unnaturally so.

"I am," Aljeron replied.

The woman reached out her hand toward Koshti, who looked up at it suspiciously. She held her hand still, until after a moment, Koshti seemed to acquiesce to her desire and lowered his head submissively. She set her hand upon his great head and stroked his thick fur. "He is beautiful."

"He is."

The woman, still stroking Koshti, looked up from him and reached out her other hand to Aljeron's face, where she touched gently the scars on his cheek. "And these, how did they happen?"

"I got them long ago."

"I did not ask when, but how."

Aljeron looked at the penetrating eyes. Despite the nondescript clothing and the rough mask, there was something undeniably beautiful about this wild creature from the northern wilderness. "A Malekim gave them to me."

"Malekim," she repeated awkwardly. "I have heard this word. You describe one of the Voiceless. Prophets have spoken of them, but I have never seen one. Few Kalin Seir have, save only the travelers who sometimes sojourn beyond the mountains in the parts of the north we have abandoned. Tell me, if one of the Silent Ones gave you this, why didn't he kill you?"

"Because Koshti killed him."

"Koshti?"

Aljeron pointed at the tiger. The woman nodded with understanding. She stood, eyes still fixed upon Aljeron. "What is your name?"

"Aljeron."

"Aljeron," she repeated after him, as she had repeated *Malekim* moments before. Then, turning away, she rejoined her friend. They left without anything further, shutting the door behind them.

"Looks like you have a fan," Saegan said.

Aljeron could feel himself blushing. "I'm sure she's just curious about my bond with Koshti."

"Sure," Evrim said. "That and your fascinating face."

"She just asked what everybody else wants to ask but are too polite to when they first see my scars."

"I don't know, Aljeron," Evrim continued. "There's interest from a woman, and then there's *interest*. I think this was the latter."

"I'm sure it wasn't," Aljeron answered quickly. "And besides, even if it was, we'll be out of here soon, hopefully, and I'll be on my way back to Aelwyn."

"If we're lucky, and Sulmandir comes, perhaps the Kalin Seir will be with us," Saegan said, smirking just enough for it to be noticeable, which was quite a bit for him. "Then maybe you'll have a chance to introduce Aelwyn to your new friend. That would be interesting."

Aljeron said nothing and lay back down on the ground, closing his eyes to make sure they understood he was finished with the conversation. He turned his thoughts to Aelwyn, but her image did not appear right away. The blue eyes of the Kalin Seir woman, however, remained vividly before him.

3

HANGING IN
THE BALANCE

BENJIAH RESTED WITH HIS BACK against the slats of
his cage. It was late morning, and the men and Malekim that
had been camped near the western gate of Amaan Sul were
gradually filtering into the column that had been moving into
the city since before sundown the previous night.

As he watched the men climb back up into their saddles,
he could almost feel the ache and weariness of yet another day
on the road. Almost, but not quite. If being locked in a
wooden cage had any advantages, it was that he hadn't walked
a single foot or ridden on horseback at all since the day he'd
been captured. To be sure, there were multiple times when
he'd have gladly stepped out of the cage to stretch his legs, but
as they moved league by league closer to Amaan Sul, he'd
learned to lie back and let the Malekim pulling his cage do all

the work. It was a small upside to his current predicament, but dwelling on such small things kept him from losing hope.

He slid his hand along a wooden slat, feeling the semi-smooth surface with his fingers. He closed his eyes and tried to imagine he was feeling Valzaan's staff. He missed carrying it, and he wondered if its loss did indeed coincide with the apparent loss of his prophetic powers. He still had his dreams, which were more troubling than comforting these days, but other than that, nothing seemed to suggest the hand of Allfather was still upon him.

A sharp pain shot through his finger, and he flinched. He looked at his fingertip and saw the dark outline of the thick, nasty splinter that had slid deep under his skin. His finger throbbed. Why had he been so foolish? The slat was rough and unfinished, not like Valzaan's staff at all. He'd gotten what he deserved.

He looked closely but couldn't see the splinter protruding at all from out of his skin. He put his finger instinctively into his mouth and sucked, and whether it really helped or not, the sting seemed to dissipate. He gnawed gently around the sore spot, hoping to find a way to secure one end or the other with his teeth, but he couldn't. Without a blade or knife to cut away some of the skin and get at the splinter, it was stuck for the time being.

As he sat there, trying not to think about his throbbing finger but only succeeding in thinking about it all the more, Malekim came walking straight toward his cage. Soon the wagon it sat upon was in motion, moving toward the column that was heading through the gate.

They joined the column, and Benjiah watched as the western gate drew nearer and then disappeared overhead. He was home. Having been within eyesight of Amaan Sul for a few days now, he was surprised by how this thought moved him. And yet, crossing into the city had wrought a change in him.

Memories of the day of his departure the previous autumn flooded him. He could see his uncles and Valzaan upon their horses around him and his mother standing in the courtyard to see them off. He had been both eager and afraid. How much like a boy he had been.

In reality he was less than a year older, but in some ways, he had aged far more than any calendar could calculate. He had passed so far and through so much, and yet as the wheels of the wagon echoed upon the flagstones of the streets, he felt it had all been for naught. He did not come home victorious, but a prisoner in a cage. Not only was he in a cage, but his mother was somewhere among the hosts of Malek, no doubt in chains. He had failed, as had their mission, and he returned to a deserted city that welcomed him with silence.

He looked around him at the empty buildings, their windows and doors mostly shut, though here and there the wind played with shutters and signs swinging on rusty hinges. The creaking of these things only occasionally could be heard above the sound of the army passing through, and he wondered if these dark buildings harbored any life at all beyond the ubiquitous mice and rats that seemed immune from all the trials and hardships of men.

"You have outlasted us all and now are master of what we've left behind," he said out loud, wondering if the vermin were brave enough to come out by daylight now that the human inhabitants were gone. If they were, he couldn't see them, nor was he surprised, for the sound of the army must have been overwhelming to any of the four-footed inhabitants who remained.

After a while they approached the central crossroads of the city, where the great north-south avenue intersected the major east-west road upon which they now traveled. These two roads divided the circular city almost perfectly, creating the four quadrants of Amaan Sul. To Benjiah's surprise, though, the

Malekim turned off of the east-west road and began to pull the wagon bearing his cage northward, away from the mass of men and Malekim headed east. There were a few other living souls on this road, but very few. He looked in the distance and could make out, though faintly, the outline of the palace. It looked as though he was really going home after all.

The splinter in his finger throbbed again, and he sucked upon it, trying to enlarge the smallish hole through which the jagged wood had passed. He threw himself into the effort, trying not to think about why he was being taken to the palace. It was a dismal way to try to kill some time, but he didn't have many alternatives.

Eventually, the Malekim passed through the palace gates into the large front courtyard. The fountain wasn't running, but the pool was full to overflowing, the result no doubt of the extraordinary storm that had inundated every last square span of Kirthanin.

The wagon, once pulled into the courtyard, was turned sideways and set along the front wall, and from where he was sitting he could see the palace only fifty spans or so away very well. If passing through the western gate had moved him, then being confronted with the place of his birth did even more so. His stomach fluttered and his body trembled. He had returned home, but not in the manner he had envisioned.

Rulalin waited for Soran at the entrance to the stable. His horse had thrown a shoe, and now that they were in a city where the right tools were available, he had availed himself of the opportunity to replace it. Rulalin watched as Soran worked deftly, betraying the skill of a man brought up to work as a tradesman. Though Rulalin, like most of the Novaana, was acquainted with the essentials of most basic domestic skills, there was no substitute for repetition to develop the kind of adroitness that Soran displayed.

Eventually Soran finished and joined Rulalin, and the two started across the courtyard toward the palace. Stepping into the hall, Soran hesitated.

"This way," Rulalin said, walking past him in the direction of the Great Hall.

"I almost forgot," Soran said as he followed.

"What?"

"You've been here before."

"Yes," Rulalin said, keeping on. "Many years ago."

They came to the doorway that led into the Great Hall, and a pair of Nolthanim soldiers were there, perhaps as guards, though Rulalin had gotten used to the idea of Farimaal's quarters being more or less unattended. Whatever they were stationed there to do, they stood aside and let Rulalin and Soran pass.

The Great Hall was much as Rulalin remembered it, though it had been rearranged by its current occupant. The formal furniture had been pushed to the side, and Farimaal's little chair, which had traveled all the way from the Mountain to the west coast of Werthanin, to the southernmost tip of Suthanin, and now all the way to Amaan Sul, sat by itself near the center of the long northern wall. In the chair sat Farimaal, slouched as usual, his legs draped over the one side and his head leaned back, seeming to stare at the ceiling.

As Rulalin took Farimaal in, a strange question popped into his mind, as though from nowhere. *What must go on inside Farimaal's head?*

Rulalin was of course familiar with the basic story of Farimaal's rise to fame in Malek's service. What servant of Malek's wasn't? This was the man who had done the impossible, single-handedly killing a Grendolai. For that feat, it was said he had received immortality, for he must be over a thousand years old. Hence the question. So much of any soldier's life was spent waiting, and how much more so Farimaal's, all those years spent in the semidarkness below the Mountain? Rulalin studied the upturned face of the dread captain and wondered what all those years would do to the mind, even if they had seemed to take no effect on the body.

A handful of soldiers sat at uneven intervals around the room, and several of the other captains were gathered in a small cluster not far from Farimaal. In fact, they all appeared to be there. Rulalin took a deep breath as he stepped into the room. He didn't know exactly how he was going to do it, but the time had come to tell Farimaal about Wylla. He hoped his failure to tell Farimaal sooner would be excused. Rulalin hadn't really been summoned before now, and he'd been preoccupied with the journey to Amaan Sul and the work of scouting the city to make sure it was indeed deserted. But if Farimaal was displeased that Rulalin had kept this information from him, well, Rulalin didn't like to think about it.

Rulalin moved toward the other captains but stopped just far enough away way that he remained outside the cluster. The physical distance he maintained acknowledged that he was a captain in their army, and from the beginning they had afforded him the respect of that position. At the same time, he was not Nolthanim, and all understood that his inclusion in their number was functional but not real.

Rulalin waited. Neither Farimaal nor anyone else in the room had shown much interest in his arrival, so whatever he had been summoned for was apparently going to have to wait. He surveyed the room, trying to imagine it as it had been the last time he was there. It was not that hard to do, but as soon as he captured the image, he wished he hadn't. Thinking of the room as it had been only brought back memories, and the memories did not set him at ease.

A figure moved into the room from another hallway. Rulalin turned slightly to see who it was, though he sensed it was

Tashmiren. Only Tashmiren walked with that swagger. Involuntarily, Rulalin's hand moved to his sword hilt.

Tashmiren moved straight through the room until he stood before Farimaal. The whispers from the captains of the Nolthanim stopped, and all in the room turned their attention to Farimaal, who turned in his chair to face Tashmiren.

"Yes," Farimaal said as he swiveled to face forward.

"The wolves and Nolthanim have passed through the city, as have most of the Malekim."

"Good. Any word from Cheimontyr?"

"Yes. Vulsutyrim have found evidence of two large groups of people leaving the city. One moving along the eastern road, as you suspected, and one branching off of that road not far from the city, heading due north."

Farimaal drew his hands together before his face. "They think those that passed north were mostly civilians, women and children and the like?"

Tashmiren hesitated briefly, seeming surprised that his information had been anticipated. "Yes, Captain, so it appears. Cheimontyr believes that the main contingent of men and Great Bear we pursued to the river, and what forces may have been added here at the city, have headed east."

Farimaal nodded. Again, Rulalin wondered what he was thinking. From the moment the city was discovered to be abandoned, the idea that the enemy had marched on to Tol Emuna circulated among the captains of the Nolthanim. Most agreed that if they were charged with setting up a defense against a force such as their own, Tol Emuna was as logical a place as any, even if Cheimontyr would make that defense moot.

Maybe the silent Farimaal, again gazing somewhat vacantly into space, was looking ahead to the inevitable battle. Inevitable, because the armies of Kirthanin would have to stand there or else surrender.

"Take word to Cheimontyr that we will march for Tol Emuna in the morning," Farimaal said, redirecting his attention to Tashmiren.

"Yes, sir," Tashmiren replied, bowing as he turned to go. He passed back out of the room without so much as a glance in Rulalin's direction.

"Captain Tarasir," Farimaal said, turning in his direction.

Rulalin felt his skin prickle at the sound of his name spoken by Farimaal. "Yes, Captain?"

"Along with the news that Amaan Sul was deserted, you sent word that certain messengers had been taken captive."

"Yes, sir," Rulalin said, noticing that his fingers were trembling as they hung at his side. Fortunately, his voice didn't appear to be affected by his nervousness.

"Well, have you discovered anything of use?"

Rulalin walked toward Farimaal's chair. "Well, sir, I actually . . . well, I had hoped to have a chance to discuss this matter with you more or less in private."

Farimaal studied Rulalin for a moment, then said without taking his eyes off of him, "You will give me a few minutes with Captain Tarasir."

The soldiers and other Nolthanim soundlessly departed. Soran, though, drifted closer to Rulalin.

"You think my directive was not meant for you?" Farimaal said, turning his gaze for the first time upon Soran.

Rulalin sensed the dangerous shift in Farimaal's voice. He had been in Farimaal's presence far more often than Soran, and it occurred to him that Soran might not realize that to misspeak at this moment could be fatal.

"Captain," Rulalin blurted out before Soran could open his mouth and put his foot in it, "I suspect his mistake is my fault. I told him that we would report to you the news about our captives."

Farimaal did not turn from Soran, but though no malice was evident, his stare was unnerving. "I summoned you, not your underling, Captain Tarasir. You requested a private audience. If either of you presume to disregard my direction again, it will prove costly."

"My apologies," Rulalin said, looking to Soran, who stood rooted to the spot, face blanched white as a sheet. He could see that Soran understood now what had been at stake. "Do you wish him to leave now?"

"My patience will not last forever."

Soran gave a slight nod and made for the nearest door. Rulalin took a deep breath. He was alone now with Farimaal, who was obviously not happy. This was not how he had hoped this conversation would begin.

Farimaal, having watched Soran exit, turned to Rulalin, his eyes cold and dispassionate despite what had just transpired. But then again, Farimaal was always cold and dispassionate. "Well?"

"Yes, well, Captain, the captives you mentioned are no ordinary captives."

"No?"

"No, at least, one of them is not. We have captured a man and a woman. The man appears to be an advisor to Queen Someris. The woman appears to be the queen herself."

"I know," Farimaal replied evenly, keeping his gaze upon Rulalin.

Rulalin nearly fell over. His knees grew weak, and he felt flush. Of all the possible responses he had expected from Farimaal, this one he had not anticipated.

"You do?" he said weakly, almost involuntarily. He knew his life was forfeit, and already he was resigned to it. The queen of Enthanin had been in his custody for a week. He had not sent word of it to Farimaal, and Farimaal knew it.

"Of course I know," Farimaal replied. "It wasn't a secret, was it?"

Rulalin sensed in the question a test, one he could not fail. "No, not from you, anyway. I thought it prudent to wait to discuss her identity until we could meet privately. This is what I had intended to do when I asked to speak to you just now. Besides, the deal we have concerning Queen Someris might not be widely known among the rest of this army, and for obvious reasons, I didn't want to risk her safety."

"The deal we have concerning Queen Someris was conditioned on her cooperation in delivering this city, and though the buildings are in my hands, the army is not. I wouldn't assume she is yours just yet."

"No, sir," Rulalin replied, for he had already guessed this or something like it would be Farimaal's position on Wylla. "All the same, though I have no power to save her if you wish her dead, I wanted to make sure she lived long enough to have a chance of being released into my care. If her identity was known, she could have attracted attention a mere messenger of the enemy would not."

"Even so, it is good that you have identified her voluntarily. Had you not I would have suspected you meant to keep it from me. Would that have been wise, Captain Tarasir?"

"No, sir."

"No, sir, indeed." Farimaal seemed to sit back a little bit in his chair and, even if only slightly, to relax. Rulalin exhaled. He felt as though the danger had passed. "Now, as I've indicated, the army of Amaan Sul and Enthanin remains at large, presumably preparing for hostilities against us. Why else flee to Tol Emuna? The queen, your old friend, has been in your custody for a week now. What help has she been to date?"

"As we approached the city, she did not conceal that it was deserted. Her report proved true, as you know."

"You consider this help?"

"We could have wasted time—"

"You waste my time. I want an answer. Will she help deliver her army into my hands or not?"

"I don't know." Rulalin said. The words escaped his mouth like a last breath slipping from the mouth of a dying man. He looked down at the floor. He knew his uncertain answer might be enough to sentence her to death right there, but he also knew he could not promise something he had no reason to believe Wylla would deliver.

"Well, let's ask her," Farimaal said, much to Rulalin's surprise. He looked up and saw Farimaal gazing past him at the far side of the room.

"Runner!" Farimaal called as Rulalin looked over his shoulder. A soldier appeared almost instantly in the main entrance. "Bring the woman captive to me."

The runner bolted, and Rulalin, who thought he had been nervous before, tried inconspicuously to wipe the sweat from his brow. Despite all his hopes and plans, this was likely the end.

The runner returned a few moments later with a pair of soldiers, who escorted Wylla in before Farimaal. Her clothes were worn and her hair bedraggled. She entered her own hall in chains, and still, to Rulalin, she was every bit as beautiful as she had been when he first saw her standing in this very room beside her grieving mother, her lustrous hair shining in the firelight. Yes, she seemed every bit as beautiful, but she also seemed proud and defiant. Farimaal would not be moved to mercy by her beauty, but her defiance could get her killed.

Farimaal watched her enter almost disinterestedly. In fact, when she came to a halt before him, he leaned back sideways in his chair and returned to his contemplation of the ceiling. Wylla looked from the almost gaunt, haggard man to Rulalin, who met her gaze levelly, though he dared not try to communicate anything. Farimaal might not be looking at them, but Rulalin was not foolish enough to assume he wasn't watching.

"You are Wylla Someris, queen of Enthanin?" Farimaal asked, not changing his posture.

A glint of accusation flashed through Wylla's eyes as she turned away from Rulalin to face her questioner. "I am."

"Your city is deserted."

"News of your army's coming preceded you, and my people fled. What did you expect?"

"I'm not interested in your people just now, but your army." At this, Farimaal turned forward and directed his piercing gaze at Wylla. "It has retreated to Tol Emuna, has it not?"

Wylla did not answer. She maintained her proud and regal posture before Farimaal's withering gaze. Rulalin was impressed, for to do so before Farimaal was no small feat. This was what he had been afraid of.

"Do you value your life?" Farimaal asked, almost casually.

"Of course."

"Do you wish to keep it?"

"Not at the price of helping you."

"What about at the price of your son's life?"

Wylla's steely demeanor cracked at Farimaal's words. She turned toward Rulalin and started at him with her chained hand upraised as though to strike him. Before she could, though, her guards restrained her.

"You cowardly wretch!" she shouted at Rulalin as they pulled her back.

"Wylla." Rulalin looked at her pleadingly, but she turned her head away in rage and defiance.

Farimaal had risen and was crossing the floor of the Great Hall to a stairwell on the near side. "Come and see," he said as he started up the stairs.

Rulalin followed the small party as the soldiers led Wylla up after Farimaal. Upstairs, some distance down the narrow hallway, Farimaal turned into a small room, what had no doubt been the quarters of a palace steward, Rulalin thought. He waited at the lone window for the soldiers to bring Wylla to him. Rulalin came up behind them and peered out to see what they were looking at.

He saw it immediately, of course. Benjiah's cage had been wheeled onto the palace grounds and rested along the wall beside the gate that led into the city proper. A detachment of soldiers was grouped around the cage, and Rulalin saw right away that these were not the men that he had charged with the watching of Benjiah. The boy had been removed from his care.

"A different sort of homecoming," Farimaal mused as he looked out the window. He stepped away to make sure Wylla's own view was clear, though Rulalin was sure the move was not necessary. Wylla was crying silently, and Rulalin could see her eyes straining to catch sight of Benjiah.

"The soldiers wait only for a signal from me, and your son's life will come to an abrupt end. He is your son, is he not?"

"He is," Wylla said quietly.

"I ask again, are your soldiers headed toward Tol Emuna?"

"They are."

Rulalin felt hope returning. *Good. He all but knows this anyway. Don't throw your life away in needless defiance over things that you can't keep from him.*

"And the soldiers and Great Bear that came to Amaan Sul from the river? They are on their way to Tol Emuna?"

"Yes."

Farimaal started away from the window and motioned to the soldiers to bring Wylla. She was reluctant, trying to linger, but they pulled her away. She stopped resisting and followed them back downstairs. Once back in his wooden chair, Farimaal resumed his nonchalant sideways position. Wylla stood again before him, no longer proud and defiant but dejected and broken. "You will help to gain for me the surrender of Tol Emuna when we arrive, or you will die, though not before I make you watch your son die in a more painful manner than you can conceive. Now leave, all of you."

Rulalin followed the detachment of soldiers though the city, at a distance, all the way to the place just outside the eastern gates. Wylla was reunited with Yorek and placed under guard. Having made sure of her location, he returned to find Soran. There were details that needed to be taken care of so that they were ready to leave in the morning, but they would need to be placed in Soran's hands.

It took longer than he had hoped to see to what was essential, but at last he was able to return to the place where he had left her, though it was well after dark. He moved noiselessly among the Nolthanim, most of them curled up on the ground getting a little sleep before dawn brought another long day on the road. He found Wylla's guards, huddled together a few spans from the prisoners. Though he had no idea if they'd let him pass, he nodded as though he expected them to respect his authority and grant him access. They did.

He found Yorek and Wylla asleep on the ground, and for a brief moment, he debated leaving her to sleep in peace. They would no doubt be required to walk all the way to Tol Emuna, and part of him wanted to let her gather strength. Another part, though, knew he could not let the events of the day pass without at least an attempt to set the record straight. In the end, he reached down and shook her gently until she stirred. He had to talk to her.

She opened her eyes and for a moment struggled to see who was crouched over her in the dark. There came, though, a moment of recognition that was unmistakable, when a cloud passed over her and she turned away from him.

"Wylla," he whispered. "We need to talk."

There was no answer.

"You did well today," he persevered. He had expected this conversation to be tough, and if she would not reply, he would at least say what he needed to, knowing that she would hear it even if she was unwilling to speak. "There is no sense trying to hide from him the things he will learn anyway. They had tracked the movement of the army out of Amaan Sul already, and they were basically sure that Tol Emuna was their destination. He was just testing you."

"I know that. I'm not a fool." Wylla lay with her face turned away. Rulalin said nothing to this, and after a moment she continued. "You betrayed me to him." The words were clear and her voice cold. "One would think you've had your fill of treachery in your miserable, pathetic life, but it seems your taste for it is ravenous."

"I did not betray you," Rulalin said, his voice rising enough that Yorek began to stir. He regained control of himself and the old man settled back into sleep. Rulalin continued once more in a controlled whisper. "I was summoned before Captain Farimaal moments before you arrived. I don't know what you know of him, but he is Malek's right hand and not to be trifled with. I had not told him about you, but I knew it had to be done, lest he find out and know I had been keeping it from him. Anyway, my point is, when I told him, he already knew."

"How?" Wylla said, her voice challenging Rulalin.

"I don't know. I was stunned. I thought I was the only one who knew."

"You and your little friend. Maybe he told."

"Soran? Never. He wouldn't. Look, Wylla, I don't know how Farimaal knew who you are, and I don't know how he knew who Benjiah is, but he didn't find out from me. I'm telling you,

I would have told him if he'd asked. I wouldn't have tried to keep it from him if I even thought he suspected, but he never said anything and I didn't offer."

"Why should I believe you?" Wylla asked. "You haven't even let me see Benjiah since I first arrived. You're playing a game with me. I don't know what it is just yet, but I know better than to trust you."

"The only game I'm playing," Rulalin whispered even quieter than before, "is the deadly game of trying to appease my master just enough, of trying to demonstrate my loyalty just enough, to secure the only thing left in this colossal wreck of a world that I care about, namely you. And as for Benjiah, I haven't let you see him again for a variety of reasons, and as of today, I don't even know if he's still under my care. Those soldiers that surrounded him in the palace courtyard are not under my authority. It could be that Farimaal has removed him from my oversight. I don't know."

"He is lost to me," Wylla said.

"Don't give up," Rulalin pleaded. "You may yet be reunited to him, if you will but cooperate."

"You know this? You have the authority to grant it?"

"Of course not."

"Then why do you offer what isn't yours to give?"

"Farimaal has promised your life to me," Rulalin said, urgency in his voice. "I swear it!"

"My life?" Wylla answered. "Why should I care about my life? I am a widow, thanks to you, and queen over nothing, again in part thanks to you. What about Benjiah's life? Has this Farimaal guaranteed that to you?"

Rulalin found her wide eyes in the shadows. "No."

They sat in silence, then Rulalin added. "I won't lie to you, Wylla. At this point, I don't think I have any say in what happens to Benjiah, and I can't promise that if you cooperate he will live."

Wylla turned toward the city and sat up straighter than she had as yet. In the distance, through the darkness, a flickering of light could be seen. "Amaan Sul is on fire," she said.

Rulalin followed her gaze toward the palace in the northernmost quadrant of the city. Something like flames rose up through the dark. It was not his city, but the thought of the palace on fire made him sad.

"The palace," Wylla said.

"Looks like it," Rulalin answered. "For now, at least, it looks as though it is only the vicinity of the palace."

"The palace is connected to the rest. It is only a matter of time."

"Yes, but the palace walls may serve to slow or stop the fire," Rulalin replied. "The city may yet survive."

"Oh, Rulalin," Wylla moaned, putting her head down in her hands to cry. "Why do you work so hard to console me? Who are you? How can you be this person that you have become? There, in that palace, you said you loved me. What's more, you want me to believe, even now, that you still love me and always have. And yet here you sit, watching my palace burn, and if they'd cut my son to pieces today, you would have watched that too."

"I cannot save your palace, and I am not able to save your son. I will not, though, sit by and watch anything happen to you. I will save your life if I can, but I don't think I can do it without your help."

"My help? You want my help?"

"Yes, of course."

Wylla looked at him in the darkness. "If it will cost me as much to receive your help as it has cost you to offer it, I will have none of it."

Through the night, Benjiah lay in his cage and watched the flame and smoke rise from the city. By morning, the flames seemed to have dwindled considerably, without having spread too far from their point of origin. He knew enough about the behavior of fire, however, not to assume its spread was over, for fire could appear to be dormant only to flare with renewed rage and rancor. Even so, he was hopeful that Amaan Sul might yet escape complete destruction.

The great army of Malek was again on the move, and the wagon on which his cage rested was rolling away from the city. He knew it was always possible he might return, but he wasn't taking anything for granted, save the two visions that had burned themselves into his brain: the image of the great white square with the explosion of water, and the image of himself chained between two poles before a vast assembly. The last of these did not leave much hope for him that he would live long beyond it, which is why he didn't assume he'd live to see Amaan Sul again.

He felt the darkness wash over him, more powerfully and oppressively than at any point before. He had come home in a cage only to see his city deserted and the palace set on fire. He had wielded enough of Allfather's power to raise a wall of earth and hold back this entire army, but now he could not shatter a few wooden slats and get himself out of this cage. Whatever Allfather had wanted from him, he was used up and discarded now. He was forsaken.

Forsaken. Even as the word echoed in his mind, something happened inside. He felt a wash of light and warmth come over him. He felt almost giddy with it, and closing his eyes he felt a rush of wind as he saw the city of Amaan Sul from high above. Small fires flickered here and there, and many buildings around the palace seemed burnt out and charred, but the worst of the fire seemed to have passed.

He sat up and opened his eyes. The city disappeared, and he was once again in the cage and rolling steadily away. He blinked and rubbed his eyes, excitement welling up inside of him.

Relax. Try again.

He closed his eyes once more, and almost before he could consciously try to find the windhover in his mind, he could see the city from above again. This time he could see the palace, and the shock of it was enough to take the edge off his joy, for it was almost burnt beyond all usefulness. It was almost lost, but not quite. He opened his eyes again, his heart racing. He was not forsaken, not yet.

All hope is not gone.

THE SUN-SOARER

WARMTH.

The feeling of warmth was marvelous. Aelwyn could not remember the last time she'd felt this way in the morning after sleeping outside. So much rain and so much cold all the time, but this, this was glorious. She'd felt the change coming. They all had. Last night the sun had gone down, so to speak, but the night chill did not come. Murmurs had rippled through the camp. Spring was coming. This morning the rumor felt like a fact: Spring was here.

It was illogical to think that the warmth was a good omen. No one had ever conjectured that all the rain was about making the world cold. The rain had clearly been about making the world wet, very wet. The world was still very wet. A month after the cessation of rain, farmlands still looked like marshlands, and the small streams still looked like swollen rivers. What's more, the strength of the enemy did not appear to depend in any way on cold. From all they knew, Black Wolves, Malekim, Vulsutyrim, and the men who served Malek (Aelwyn disliked calling them Nolthanim; none of them had ever lived in Nolthanin after all), each seemed to be just as formidable in good weather as in bad. No, it was illogical to find hope in warmth. Warmth could not save them.

Illogical, perhaps, but hope came with the warmth nonetheless. It rippled through the camp in the form of smiles and chatter and discarded cloaks. It showed in the way weary men and women stepped more vigorously into their saddles, saddles they'd dropped heavily out of the previous evening. It showed in the way the camp packed up quickly and efficiently, and in the way the column advanced just a half step faster toward Tol Emuna. It showed in the way music came unbidden from somewhere deep inside. Aelwyn found herself humming, something she hadn't done in ages.

When she was a little girl, her father had always sung to her at bedtime. In the darkness of her room, he would sit beside her and sing, serious songs or silly, depending on his mood. His big warm hand resting reassuringly upon hers, and the sound of his voice singing over her head—it was one of her favorite memories. It was no surprise, then, that humming and singing to herself had always been a mark of her mood, a sign of happiness, and on a day like today, a sign of hope.

> *Said the swallow to the sunflower*
> *And the jackrabbit to the juniper,*
> *Said the magpie to the melon patch*
> *And the chipmunk to the chestnut tree,*
>
> *Open your eyes, lift up your head*
> *The morning's come, get out of bed.*

Said the whippoorwill to the winding road
And the groundhog to the grassy plain,
Said the furry fox to the flowing stream
And the rogue raccoon to the rolling hill,

Sigh no more, be not sad,
The spring has come, awake, be glad.

"What's gotten into you today?"

"Good morning, Sister," Aelwyn said as Mindarin rode up alongside her.

"Spring fever got you too?"

"Doesn't it have you?"

Mindarin smiled, secretively, and whispered, "Yes, a little, but don't tell. It would ruin my reputation."

"Improve it, you mean."

"I guess that depends on your point of view."

"I was just going to ride up to find Kyril and her girls. I feel like sharing this warm morning with the vigor of youth."

Mindarin groaned. "Vigor of youth. The young one never shuts up. How can you bear it?"

"Mindarin!" Aelwyn said, half laughing, half shocked.

"I'm serious," Mindarin replied. "I've known some talkers in my time, some who'd been at it for decades, perfecting the art over a lifetime of practice, but none of them could have kept up with this one."

"She's just a kid. Not only that, she's a kid who hasn't seen her father in a long, long time. She only knows he's been sent on a mission into a part of the world that makes most men tremble. I think her ability to be cheerful is remarkable."

"It may be, but that doesn't mean I should have to be subjected to it."

"Suit yourself," Aelwyn said, "but I'm going. I liked Kyril from the moment I met her, and the girls, and I want to ride with them today."

Aelwyn spurred her horse on as she moved to the side of the road to advance. She didn't think Kyril would be that far ahead. Mindarin called after her. "Aelwyn!"

She slowed down and turned. "Yes?"

"All right, you win."

"I wasn't out to win anything. Don't come if she bothers you. I'll see you later."

"No, I'll come. I was hoping to see Nyan today, and she's probably farther up as well."

"All right," Aelwyn said, then pressed on as before.

They rode up along the outside of the column, and Aelwyn noted that she was not the only one feeling musical. Men and women alike rode whistling, singing, humming. It was testimony to the irrepressible nature of hope that something so small as a slight shift in the temperature could rekindle its embers. They were still on the run, marching toward a great rock city that was to serve as their fortress. Their enemy had to date suffered no really serious defeats, even if the intervention of dragons and prophets had on occasion slowed their progression. Aelwyn doubted that the stone out of which Tol Emuna was carved would be more successful than the dragons and the prophets, but such was the nature of warmth and hope that she too felt what defied all logic.

Before long they caught sight of Kyril, riding alone. Aelwyn greeted her as she and Mindarin flanked Evrim's wife. "Kyril, how are you this fine spring morning?"

Kyril turned to smile at them, and Aelwyn saw instantly that she had been crying. "What is it, Kyril?"

"Nothing, Aelwyn," Kyril said. "It is a fine spring day. A beautiful day. Don't mind me."

"Yes, the weather is beautiful," Aelwyn replied. She was unsure whether to press further. She liked Kyril and wanted to know her better, but she didn't want to pry. "Where are the girls this morning?"

"They're riding ahead with Karalin. They wanted to go forward a bit and watch the Great Bear, and Karalin offered to take them."

"Do you mind if we ride with you?"

"Not at all. Join me."

A slight breeze from the south picked up, blowing warm air and the fragrance of fresh growing things. Aelwyn marveled. All that rain, and yet the natural world seemed not to be destroyed, though Aelwyn always thought it fragile. There would be grass and flowers and blossoms this spring. The resilience of Allfather's creation was remarkable.

"There's little in this world to compare to the smell of spring," Aelwyn said, trying again to prompt conversation.

"Yes," Kyril agreed. She hesitated, but continued. "It always makes me think of the spring Joraiem went to the Summerland. It was the year I came of age, the year Evrim sought my hand. It was the best time of my life."

The loneliness in her voice touched Aelwyn deeply. Tears came to her eyes. "Kyril, I'm so sorry."

Kyril nodded. "You know, it's like I lost them both the day Rulalin killed my brother. Joraiem I lost immediately, of course. I never saw him again. Evrim, I lost ten years later. The war started, and Evrim went. Since then, well, I've felt like a widow most of the time, never sure if he's alive or dead, always wondering when this will end and if we'll ever be a family again. Not much chance of that now, I guess."

"Maybe not much, but there is a chance," Aelwyn said quietly.

"Maybe," Kyril replied, "but between his predicament and ours, the odds that I'll see him again just aren't very good."

Aelwyn did not know what to say to that, and even Mindarin was quiet, looking blankly at the road. "It is hard to be so far away from those you love, not knowing how they are."

Kyril reached over and put her hand on Aelwyn's. "I'm sorry, Aelwyn. I know you must worry about Aljeron too. I didn't mean to quench your good spirits."

"No, its all right. I know things don't look good, and the waiting is terrible. I wanted you to know you're not alone."

Kyril smiled again. "You know, Aelwyn, I really hope Evrim and Aljeron both make it out of there. I hope they come home, and that somehow, some way, we make it too. I'd like to sit down to dinner in a happier time, the four of us, and enjoy a good meal, laughter and music. I don't know why no one snatched Aljeron up sooner, but good for you for looking past . . . well, for looking past his scars both inside and out, and for seeing what he is and could be."

"That would be wonderful, spending an evening together in a time of peace, that is. May it be so."

"So may it be," Kyril answered, and on they rode.

Three riders came thundering along the outside of the column. Two swept past and continued on their way, while the third rider approached the three women. He slowed when he saw them, reining in his mount and checking his pace. "Kyril Minluan?" he asked, looking at Kyril.

"Yes?"

"Two men have joined the rear of the column. One of them has asked for you."

Kyril looked at Aelwyn and Mindarin, then back at the rider. "Is it my husband, Evrim Minluan?"

"I don't know either of their names, but I don't think so. They are both older and said they had recently arrived from Suthanin. They look a bit ragged from the journey. Refugees, no doubt."

"And one of these refugees has asked for me?" Kyril asked, both disappointment and confusion in her voice.

"Yes. They talked to my captain for a while when they first arrived, and then I was sent for you."

Kyril, looking a little mystified, turned her horse around and started after the messenger. Aelwyn likewise turned around. "We'll come with you."

Soon all three were riding behind the soldier, back along the column. Aelwyn's heart beat quickly. Like Kyril, the first place her mind had gone at word of two men arriving was to Aljeron and Evrim. For the briefest of moments, she'd held her breath in wonder at what seemed like an instantaneous fulfillment of her deepest wishes. She had not had time even to hope for what Kyril had suggested, so the disappointment had not been overwhelming, though now she felt disappointment and excitement in equal measure.

Their guide slowed, and looking past him they could see a small cluster of men beside the road. Two sat on horseback with a captain of the Enthanim, one with a bushy beard of black sprinkled with grey and the other, older and clean-shaven. Both watched their approach. Suddenly, Kyril spurred her horse on, and she galloped toward the small fellowship.

The older of the two men dropped from his horse, as did Kyril. Soon she was in the arms of the older man, clinging tightly to him. Mindarin and Aelwyn came upon the tender scene and dismounted quietly a few spans away.

"Father," Kyril said at last, still holding him tight.

"Daughter."

After another long moment, Kyril finally stepped back from Monias and looked from him to his traveling companion and back. "What brings you all the way out here?"

"To see you, you and the girls, as well as your brother and the rest of my family."

Kyril glanced around, scanning faces. "But Mother . . . you left her at home?"

Monias put his hands gently on her arms. "She's dead, Kyril."

"Dead?"

"Yes, she died near the end of winter."

"Winter?" Kyril echoed, her voice sounding distant and hollow, as though the word did not have meaning.

"Yes," Monias replied, "and with her gone, there was nothing left for me in Dal Harat. Nothing, you see? I decided to come, to look for my family, and Allfather has brought me safely to you at long last."

Kyril set her head upon Monias's chest, and he stroked her hair and whispered comfort to her. Behind them, horses approached. Aelwyn turned to see another rider leading Karalin and the two girls, Halina and Roslin.

The news from Dal Harat was difficult for the girls, and both began to cry with loud sobs. Monias pulled them close once more, this time seeking to comfort even as he had sought to welcome. "Weep for our sadness, but do not weep for her. She lived well and loved much, you grandchildren as much as anything or anyone else. She has finished her race and is at rest."

"And you, Father?" Kyril said as Monias stood back up with one granddaughter clinging to each side of him. "How are you faring?"

Monias looked at her. "I am better, now, for I have found you alive and well. At least, as well as anyone might be in these dark days. It was hard at home, too hard. Everyone I loved and would have found hope in was somewhere else. There were times when I thought I'd never find you, but seeing you all now, I know that coming was the right choice."

"I'm afraid that you've walked right into the path of the enemy," Kyril said. "You were probably safer in Dal Harat, at least for a time."

"Perhaps, but I will happily face whatever is coming in the company of my family."

"You've missed Wylla."

"No, I saw her on the way."

"You did?"

"Yes, a few days southwest of Amaan Sul. She was on her way to find the camp of the enemy and Benjiah."

Silence prevailed until Kyril added at last, "I half hoped that she would change her mind and follow us, that she would at last see reason."

Monias shook his head. "She seemed determined to ride on. As for reason, what seems like madness to one is reason to a mother's heart. Were your places reversed, you might well have done exactly as she did."

"Maybe," Kyril answered. "At any rate, I hope she has not paid a high price for her boldness."

"I know no more than I have told you." Monias continued. "I know Evrim has gone into Nolthanin with Aljeron, but I had hoped to find Brenim among the army here. Is he all right?"

"Yes," Kyril said, looking back up the column. "He was likely up near the head of the column with the scouts. If the third rider who was sent out went after him, he will likely be here soon."

"Good," Monias said. "I have now seen both of my daughters and my granddaughters. I would like to see my son as well."

"Father?" Kyril said.

"Yes?"

"Brenim . . . well, a lot has happened since he rode from Dal Harat seven years ago. The war . . . it's changed him."

"Much?" Monias asked.

"Yes, Father, quite a bit."

"As a war must, I suppose," Monias said. "There is more you wish to tell me, Daughter?"

"I fear you will find the changes difficult. He's become hard, bitter. The war is devouring him. Hatred of Rulalin has become hatred of most things."

Monias nodded soberly. "I am saddened but not surprised. It is the nature of war to destroy, one way or another."

The sound of riders approaching from the front of the column once more drew their attention, and sure enough, Brenim and another soldier came on, riding hard. Unlike Kyril and the girls, Brenim did not see his father. As he came to a halt, he looked down upon them, "What is going on back here? Why have I been summoned?"

Monias stepped toward him. Brenim dropped from his horse, tears springing to his eyes. "Father?"

"Son."

Brenim looked past him at Garin and the other Enthanim soldiers. "You've come alone."

"I have."

"Mother's dead."

"Yes."

He stood, arms hanging limp at his side, and Monias took him in his arms and pulled him close. He cradled Brenim's head and whispered into his ear. "She wanted me to tell you how much she loved you, Brenim. She only wished she could have held you again and told you herself."

Brenim rested his forehead on Monias's shoulders and cried, really cried. Racking sobs shook his whole body. "My son," Monias said, stroking his head. "It's all right. It's all right."

Aljeron sat with his back against the wall of the long, low house. It was their third day here, and despite the suggestion that perhaps they would be allowed out for some fresh air and exercise, it hadn't happened. All that time without shelter in the snow, he wouldn't have believed he'd be sitting under a solid roof, daydreaming of being in the open air, but such was the fickleness of fortune that this was exactly what he now craved.

"Valzaan," he said, leaning over and looking at the prophet where he was sitting out in the open floor, legs crossed, eyes closed and head erect.

"Yes?" Valzaan's eyes remained closed.

"What do you make of our captors?"

The prophet's eyes opened at this, and he turned as though to look at Aljeron. "What do you mean?"

"Well, their strange talk for one, their issues with Blade-Bearers for another. Just generally, what do make of them?"

"Their strange talk is hardly surprising. They've been an isolated enclave since the end of the First Age. Linguistic anomalies are to be expected. I would have expected more, actually.

"As for their obsession with Blade-Bearers, that's interesting but perhaps not surprising either. They attribute the ruin of their people to Andunin's acceptance of spears and swords from Malek. What's more interesting to me is the way they've rejected the metal of Malek's weapons but not the weapons themselves."

"What do you mean?"

"I mean that they appear to be as deadly with spears of wood as any Nolthanim follower of Malek would be with metallic spearheads. They've rejected the metal that made the blades, but they've embraced the basic idea of weapons for killing. In fact, they seemed to have made training to kill a central aspect of their cultural identity."

"They do seem somewhat warlike," Evrim said.

"Somewhat," Valzaan echoed. "Further testimony to the deceptiveness of man's heart. Malek made blades of metal because metal is efficient for killing, but metal is not the main problem. The problem lies in the hearts of men. The Kalin Seir seemed not to see this basic contradiction."

"Are you going to say something?" Aljeron said. "I hadn't thought of it like that, and maybe if they got your point they'd recognize there's nothing wrong with my wearing a sword. Maybe they'd see there wasn't any point to keeping us in here."

"There's little chance that I'd persuade them of anything, not after all this time and all the importance they've attributed to metal blades for centuries."

"That's too bad," Aljeron said. "It would be nice to be vindicated. I don't like being suspected of service to Malek."

The door to the house opened, and the Kalin Seir who had been charged with feeding them entered with breakfast in their hands. This group included the woman who had conversed with Aljeron. She had not spoken to him yesterday, other than to mention that the elders were debating whether to let them out to exercise, but even so, she watched him each time she entered with the others to tend to their meals.

This morning, after placing their breakfast on the lone table and taking the old plate away, she spoke directly to him. "Aljeron?" she said, using his name for the first time.

"Yes?"

"The elders say that today, after you have eaten, you may all come out. They are sorry that you were not let out yesterday. There was a disagreement over you."

"It has been resolved?"

"I do not know, but today you may come out." She stooped before him. "You must not, any of you, try to escape. You must not try anything, even if tempted. You won't succeed and will likely die. Be patient. Show the elders that you may be trusted, and I believe all will go well with you."

"If we show we can be trusted, will we be given our freedom?"

"I cannot promise that, but I think so."

Aljeron leaned forward. "Naran is the only Kalin Seir that we know by name, and we have not seen him since the day we were locked in here. Who are you?"

"I am Keila," the woman said, but even with the mask on, Aljeron could see that she was embarrassed to answer the question. "I must go."

She rose and quickly exited the building. Aljeron moved with the others to the table to grab breakfast, and he could not help but notice the smirks on Evrim's and Saegan's faces.

"What?" he asked.

"What do you mean *what?* You know very well what," Saegan scoffed.

"We told you," Evrim said.

"Aljeron," Valzaan added. "Even I can see that the woman has taken a particular interest in you."

"All right," Aljeron said, knowing his face must be as red as Keila's. "So what if she does? That's not my fault."

"Hey, no one said it was anybody's fault," Evrim replied. "Don't be defensive."

Aljeron turned his attention to the breakfast, muttering as he took his share of the food and then some.

"Valzaan," Saegan said, no doubt looking for a way to shift the conversation away from Aljeron's admirer. "What do we do now? They're going to let us out into the open, but there's no evidence that we're any closer to being set free."

"What do we do?" Valzaan echoed Saegan's question. "I guess we wait. Allfather knows as well as we do, better even, how much time is pressing. As far as I can see, there's nothing for us to do but wait."

The door opened midmorning, and one by one they filed outside. Many Kalin Seir gathered to look at them. In fact, they were quickly surrounded by a great throng of people, jostling for position to get a good view. Aljeron noted a complete lack of fear in the eyes of any of the men or women or children that he saw. Whatever bearing weapons with metallic blades implied to these people, they were not concerned enough to disarm Aljeron and his friends, or to appear alarmed at the sight of those weapons dangling from their sides.

Apparently, Aljeron and Koshti were of special interest. Word of the bond between them had spread, no doubt, and the Kalin Seir maneuvered to study the man and his tiger. Snow leopards moved among the Kalin Seir, and before long, a small number of them were playing with Koshti. The great cats cuffed one another and there were play-bites as they rolled in the snow together. The Kalin Seir who were close enough laughed, as they watched the spectacle of tangled fur and barred teeth.

Eventually the crowd thinned as many of the Kalin Seir returned to their business. When they began to dissipate, Naran appeared out of the crowd and approached them.

"The elders are at an impasse."

"Concerning us?" Valzaan asked.

"Yes."

"They don't believe our story?"

"No, I think that they do. The problem is that you are Blade-Bearers. They don't want to keep you like prisoners, but they can't seem to let you go either."

"So what would they like from us?"

"I don't know," Naran shrugged. "I am sorry that I don't have better news. If it were up to me, I would let you go, but it isn't up to me."

"Can you give us any hope here?" Evrim asked.

"Yes, the elders seem to have shifted their favor in your direction, just not enough to let you go completely, and there doesn't seem to be any middle ground. You are either under guard or you are free to go. There is no third alternative."

"Well," Aljeron said. "If they've shifted our way, maybe they'll shift more. Maybe they'll let us go."

"Maybe, but from what I've heard, the elders holding out against letting you go are insistent that Blade-Bearers cannot be set free, not without more compelling evidence."

"So the hope isn't so hopeful after all," Evrim countered.

"You might even call it hopeless," Saegan said softly.

"Hopeless?" Valzaan said, and there was a strange quality in his voice that drew the attention of the others. "Nothing is ever hopeless. Look!"

All the men turned as one to follow his outstretched arm, and they gazed into the sky. They did not see, at first, what Valzaan meant them to see, but soon the distant golden gleam of the approaching dragon became clear, its mighty wings beating the clouds.

A moment later, Sulmandir flew low over the village of the Kalin Seir, the trees bent low by the wind his wings created. Shouts of wonder rose from the Kalin Seir, who stood wherever they were, staring up at the dragon who rose suddenly, then began to circle, slowing and descending.

"The Sun-Soarer!" Naran cried out, looking from Sulmandir to Valzaan and back into the sky. His cry was picked up and echoed all across the clearing, where the Kalin Seir waited and watched in wonder.

Then, just like that, Sulmandir dropped onto the ground in their midst, his magnificent wings outstretched so that many Kalin Seir had to dodge, having underestimated the great breadth of his wingspan. Sulmandir held his head high, regally, looking down on them all. He retracted his wings and stood tall, waiting.

The elders made their way through the quickly gathering mass of Kalin Seir to the place where Valzaan stood calmly, below the uplifted head of the dragon. Sulmandir did not acknowledge them, and they did not speak, content for the moment merely to observe. Valzaan lifted his head in the direction of Sulmandir's silent form.

"Father of Dragons," Valzaan called from the ground, "who am I?"

"You are Valzaan, prophet of Allfather."

"Who are you?"

"Sulmandir, the firstborn and Father of Dragons."

The elders of the Kalin Seir fell prostrate before Sulmandir. Except for Valzaan and those who had traveled with him, everyone dropped instantly to the ground and lay face down.

"Rise!" Valzaan called out to them. "Sulmandir, the Sun-Soarer, is but a servant of Allfather like you. He is mighty, yes, but he is not to be worshiped."

Hesitantly, the elders rose, and gradually, the rest of the people did as well, but Aljeron could see that they were uneasy in the presence of this legend, much as he had been not many days earlier.

Valzaan lifted his voice, looking from the elders to the crowd as he cried. "People of the north! True sons of Allfather. Today the prophecy of old is fulfilled in your midst! The Sun-Soarer is come. You see him with your own eyes. Is it not time to re-enter the world of men? March with us to the mountains in the south and beyond. March with us to war. We go to face Malek and fight, to rid this world of him and his creations, once and for all. Stand with us against the Traitor-Titan, against the Forge-Foe. Regain your lost honor and cast away your shame! Leave behind your past and the betrayal of your brothers and come. So says Allfather!"

If Valzaan was hoping for a dramatic effect upon the assembly, he could not have been disappointed. Murmurs and excited chatter rippled through the crowd, and even the elders were visibly stirred. One of them grabbed Naran and pulled him close so that he could be heard over the rising din. When the elder let him go, Naran leaned his head in to address the waiting men. "The elders believe. The day has come. We will march with you and join this battle. The muster is begun."

Aljeron had no idea how official word of the elders' decision spread, but it did spread, and quickly. In what seemed like no time, a sort of organized pandemonium broke out as men and women began to move with alacrity and determination, each one to his or her own home to prepare.

"What's happening?" Aljeron asked, leaning in toward Naran.

"They are preparing to march."

"Will they be ready by morning?" Aljeron asked.

"Morning? You mean tomorrow?" Naran said, looking confused. "They will be ready within the hour."

It was Aljeron's turn to be confused. No army at his command had ever prepared to march so quickly. "Will they all come?"

Naran shook his head. "The men and women of fighting age will come, they and their battle brothers."

"How many are there?"

"About fifteen hundred of both," Naran said. "Now you must excuse me, but I must prepare as well. There isn't much time."

The army of the Kalin Seir, some fifteen hundred men and women with a matching number of snow leopards, was indeed assembled and ready to march in less than an hour. Aljeron had watched in amazement, having no real preparations to make himself. Weapons, gear, food, all the things they could carry on their own backs, had been brought together, neighbors providing for the needs and wants of those who were lacking. The elderly and the children ran errands here and there, aiding wherever they could.

The good-byes were brief and free of tears for the most part. Aljeron could see the excitement that this expedition represented even in the eyes of those left behind. Perhaps later, when the days turned into weeks and those they loved had not returned, perhaps then they would feel the sorrow of such separation. Not yet, though. Now they seemed cognizant only of the fact that the Father of Dragons had appeared from the sky, that a prophet of Allfather had summoned them to war, and that at long last a chance to free themselves of the shame that they had borne for two millennia was now come. There were hugs and kisses and waves, and just like that, the army was on its way, weaving through the woods that surrounded their hidden village, working south toward the plain that lay between them and the Zaros Mountains.

There were no horses. All of the Kalin Seir were on foot, like their battle brothers. Aljeron and the others, having come on foot all the way from Harak Andunin, were not happy about setting out on foot again, but they did not complain. They were not under guard and had been treated as free men and companions from the moment the order to march had been given. Sulmandir was gone now, for as soon as the army began to move out, he leapt into the sky and flew south, as he and Valzaan had agreed.

"I should be on my way," Sulmandir had said to Valzaan as the Kalin Seir began gathering their things. "The great muster of the dragons is begun, but there is much left to be done."

"I do not think there would be trouble if you left," Valzaan replied, "but if you could wait to set out with us, I think the sight of your flying on before them would give the Kalin Seir much encouragement—encouragement that might be needed in the long days ahead."

Sulmandir had agreed to wait, and his departure was marked by a great shout from the Kalin Seir as they moved out into the woods. With raised spears and fists the people ran, calling out to the Sun-Soarer as he disappeared over the treetops and into the distance. Naran, who was running with them near the head of the column, moved close to Valzaan.

"Where is he going?"

"He has work to do in the south. He is assembling an army of dragons. It may well be that we run toward the last and greatest of battles in the history of Kirthanin."

"If so, so be it."

"So may it be."

It was dark by the time they emerged from the wood into open ground, but if the company running with Valzaan had thought they might stop for the night, they were mistaken. Torches emerged here and there among the Kalin Seir, and they kept on through the darkness. In fact, if anything, the pace of the army quickened now that they ran across easier terrain. When asked when they would stop, Naran replied that hunting parties and long-range expeditions sent out by the Kalin Seir never stopped until morning light, and then only for a short rest, not a sleep. It was the custom, a demonstration of will and endurance.

"If I'd known that I would have napped while the Kalin Seir got themselves together," Evrim groaned.

"At least we know we'll make good time," Saegan replied, and they all ran on through the dark in silence.

When at last the first light of morning came, they did stop as Naran had promised. He produced water from an animal skin and they all drank as they rested. Evrim drank stretched out in the grass. In a matter of moments, light snores emerged from his mouth.

"I guess we should let him go," Aljeron said, looking down at him. "Even if he only gets a short sleep, it would be cruel to wake him before we have to."

"My leg is killing me," Saegan said. "I think I pulled a muscle on a tree root or something shortly after we left. It's been hurting all night."

"When will we have a real rest, Naran?" Aljeron asked.

"We'll stop for a full sleep tonight, probably a little after dark."

"And each night after that?"

"Yes, barring circumstances I can't foresee. The Kalin Seir are as human as you are, and we need our rest."

"Saegan," Valzaan said after a moment. "Do you have any suggestions for crossing the Zaros Mountains? Most of the passes I know of are high and difficult. Getting a whole army through will be arduous."

Saegan shook his head. "I am afraid I cannot help there, Valzaan. The Zaros Mountains are tall and their crossing treacherous. All ways through the mountains are hard and unforgiving. I think we should stick to the original plan. Let's go east to the sea and bypass the mountains. From there we can approach Tol Emuna from the east."

"We will go neither over the mountains nor around them," Naran said.

"What?" Aljeron said and the others echoed.

"We shall go through them."

"Through?"

"Yes," Naran said. "I should have said earlier, but the Kalin Seir have long used a passageway through the mountains."

"You have a way through the mountains?" Saegan said, staring at Naran in wonder.

"Not all the way through from north to south, but most of the way. When we first settled here, scouts found a cave that led through great caverns deep into the mountain. They also found a small and winding way from one of those caverns up into a mountain pass on the southeast side. That small and winding way has been guarded and maintained, and the outlet into the mountain pass closed to all who would seek it from the outside. We, however, will pass into the mountain and journey through it to the other side."

Valzaan broke into a smile so broad it lit up his leathery face. "See, Allfather knows our need of haste, does He not?"

"He does indeed," Aljeron echoed.

Not long afterward they set out again. Aljeron woke Evrim, and the latter rose grumpily to rejoin the march, though the pace at which the army ran would not under normal circumstances qualify as a march. Aljeron, despite the lack of sleep, felt his strength and energy renewed. Perhaps it was the good news of learning about the passage through the mountains, or perhaps it was just the adrenaline of his second wind. Either way, he ran with Koshti and looked down at his battle brother, who seemed to be keeping up without even trying, his great legs treading rhythmically through the snow.

As though from nowhere, Keila appeared beside him, running. At her side, a sleek, graceful snow leopard kept pace. She looked at him and smiled. Though surprised, he acknowledged her with a nod.

"It is good to run with a purpose, is it not?"

"It is."

"It is a big change for you from yesterday. You are free now, and we are not your captors, but your friends and allies."

"Yes, it is a welcome change."

Keila blushed, and Aljeron wondered what he had said to cause the reaction. "I look forward to fighting at your side, Aljeron. Beyond the mountains, on the field of battle, I will show you my worth."

"I am sure you will," Aljeron replied. Suddenly, he realized that he had to speak to her about Aelwyn. Her interest in him could not be denied, so he needed to be clear about his commitment elsewhere. "Keila, you should know that there is a woman of my own people waiting for me beyond these mountains."

Keila looked ahead at the ground over which she was running, but she did not stay quiet. "Are you married?"

"No."

"Well, then we shall see. We shall see how well she fights, and then you may judge between us. I am one of the best warriors among the Kalin Seir, either male or female. You will see."

Before Aljeron could answer, Keila had gone ahead, the snow leopard running with her.

5

TOL EMUNA

THE GATES OF TOL EMUNA towered ahead. Aelwyn
felt dwarfed by the great stone walls on either side, grey and
red and daunting even from a distance. The gates were almost
as impressive, enormous wooden barriers reinforced by steel,
or so the captains had said somewhere along the way. As she
looked at the open gates, slanted back into the city, she could
see that they were huge, for the men and Great Bear streaming
through them looked small and insignificant by comparison.

Mindarin was riding with her, as were Karalin and Nyan
Fein. Whenever Mindarin was around Nyan and Karalin, she
was a different person, softer somehow. Aelwyn knew the
three of them shared a special bond with Wylla and Bryar and
the other women kidnapped by the Malekim and the Vulsutyrim. She remembered who Mindarin had been when she
left for her sojourn in Sulare, and she remembered who her
sister had been when she returned. To be sure, she hadn't

been totally transformed. Still, her adventures took some of the edge off, and though she still had a sharp tongue, she refrained from using it much more often.

Mindarin had also become more reflective, even nostalgic, when with Novaana from that Summerland trip. Mindarin was never one to look back about most things. She'd stopped using her married name, Orlene, fairly quickly after her husband's death. She never talked about him or the years they'd spent together, and Aelwyn rarely asked. To Aelwyn, she'd just always been one of those people who let the past be the past and who focus on what's going on around them. But in present company, Mindarin had no trouble hearkening back to her adventures almost two decades before.

"These massive walls remind me of Nal Gildoroth," Nyan said.

"In size but not color," Mindarin answered. "Nal Gildoroth was darker."

"And bigger," Karalin added, "but as far as walls for a human city go, these are the most imposing I've ever seen. In that way, they do remind me of Nal Gildoroth."

"That day was so bright," Nyan said, sounding lost in a vivid memory. "Do you remember? The bright sky? The hot sun?"

"Yes. We were scared and excited, all at the same time. We had no idea what was waiting for us inside that city."

"Or what was waiting for us outside if it," Mindarin finished for them, looking at the others. "When we came out of those gates only to have that giant slam them shut behind us, I thought I was going to die right there."

"We all did," Nyan said.

"I think Bryar wanted to," Karalin added softly.

"Yes." Nyan nodded. "As bad as that day was for us, it was even worse for her. The hardest day of her life."

"Have any of you been here before?" Karalin asked.

"No."

"Not us," Mindarin answered for Aelwyn. "Have you?"

"Yes, long ago. It is imposing, but it isn't really anything like Nal Gildoroth. That was a horrid place. Everything stark and black with that awful stone. Everything so empty and bare and devoid of life."

"The creepiest thing about Nal Gildoroth was the emptiness, wasn't it?"

"Maybe," Mindarin said, acknowledging Nyan's point. "The sheer size and scale of everything was pretty spooky too. And that gigantic statue in the center of the city? That was horrible."

"Yes," Karalin continued. "Tol Emuna isn't at all like any of that. It's a living place, and the stone is all light grey or red, like the sun-burnt soil of this whole area. In its own wild way, Tol Emuna is beautiful, even if the plants both in and out of the city are scraggly and tough, and even if the soil grows more rocks than food. It is an untamed beauty. We shouldn't bring thoughts of Nal Gildoroth under these gates with us. It will ruin your first impression."

"And the people?" Mindarin said, gazing at the gates not more than a few hundred spans away. "What about them? Are they as wild and untamed as this land?"

"Well, how would you describe Saegan? This is his home, after all. I think he's pretty much representative of what I've found here."

Mindarin nodded. "He belongs in a place like this. You can see where his toughness would come from, looking at this city and the land."

"Yes, you can."

"The people here are beautiful as well as tough." Karalin smiled as she turned to survey them all. "They're straightforward and direct, and they all seem to have that inner fortitude you were talking about with Saegan, but they're generous and hospitable too. You'll see."

Despite Karalin's attempt to bring good cheer to the small company, the talk of Nal Gildoroth and the dark clouds that hung over them kept a smile from Aelwyn's face. "We've come so far through so much," she said, half to herself and half out loud.

"Yes, and the long road has led us here," Mindarin continued.

"It's a long way from Cimaris Rul and the shores of the Southern Ocean," Nyan said in soft agreement.

"Yes, and a long way from Shalin Bel, even if we'd come directly," Mindarin said.

"So many leagues you've traveled," Karalin said compassionately, looking at Mindarin with sadness in her eyes. "I'm so sorry for all you've been through."

"Well," Mindarin said, disarmed a bit by Karalin's graciousness, "as hard as it was for us, it was harder for the men fighting the battles along the way. Think of the soldiers from Shalin Bel who penetrated the defenses of Fel Edorath, only to find out their labor wasn't over. I can't begin to imagine their weariness."

"No, it is hard to comprehend."

"This army has traveled the length and breadth of Kirthanin," Nyan said. "Save only for the waste of Nolthanin."

"And some of our own have even been sent to journey across that," Aelwyn said.

"Yes, and now there is nowhere else to go."

"No, there is nowhere else."

They rode under the gate, and Aelwyn looked up at the thick stone arch that formed the top of the gate when it was closed. *Here we will stand, or here we will fall.*

Caan watched as Gilion tried to brush, flick, and scrape away the reddish mud that had affixed itself to his pants as he rode, but it clung tenaciously. It simply would not be removed. Caan looked down at his own bespattered clothing. He did not feel the least concern over trying to be rid of the mess, evidence of their passage through rough terrain. He knew Gilion couldn't look upon such things with the same eyes. He felt an inner compulsion to be clean and tidy, which is why even after so long on the road, his hair and beard and even his clothes, as much as was possible, appeared well kept and properly groomed. No doubt compared to the rest of them, Gilion must have looked like a newcomer to the army, though of course he'd logged as many leagues in this sojourn as any of the others and more than most.

"It's not going to come off," Caan said at last, though he didn't really expect his words to have any effect.

"I'll wash it off when we're settled in the city," Gilion said, but as Caan expected, he didn't stop his efforts to be free of it now. "This mud is more like clay than dirt. I'd forgotten just how unfriendly and barren this place was."

"Not so unfriendly."

"Not the people, the place," Gilion corrected. "Perhaps *unfriendly* was a poorly chosen word. Maybe *rugged* or *remote* or *wild* or something else would have been better."

"Either way, I get your point. A tough place to stay suitably clean," Caan said with a smile on his face.

"Yes, quite," Gilion replied curtly, at last lifting his head. He looked at the men filing past into Tol Emuna. It was late afternoon, early evening, and though the days were slowly getting longer, the light of this particular day was almost gone.

"We're almost inside," Caan said after a moment.

"Yes. That at least is some relief."

"Some." Caan grimaced. All the way from Amaan Sul to Tol Emuna, he'd avoided most questions of what to do once they got there, answering simply that they needed to get here safely first before they started worrying about what to do then. Even after Eliandir and Dravendir brought word that Malek and his forces were perhaps a week behind, he still feared that they would close the gap once they crossed the Kalamin. He had been almost sure of it, but here they were, and they had not been caught. *They're not afraid of us or these walls. And why should they be? From the ruined walls of Zul Arnoth to the towering walls of Cimaris Rul, we've found none that could keep them out.* The image of Cheimontyr, his great hammer held over his head, appeared in Caan's mind's eye. He'd avoided all questions about what to do next, because he didn't know what they could do.

"Thirty-five thousand men," Gilion said almost under his breath. "What an army!"

"With some thirty-five hundred Great Bear," Caan added. "A Great Bear might not be quite worth ten men on the battlefield, but they're close. They almost double our fighting strength."

"And still we don't know how to fight this battle," Gilion said, looking intently at Caan, who turned to meet Gilion's stare. "We can admit it out loud now, can't we? We're here and out of reasons not to do so."

Caan nodded. "We can admit it, as long as there's no one around but us to hear it."

"Fair enough."

"Any great ideas?"

"Great? No. Ideas? Yes. Given the strength aligned against us, I don't know that there are any great ideas to be had."

"I was afraid you'd say that," Caan said. "I just can't see how to fight this battle, Gilion. At least, I can't see how to win it."

"Winning may be out of our hands. With Allfather, anything is possible, but I'm not His prophet and I can't speak for Him in this matter. There just aren't any guarantees."

"There never are guarantees in war," Caan said. "I've always known that. I just don't know how to plan for an enemy who wields more power than I can imagine. How do you assess such strength? How do you prepare for it? How do you create contingency plans when the contingencies defy logical calculation or anticipation?"

"I don't know."

"Neither do I," Caan shook his head. "If you told me a year ago that I'd be here with thirty-five thousand men and a tenth as many Great Bear, and if you told me that I'd have no idea whether I could hold Tol Emuna with such a force, I would have laughed in your face. An army like this? I'd have told you I could hold any city in Kirthanin, let alone this one. But here I am, with no idea whatsoever about what to do."

In the western sky, two golden forms appeared, approaching Tol Emuna quickly. Caan looked up at them, relieved. He hadn't had a report from them for a while, and now at least he'd know where the enemy was and how much time his people had. That would be one less surprise.

He dismounted as the dragons circled above the muddy ground beside the road. He and Gilion both walked out toward them, and as they did, he saw Sarneth approaching from the Great Bear that had been moving toward the gate. He stopped and waved to Sarneth.

"May I join you?" Sarneth called as he drew nearer.

"Of course," Caan answered, smiling.

The trio approached Eliandir and Dravendir. Caan looked at their mighty forms and thanked Allfather one more time for their presence with his army. With a rear guard of two dragons, he'd been able to move all his scouts up in the column. Both as reconnaissance for the army and as protection for the rear, the dragons could not be equaled. From the moment of their appearance beside the Barunaan, they had been invaluable to the movement and survival of his army.

"Eliandir, Dravendir," Caan said, nodding his head to acknowledge them. "Welcome to the gates of Tol Emuna. What news?"

"Malek's host has moved quickly from Amaan Sul." As usual it was Eliandir who brought the report. There was some form of rank or deference between these two, but what it was exactly or how it worked, Caan didn't know. "They are at most three days and nights away."

So, they had cut the week's head start by more than half. Just three days, and they would be here. And why not? Why wait longer? What was the difference between three days and three weeks? No more men were coming. No more supplies. Waiting longer would just make the Kirthanim more vulnerable to a siege. Let the enemy come. But Caan said, "Thanks for the information. We will ready our defenses and prepare the city accordingly."

Caan thought that would be the end of the exchange. Neither Eliandir nor Dravendir were given to idle chatter. Neither Eliandir nor Dravendir moved, though, and both continued to gaze at the men and Great Bear at their feet.

"What is it?" Caan inquired.

"We encountered one of our brothers when we were checking on the location of the Kumatin, for the creature remains active in the Kalamin River between the Kellisor Sea and the coast."

"Yes?" Caan replied, excitement growing inside of him. Any word of another dragon was encouraging.

"A muster of the dragons is underway. Word of Sulmandir, our great father, appearing from the northlands, is spreading throughout Kirthanin. Many dragons who have long hidden from the eyes of men are rising and leaving their mountain gyres. Many who have not felt the breeze beneath their wings for hundreds of years have taken to the skies. The dragons are waking."

Neither Caan nor Gilion nor Sarneth for that matter, said anything. Caan stared blankly up at the majestic face of Eliandir, as the red dragon gazed down at him, his great golden eyes as inscrutable as ever. The information rolled around inside his head, and he knew it to be momentous, but the dragon had communicated with all the fervor and passion with which he might order his water pitcher refilled at the local inn.

At last the spell began to wear off, and Caan turned to read the look on Gilion's face. Even there, in the contemplative and controlled visage of his old friend, was a giddy joy that confirmed he had not misunderstood the message.

"A muster of the dragons?" Sarneth said at last, the first of them to speak.

"Yes, an assembly has been called for, to see what strength remains among the children of Sulmandir and to hear what our great father has to say."

"Sulmandir," Caan said, the name awkard on his tongue. "Aljeron's quest was not in vain."

"It would seem not," Sarneth replied.

Almost involuntarily, the north drew each of their eyes. The two men and the Great Bear looked across the northern plains of Enthanin in the direction of the Zaros Mountains. Caan wondered where Aljeron was now and how many of his party had made it.

"I thought it a waste of time," Gilion said, and Caan could hear the shame in his voice as he murmured his confession.

"So did I," Caan said, nodding to his friend. "Foolishness, in fact, if the instruction to go had come from any other than Valzaan. And yet, this foolishness might be our salvation."

"Thanks be to Allfather," Sarneth added.

"Indeed," the men echoed.

"Eliandir?" Caan said, looking up at the dragons. "Will the dragons be able to be here in three days? Is help coming?"

"I don't know," Eliandir replied. "I don't know when the muster will be complete, or what they will decide to do when they meet."

"You don't know, but can you guess?" Caan asked, plaintively. "Obviously, I can't plan on the aid of the dragons as I look to our defenses, but if you think it likely they will be here, it would make a difference."

Eliandir lowered his head a little bit. "I would not count on their appearance in three days or less. I understand why you ask, but I cannot say. Dragons do not feel urgency the way that men do. This I had forgotten over the long years of our retreat. And yet they are not unaware of your need. That Sulmandir has come forth at all and called for the muster shows that he desires we sleep no longer. I think dragons will come. How many or when, I cannot say."

Caan nodded. "You cannot tell me any more than you can tell me. Thank you, thanks to both of you."

Both Eliandir and Dravendir leapt from the ground and began to circle back up into the sky. Caan slapped Gilion on the back. "Hear that, old friend? Help may be on the way."

"Help is almost certainly on the way," Gilion replied, "but when will it get here?"

"That's the question."

"I still don't know how to fight this battle."

"Nor do I, Gilion," Caan said, turning back toward Tol Emuna, "Nor do I."

"If I might have a word," Sarneth said, and both men turned toward him.

"Yes?" Caan asked.

"That's actually why I was looking for you two, even before we spotted Eliandir and Dravendir."

"Go on."

"If you were referring to the defense of the city," Sarneth began. "I have an idea."

"Well, we're certainly open to ideas," Caan said.

"To kill a snake, you need to go for the head."

"Malek?" Gilion asked, incredulous.

"Yes, I suppose Malek is really the head, but that wasn't what I meant," Sarneth replied. "The visible or symbolic head is the Bringer of Storms. Kill Cheimontyr, and we may just win this war."

Caan stared at Sarneth for a moment. "You may be right about that, but how do we do it?"

"I have a plan, though it isn't without risk."

Aelwyn leaned closer to Pedraal, who was riding beside her over Tol Emuna's streets. "Who is this Carrafin again?"

"His official title in Tol Emuna is Captain of the Rock. He's the chief military officer of the city."

"But he is answerable to you as captain of the armies of Enthanin?"

"Yes, technically. There's a delicate balance between respecting the near-autonomy of Tol Emuna and asserting the rights of the Enthanin monarchy. Wylla is queen of Enthanin, but the royal family has been associated with Amaan Sul for so long, it is sometimes forgotten by those outside Enthanin, and even by some within, that she rules not the city but the whole domain."

"So that's why he's not very warm toward us? It's an authority squabble of sorts?"

"No, actually," Pedraal answered, looking over at Carrafin and his wife, Eluann, who sat on horseback, talking to Monias and Kyril. "You'd probably never find Carrafin warm, as you call it. What goes on in Carrafin's heart is probably known only to himself and maybe his wife. He's as stony as the city walls, but he's not being difficult in any way. He knows we had to come and has been a great help to us since we've arrived, working hard to accommodate so many of us."

"Will there be room for everyone?" Aelwyn asked.

"Yes, one way or another. Some will bed down in homes or shops or other buildings. Others will sleep outside in the streets, as long as the dry weather holds. Also, as you can see, the buildings of Tol Emuna have flat roofs, much like Shalin Bel. Many will sleep on the roofs."

Aelwyn took another good look at the city. As they rode in, she'd focused mainly on the people, their simple and drab garments, their serious but not unfriendly faces. Now she looked again at the low square buildings. The square open windows with propped-up shutters to allow the warm evening breeze through seemed inviting, despite their simple appearance. The houses, like the rest of the city, were reddish-grey like the stone of the mountainous rock on which they were built. Another thing that she couldn't get over was the remarkably steep pitch of some of the city streets. Every city she knew well had been built on relatively flat ground, but here the streets rose and fell like sand dunes by the ocean. One had no sooner ascended to the top of some hill than the street dropped away just as suddenly. Some of the square houses seemed to protrude right out of the side of these hills, and Aelwyn imagined that burrowing into the side of these rocks must provide a cool refuge when the hot blasts of summer wind blew across the desertlike plains.

The reddish hue of the rock was reflected in the evening sky. Aelwyn didn't know if this was a normal effect or if the strange play of the twilight on the grey clouds reproduced the redness across the horizon, but it was fascinating to look back over the plains and see red-grey filling both land and sky.

As Aelwyn stared out over the city, a rider came hard up the stone street to the place where they were gathered, and the Captain of the Rock was taken aside. Aelwyn looked at her sister, who sat with her eyes closed in her saddle, her chin slowly slipping toward her chest. Just at that moment, Mindarin's head snapped upward and she opened her eyes and looked at Aelwyn, smiling faintly.

"Tired?" Aelwyn asked, holding back a smirk.

"Very." Mindarin yawned. She straightened and ran her hand through her hair, then rubbed her tired eyes with her free hand. "I'm glad we've reached the end of the road. No more riding sounds pretty good."

Pedraan nudged his horse closer to his brother's. Looking back over his shoulder at Carrafin and the rider, he whispered, "I wonder what they're talking about."

"I don't know," Pedraal replied. "If it is at all relevant to us, I'm sure Carrafin will let us know."

The brief meeting between Carrafin and the rider ended as the man headed back the way he had come. Carrafin turned back to the small cluster of waiting riders. He looked to the twins, "Pedraal and Pedraan, may I have a moment with you?"

Carrafin took the brothers aside, and Mindarin looked at Aelwyn and rolled her eyes. "We're going to know what's going on eventually. I don't know why they don't just tell us. Soldiers and their chain-of-command obsession."

The discussion between Carrafin and the twins lasted a little longer than the discussion with the rider, and when they were finished, the three men returned to the waiting company and began to make noises about not being able to linger and needing to make sure everyone was taken care of for the night. Even so, as they began to move on, Pedraal motioned Aelwyn to come aside even as Pedraan pulled Kyril aside only a few spans away. Mindarin huffed and pointed her horse toward her quarters.

"Pedraal," Aelwyn said quietly, "what is all this silent whispering about? What's going on?"

"Eliandir and Dravendir have brought news to Caan."

"Yes?"

"Well, we're not ready to make a general announcement yet, but Pedraan and I thought you and Kyril should know."

"Know what?" Aelwyn asked, her heart beating fast. There was only one reason she could think of that there would be news of special importance for her and Kyril alone.

"Apparently, Sulmandir has called for a great muster of the dragons."

"Sulmandir?"

"Yes."

Aelwyn felt tears coming to her eyes. "Then he is alive, and Aljeron has found him."

"We don't know. It would certainly appear that if Sulmandir has come forth, at least some among their number reached Harak Andunin. More than that I can't say for sure, but we thought you'd like to know."

"Yes, thank you, Pedraal," Aelwyn said, turning to see how Kyril was taking the news.

Kyril was talking quietly and intently with Pedraan, and after a moment, she turned to look for Aelwyn. Aelwyn smiled through the twilight at Kyril, who smiled back, a tender glance that spoke of both joy and relief. Later, when the chance arose, she would speak to Kyril further. They didn't know that Aljeron and Evrim were alive and coming back to them, but at last there was something beyond conjecture, something concrete to discuss.

A pair of torches burned brightly on either side of the simple flat roof, illuminating the small gathering. The flames flickered brightly, sending sparks and small plumes of smoke curling into the darkness. Aelwyn sat on the comfortable wooden chair and leaned back, looking up into the barren night sky. She missed the stars. On a warm spring night like this, there should be tens of thousands, some brilliant in their brightness and others faint in their distant grandeur, but there were none. The storm was over but the clouds were not gone.

Perhaps the storm wasn't over. It might just be on hold. It was a gloomy thought, but if the rain was a tool in the hand of the enemy, he might just be waiting to see if he needed it again.

What if Malek wins? Will the clouds disappear and the sun and stars return? It seemed to Aelwyn an odd possibility. That Malek's conquest of Kirthanin could signal the return of light was a jarring thought. Metaphorically at least, Malek's third coming had often been referred to both in prophecy and in common speech as his attempt to cover Kirthanin in darkness. This he had done, not metaphorically but really, but would it stay that way forever if he won? His purposes accomplished, would the Bringer of Storms release the clouds from their service to his master's will, and would the weather patterns of Kirthanin return to normal?

A warm wind blew across the roof and ruffled Aelwyn's hair. Malek's control of the weather, or at least Cheimontyr's control, did not appear to be complete. The coming of cloud and rain, the maintenance of the cloud cover, these things had defied all expectation, but the seasons were progressing as expected. The world had grown cold when it was supposed to, and now it was growing warm once again. Were the seasons themselves a sign? Were they evidence that a greater hand than Malek's held the world in its grip, that storms would come and go, some large and some small, but nothing could shake the surety of the sun's rising and setting, the seasons' waxing and waning?

Aelwyn hoped so. Not much in the last half year gave her hope, and even with the news earlier that Aljeron might well be alive, that didn't necessarily mean this war would soon be over and Aljeron returned safe and sound. And yet, if anything could bring hope to their immediate situation, surely it was the possibility that dragons, perhaps many, might come to their aid. And what's more, if anything bore witness to the fact that Malek had not wrested Kirthanin completely from Allfather's sovereign hand, surely it was the spring that was creeping over the land, blowing hope with each warm gust of wind.

Aelwyn looked around. Mindarin sat quietly beside her, and nearby, Karalin and Nyan were talking quietly as they looked out over the city. A sound behind them revealed Kyril's arrival as she reached the top stair and stepped onto the roof. Aelwyn smiled to greet her and indicated to the open chair beside her.

"Are you alone?" Aelwyn asked.

"Yes."

"Your father didn't want to spend his evening with a gathering of women?"

"Probably not, but that wasn't what kept him from coming. Even though he protested that he wasn't wise in things military, he was invited by Caan and Carrafin to come with Brenim to the council tonight."

"Men and their councils of war," Mindarin said. "Am I the only one here who gets nervous at the thought that our fate appears to be in the hands of a room full of men?"

"Bryar is there," Kyril said.

"Yes, that's true," Mindarin conceded, "but I'm afraid she's hopelessly outnumbered."

"Even if Father hadn't gone," Kyril continued, "I doubt he would have come here with me. He would have excused himself for one reason or another, then walked through the city on his own."

Aelwyn and the others nodded. They sat in the small circle of chairs, the torches casting their shadows on the roof.

"Well," Aelwyn said after a moment, "I'm assuming all of you have heard the big news by now, even though you were probably told not to spread it."

She looked around, and the others nodded. "Have any of you heard where or when the dragons might arrive?" Karalin asked.

"No," Aelwyn replied, and the others shook their heads as well. "What help they will bring seems to be unknown. At least, Pedraal acted like he didn't know, and I believe he really didn't."

"It would seem to suggest Aljeron made it to Harak Andunin and is all right," Kyril said, looking at Aelwyn. "And hopefully that means Evrim is too."

"It could, though we have to concede that their mission could have succeeded even if some of them didn't make it. For that matter, Allfather could have summoned Sulmandir without anyone making it, but," Aelwyn hastily continued, not wanting to squash her own hope or Kyril's, "it seems logical to think that Sulmandir's return at this time is not a coincidence. Aljeron left to seek and find Sulmandir, and now Sulmandir has appeared. Let us hope they have succeeded and are on their way back to us even as we sit here."

"Wouldn't it be great to see them come riding through the gate together?" Karalin said, smiling broadly.

"Oh yes," Nyan agreed. "I haven't seen Aljeron in so many years. And you said Saegan was with them as well, right?"

"Yes, he is," Mindarin said. "Let us hope that all of them will shortly be back, though we must remember that the northern reaches of Nolthanin are still a long way from here. They could be safe but far away, too far to reach us before Malek does. It is a big world out there."

"Yes, it is a big world," Aelwyn agreed, "even if trying to find a place to hide from Malek's wrath has made it feel small."

"Well," Nyan said, "no one is hiding anymore. We're here, and he knows it and will be here soon too."

"I'm almost glad," Kyril said. "This needs to end. We'll never be stronger than we are now, especially if the dragons are really on their way."

"And we'll never find a place stronger than this one," Karalin agreed, sounding more optimistic than the others.

"Here is where we win or lose," Mindarin said, putting into words what they were all feeling.

Aelwyn stood. "Well, the men have gathered to do their thing, and we have gathered to do ours. We might as well be about it."

She pushed her wooden chair back and knelt on the smooth stone of the roof. The others knelt as well, and reaching out, she took Mindarin's hand on the one side and Kyril's on the other.

For a long time they knelt, the five of them, their heads sometimes bowed, sometimes lifted, staring into the heavens.

There was complete silence, and in each of them their unutterable groans and cries rose wordlessly from their weary and troubled hearts.

When a long time had passed, they rose to their feet, still holding hands in a circle. Aelwyn scanned them as they stood. "Whatever plan the council decides upon tonight, we will do all we can to support them. When the battle comes, we will hold the hands of the dying and give aid to the living. We will face what must be faced and do what must be done, agreed?"

"Agreed."

Amontyr and Nirotyr crouched in the sparse light of dawn in the deep snow of the mountain pass. They had passed through the worst of it and were now descending on the southern side. By that evening, they should be on level ground again and on their way across the plains of Enthanin to join their brothers.

"I will be glad to be out of the snow," Nirotyr said.

"Yes," Amontyr replied. "Spring is coming. The warmth will be a relief after our time in the northlands."

"Oh yes, it will be," Synoki said from behind them. They turned to see the man, wrapped tightly and waist deep in snow, coming up behind them.

"You are awake," Amontyr said. "We can be off."

"In a moment," Synoki said, walking between them to also look down over the mountain and the plains. "I'd like to enjoy this view too, as well as the peaceful stillness of the early morning, before I'm placed on one of your shoulders for another long day of being bounced incessantly from dawn till dusk."

"I'm sorry for your discomfort," Amontyr said.

"It can't be helped," Synoki said, waving off any further attempt at apology.

Synoki looked out at the snow and the red-grey rock and soil in every direction. It was fortunate, in a way, that Tol Emuna was to be the place of the last great battle. Knowing what he now did about the child of prophecy, it could have been worrisome to know the boy was somewhere deep in Suthanin, many weeks away, even for the supernaturally strengthened feet of a pair of Vulsutyrim. Tol Emuna, though, was far closer. It would not be long now, and he would return to his army, and then all would finally be accomplished.

"Master?"

"Yes?" Synoki answered.

"Are you ready?"

Synoki turned to them and smiled. "I am."

As Amontyr lifted him onto his massive shoulder and started moving through the pass, continuing their descent out of the mountains, Synoki looked out over the plain again. *Yes, I am your master, and soon all living things in Kirthanin will know me for their master too. My time has almost come.*

THE FURY OF THE
GREAT BEAR

"I'm sorry, Yorek."

"Don't apologize, Your Majesty."

Wylla wiped her tears away, tears that had slowed but not stopped. They had been walking all day, and when the rain started again, she'd been too weary and focused on keeping up to let it get to her. Now that they had been stopped for the better part of an hour, though, the emotion of the storm's return caught up with her, and the tears had begun to fall.

"It's this rain," she said, looking at the concerned face of Yorek that was turned upon her with kindness and sorrow in his eyes, "but it isn't just the rain."

"I know," he said. "The rain is just the proverbial grain that tips the scales, one more thing to weigh down your burdened heart."

"Yes," she said, rubbing her eyes with a sleeve that was already soaked by rain. "Today is one of those days that I find myself wishing with all my heart that I wasn't a queen."

"Yes," Yorek nodded. "The weight of privilege and the responsibility of wise rule."

"I remember walking through the city with you when I was a little girl," Wylla said, resting her head against Yorek's shoulder. He put his arm around her and caressed her hair gently, and for a moment she almost could have closed her eyes and imagined that she was a little girl again, sitting on Yorek's lap in the palace. The memory cheered her and her voice grew less shaky. "Girls in the city would stand in clusters as we passed, holding onto their mothers' legs, just staring at me. I could see already there was distance that separated them from me. There was a gulf. Worse than that, I could see already that they thought I was the luckiest little girl in the world. I bet most of them, when they were at home with their friends, pretended to be the princess, the heir to Enthanin's throne."

"Probably."

"I was blessed to be born into the royal family, Yorek. I know that," Wylla said, as though answering an imagined accusation.

"Yes," Yorek said, understanding what she meant. "But it was a blessing that came at a price."

"It did, and I'm still paying it. I lie awake at night sometimes and wish that I was ordinary, that Joraiem had been ordinary, that Benjiah was ordinary. Maybe Joraiem would be alive. Maybe Benjiah would have a brother or sister. At least we wouldn't be here, captives."

"Do you really think so?" Yorek asked.

"Yes, why not?"

"Because the passion that drove Rulalin to kill Joraiem is not limited to the Novaana. Such envy could have struck its fatal blow, destroying even a marriage between 'ordinary' citizens. And Benjiah, well, who's to say Allfather wouldn't have called him if he'd not been a prince? His royal birth may or may not have anything to do with it, and if he'd been captured in the fulfillment of his duties, your maternal bonds, even as an 'ordinary' citizen, might well have led you here."

"Maybe, but no one could try to coerce me to betray the people of Enthanin in order to spare my son's life."

"That is true. You would be completely expendable, as an ordinary person, in which case you'd probably be already dead."

Wylla sat up. "You're no fun, Yorek. Here I am trying to indulge in self-pity, and you've ruined it for me."

"Sorry."

"Now its your turn to stop apologizing," Wylla said, smiling for a brief moment. She leaned back against his arm and whispered, "I'm so glad you're here with me. I just don't think I could have faced this alone."

"I'm glad I could be here."

"Are you?"

"Of course."

"Don't you wish, with every step and every league we travel, that you'd stayed as far away from Amaan Sul as possible?"

"Absolutely not. Why would you say that?" Yorek looked at her quizzically, and Wylla could see his surprise was genuine.

"Yorek," Wylla said, incredulous. "They're going to ask me to try to convince the Enthanim from Amaan Sul and Tol Emuna, and probably the whole army of Kirthanin, to surrender. They've made it clear. Benjiah's life depends upon it."

"So?"

"So? I can't do it! I won't do it! I'll never do it! And when I don't do it, they'll kill Benjiah and me."

Yorek nodded slightly, tears appearing in his eyes for the first time since they'd left Amaan Sul. "I know."

"And that means they'll almost certainly kill you."

"I know that too," Yorek said.

"Well? Don't you wish you'd never come back? Never entered my service? Never come to Malek's army with me in search of Benjiah?"

"Oh, Your Majesty, my dear, dear Wylla," Yorek said tearfully. "You need not worry for me. Life has not been so kind to me that I will greatly miss it when it's gone. I do not fear death. I count it one of my chief joys in all the years Allfather has given me, that I have a second chance, the chance to serve you in my old age. If I end my days easing your pain and sharing your burdens, I will count my life well spent. I regret many things in my life, but not anything since the day I returned to the palace of Amaan Sul and entered your service."

Wylla put her arms around Yorek and hugged him. "For your faithfulness to me, I thank you."

"You're welcome."

"It may not be hopeless for us yet," Wylla said after a moment. "It may be that perhaps, just perhaps, Rulalin will be able to help us."

"Perhaps."

The rhythmic drumming of the rain on the top of Benjiah's cage made him sleepy. The monotonous rolling of the cage and cart had come to an end for the day at last, and with his world at rest again and the soothing sound of the rain, he closed his eyes and slipped into darkness.

The darkness gradually cleared and he found himself standing on a raised platform. The sky was gloomy, for the clouds were as thick as ever, thick and black and relentlessly shielding everything from the full light of day. Rain fell, but it was light and he barely noticed the tiny drops when they struck him.

What he noticed was the vast assembly, a sea of faces that he could both see and not see at the same time. The enormous crowd was familiar, spread as far as he could see in any direction, but he could never see them in any detail. Something always shrouded them from scrutiny. He noticed the iron manacles tightly fitted around his wrists and connected to heavy chains, which held his arms outstretched at an angle above his head, almost taut. He felt the weariness of trying to hold himself up mixed with the pain in his sockets when he tired and sagged, feeling as if they were dandelions pulled by a child from the earth.

He looked beyond his arms and the chains to the two great poles that rose from the wooden platform. They were thick and tall, probably a full two spans, with large iron rings that the chains were firmly attached to near the top. He looked at them and winced. Even if he had strength left in his arms, he knew that under his own power and with his own strength, he would never have been able to pull the chains from the rings or the rings from the poles.

He hung his head in despair. Silently he begged for just the smallest fraction of Allfather's power to flow through him, that he might break free and be spared this ignominy. He pleaded. He implored. Nothing happened. He opened his eyes and looked up to the heavens, and the world grew dark again.

Benjiah opened his eyes and sat up, rubbing his arms, which ached with remembered pain. It was much later now, and twilight rested on the land. The whole army would be at Tol Emuna by tomorrow, midday at the latest. He had himself seen the almost mountainous red-grey rock out of which the city was carved in the distance as the cart with the cage had rolled to a halt.

Suddenly, another detail from his vision came back to him. The plain on which the vast assembly stood was red-grey. It was here, outside the walls of Tol Emuna, that the vision would become reality.

The realization was chilling. He didn't know why he hadn't understood it before, but it had been some time since he'd been to Tol Emuna. He tried to remember his last visit. It was about the same time as the outset of the war between Fel Edorath and Shalin Bel. So long ago.

He leaned back against the slats of the cage, wide awake now. Any vestige of sleepiness was gone, even though the rhythmic drumming on the top of the cage continued. He stared out of the slats that faced Tol Emuna, though he couldn't see it through the darkness. Reaching the city had taken on a whole new meaning. He was rolling onward, onward toward not just the city, but the poles and the chains, toward the pain and the humiliation.

The vision had been so clear, persistent and haunting of late, that he found it hard to believe it betokened anything but his death. In fact, he would have been sure, sure past any doubt, had it not been for one thing. One piece, one fragment of the repeated vision that had haunted him even before he knew who he was, before he'd been enlightened about his calling, remained unexplained. He understood now the images of rain, the bright and searing light, the wooden cage. He understood all of them, very well indeed. But the city, the great white city, that part of the vision had not yet come to pass. He had not walked the empty streets or stood in the great open square beside the low white wall. He had not stood there as water came, welling up over him and around him.

Until this moment he had figured that if the second vision was of his death, the fulfillment of the first vision, the vision of the city, would come before he found himself chained to those poles. Now he knew that the chains and poles were imminent. He could see no escape from this cage. Perhaps this meant he would survive the chains and the poles. Perhaps they did not represent his death. Perhaps in some unforeseen manner he would be rescued.

And yet he was troubled. His head fell upon his knees as he drew his legs up underneath him. Deep inside, he felt that the image of the empty white city and his death were related, and now he wondered if he could see how. Perhaps the water and the white city had never been a vision of something awaiting him in this life. Perhaps he was being given a glimpse of the greatest of all mysteries, of what lay beyond the pale of this temporal existence. Maybe the white city was the place where Allfather granted new life and peace to the faithful dead. If that was so, then the poles and chains might still represent his dying. Perhaps they were in fact a glimpse of the portal by which he was to leave this world, only to rise in that one.

Perhaps.

Aelwyn and Mindarin stood on the roof in the rain. It was only drizzle, their wet and matted hair stuck to their faces and necks.

"Any chance it's a coincidence?" Aelwyn asked.

"Not much," Mindarin answered.

Aelwyn looked into the gloomy sky. "We're not on the ocean or near a river. Why would Malek want it raining here?"

"I don't know. Maybe it's an assault on our will. Any hope or optimism that the dry weather and warmth brought me between Amaan Sul and Tol Emuna is about gone. If the rain has the same effect on the soldiers, how much do you think it will affect their will to fight?"

Aelwyn shook her head and shrugged. She turned from her sister and looked back out over the city, toward the great wall. Word had come that the foremost ranks of Malek's army had arrived and were stopped at some distance from the city, so the wall was soon to be tested. It was strong and it was mighty, but Aelwyn was not at all sure that it could keep Malek out.

Her mind wandered north. Her thoughts soared high above the red-grey plains toward the Zaros Mountains and beyond them toward the Nolthanin waste. She'd never been there, or even near it, but she imagined a bleak and barren land, perhaps still covered in the winter snows. She had hoped Aljeron would somehow arrive, almost magically out of nowhere, riding through those front gates before Malek came.

She had felt intuitively that he was rushing to be here, to return to her, but if that was so, Malek's forces now lay between them. What hope she had of surviving this siege to see him again, even if he was coming, she couldn't guess and didn't want to.

"He's out there, Mindarin, I can feel it."

Mindarin put her arm around her sister. "I think the odds are good. If Sulmandir is gathering the dragons, the most logical explanation is that Aljeron made it to Harak Andunin."

"But if he's coming back, if he's on his way here, what will he do? Malek's army has cut off his access to the city."

"Aelwyn," Mindarin said hesitantly. "I don't want to discourage you, but we don't even know if he knows we're here. When he left us, we were on a ship off the coast of Col Marena, about to head south."

Aelwyn's heart sank. The inevitability of this logic, that Aljeron would go looking for them where he had expected them to go, south toward Cimaris Rul, had danced around the edges of her reason, but she had pushed it away, not wanting to face it. She felt the force of this reasoning now, and yet she did not despair. A peace that calmed her mind and heart washed over her like an ocean wave, and she put her own arm around her sister. "If he is alive and well somewhere in this world, whether near or far, I am happy."

Caan stood with Gilion on the top of the guard tower, a high pinnacle of rock that overlooked the entire city and plain. Carrafin had been there with them, but he left to see to a matter in the city. In truth, there wasn't really any need for Caan and Gilion to remain, for the numbers of their foe were beyond their capacity to accurately count from this distance.

"So many," Caan said, staring as though entranced with the vast host assembling well beyond bowshot on the plains. "It's as though they lost none of their strength in any of our battles to this point. They seem almost more numerous."

"Perhaps they held some of their forces in reserve," Gilion replied. "No need for that here."

"Yes, this is our last chance to turn the tide of this war, and they know that as well as we do." Caan looked up from the gathering host to the sky. The storm, though discouraging and inconvenient, seemed oddly appropriate, and he did not resent it. Even so, he had no wish to be soaked when he could be dry. There would be a time when it was unavoidable. Soon enough, no doubt. "Let's go in, Gilion. I don't want to be drenched."

They turned from the wall and crossed to the narrow door that led to the winding stair that would take them down through the towering stone to their quarters. Passing from the fading gloom of the dying day into the brightly lit stairwell made them squint until their eyes had grown accustomed to the flickering brightness of the torches. Once below, they stepped into the quarters they were sharing, poured drinks, and sat down at a sparse stone table. All food in the city had been immediately rationed upon their arrival, though all of the officers expected the war to be over, one way or another, before food shortages became an issue.

"No word from Eliandir and Dravendir," Gilion said, mopping his face and drying his mustache with a small, dry cloth.

"No," Caan answered.

"If they don't come soon, there won't be any point in coming at all."

"Oh, I don't know about that, Gilion." Caan frowned. "I think they'll engage Malek's host when they're ready, whether we're still holding out here or not. I find it at least a little comforting to imagine their victory celebration after our demise being interrupted by the full fury of the dragons."

"I'm glad it comforts you," Gilion said. "I'd be more comforted if they arrived predemise."

"True, but that is out of my control and not worth my worry." Caan rose and walked to the large window. Its vista looked out over the wide avenue that ran in front of this military headquarters. Messengers moved quickly to and from the building, and there was a general sense of purpose in the strides of all who passed by below.

Caan leaned on the windowsill and peered out through the rain. Not long now and it would be completely dark. How much larger would the host out on the plain grow during the night, and when would the Vulsutyrim come, and with them the Bringer of Storms and his dread hammer?

"Should we have agreed to this plan?" Caan asked, continuing to look out of the open window.

"Second-guessing the wisdom now?" Gilion asked.

"Aren't you?"

"I second-guessed it from the start, but when there aren't any good options, all you're left with are plans that leave you doubting your sanity."

"The payoff is enormous, but the risk is big too."

"Sarneth knew that."

"I know, but after seeing Malek's hosts making camp, I almost wish I could get word to him to call it off."

"We're past the point of no return now."

"I know," Caan said, turning away from the window. He walked back to the table and looked down at Gilion. "And we're past all time for timidity and delay. I've made a decision. I want all our archers in place upon the wall, or at least ready behind it to take their places, and I want everyone else ready to march at a moment's notice. Whether Sarneth's mission goes well or ill, this may be our best chance to hit the enemy hard. We both know that even Tol Emuna's walls won't keep him out. If the Great Bear fail, Malek will smash his way in here and we'll be hemmed in completely."

"But if they fail and we're outside the city, we won't last the night."

"We may not."

"Shouldn't we play the odds? Isn't our chance of surviving until the dragons come at least a little better if we stay put?"

"I didn't march all this way just to cower here, hoping the dragons will save me," Caan said slapping the table with his open hand, his eyes blazing. "The Great Bear are going to hit with everything they have, and I want to be ready to follow up with everything we have. I will not forsake them. Win or lose, the enemy will not forget this night."

Gilion looked impassively at Caan. "It's your decision."

"Yes it is, and I've made it."

"I'll let the others know. It shouldn't take more than an hour to be ready."

Gilion stood and crossed to the door. As he opened it, Caan called after him. "Gilion?"

Gilion turned and stood quietly.

"Thanks."

Gilion nodded, his face softening, and he stepped briskly from the room.

Caan returned to the window. The street below was noticeably darker than it had been just a few moments before. Streetlamps were lit, and the constant traffic to and fro now cast furtively darting shadows across the stone streets. It was going to be a long night.

Sarneth was soaking wet and filthy, sitting in the hastily dug out trenches that ran for almost a league well north of the main road to Tol Emuna. He was in the middle of the Great Bear line, along with the Taralin elders, Kerentol and Parigan, Turgan from Elnin, and the young warrior Elmaaneth, who reminded him so much at times of his own son, Erigan. He looked back over the dark plains north of their position toward the Zaros Mountains and wondered, not for the first time, if his son was all right.

He would have enough to worry about this night without worrying about Erigan. It wasn't Erigan lying in ambush with only thirty-five hundred Great Bear while the full force of Malek's hosts moved steadily eastward along the road just a half a league south of them. It wasn't Erigan who was about to lead an attack against that force, an attack that had little hope for success and less for survival. Even if they were able to strike hard enough to kill Cheimontyr, what hope did they have that they would be able to fight their way back to the city? Not much was the answer, and all of them knew it.

And yet, despite this, there had been no opposition to Sarneth's plan from the moment he brought it before the others. Cheimontyr had to be stopped if they were to have any hope at all, this much was clear. If they succeeded, if Cheimontyr and most of his brothers fell tonight, then the men might stand a chance against the Malekim and Black Wolves. If the Great Bear succeeded tonight, their draals might be spared the destruction that Malek no doubt planned for them, for none of them believed that this war would end here at Tol Emuna. Malek would burn his way through Elnin and Lindan and Taralin. Sooner or later all the draals would be destroyed, and those woods would become the dark places that Gyrin had become.

Just thinking of Gyrin stirred the embers of fury that glowed in Sarneth's heart. Corindel might have betrayed the location of the Gyrindraal, but it was Malek and his hosts who raided, pillaged, burned, and destroyed it. The tale of its destruction lived on in his memory, passed on in his family from father to son, a tale so gruesome when told in its fullness that it made one sick to the stomach. Even the most gentle Great Bear alive felt the low simmering of rage that ran now in their blood when the story was told. It was this story he had called to mind two nights ago when he stood before the gates of Tol Emuna to prepare his army for this ambush. They would strike Malek's hosts with all the power they possessed, with all the fury that a thousand years of pent-up desire for vengeance could manufacture in the hearts of All-father's patient yet powerful woodland keepers.

With this grim reminder in view, they had marched hastily through the night to their current position and dug like mad in the rain-softened earth beyond sight of the road. In this the rain of the previous months had been their ally. To dig a trench of sufficient width and depth to house them all would have been almost impossible had the ground near Tol Emuna retained its usual dry hardness. As it was, they dug quick and sure, smearing much of the red-grey soil they removed into their coats to make sure their bodies were flecked with the colors of the wide plain. Should even the most clear-sighted enemy be able to see a Great Bear in the distance, the camouflage was sufficient to prevent recognition. It was further hoped that their approach to the Vulsutyrim, whether by day or by night, would be shielded to at least some degree beyond what they could ordinarily have expected.

Despite their hope that even an approach by day would be disguised, Sarneth had hoped and expected that the attack would commence that night. He looked to the sky and saw that it was showing signs of morning. Since midday the previous day, the army of the enemy had been assembling, and he would not have thought it possible that the Vulsutyrim had not yet passed by, but no word had come from their advance scouts, and now the morning could not be so much as an hour away.

Almost as though in answer to his wish, one of the scouts came scrambling over the top of the trench and dropped in beside him.

"They are come."

"All together?"

"Yes, the Black Wolves, Malekim and now also the men on foot and on horseback have passed by. The Vulsutyrim are almost even with us on the road. It is time to go."

Sarneth scrambled up to the top of the trench and gave a long, low growl that was deep like a rumbling in the earth but echoed and vibrated along the ridge of the trench in both directions. Echoing deep, low growls rolled along the trench in both directions, and soon the whole body of Great Bear, five to ten deep along the whole half a league, stood in the faintest glimmer of the morning light. Sarneth dropped to all fours and began to run, his great paws tearing up the soft earth as he moved steadily faster across the great open space.

His heart began to beat faster and faster. He could feel the fury in every footfall, and the adrenaline of rage pulsed through him. The ground slipped away quickly, and before long, he could make out the enormous forms of the Vulsutyrim, immense and powerful, striding along the road.

A loud and powerful horn call pierced the darkness, and Rulalin was shaken out of his reverie. He was tired, very tired. With their close proximity to Tol Emuna, Farimaal had ordered them to march through the night. He would not camp at a distance from the city, just in case the Black Wolves and Malekim all the way forward were attacked, as unlikely as that might be. So Rulalin had been forced to drive his men, now marching near the rear of the column, to travel through the night until they had just about reached their camping place. He allowed himself to think about the sleep that was almost his, when this horn rudely interrupted his meditation and summoned him back to reality.

The horn blew even louder, piercing his daze and drawing every Nolthanim man within eyesight to look back through the darkness in the direction of the Vulsutyrim at the rear. He had no idea what the call could mean, but had they been on the battlefield, it would have sounded to him like an impassioned cry for help.

He suddenly understood the unsettling nature of the horn call. It was what his mind had automatically assumed it could not be, a cry for help. As impossible a thought as it was, it had to be. He summoned a messenger and dispatched him to Farimaal. The gist of the message was simple: *Trouble in the rear, come quickly.*

He began to mobilize his men. He got them organized and dispensed his captains to make sure all were mounted, armed, and ready to ride. As he was doing this, a second chilling thought occurred to him. Just like that, he had ordered every man under his control to turn around, to face west, leaving their backs exposed before the city.

He summoned another messenger and again dispatched him quickly toward the city. The gist of this message was also simple. *Beware attack from the city. This could be a trap.*

At just that moment, Soran, who had been riding near the very rear of his men, came galloping forward in the breaking dawn, seeing Rulalin too late to stop until he was several lengths past him. He reined in his horse, turned around and rode up beside his friend.

"What's going on, Soran?"

"Attack."

"We're under attack?" Rulalin asked, incredulous.

"Yes, Great Bear have struck the Vulsutyrim hard from the north, thousands of them."

"Great Bear!" Rulalin said, looking up as though just the mention of the word could help him to see through the dim light.

"Yes, you need to send word for help."

"I already have."

"Good, then come now, with every man under your command."

"We're coming."

Rulalin stood in his stirrups and shouted his orders. In a matter of moments every Nolthanim under his command was thundering westward down the road and beside it.

Before long they began to encounter Great Bear, and for at least the first few moments, they had the benefit of coming from the side into a mass of the beasts, who were pouring over the road. Rulalin's own horse almost struck headlong into one of them, and before the Great Bear could pivot to wield his massive staff in Rulalin's direction, one blow from which would have killed Rulalin or broken the back of his poor horse, Rulalin struck a slashing blow to the Great Bear's elbow. He drove past, aware that he wasn't pushing through a human army at all, and that he would have to be nimble and think quickly to keep himself alive.

The initial blow they struck against the Vulsutyrim had been as successful as Sarneth could have hoped for. Few of the giants had seen them coming, and the force of the moving mass of Great Bear had driven many of the Vulsutyrim sideways into their brothers. The sweeping stroke drove almost all of them from the road.

Almost all of them, for some of the Vulsutyrim had already passed the place where the Great Bear struck. Even so, the left flank of the Great Bear quickly wheeled eastward, staffs whirling, and engaged these giants even as they turned to see what had swept over their brothers.

Sarneth was caught up in the mayhem of it all, the seething mass of Great Bear now striking furiously at the bodies of the struggling giants. While some of the Vulsutyrim had been borne down to the ground under the weight of their attackers, then bashed and beaten by staffs, and ripped and torn by claws and teeth, fewer fell than Sarneth had hoped for.

What's more, the staffs were less effective against the Vulsutyrim than against any of Malek's other servants. While a solid blow from a Great Bear's staff would crush the head of a man or wolf, or even the head of a Malekim, the thickly muscled bodies of the Vulsutyrim seemed far more impervious to the force of their blows. Perhaps their bones were simply stronger and more durable; perhaps the many layers of muscle provided an insulation that kept them intact. Whatever it was, without the sharp blade weapons of men, it was harder to crush and kill any one Vulsutyrim than Sarneth expected, especially when they closed ranks and stood side by side. The Great Bear had killed a dozen or more giants in their initial assault, at least, but already the Vulsutyrim were stemming the tide of that charge, wielding their massive curved swords and metal weaponry, dropping many a Great Bear in his tracks and beginning to surge toward the road with a push of their own.

The sound of men calling above the din came from the west, and Sarneth knew that help was coming to the Vulsutyrim. It couldn't be too long before Malekim and Black Wolves also arrived, and then they would have the entire host of Malek to fight, and they would be drowned in the sea of blades wielded against them. He needed to rally the Great Bear in the direction of Cheimontyr, but he couldn't see exactly where that was.

Then, as though in answer to a prayer, a massive hammer was lifted to the sky in the distance. Lightning rippled laterally through the clouds, seemed to gather in a surging mass above the fray, and fell from on high, striking the hammer and illuminating the spite-filled face of the Bringer of Storms.

It had been meant to intimidate, but it served as a rallying signal for every Great Bear on the plain, and reacting as one, each Great Bear beat even more furiously against the faltering mass of Vulsutyrim, surprised by the adverse effect this display from their captain had inspired. Sarneth opened his mouth wide and roared, a furious and ear-splitting roar. It too spread across the plain and before Sarneth knew it, he was leading the mass of Great Bear, no longer trying to kill the Vulsutyrim between him and Cheimontyr, but trying to beat them off so he could get past them.

A knot of some fifty Great Bear followed him, pushing through the bewildered Vulsutyrim, who used their cruel blades now mainly in defense, trying to stave off one attack after another. The wave of Great Bear seemed to surge past them, pushing ever further in the direction of their captain.

Men on horseback entered the scene, and Sarneth greeted a rider with a blow from his staff that lifted the man right out of his seat and flung him ten or twelve spans through the air. Sarneth's companions likewise struck hard at the charging riders, sufficiently forcing them to veer north into the larger body of giants and Great Bear that Sarneth had left behind.

Another surge of lightning fell from the sky and struck Cheimontyr's hammer, which by now was not nearly as far away. However, this display was not just for show, and immense balls of lightning lashed out from the hammer and Cheimontyr's hand in their general direction. The fire streaked by with such blazing heat and fury that Sarneth and most of those with him dropped to the ground to avoid being burned to death. Sarneth could hear the screams of Great Bear who were struck and scorched by the flaming balls.

Once more the fury in his blood drove him to muster his willpower and master his fear. They had come too far to be defeated now. If he could regain his feet and renew the charge, he knew that the warriors who followed after him would likewise rise and follow. He looked at the group that was following him, and his eyes fell first on the semi-charred body of a Great Bear who had not been able to dodge the low flying lightning strike. It was Elmaaneth. His right arm and shoulder had been blown completely off, leaving his blackened body in the mud and mire, his eyes open and staring emptily into the sky.

Sarneth leapt to his feet and began to move, dodging deftly the sweeping stroke of a Vulsutyrim's sword. He rolled in closer to the giant to get inside the natural arc of the weapon and to strike a terrific blow across his knee. The creature howled in pain as Sarneth heard a popping sound and as the giant stumbled. A swarm of Great Bear swept over him, beating his body as though in unison as he tried to shield himself from the blows with his arms and hands.

Sarneth moved on. He could see Cheimontyr now, only a handful of Vulsutyrim between them. He growled again, and the small assault band of Great Bear moved forward, again seeking to bypass more than engage the giants between them and the Bringer of Storms. These giants, though, no doubt aware that they were their captain's last line of defense, would not give ground, and for a moment, the bears' attack stalled. They were held by the vicious counterstrokes of these five or six Vulsutyrim, who drove against them furiously. Sarneth felt himself and the others giving way, and he began to despair that they would be able to regain the upper hand. At that moment, another hundred or more Great Bear came charging from the north. They had managed to separate from the main engagement and arrived to give aid. Sarneth looked to them as they came up alongside and began to push the giants back. Turgan, the warrior of Elnin, was leading them, his proud head erect as his staff flashed through the growing light of dawn, inspiring the Great Bear to push harder.

Sarneth motioned to those with him to circle around the edge of the engagement between Turgan's group and the Vulsutyrim. They would strike at Cheimontyr from the side.

The move took them almost into completely empty terrain, soft and wet where no foot had fallen yet in the battle. As they circled toward the place where Sarneth had last seen Cheimontyr, Sarneth found him with his side to them, wielding his great hammer in defense. The charge by Turgan and the others had penetrated the defenses of Cheimontyr's guard, and he was fighting now in his own defense.

It was an awesome sight. Cheimontyr struck left and right with the hammer, and everywhere the hammer made contact with a Great Bear, the Great Bear crumpled around the hammerhead and was flung away into the darkness. Some were able to get close, but none reached him, and the surge was dying as other giants rallied to Cheimontyr's defense.

Sarneth approached rapidly from the side, and an impassioned cry from one of the giants gave warning just as Sarneth struck the Bringer of Storms with all his might. It had been directed against the small of his back, but Cheimontyr had turned at the last moment and Sarneth hit him in the side, just below the hammer. He heard a grunt from the giant, and then Sarneth leapt clear and rolled across the ground to dodge the fierce counterblow Cheimontyr tried to deliver. Sarneth rose and circled to see if any of those following him had likewise been successful in striking their target.

What he saw brought despair to his heart. A swarming mass of Black Wolves, flying across the ground like a mighty wind, thousands and thousands of them, running silently upon their massive padded paws, had swept over most of the Great Bear. Only a few remained upright before the giants, and the Vulsutyrim were ready for them.

Sarneth had little time to take this in, for a wave of the black ocean was rolling toward him, and a moment later, despite his furious self-defense, he was borne down to his knees and pushed over on his back, crushed under the weight of twenty or thirty wolves ripping his fur with their claws and cutting him open with their teeth.

7

MY BROTHER

THE GATES OPENED, and as the Kirthanim soldiers from the various cities and armies poured out, Pedraal looked up at the grey light of dawn just barely illuminating the road. Men on horseback rode quickly down to make room for the rank upon rank of foot soldiers that would come after, men from Fel Edorath and Shalin Bel, from Cimaris Rul and Amaan Sul, and men from Tol Emuna and even Kel Imlaris, as a small detachment had come north in answer to messengers from Amaan Sul sent long before. Pedraal gazed out over the heads of the men on horseback, breathing in the smell of a wet spring morning. It was a good smell, a green smell, a smell of things new. It was as good a day as any other to march to war. It was not so warm as to raise a sweat just standing there, nor was it so cold as to make him shiver. It would not be so bright as to make him squint in glare of the morning sun, nor would it be so dark as to cause his eyes to strain. It was a fine morning to fight. It was a fine day to take one last stand, if indeed this was their last hurrah. It was a fine day to kill or be killed, to wield the blade or surrender to it, as Allfather ordained.

Outside the gate, the hosts of Malek waited. The hare was cornered at last, and he must find a way to kill the fox or die.

Pedraal knew what the Great Bear had gone to do. Their success would be critical. The sound of distant battle made it clear that the enemy had been engaged. What was less clear was what the men would find when they marched out to meet their foe. What lay beyond his vision was for the most part a mystery.

What Pedraal knew, as he looked to the grey dawn, was that it felt good to be attacking. He wasn't the retreating type, and he hadn't ridden through Gyrin to Shalin Bel with the expectation of doing little but ride, march, and run before the enemy. He wanted to stand on his own two feet, his battle-axe in hand, and face the enemy on ground of his choosing. That was why he had passed up the offer of horses, he and Pedraan, who stood beside him. They weren't horsemen and they knew it. His battle-axe and Pedraan's war hammer were both meant to be wielded from the ground. Today they would stand side by side among the men of Kirthanin, and they would do what they had spent the better part of their life training to do. They would fight.

"It is a fine day to go to war, my brother," Pedraal said grimly.

"As good as any," Pedraan answered.

"Indeed, and better than most."

"Yes. With any luck, the enemy will be distracted and we'll drive a wedge into their ranks and create a wave of confusion that will ripple throughout their host."

"And if Cheimontyr is fallen, hopefully they will be unable to regroup and chose rather to withdraw."

"So the theory goes."

"So it goes."

"And if not?" Pedraan looked at his brother.

"Then it won't, and we'll still hit them as hard as we can before we fall." Pedraal held Pedraan's eyes. "If things go badly, Brother, I have your back."

"And I have yours," Pedraan answered. "Pedraal?"

"Yes?"

"If it comes down to it, if things don't go well for me but you make it back, take care of Karalin, will you?"

Pedraal nodded. "You know I'll take care of her if need be, but it won't be necessary. You have a lifetime ahead of you to take care of her."

"I hope so."

"She came to you in the night, before the call to assemble at the gate came."

"She did."

"How was she?"

"You know," Pedraan smiled. "She was warm, encouraging, supportive and gentle. She hugged me tight and wished me well."

"She's a steady one," Pedraal said, returning Pedraan's smile. "Whatever did you do to deserve her? You're an idiot."

"No one knows that better than me." Pedraan laughed. "I've never claimed to deserve her and never will, but she loves me all the same."

Pedraal reached over and clapped his brother on the back. "We'll stay together like we always do, and when the day is done, we'll be fine. It's whoever or whatever is waiting out there that should be worried. We may only be men, but we'll show them what men can do on a battlefield."

The horses had all passed by, and Pedraal stepped out from the wall beside the gate and motioned to the officers to follow him out of the city. Shouldering the battle-axe for quick marching, he set out at a slow jog. Pedraan ran beside him, likewise staring at the back of the horsemen drawing away. The road felt good under his feet. They weren't using it to run away, not today.

Pedraal breathed rhythmically, but quicker than normal in his discomfort. He wasn't one for running, whether long distances or short. He did it when he had to, but it never felt natural. His bulky frame was equally ill-suited to riding on a galloping horse, so he preferred to walk. He could walk all day at a good pace without feeling tired. All he had to do was run a hundred spans, though, and he always wished he could stop. Stopping today would mean stopping to fight, but that was all right with him. Nothing in the world felt as natural to him as swinging his battle-axe.

Up ahead, the horsemen and scouts looked as though they had encountered the enemy, though their line was broad and stretched almost as far as he could see in either direction. He could vaguely make out what appeared to be a slight change in pace, a slowing down and perhaps even a staggering of the line. They were still pressing forward, evidence, he hoped, that they were making headway.

"Looks like its time to ready our weapons," Pedraan said, confirming that the battle was joined.

"Looks like it," Pedraal answered, lowering his axe slightly and shifting his grip so he'd be ready to wield it as soon as need arose.

There could be no doubt of it now: The riders were mired in combat. He saw now, here and there, the towering silhouette of a Malekim amid the riders, great curved blades flashing in the dull morning light. He heard the howling of Black Wolves too, and as they drew closer, he could see their sleek black forms darting to and fro, trying to avoid being trampled by the horses' hooves.

Pedraal looked back. A wave of foot soldiers, wider and deeper than the line of horsemen, was sweeping across the plain. Some twenty-five thousand men at least followed them, and they would hit the enemy in a condensed mass. He turned back around, looked for a spot between the horsemen where he could focus, found it, and drove into the seething chaos with his axe held high. A Malekim turned too late to avoid his stroke, and Pedraal drove one side of his axe-head deep into the Malekim's chest. Prying the blade out with a quick pull, he struck again to be sure of the kill, then moved on.

Pedraan came behind him, and for a moment, there was a frenzy of strokes from both the battle-axe and war hammer. Several Black Wolves moved in and out around them, and though the speed of the creatures gave them some difficulty, there wasn't enough room amid the mayhem for the wolves to take full advantage of their superior agility. Pedraan broke several of their backs with the hammer, the crunching of their bones rising above the din even as Pedraal made short work of several others. When the flurry of attacks from the Black Wolves was over, the brothers proceeded, working their way slowly toward the front of the line.

The way grew increasingly difficult. The density of the battle increased, span by span, until there was little more than a logjam of men hewing and hacking against wolves and Malekim, who for their part fought ferociously against the great tide driving at them from the city. In the confined space, Pedraal felt a sword tip slice across his bare shoulder. He whirled with axe held high to defend himself against the counterstroke only to find that he'd been wounded by the follow-through of a horseman facing the other direction. He was about to lower his axe when he saw a Malekim charging laterally at the horseman. Separated from the creature by the horse between them, he watched helplessly as the Silent One brought the horseman down.

Pedraal stooped to avoid being seen as the horse, now riderless, moved off in a random direction through the crowd, and then Pedraal sprang toward the Malekim and drove the battle-axe into his back. The Silent One whirled so sharply the axe-handle was yanked from Pedraal's hand, and he stood facing the creature, weaponless. Even so, just as the Malekim was about to swing with his sword, a horseman rode him down, the great forelegs of the horse striking the Malekim in the head and shoulder as it kicked. Pedraal leapt across the fallen creature and grabbed the axe-handle, pulling it out with a swift jerk. Then, as the creature struggled to get onto its hands and knees, Pedraal dealt it a death-blow to the head.

"That was close," Pedraan said coming up beside him.

"Too close."

"Try to hold onto your weapon, Brother," Pedraan added. "It really makes fighting Malekim so much easier if you do."

"Good advice," Pedraal answered.

They looked around at the battle, furious and bloody and mired down as far as they could see. "You know what's missing?"

"What?"

"Men."

Pedraal suddenly realized he hadn't encountered anything but Malekim and Black Wolves. "That's not good."

"No."

"No Great Bear with us, and our archers with their cyranic arrows on the wall to guard any retreat, and we've struck straight into the heart of the Voiceless. We won't be able to hold on here for long, not without help."

"Probably not."

"I guess we keep going as long as we can."

"I guess so," Pedraan replied, wiping sweat from his brow, "there should be plenty to keep us busy."

"Indeed," Pedraal answered. "Plenty of blood and death, enough even for us."

"Come," Pedraan said, raising his hammer, "the morning is still young, and there is much still to do."

Pedraan plunged ahead, engaging immediately with a great brute of a Black Wolf, his jaws wet with blood. Pedraal came after, feeling the battle frenzy and fever boiling within. It was a feeling hard to recapture in the quiet moments after the battle, let alone weeks or months beyond it, but it was a remarkable mixture of excitement, adrenaline, fear, and passion. It was terrifying and electrifying all at the same time. It was extreme consciousness of the fine line between life and death that a soldier walked in battle. It was, in a sense, the tangible taste of life itself.

Pedraal knew it was past midday. He could not see the sun as it made its way across the sky. He could not see any perceptible shift in the grey clouds and the steady rain that fell upon the bodies of the living and the dead alike, upon man and horse, upon Malekim and wolf. Even so, Pedraal knew it was past midday. They'd been engaged in battle for hours. His aching fingers, struggling to maintain their grip on his battle-axe, told him. His aching legs, weary from the quick footwork required to stay alive in the thick of battle, told him. His aching shoulders, exhausted from wielding his battle-axe faster and more furiously than ever before, told him. Beyond all these physical ailments though, the toll of the day on his mind—the intense awareness of every movement, of every sound and sight, the constant necessity to act first and think and process later—he carried with every step, and these things weighed on him as much as the battle-axe.

Things were not going well. He couldn't see the whole battlefield from where he was, but he didn't need to. The mass of men around him had thinned considerably. It was hard to move in any direction without needing to step on or over the bodies of the dead or dying. It had been ages since they'd moved forward, and he found himself driven backward, step-by-step, slowly retracing in his whirling dance of death the ground covered so easily that morning.

He'd seen many fall, but Pedraan was still with him. They'd survived a tense moment earlier, when a wolf managed to pull Pedraan down and take a bite out of his forearm. Pedraan rolled over on the wolf and grabbed its head with his bare hands and smashed its skull to bits against the death-hardened corpse of a Malekim. The blood from Pedraan's wound had eventually stopped, a messy clot periodically opened by the great swings of his war hammer, but like Pedraal's shoulder gash, it was a wound that could wait.

Suddenly, there in the desolation of that place, a horseman rode into Pedraal's view and the horse reared as the rider fought to keep it under control. Pedraal saw Caan looking down on him, his face grim and hard and his sword, a First-blade, soaked with blood.

"Pedraal," Caan called. "We have to fall back. Without aid, there's nothing more we can do."

"We're committed, fully," Pedraal shouted. "Why not finish what we've started?"

Caan did not answer straight away as he struck wildly at a Black Wolf on the other side of his horse. Pedraal didn't see the blow fall, but he could see the creature drop to the ground below the horse, and Caan spoke while still watching the other direction.

"A good soldier knows when he's lost, Pedraal. Prepare to fall back."

Despite his exhaustion, the command was like a slap in the face. Even as he'd been giving ground, he contested every span, every hand-length the enemy won. To retreat now would be to give it all back. To retreat now would be to surrender, not just the day, but the war. That much, even in his weariness, Pedraal knew. If the Great Bear had failed, as they had failed, they were finished. They were finished. Kirthanin was finished, at least Kirthanin as they knew it was.

"All right," Pedraal said, and the words sounded strange and alien to his ears, as though his body had answered independent of his silent, internal protest.

Caan started to move off but stopped, and Pedraal saw him stand up in his stirrups, looking sideways across the field toward the north. He pointed with his free hand and called to Pedraal. "Look, do you see?"

Pedraal looked, but from his place on the ground, he could see nothing. "No, what?"

"Great Bear," Caan said excitedly. "They're fighting their way from north of the road into the heart of the battle."

Pedraal felt a resurgence of hope. He'd seen what Great Bear could do against Malekim. "How many?"

"I can't see how many," Caan said. "They are worn and dirty, ragged like I've never seen a Great Bear before, I can tell you that."

"Then let's go to them," Pedraal replied, moving north past Caan's horse. Pedraan and Caan came after, and together the three of them fought their way north.

The resurgence of hope Pedraal felt was visible around him. The men on foot and on horseback fought with renewed vigor. He saw more than one man, hard-pressed but a moment before, counterattack with new energy and zeal. He felt the change in himself. He stepped more lively, and the next wolf he encountered he struck so hard he all but cut it in half with a single blow. He hadn't engaged the enemy that hard in hours.

Moving closer to the band of Great Bear, however, some of the optimism began to dissipate. Caan had been right about their appearance. They were haggard in the extreme. Mud and mess and blood in equal measure matted their fur. Several fought with staffs that had been shattered into fragments of their former size and strength, and Pedraal watched as one Great Bear drove the broken end of his staff like a stake into a Black Wolf.

Beyond their shocking appearance, Pedraal was disheartened by the realization that their numbers were few, very few. In the group ahead, there were perhaps a couple hundred, spread out, fighting furiously, drifting steadily cityward as they came. Pedraal evaded a wolf and ran across the open space between him and the nearest Great Bear.

"You're a welcome sight," he said. "What news from your mission?"

"We've failed."

"Failed?"

"Failed. Cheimontyr lives. We've been routed, utterly. We must all fall back to the city. The Bringer of Storms cannot be far behind."

Pedraal stopped and stared, trying to comprehend the words. Caan did not seem fazed, however, and in a moment blew several mighty blasts from the horn that dangled around his neck. Echoing calls from similar horns resounded across the field, and now the Great Bear and men and even Pedraal all moved east, back toward the city, back toward the walls, back toward the gates from which they'd come.

If Pedraal had any idea that moving east would be easier, it wasn't, at least not initially. They had fought their way so far into the mass of Malekim on the plain that trying to get out was as bloody as getting in. Caan drifted off, further north, conversing between violent encounters with some of the other Great Bear. Pedraan was ahead, and his war hammer flashed back and forth, clearing a path through the foes that were surprised by the men and Great Bear coming from behind them. The bulk of the Great Bear were on their left, and they ploughed somewhat more efficiently through the enemy, so much so that the men's course became that much more difficult as Voiceless trying to avoid the surging tide of Great Bear ended up in their path.

So it was that Pedraan found himself in a tenuous place. A handful of Malekim fleeing the fury of the Great Bear spotted

Pedraan wielding his hammer against one of their brethren. Heartened to find him but a man and somewhat isolated, they moved forward in concerted attack.

Pedraal understood immediately the danger his brother was in, and he sprang forward with a burst of energy and speed. Pedraan began swinging the hammer in a crazed and manic fashion to keep them all at bay. When he saw Pedraal approaching with his battle-axe raised over his head, he moved aside and struck an absolutely crushing blow to the Malekim in his way even as Pedraal buried the axe in the back of another. Wrenching the blade free, Pedraal saw Pedraan knocked back by a stiff blow from one of the Silent Ones still on his feet. Horrified, Pedraal saw his brother stumble across a body and fall upon his back. A pair of Malekim between the brothers raised their curved blades to finish Pedraan.

Pedraal struck harder and faster than even he would have imagined possible, and his stroke sunk about halfway into the small of one Malekim's back and sliced all the way from right to left, where the blade emerged again. Pedraal redirected his effort and managed to disable the sword arm of the second Malekim. The first dropped to the ground, but the second was only stunned. Pedraal reared again and drove him down with a furious blow, then pulled free once more and struck the Malekim he had just dropped a moment before.

Neither of them had managed to take a swing at Pedraan, and now both lay dead at his feet. He felt a rush of adrenaline and joy as he looked down at his startled brother, a look of fear and wonder in his eyes, trying with his great war hammer in hand to get up. Pedraal smiled as he looked down and reached out his hand to help Pedraan up.

"That was impressive, even for me," Pedraal said, joking.

No sooner had the words passed his lips when a sudden and excruciating pain ripped into his back. Agony washed over him like a wave crashing on the beach, and he tried to understand what had happened but could not.

Pedraan saw it all, even the Malekim that Pedraal did not. From his seat there on the ground he saw it all with terrible clarity. Pedraal, oblivious to the form of the furious Malekim running toward them, had moved swiftly and successfully to cut down the two Malekim, and for a moment Pedraan thought that maybe his brother would be all right. He'd killed them so quickly that there was still time for him to turn and defend himself, but he never turned. He didn't appear aware at all. Pedraan was frozen, caught between the urge to leap up to defend his brother and the urge to scream for him to turn around. In the end he was unable to do either quickly enough. Pedraal stepped forward, a smile on his face, hand outstretched and a glib remark on his lips, and the Malekim had buried his sword in Pedraal's back.

Pedraan stared now at them both, transfixed by the shock and horror of the scene. Pedraal's eyes remained open, but they were lifeless and empty. They rolled up in his head eerily. His legs buckled and his body began to waver. Had it not been for the sword still stuck in his back, now artificially supporting him, he would have toppled immediately. His great battle-axe wavered in his hand. The death grip was not enough to maintain its hold, and as the fingers slackened, the axe tilted and then tumbled to the ground.

The Malekim, now peering down at Pedraan, cautiously rose to his knees and withdrew the blade. Pedraal fell forward with a thump. Pedraan sprang. He didn't rise and run, he leapt, determination mixing with unabated hatred and fury as he crossed the scant distance between them with the speed and agility of a smaller and younger man. The Malekim was waiting for the attack and swung his great curved blade, hoping to cut Pedraan down mid-lurch. Pedraan, his hands high up the long handle of his war hammer, swung down to block the attack with a short, powerful stroke. He swung with anger, with passion, with desperation, and with complete focus on striking the blade straight on with solid center of his hammerhead. The clang that resulted resounded across the field. Pedraan had intended to knock the sword from the Malekim's hand, but instead, he had broken the blade off in the middle. The shattered blade tip flew shimmering several spans, and the Malekim looked up in disbelief. Pedraan pulled the war hammer in and quickly jabbed straight ahead, punching the Malekim in his exposed chest with the top of the hammer.

The Malekim stumbled back as Pedraan made sure of his footing. There must have been something in his eyes that the Malekim saw, for the Malekim, after steadying himself, started to turn to run away. He didn't get very far.

Pedraan, now sliding his hands down the long handle away from the head, took three steps as he wound up for the killing blow, then swung with as much force as his muscled body could muster. The blow caught the fleeing Malekim right in the side of the head and shattered it with brutal efficiency. The creature swayed sideways and dropped to the ground. Pedraan came up to where he lay and without hesitation struck his fallen body three more times, mangling it almost beyond recognition.

After the last blow, he turned to look at the place where Pedraal had fallen. His brother lay still, face down, the battle raging beyond them, but nothing moved within half a dozen spans of where he lay. It was as if both friend and foe alike had marked the resting place of the deceased and moved elsewhere out of respect. He knew this was not the case, and that the relative quiet that surrounded Pedraal's body would not last, so he jogged to the place where he lay.

He stooped beside him, resting his war hammer on the ground. He took up Pedraal's head and shoulders and cradled him gently in his arms. The skin was still warm to the touch, but his head was limp and lifeless. He took his fingers and brushed closed the eyelids to hide the empty eyes, then bent over to kiss his brow. He whispered as he kissed him, "My brother."

Suddenly he was crouching with his legs bent and his arms gripping Pedraal's body, and with a mighty heave he lifted it. It took a couple tries to get Pedraal settled over his shoulder, but he did, despite the protests of his shoulder and legs, now feeling the weariness of the struggle, and despite the fire from his wounded forearm, which was seeping blood again. Even so, he got Pedraal set and held him tight with his strong arm, preparing to head for the city.

He started to squat so he could take up his war hammer with his free hand. He stopped. The war hammer was lying criss-crossed upon Pedraal's battle-axe, their handles both streaked with the blood that had flowed freely all morning. He looked at them and hesitated, a sudden, vivid image from the distant past rushing over him.

He saw the wide blue sky with great puffy white clouds floating lazily along. He felt the wooden deck of the *Evening Star* under his feet, and he could feel it rise and fall almost imperceptibly above the rolling waves. He saw his brother, only nineteen years old, standing tall and strong with his shirt tied around his waist. Pedraal was holding the battle-axe for the first time. Caan had just given them their "gifts" and instructed them to master these as they headed for the Forbidden Isle. Both weapons were clumsy and awkward in their hands, and the brothers laughed at one another as they practiced the swings and strokes that Caan tried to show them. He was leaning on the handle as the war hammer rested on the deck, and Pedraal was holding his battle-axe lovingly below the great double-blade. He was running his fingers along the side of the blade, feeling the cold smoothness of the steel.

"I will master this," Pedraal said, looking at his brother. "So will you."

"I know."

"Provided we live long enough to have the chance."

"Yes," Pedraan had answered, "provided we do."

The memory slipped away and grey rainy skies replaced the blue. He looked down at the war hammer and battle-axe. *No.*

At first that was the only clear thought in his head, just a no. Even so, it quickly gave way to more. *Too much of my life has been dedicated to that hammer, too much of both of our lives. I don't need it anymore. I don't want it anymore.*

He began to jog across the battlefield, southeast toward the road where it would be easier to keep his footing. It would not be easy to navigate the field with his brother on his back, but he'd make his way. He would make his way, and he would not look back.

Caan looked over his shoulder at the rear guard of riders and Great Bear, trying to protect the retreat of the others. Gilion was with them, directing their movements with crisp efficiency, barking out orders to the scouts and riders to move here or there, keeping order in their retreat.

Caan looked to the moving mass of foot soldiers, pressing ahead of him toward the city. The great gates were open, and many had already passed within. Looking up from the men to the city walls, he thought about the archers waiting for his signal. *Not yet. The enemy is still too far removed.*

It must have been midafternoon already, perhaps Ninth Hour by now. Caan knew they had done well to stay in the field of battle as long as they had, given the loss of Great Bear and the numbers arrayed against them. They had fought so hard and so valiantly, that the word *failure* didn't seem to apply, and yet how else to understand the day? Cheimontyr was alive, the Great Bear were decimated, and an unknown but vast number slain from his own army of men now littered the battlefield. They had struck with all they had, but all they had proved insufficient. Now there could be little doubt that they were finished.

He looked to the sky beyond the approaching Malekim, for a swirling cloud of darkness seemed to be forming in the distance. Lightning began to flash laterally above them, illuminating the clouds. A deafening peal of thunder rumbled in the heavens. The rain stopped, as though the moisture was being sucked back into the clouds, or as if the sudden burst of electrical heat and energy had dried them up. Far away, beyond what Caan could see of the fighting, a single, brilliant flash of lightning fell from the sky.

Cheimontyr was coming. There could be no doubt. The moment Caan had feared since he first learned of the Great Bear's failure was at last upon him. The men who had ridden to the aid of the Vulsutyrim and, more importantly, the Vulsutyrim themselves, would join the battle. They must move faster.

He rode to Gilion, who was not surprised to see him. "You saw it then."

"Yes, how could I miss it?" Caan said.

"He's coming."

"And we have to be going." Caan took Gilion's arm. "I have to give the signal to the wall."

Gilion looked over his shoulder at the city. "We're still too far out."

"Then you have to give the signal to retreat. You've done your best. Give the signal."

For a brief moment their eyes met and Caan held strong, meeting Gilion gaze for gaze. At last, reluctantly, Gilion gave the command. He called out the signal, then gave four quick blasts on his horn, and the men and Great Bear began to disengage.

Caan was already riding toward the city. He lifted his own horn to his lips and blew with all his breath. He pulled to a halt, stood in the stirrups, and waved to the small observation tower upon the wall beside the gate. In answer, a flaming arrow was raised and fired in a great arc over their heads. Caan knew they were gauging the distance to the enemy so they could use their first volley more efficiently. Caan turned to see the men on horseback and the Great Bear coming more swiftly than he had imagined, and behind them a swelling wave of yelping Black Wolves and running Malekim. They sensed the opportunity to turn the retreat into a rout.

At that moment, the whistling sound of a thousand arrows cut through the air, and the sky darkened. Though the riders ducked in their saddles, a few men and horses were struck by the arrows that fell short, and Caan felt a stab of pain inside. He had known when he gave the order that some of his own men might die. The arrows would be cyranic, and any man so pierced, no matter where or how slight, would not survive. Seeing his men slide and fall from their galloping horses, slain by their own countrymen and brothers in arms was difficult to endure. It had been necessary. That alone gave him a modicum of comfort.

For a brief moment, the wave of Malekim and wolves hesitated, giving more separation to the retreating men and Great Bear, which was exactly what the Kirthanim had needed. Caan again blew his horn with a mighty blast, and an instant later, a dozen flaming boulders, hurled by the great catapults of Tol Emuna, flew and came crashing down, some in the space between the army and enemy, where they sat burning brilliantly in the muddy field, some in the midst of the enemy. They landed with a thud and with many howls of pain from the wolves. The separation between the parties grew a little more.

He rode hard for the open gates, now looming large indeed, perhaps fifty spans ahead. Most of the foot soldiers were in, and the riders and Great Bear had caught up to the rear of the column moving on foot. He let the men on horseback move past him, and soon he found himself at the outer extremity of the retreat. The Malekim and Black Wolves were coming more cautiously, the arrows and flaming boulders having unsettled them. And yet the lightning in the sky had not slowed, and from the sound of the rumbling, the Bringer of Storms was drawing closer. Caan didn't know how close he needed to be to strike out at the city walls as he had at Zul Arnoth, but he expected the giant to strike at any moment. He had no idea if getting his army behind the walls would actually give them any protection, but it was all he could do.

At that moment, as though in answer to his fear, great bolts of lightning fell from the sky. They seared the soaking grass, and thick plumes of grey smoke curled up into the sky wherever the soggy ground had been struck. A handful of men on horseback were blown off their steeds and charred instantly. A strike hit the ground only a couple spans away from Caan, and the searing light and heat made his horse rear, throwing him violently to the ground.

He fell with a thud and pulled himself up instantly. The horse bolted, and running after it was not an option. He drew his sword and moved hastily backward with the retreating men.

A second great volley of arrows flew. He was grateful for the restraint of the archers. They were under Carrafin's direction, and the captain had played it well. Rather than firing again while the flaming boulders had made the enemy momentarily immobile and thereby more vulnerable, he had held them off until now, when the lightning strikes inspired their renewed attack. Unleashed now, this second attack would hopefully slow them down again.

It did. He could see many in the black rolling wave of the enemy stumble and fall, and others behind came on more cautiously, looking up to the sky for signs of more danger. They were not disappointed, for the arrows were followed by another volley of the flaming stones, the catapults having been adjusted for the shorter distance. Even so, the stones fell several spans behind the front lines, and Caan knew that they could be adjusted no more. They could not launch effectively over the walls at an enemy this close.

Fortunately, the army was now all but inside. The last remnant of retreating men and Great Bear were passing through the gates now, and Caan ran to join them. Once through the great gate, he signaled to the men with mules on either side who worked the great gearbox to pull it closed. He heard the whistle of arrows again, and he turned to see through the steadily closing gates a flurry of Black Wolves, many brought down by the arrows from above.

With a crash, the gates closed and his view of the outside world disappeared. He moved hastily through the mass of men and Great Bear, doubled over to gasp deep breaths of air. He found Gilion quickly.

"You must ready them for the breaking of the gates. It is the most vulnerable part of the city, and whether the walls hold out against Cheimontyr's power, the gates likely will not. We will be breached."

Gilion nodded and moved away. Caan went to the foot of the stair that led up to the observation tower beside the gate. Though tired and sore, he pressed up the great stair. He was driven by a great need to see what was happening. He knew the enemy was still coming. He knew that among them were the Vulsutyrim and Cheimontyr. He knew it, but he felt drawn to see it.

When he reached the top of the wall, he was stunned by what he saw. The Malekim and Black Wolves had not advanced. If anything, they had dropped back so as not to be such easy targets for the archers and catapults, although both had ceased their firing to save ammunition for the assault. What stunned Caan was how great the army of Malekim and Black Wolves remained. He knew they had slain many, but many more lived. What's more, a great host of men on horseback was moving up the outside of the formation, and behind them moving quickly came the Vulsutyrim. He could see their great forms towering over even the Malekim, moving through their midst. A great dark arm raised the hammer, and the lighting fell. It struck the hammer and a dozen balls of light shot out over the heads of the Voiceless into the open field between the city and the army, making the weary ground smolder even more.

Caan squeezed between two archers and looked out over the wall. Thunder rumbled incessantly in the sky, and the flashing of light within the clouds was spectacular. He looked beyond the gathered army, with one last whim of hope that perhaps the golden forms of dragons would be visible on the horizon, but he found nothing. He looked back down in despair.

Cheimontyr made his way all the way up to the front and stood there with a guard of Vulsutyrim holding great wooden shields. Caan imagined they were to block any aerial attacks that might come from the city. Caan held his breath, waiting for the hammer to rise and the brilliant blasts of power to streak across the intervening space and crash into their walls. He waited, but it didn't come. Nothing came. In fact, the swirling clouds began to settle down, the thunder quieted, and the flashes of lightning ceased. Inexplicably, after standing and gazing at the city for a few long moments, Cheimontyr turned and walked away. The Vulsutyrim followed, and soon thereafter, so did the men, Malekim, and Black Wolves.

The rain began to fall in a steady drizzle. Caan looked down from the walls in relief and disbelief, both in equal measure. After a moment, he turned and headed back down the stair.

8

THE HAND OF

ALLFATHER

THE ZAROS MOUNTAINS loomed larger day by day until at last it was clear that today the party would reach them. Aljeron did not understand just where this secret passage into the mountain began, so he was eager to see the mystery of this place long kept by the watchful guards of the Kalin Seir.

As the Kalin Seir and snow leopards slowed from their run to a walk, and as the walking slowed to a leisurely pace, Aljeron realized that somewhere up ahead, the mass of Kalin Seir and their battle brothers must be funneling through an entrance of some sort, for nothing had slowed them yet on this journey, and Aljeron did not believe anything short of an actual physical barrier could have done so.

Naran was close by, and he approached Aljeron and Valzaan and the others. "We're there, and in good time. The war party has moved quickly. We should all be inside by nightfall."

They had been running through a canyon that narrowed and deepened at the same time. On either side were snow covered rocky ascents in patches, and Aljeron was glad they weren't going to have to try to scale any of those. And yet, as he looked ahead over the crowd of Kalin Seir, he could see that they were still some distance from the place where the canyon must enter the mountain.

"Naran, it doesn't look as though the front of the column has actually reached the mountain yet, but we've slowed. What's going on? Is there some impediment ahead?"

"Yes and no," Naran replied. "What you cannot see yet is a steep ravine that crosses this canyon. This ravine is so narrow on our right that you could leap across it, and yet as it runs closer to the mountain, it widens. At the base of that ravine, a pathway leads into the mountain, and those at the front of the war party are already descending."

"Ravine," said Evrim, looking none too happy, memories of Harak Andunin no doubt returning. "That doesn't sound like fun."

"How far to the bottom?" Saegan asked.

"It is a long way down," Naran answered. "A narrow path leads down from the top, and this is the way some of our people and all of our battle brothers will descend. It is a difficult path and steep, but take your time and you will be all right."

"Some of our people?" Aljeron said. "What about the others?"

"They will go down a more direct way."

"What way?"

"They will descend by rope, straight down the side of the ravine. It takes but a moment if you know what you're doing."

Aljeron, who had no great love of heights, was inwardly relieved that it would be natural for him to go with Koshti, who could not take this other way. "I will stick with Koshti on the narrow path."

THE HAND OF ALLFATHER 385

"I'll come with you," Evrim said. "I may have made it up Harak Andunin with only one arm, but this rope-into-the-ravine business sounds out of my reach."

"I also will come with you down the path," Valzaan said. "I am old enough to appreciate the value of keeping my feet squarely on the ground and keeping the ground squarely under my feet."

"How narrow is the path?" Erigan asked Naran.

"Narrow, but I think you will be fine," Naran answered. "I have watched you move and know you are nimble, despite your size."

"I guess that leaves just me to try the rope," Saegan said, looking at the others, who looked a back at him with mild surprise.

"Are you sure?" Aljeron asked. "Not going to stick with us?"

"I'll see you at the bottom," Saegan said, adding wryly, "whenever you get down there. The rope sounds like too much fun to pass up."

When at last they had progressed far enough to see the ravine, each peered over the side into the darkness. Far down, indeed farther than they had anticipated, they saw the red-haired heads of the Kalin Seir moving along the bottom toward the base of the mountain. Nearby, a half dozen ropes were firmly tied to great rocks. A Kalin Seir stood by each rope, looking down after the men and women descending, bouncing off the ravine wall with their feet and gliding down the rope as they let it slip between their tough and leathery hands.

"Ouch," Evrim said. "Even if I had both my arms, I'm not sure I'd want to try that. Looks like a sure way to get a severe case of rope burn."

"Ah, it doesn't look that bad," Saegan answered. "Watch."

He walked up to one of the Kalin Seir who was monitoring the ropes, and after getting a pointer on how to hold the rope and go over the side of the ravine, he dropped over the edge. They watched as he nimbly descended, apparently every bit as comfortably as the Kalin Seir. He was quickly lost in the shadows of the base of the ravine. The others turned away, following the line of Kalin Seir and snow leopards who were setting off down the narrow path.

The path was steep, but Aljeron found it not so difficult as to be worrisome. He kept his eye on Koshti, though, watching carefully where the tiger chose to set his feet. He had found, over the years, his battle brother to be a nearly infallible guide when it came to finding sure footing. In the end, all of them arrived at the floor of the ravine, safe and sound.

The narrow floor was just wide enough for two to walk side by side uncomfortably, so they did not move quickly. They walked in silence, and Aljeron peered up at the impressive view. The walls of the ravine ran upward, on and on, so far it was hard to fathom what force could have cracked rock like this so deep into the ground. The sky was visible above the surface of the ravine, as though someone had taken a grey paintbrush and made a jagged streak across a black canvas. Behind him the streak was very narrow, but before him, the streak widened.

After a few moments, they came upon the place where the ropes dangled all the way to the ground, and Aljeron saw that as above, Kalin Seir manned each of them, helping those descending to gauge the distance to the bottom through the darkness and dismount safely. Men dropped from the ropes as though falling from the sky and merged with the men and leopards already on the floor. Not far ahead, Saegan leaned against the ravine wall beside the river of Kalin Seir, grinning as they approached.

"You were right, Evrim," he said as they drew near. Holding out his hand, they could see a nasty looking red mark across his palms.

"Looks painful."

"It stings a little."

"Was it worth it?" Aljeron asked, frowning.

"You better believe it," Saegan answered without hesitation. "I'd go back up and do it again if there were time."

Aljeron rolled his eyes and shook his head. "That would be great. You could lacerate both hands even more and be totally useless with your sword when we get into battle."

"Don't you worry about me," Saegan said, a little testily. "I'll match you stroke for stroke, or anyone else in this army for that matter."

"Enough, you two," Valzaan said, like a father breaking up a pair of quarrelsome brothers. "You weary my ears with your nonsense. We're all down here now, regardless of how we got here. Let's move on."

Aljeron noticed that though the ravine had widened to accommodate perhaps four men abreast, the visible streak of sky was beginning to narrow again. After twenty or thirty spans, it closed to all but the thinnest sliver of light, and then disappeared entirely.

"Does anyone else, knowing that Malek dwelt for so many years under Agia Muldonai, find it a bit creepy to be going into the mountain like this?"

"We are going into a mountain," Valzaan said, "not the Mountain. There is a big difference. Malek's abode was hundreds of leagues west of here."

"Even so, it feels strange," Aljeron said. "This is the same mountain range."

"True," Evrim echoed. "Now that you mention it, it does feel a bit odd to be passing into one of these mountains."

"I don't suppose it would even matter if we were passing through Malek's domain," Saegan said. "Surely those halls and tunnels are even emptier than these are likely to be, now that he has loosed his army upon the world."

The darkness deepened as the open sky fell farther and farther behind. The Kalin Seir produced torches, burning brightly and casting their shadows against the dim walls of the ravine, which had now become a cave. As Aljeron looked up, he fancied the roof wasn't quite so far above him, and he wondered how far down it would come and how tight the walls would get.

"The last time I traveled far down below the earth was on the Forbidden Isle, and that is not a pleasant association."

"Shh," Valzaan said firmly. "You should not mention that here, even if the memories come to mind unbidden."

"Why not?"

"Our credibility was hard enough to establish with the Kalin Seir, just because some of you wear swords. I'd rather not give them another reason to suspect that we are not who we say we are."

"The story would be easily enough explained, and we could surely not be doubted, now that Sulmandir has come."

"Maybe, but I'd rather not have to explain it, so do as I ask and speak no more about it."

They caught up to Naran, who was a little bit ahead of them. They joined him and continued deeper into the mountain.

The tunnel widened as they progressed, so that there was room for perhaps ten abreast, and soon they were moving as a column once again. They jogged along the essentially smooth stone floor, which was hard under their feet after the damp, springy turf of the open plain. It felt good to have truly solid ground underfoot at the moment, but Aljeron knew that if their journey through the mountain required too many days of running on stone, he would soon miss the softness under his feet. In any case, he knew he would miss the increasing warmth of spring upon the land, for the farther into the mountain they went, the cooler the air felt upon his exposed cheeks and hands.

Despite the absence of natural light, the torches pushed back the darkness. The walls were grey and rusty red, and they rose many spans on either side. The roof was also illuminated by the plentiful light, rising and falling irregularly so that at times it seemed no more than two and a half to three spans above them, and at other times perhaps four or even five spans up.

Aljeron had not seen any other tunnels or passageways since passing inside the mountain. Once in through the entrance at the bottom of the ravine, there was but one way to go. He wondered about the first Kalin Seir to come here and about how they had discovered the entrance at the bottom of the ravine. Had they gone looking for a way into the mountain? Had it been by chance? Had they climbed down or survived a fall into the ravine? Once in, had they gone forward, deeper and deeper, alone in the dark looking for who knew what? It was eerie enough for him to be in this place with many others and with the assurance that eventually the way led to the southern side of the Zaros Mountains. He couldn't imagine making this journey when the way was unknown and the darkness deep and deepening on every side.

"Valzaan?" he asked of the prophet, jogging along beside him.

"Yes?"

"You've never been inside this place?"

"Never," he answered, face straight ahead. "Had I been in here before, I almost certainly would have found the Kalin Seir or been found by them."

"True," Aljeron agreed, feeling silly now for asking an obvious question.

"And yet," Valzaan continued. "I have sojourned in the Zaros Mountains and into Nolthanin in this general area before. Perhaps I have passed not far from Kalin Seir but never known it. Maybe I have even been seen by the grandfathers or great-great grandfathers of these who run beside us, who knows?

"No, I have never passed this way before, and though I have not passed below the Zaros Mountains until now, I have passed through many of the deep places of the earth and sea."

"Like the struggle with the Kumatin that took you into the great deep?" Aljeron asked, wondering not for the first time what adventures Valzaan's long years contained.

"Both like and unlike that," Valzaan replied, "but I would not speak of that now, for the mention of that name reminds me that the creature still inhabits the flood-swollen rivers of Kirthanin. I may yet have to face him again."

They jogged on, and Aljeron, his mind awakened by many questions that swirled around in his head as they ran, continued. "Do you think that perhaps Malek made these tunnels as he made the tunnels under Agia Muldonai?"

"He did not make the tunnels under Agia Muldonai, at least he did not make all of them. The springs that flowed up out of the deep to feed the Crystal Fountain in Avalione, the springs that burst forth at the bidding of Allfather, they created some of the tunnels beneath the Mountain. Others were there, already empty, from the very beginning. From early on in the First Age, Malek would venture into those tunnels, and it is there beneath the Mountain that he erected his first forge. It is also there that he became, of all the Titans, the master maker and craftsman, and it is likely there that he first bent metal to his ill-conceived purposes. Of course, much of his work for the Nolthanim was undoubtedly carried out at the forge you saw by the Great Northern Sea, far from the watchful eyes or sleeping suspicions of his brethren.

"The tunnels under the Mountain he did not make, but he made them deeper and expanded them in many directions to house the remnant of the Nolthanim, along with the Vulsutyrim and his new creations. Those tunnels must be labyrinthine, stretching farther than we can begin to imagine both down and out, perhaps well beyond the actual breadth of the Mountain itself. Perhaps one day, when Malek has been defeated, the Mountain cleansed and Kirthanin restored, perhaps then some will venture down into his old hiding place. Then we will know the extensiveness of his hidden home.

"These tunnels may be as unknown to Malek as they were to me. Who can say what Malek has or has not discovered about the secret ways beneath the earth? Even so, I would venture a guess that he did not make them."

"Then have they always been here?"

"Always?" Valzaan asked. "No, not always, for they have been here at the most since Allfather spoke the world into being, and the world has not always been here either. And yet, it could be that when Allfather made the world, this place was formed at the same time. In fact, I wouldn't doubt that there are many places like this one, relatively unchanged since the beginning of the world."

"The enormity of this place reminds me of how small I am," Aljeron said after a moment of reflection. "So much lies beneath this single mountain, and yet this is only a fragment of the whole range, which is only one little piece of Kirthanin. The vastness of the world is overwhelming, and yet Allfather created all of it, giving it shape and form and creating life. It is too much for me to comprehend."

"To stand in awe of He who made both the world and you is a good and right thing to do."

"I should probably do it more often," Aljeron conceded.

"There are many things we should all do more often," Valzaan replied. "For now, simply take stock of the truth you have rediscovered rather than letting it pass away as you bemoan the fact that you needed to rediscover it."

Their conversation ended abruptly as the tunnel also ended, opening suddenly into a great wide cavern. The cavern was spectacular for many reasons beyond its enormity.

The first thing that stood out to Aljeron was that it was brightly lit and there were people gathered in the cave waiting for them. The Kalin Seir who had reached this place ahead of Aljeron and his companions stood catching their breath before this small assembly, who clearly were not part of their war party, for they carried no packs or torches and wore warmer cloaks and a different kind of shoe, thicker soled and lined with some kind of fur.

The second thing that stood out to Aljeron was the existence of perhaps a dozen buildings in the cavern, most of them grouped around a central open area like a village surrounding its central square. Torches on tall slender poles burned all around the buildings and open area, and as Aljeron came to a halt and took a deep breath, Naran drew closer.

"We will stop here for tonight."

"Good," Evrim replied. "It seems like an ideal place to get some rest."

"It is, and it is the last such place we will encounter between here and the enemy. I would guess that already messengers have been dispatched to gather up all of my people who dwell here. They will join us, bringing whatever food and weapons they have with them."

"No one will be left to watch and protect this place?"

"This place has long been watched and protected because we believed that one day it might serve precisely this purpose. Now that this day has come, we have no reason to watch any longer. If we are successful and the enemy falls, there will be no one left to harm this place or our home north of the mountains. If we fail, then we will not return this way again, and our home will lie vulnerable to the enemy whether he goes under the mountains or over them."

"So they will all join us," Aljeron said, half to himself as he looked again at the cluster of Kalin Seir.

"They will."

"This place looks pretty comfortable," Saegan said. "It's impressive."

"Yes," Naran answered, smiling. "It has come a long way over the years. I am told that the first outpost sent here had little more than straw mattresses and a fire ring. Now we have houses and buildings for storage, and running water has been diverted from elsewhere beneath the mountain into a large cistern that stays full of clean, cool water year round. When the elders send out a new company to take up this post each summer, there is no grumbling, for life in the mountain is good."

Aljeron leaned over to Evrim and whispered. "Surely he can't really mean 'no grumbling,' can he? Every order to leave home we've ever given has always been accompanied by at least some grumbling, right?"

"Indeed," Evrim said, then added, also whispering. "Maybe the Kalin Seir like their elders more than your men liked you."

Aljeron laughed. "I shouldn't doubt it."

It soon became apparent that their evening meal was to be a big affair. Since the outpost was being abandoned and it was not convenient to take all the supplies with them, there was much that would need to be consumed or go to waste, and there were plenty willing to do the consuming. So, those Kalin Seir who had been stationed inside the mountain started preparing for a feast.

Meanwhile, many of those who had been in the war party set up an impromptu competition in archery and spear throwing. From what Aljeron could see, the object of the competition was simple. One of the Kalin Seir would shoot or throw his spear into the large wooden wall of one of the larger buildings, and the others would compete to see who could put their arrow or spear closest to it. They started out at distances that seemed not too difficult to Aljeron, but quickly the competition moved farther back, and Aljeron was greatly impressed by their accuracy.

He was also greatly impressed that with both bow and spear, Keila was clearly one of the better competitors. As the pool of participants was gradually whittled away by a mutually agreed upon but varying rate that Aljeron did not fully understand, Keila remained among the half dozen or so left. What was at stake in the contest, if anything beyond honor and pride, Aljeron couldn't tell, but the remaining Kalin Seir competed with intensity.

Whatever went to the winner, Aljeron never did see, for Keila was eliminated after a few more rounds, and while the last three contestants pursued victory, she stalked off from the assembled crowd of onlookers. Aljeron followed her.

He came upon her, sitting by herself on a bench at the outskirts of the little grouping of houses, on the side where long tables, covered with food, were being prepared for the feast. He walked over to where she was sitting but did not join her on the bench.

"You did well," he said. "I was very impressed."

Keila looked up, but Aljeron could tell right away that she wasn't glad to see him. A look that he thought might be anger flashed through her eyes as she rose from the bench, nodded slightly in acknowledgement of his compliment, and then turned and walked away.

Aljeron did not follow her this time but looked after her for a moment baffled, wondering if he had somehow offended her by congratulating her despite her defeat. After a moment he rejoined the others, who were spending the time before the feast resting their weary feet and talking of many things, none of them serious.

The feast was as good or better than Aljeron had imagined it would be, and when they were finished at last, he curled up on the dry but hard floor not far from one of the fires that were scattered throughout the big cavern. He had gathered enough information during the feast to know the next day would be long. They had a fair distance still to go through a series of increasingly narrow tunnels. Then, once they reached the outside, they would be a third of the way up a mountain pass, and they would need the rest of the day on into evening to traverse it to the plains south of the Zaros Mountains. In order to get down to level ground by nightfall, they would need to set out before sunrise. The time they set out didn't make any difference in terms of the light they would have to travel by, not in here, but it made a difference in that they wouldn't get a full night's sleep. So Aljeron tossed and turned, wanting to go to sleep but frustrated that he couldn't. Eventually, the crackling of the warm fire and his full belly won out over his anxious mind and the hard floor, and he drifted off at last.

As Aljeron slept, he dreamed of his home in Shalin Bel, the cozy fire and large soft bed in his sitting room. He dreamed of his windows open on a warm summer's night and bright stars twinkling high in the darkness. He dreamed of laughing voices floating in the open windows from the city, and he knew a celebration of some kind was spilling out of the homes and inns into the streets. *Perhaps it is over, this interminable war. Perhaps there is peace once more, peace forever.*

A hand shook him stiffly, and he opened his eyes to see Saegan crouched beside him in the relative dark. It took a moment, but he remembered where he was and quietly rose at once to his feet. Valzaan and Evrim were already up, as were Erigan and Koshti. The Kalin Seir talked softly among themselves, and in a moment, the head of the column started forward, leaving the cavern by a smaller entryway then the one they had entered the previous day. Before long, the motion of the column as a whole had rippled back to the place where he and the others stood, and reluctantly, Aljeron felt his feet step forward with the rest. After their long run from the home of the Kalin Seir, he had enjoyed their brief reprieve.

The tunnels through which they ran did grow steadily narrower, as Aljeron had gathered they would, and they also rose gradually so that they ran at an incline most of the morning, except for in rare places where the ground leveled out for a space before tilting up once more. The pace of the Kalin Seir war party slowed bit by bit, more from the increasingly compressed quarters than from the upward bent of their road. The column thinned from half a dozen abreast to half that number, and for a time Aljeron and Koshti ran behind Erigan alone, who on all fours was wide enough to preclude anyone else from running comfortably beside him.

Even so, they never came to a complete halt, and for hours they ran with no variation to the scenery. On occasion they passed small alcoves, whether there by nature or carved from the rock by the Kalin Seir, Aljeron couldn't tell, though their walls seemed smooth enough. What he did not note, not anywhere along the long passage upward, was anything even remotely like a side tunnel leading in a different direction. He couldn't believe that from the depth of the narrow ravine north of the mountain, all the way through and up to the pass on the southern side, the way was unvarying, and yet he had seen no evidence to suggest otherwise.

The farther up they went, the more the narrow tunnel seemed to curve and wind, until at last it became somewhat challenging to follow the light of the nearest torch, which always seemed to be appearing for a moment only to disappear around the next bend. Aljeron cursed the intermittent darkness under his breath and began to hunger actively for even the gloomy light of the cloud-filled sky.

When they emerged from this dark tunnel, they would be in Enthanin, out of Nolthanin at last. Despite the difficult days that might lie ahead, it was hard not to be excited at the thought. His mind wandered back over the spring and winter, through the rough terrain and constant snowfall, all the way back to the day they'd landed on the ancient quay of Avram Gol. He thought of young Tornan and Karras, the soldiers they'd rescued from the charred remains of Col Marena only to lose along the way; of Arintol, likely still buried beneath the snow where they laid him after he fell to the Vulsutyrim. He thought of the traitors Synoki and Cinjan, one of which had received what he deserved and the other who would in time. Oh yes, Synoki would be made to pay for his long history of deceit and destruction.

He thought of the Red Ravens and the Snow Serpent, creatures that had been so real when he encountered them but now seemed at a distance like impossible creatures of myth, though Evrim's lost arm testified to their existing in fact. He thought of the endless snowfields, of Andunin's vast white plateau, the great Water Stone in the midst of it, the freezing cold waters of the Great Northern Sea and the blessed sight of the Tajira Mountains and Harak Andunin itself. All these memories blurred together, the recollection but a few fleeting moments now, though at the time they had seemed to be the fabric of a nightmare woven of numberless days and nights spent in cold dampness far from home and bereft of hope.

They'd come through. He and Saegan and Evrim, even with his wound, along with Erigan and Koshti. They'd even picked up Valzaan, whose return was in itself as welcome as their successful expedition to Sulmandir's gyre. They had survived and passed south all the way to the border of Enthanin, but three days shy of Midspring, though any thought of the seasonal feast and Mound rite had been as far from him as the memories of life before Nolthanin. Now that he expected to emerge imminently into the world below the mountains, below the wild and forgotten lands of the north, consciousness of how far into Full Spring they had already come sprang unbidden into his mind.

What was going on in Tol Emuna? Was the city besieged already? If so, did it still stand? Was there anywhere in Kirthanin where the children looked forward to the feast of Midspring with hope and enthusiasm rather than fear? Maybe not this year, but there would be again. He had dreamed of celebration in the night, and of peace, and he pressed on harder in the hope that he ran toward the fulfillment of that dream.

It wasn't long after these thoughts raced through Aljeron's head that the party emerged, suddenly and unexpectedly, through a narrow opening onto the side of the mountain. The top of the tunnel dipped down so that Aljeron had to bend over and Erigan had to more or less squeeze under it, out through a hanging tapestry of white that blended perfectly with the year-round snow, concealing the entrance from any prying eye. Had anyone been watching that day, though, they would have been amazed as both men and animals came pouring out of what seemed to be the snowy side of the mountain. They poured out into the open air, paused to breathe deeply of its freshness, and then plunged onward, making their way steadily down the pass through the shallow snow that clung to the cold decline.

However, one cluster that emerged out of the mountain did not go on immediately. When Saegan and Evrim had come through the mountain after him, Aljeron turned and looked at them, seeing in their eyes the excitement that he felt inside.

"We made it," he said, smiling, and he held out his arms to them, embracing both firmly and warmly.

Tears were in Evrim's eyes as he clung to Aljeron with his only hand, and Saegan stood silently, just nodding over and over.

"I didn't think I'd live to see this," Evrim said. "I can't believe we made it back."

"You have done well, all of you," Valzaan said, approaching the men. He placed a wrinkled but strong hand on Aljeron's shoulder. "You especially, Aljeron, for you did what I asked of you upon the shore of the Bay of Thalasee, even though it must have seemed to you at times as though it would have been better to head south with your men."

"At times," Aljeron said, laughing now to look back at the frequency of that very thought.

"Your mission was not without cost," Valzaan continued. "But it has also been more successful than either of us could have envisioned. Sulmandir has awakened, and a lost remnant of the Nolthanim has been found. Both have journeyed south with us to join the war against Malek. Now let us not lose heart, for difficult days still lie before us and there is much left for us to do."

With that the prophet took a long stride into the soft snow, which lay little more than ankle deep in the pass now that a few hundred Kalin Seir had passed through it. The wild white hair of the ancient seer fluttered behind him. Aljeron and the others ran after him, glad to feel real wind upon their faces and to be pointed downhill at last.

As he ran, Aljeron turned his face upward to drink in the natural light. Even the lesser light of the cloud-filtered rays seemed brighter when reflected upon the snowy mountainside, but looking up to the clouds directly relieved his eyes from the glare. How fine and delicate his eyes were! He thought of the frustration he had felt running in the near dark not an hour before and compared it to the difficulty of taking in the unbroken whiteness of the daylight as they ran down the mountain.

Looking up to the sky to provide even momentary relief from the landscape was not long sustainable. The ground underfoot fell away in places, and running down the pass was at times treacherous. *Running* was perhaps a generous word for what they were doing, for in places it was more like sliding and jumping, as they slid through the snow only to leap forward when the slide came to an end. A few times Aljeron would slip and skid down on his backside for a span or more before his momentum carried him back up to his feet, and he would have felt awkward about this had it not been happening with regularity among the Kalin Seir. Only Koshti and the snow leopards seemed able to maintain their footing as they ran, for even Erigan lost his balance from time to time and skid along with the rest of them.

In this way they ran and leapt and tumbled down the mountain. Aljeron felt a rush of energy and excitement he hadn't felt in ages. It was being out of Nolthanin. It was moving downhill through the snow. It was thinking of returning to his men and rejoining the main campaign of the war against Malek. It was the realization that if she was out there waiting, he might just live to see Aelwyn again after all.

A vision of her came to him there in the snow, there on the mountain. It seemed like so long ago that he'd bid her farewell. He could see her now, standing elegant and lovely upon the ship's deck as he prepared to disembark with the others. He could see her leaning on the side of the ship, waving slowly and fondly as they rowed away. Now every step down the mountain brought him closer to her, and he ran on with renewed zeal and vigor.

Not long before sunset they reached the bottom, more or less, having emerged below the snowy portions of the pass some time before. They kept going until they put a little distance between themselves and the base of the mountain. There they made camp for the night. Despite the exhilaration of the downhill run, Aljeron felt the weariness of the day. He was glad to sit down and enjoy the warmth of the fire.

Evrim sat beside him, and Aljeron leaned over and whispered, "Think much of Kyril today?"

"All the way down the mountain."

Aljeron nodded. "I thought so."

"And you," Evrim started, "thoughts of Aelwyn?"

"Absolutely. She's become more like home to me than home itself."

Evrim smiled, and they sat in quiet as the darkness deepened.

"How far to Tol Emuna?" Erigan asked Valzaan.

"A few days," Valzaan answered, leaning over to Saegan. "Wouldn't you say?"

"This close to the mountains, I can't know exactly where we are," Saegan answered. "When we move off a little way tomorrow, I'll have a better idea. But yes, I'd guess that at our current pace, we could reach the city by Midspring or the day after."

"Have you seen the city?" Aljeron asked Valzaan. He hadn't asked before, because he figured Valzaan would tell them anything they needed to know. But being on this side of the Zaros Mountains at last, he couldn't resist any longer.

"Yes," Valzaan answered after a moment of hesitation. "As we ran down the mountain today, I found a windhover near the city."

"Well?" each of the other men said more or less together when the prophet did not continue.

"A vast host is already encamped a short distance from the front gate, though all have not yet arrived. From what I could see, I would guess that the numbers would only swell through the night."

There was silence from the others, and Aljeron had a sudden vision of what a vast host swelling might mean.

"We'll need to tell Naran and the Kalin Seir," Saegan said after a moment, hiding any anxiety he might be feeling about the fate of his home and about being cut off from it now by Malek's army.

"Yes, I know," Valzaan said, sighing. "I was just going to warm up for a few moments first."

"Was there anything else, Valzaan?" Aljeron asked, for when he looked carefully at the prophet's face, he had the distinct impression there was more.

"An ambush of Great Bear is lying in wait north of the main road leading to the gate, some distance from the city, watching the late arrivals come."

"An ambush?"

"Why?" Evrim started, "What hope can there be in that?"

"I don't know what they have planned," Valzaan replied. "I can only tell you what I have seen: several thousand Great Bear lying in the fading light of evening, waiting for something. For what exactly, I couldn't say."

Aljeron scratched his head. "With Caan and Gilion, and officers from several armies, not to mention Sarneth and elders of the Great Bear, we have to trust that there is a good reason for what they're doing, even if we don't see it."

"Indeed," Valzaan said, rising to his feet, "we have little choice."

Aljeron passed a restless night. Gone were the dreams of Shalin Bel, celebration, and peace. Instead a series of passing images, disjointed and discomforting, disturbed his slumber. He dreamed he was tumbling down the mountain, really tumbling, falling head first and being bounced and battered by the hard rock beneath the snow. He dreamed he was standing at a distance from Tol Emuna, a great and innumerable host between himself and the city. He dreamed that he was on horseback on the Andunin Plateau, riding into a snowscape that stretched as far as his eye could see, and when he turned to see if the others were following, he found that he was alone.

Waking in the dim, dusky light of early morning was a relief, even if he felt sore from the previous day's run. A light rain was falling, and he groaned at the memory of all the rain and snow they had endured. He hoped this was not anything more than a normal shower, though a normal rainfall was almost a distant memory. He rolled over and rose immediately to his knees, arrested by what he saw.

Valzaan was prostrate on the ground, his face in the grass and his hands pressing his thick white hair to his head. His body was tense and seemed to Aljeron contorted. He hesitated for a moment, unsure whether to go to him.

"Valzaan?" he asked, starting to rise to his feet.

Valzaan didn't answer, but his head jerked up. His blank white eyes were wide and staring, and Aljeron was a little unnerved. Valzaan raised his right hand high above his head as he stood.

By this point, the attention of the others as well as a few nearby Kalin Seir had been drawn to the curious scene. "Valzaan, what is it?"

"I have had a vision," Valzaan replied.

"Of what?"

"I saw thick darkness and a furious storm. Lightning rippled through the heavens and passed between the earth and sky. Cheimontyr was there, his countenance furious beyond all description. Power rippled through him. Lightning flew from his hand and everything I saw was lost in the blazing whiteness of the strike.

"A voice, the voice of Allfather, spoke into the dazzling whiteness, and this is what He said.

" 'The battle for Tol Emuna is engaged. The Great Bear are moving to strike down Cheimontyr, and they will fail. His fury will be awakened and directed at the city. He will move to destroy it before the day is over and will succeed unless I hold back his hand and preserve the city.

" 'This I will do by the means I will make known to you, but you must understand what is happening, that you may testify to my work on the city's behalf. The assembly of dragons under Sulmandir has been delayed in coming by my own hand, that it may be clear to you that the city's salvation this day is from my hand and my hand alone. Know this and speak it.

" 'Cheimontyr will not fall today, because his time has not yet come. His power, the power he was granted by Malek, power granted to Malek at the hour of his creation by me, is sufficient to destroy the walls of Tol Emuna. However, if you hold your right hand above your head until the light of day has passed, I will hold back his hand and avert his wrath and spare the city. He will not attack, and those within the city will not be overrun.

" 'This is to be a sign to you and to the Kalin Seir and to those within the city who survive until you come, that you and they may know what has saved them. I am present and active, I reign over all, and I have not abandoned nor forsaken you. This is to be a sign to be remembered forever, for on this day I will save the city, and you will know that I am greater than him whom you fear and must face.' "

Valzaan stood, his right hand still high above his head. Aljeron and the small circle that surrounded him just stared.

"What should we do?" Aljeron asked after a moment, awkwardly.

"Run beside me, for we must run. Allfather has promised to spare the city from Cheimontyr, but that doesn't mean that the battle will end well for our friends. We must run, and you and Saegan must run with me. Take turns helping to hold my hand high when I grow weary, for it will be a long day and I'm going to need help."

It didn't take long for word of Valzaan's vision and prophecy to spread through the camp, and Valzaan was brought to the front to run with the leaders of the war party at the head of the column. They ran all morning and through lunch and on into the afternoon, not resting or slowing in their pace. Aljeron and Saegan ran beside Valzaan, taking turns holding his right hand high above his head. Aljeron ran and helped until his own arm felt too weary to lift above his waist, but he did what had to be done and gladly rested every time Saegan took over. The stints they both took helping Valzaan grew increasingly shorter, and the changing of positions more frequent as the day passed.

They kept running, south and east, their eyes ahead but their thoughts behind as they waited for the sun to set. They cursed inwardly the lengthening days of Full Spring and for once in their journey craved the coming darkness. It came at last and they slowed their pace, stopping at long last to rest.

When the darkness was complete and nightfall undeniable, Aljeron let go of Valzaan's hand, and the prophet lowered it gingerly, his old joints cracking. Many surrounded him, waiting for a word.

"Is the city all right?" Saegan asked finally. "Can you see?"

"The city is all right. Cheimontyr has turned away. It will not fall tonight."

They breathed a collective sigh of relief, but Valzaan continued. "The walls stand, but the army is defeated and most of the Great Bear slain. Another battle like today's will be unthinkable. They cannot take the field again against Malek's hosts, and they know it."

9

AN ULTIMATUM

AELWYN PAUSED TO wipe her hands on the apron she wore, though there wasn't really much apron left that wasn't already drenched with the blood of the wounded. She looked around her at the volunteer men and women moving among the bodies, arranged as carefully on the floor as time and the hecticness of the day allowed. Most of the injured soldiers still in the room were alive, since they tried to remove the dead quickly, mostly for the morale of the wounded but also for the morale of the workers. It was their goal, all those volunteering here, to try to bring relief into the midst of so much anguish, both physical and emotional. The mayhem had subsided a bit, as the closing of the gates had slowed the influx of new patients. But she knew that for every wounded man within, there were more out there on the field, where no help could reach them or provide comfort during the creeping hours of this long, dark night.

She took a deep breath and gathered herself. She had no idea what time it was or how long she had been at this. Early in the day, the first trickle of wounded men began to flow into the city. She and the others were prepared, for they had secured space from the city council, clearing out large rooms in buildings near the gate that were on the first floor and easily accessed. They had gone throughout the city and collected cloths and towels, and many boys too young to fight but old enough to wish they could volunteered to bring water to each of the collection points.

Early on, the flow of patients was manageable. Many women had traveled, some of them all the way from Shalin Bel, though many had been added at Col Marena and Amaan Sul, to be here just for this reason. Of course, many women of Tol Emuna also silently joined them, simply coming alongside. These were accepted with gratitude, and there was little need for overt organization, as all seemed intuitively to observe what needed to be done and do it.

The task had not remained manageable for long, however, for as the day progressed and the frontline of the fight had receded, the number of wounded that returned to the city grew exponentially. They flooded in faster than they could be attended to, and before long all the prepared places were full and men were being laid in the streets and alleyways around these places for blocks. More and more people in Tol Emuna were pulled into the extensive task of caring for them. The towels and cloths were used up and the collected water ran out, and now men, women, and children moved frantically through the streets, getting whatever supplies they could. Aelwyn heard that a local seamstress and dressmaker had opened her shop and began doling out strips of linen for the wounded from all the bolts of cloth in her store, beginning with the finest and most expensive because it was the softest and would be the most comfortable.

Despite stories like this one of extreme generosity and self-lessness, tensions and tempers began to run high as the day grew to a close and the full-scale retreat into the city was on. Volunteers had barely enough room to maneuver through the packed rooms and streets and often found themselves frustrated by their inability to get the assistance they needed and had received so readily earlier in the day. They were constantly trying to drag or lure other volunteers away from their current tasks, even as these other volunteers were appealing to them to do the same.

Through it all, Aelwyn and Mindarin worked steadily, only speaking when verbal communication was absolutely necessary. There seemed to be an unspoken understanding between them that there wasn't enough physical or emotional energy to spare even for words. So they worked on in desperate silence, holding at bay all the feelings and words and emotions that had stirred within them throughout the long, painful travesty of the day.

Now the tide had receded. Many men left on the street until well after dark had been moved inside. Aelwyn knew this was in part due to the fact that so many of those inside earlier had died. She stopped herself every time she began subconsciously to recount the number of times she'd examined a new patient and found his wound fatal. The faces still flashed before her, ashen and alone. They were often her age or older, but in their final hours, they were all her children. She would mop their brows and whisper words of peace into their ears in the hopes that somehow they could hear and understand and not be afraid of the journey they would soon be taking.

Aelwyn looked around. The clean grey stone floor of that morning was gone. It resembled now the floor of the butcher's killing shed, and suddenly she was overwhelmed. The tears that she had suppressed all day came unbidden, and she raised her hands to her head, afraid that if she couldn't stop the tide of emotion that was now beginning to rise within her, she would collapse then and there.

She felt a hand upon her shoulder, and an arm was slipped around her. Mindarin's voice came gently to her ear. "I know, Aelwyn, I know. Hold onto me."

And she did. She lowered her head and put it on Mindarin's shoulder, taking hold of her sister tightly for fear she would fall if she did not. She held onto her and cried, and all the while Mindarin steadied her and whispered soothingly that it would pass in a moment.

It did. The tide of tears reached its peak, then subsided, and after a few moments, she wiped her eyes and stood straight again. "Thanks."

"You're welcome," Mindarin replied, and her voice was calming although there was no smile. "This is madness, this place."

"Yes, but we swore we would do what needed doing."

"And we've done it. All day. The battle is over and we're still doing it, and we'll do it again tomorrow. That's why we need to get some rest, both of us."

"I know."

"We'll be no good tomorrow unless we do."

"I know, we just haven't worked out a system of rotation yet. We didn't look that far ahead, and there is still so much need."

"Well," Mindarin said, "we're as close to being in charge of this mess as anyone, so if we don't look to it, it may not get done."

"All right," Aelwyn said, wiping her eyes with her upper arm, one of the few places still relatively free of blood. "Let me take a moment or so outside first, then we'll figure it out. I need some air."

Mindarin nodded. "Take the time you need."

Aelwyn walked out into the warm spring night. The rain still fell, slowly, but it did not evoke the terrible memories it had first brought her upon its return. Now, instead of thinking of the long dark days on the road, she thought only of the power of the rain to make her clean. She raised her hands to the sky and let the water soak them, then lowered them in front of her and scrubbed furiously, manically. She scrubbed and scrubbed and the blood not yet dry washed off and the layer beneath that flaked and washed off and the layer beneath that did as well, and still her hands were not clean. She scrubbed some more until she knew it was futile. She dropped her hands to her sides and rubbed them on her cloak beneath her apron, no longer caring if it was stained, and started walking down the street.

The lights of the city seemed dim, as though in reverence for the day's defeat both inside and outside the walls. Some of the wounded still lay propped up against the front wall of the building, and a pair of Tol Emuna matrons walked among them, seeing what they needed. Aelwyn scanned them with her eyes and walked on.

A little farther down, she noticed a narrow alley running between two large buildings, a passage connecting the larger thoroughfare she walked upon with one of the city's many smaller roadways. Light from a window in the side of one of the buildings flickered upon a curious scene. A pair, apparently craving solitude, were camped out in the alley. One was sitting, back against the wall with legs stretched out in front, and the other was lying on his back, immobile.

It occurred to Aelwyn that these also might be wounded men perhaps lost in the shuffle and forgotten during the confusion of the day. She had come out for a moment's peace, but first she would check to see that they were all right.

She started down the alley toward the pair, but neither moved or looked up at her. She hesitated a span or so away, suddenly losing her nerve in the close quarters of the shadowy place.

"Are you two all right?" she asked from where she was.

No answer, and she wondered now if they were dead. Another light in the building opposite the two men appeared in a window, casting rays into the alley. Aelwyn gasped.

"Pedraan?"

The figure that was sitting against the wall looked up at her, his eyes empty and staring. He did not speak.

She ran to them, and stooping over the prone body of what she realized was Pedraal, saw immediately that he was dead. She took his cold, stiff hand gently in her own and stroked it tenderly with her fingers. She turned to Pedraan, who was staring down at his own feet, rain dripping off the ends of his saturated hair. "Pedraan, I'm so sorry."

Still, he said nothing. He didn't speak, didn't move, and didn't acknowledge her or her words at all. Aelwyn searched for something to say or do, and finding nothing, turned back to Pedraal. The front of his cloak was stained dark with his blood, and she didn't look to see the wound that had killed him. She'd seen enough that day to imagine it. He'd been so full of life, both of them had, and now the faces of both the living and the dead seemed to have lost the spark that animated them.

"Karalin," Aelwyn said out loud. She turned to Pedraan. "Stay here with your brother, Pedraan. I'll go find Karalin."

At the mention of his beloved's name, Pedraan turned and looked at Aelwyn, and she knew that perhaps for the first time since she'd come down the alley, he was really seeing her.

"Pedraan," she said putting her hand now on his. "I'm sorry about Pedraal. Just stay here until I can come back with Karalin."

She didn't know if it was the touch of her fingers upon his or if it was the repetition of Karalin's name, but Pedraan began to cry.

Synoki pushed past the startled soldiers at the entrance to Farimaal's tent before they realized who it was and could get out of the way. They fumbled with apologies as they stepped back. He entered the tent, fire in his eyes. "What is the meaning of this?"

Farimaal was not alone, and those who were there, a handful of the Nolthanim captains, turned to see who had come barging in. They saw and stepped aside even as Farimaal noticed who it was and came walking toward him, saying nothing. The fear of the others was palpable. Farimaal, though, even when caught off guard, showed no sign of anxiety.

"Why is Tol Emuna not reduced to rubble?" Synoki asked. "The city walls stand. The gate is intact. I saw, even from a distance, the enemy army on the run. I saw Cheimontyr marching on the gate, majestic in his fury and wrath. I waited for the strike that would shatter the gates and break down the wall, but it never came. Never. What's going on?"

"That's a question for Cheimontyr, Master," Farimaal answered.

"I'm asking you."

"The Bringer of Storms neither answers to me nor explains himself to me."

Synoki stepped closer to Farimaal. "I will speak to him, believe me, but right now I am here with you, and you will answer my question. What happened?"

Farimaal shrugged. "I too was waiting for the hammer to fall, and when he turned and walked away, I was as surprised as anyone. I sent a messenger to the camp of the Vulsutyrim, but Cheimontyr would not speak to him. The message he passed on through one of his brothers said only, 'Not tonight.'"

"Not tonight?"

"Not tonight."

"What does that mean?" Synoki said, disgust and annoyance evident in his voice. "Why not tonight? Tonight was perfect. They were broken and defeated. Their time was up and they knew it. Delaying can only give them hope."

Farimaal said nothing to this, and Synoki turned and paced, limping, back and forth in the middle of the tent. The Nolthanim captains sidled quietly to the tent flaps and disappeared, but Synoki took little note of their departure. At last, he turned back to Farimaal, now that the two of them were alone.

"So, what is your plan then, seeing that the city is not yet in our hands?"

"The same as it was before."

"You plan to use the traitor?"

"Yes."

Synoki waved his hand dismissively. "His usefulness is surely past. The men in command of that army hate him almost as much as they hate me, probably more since they once knew him and considered him one of their own. If anything, sending him will only strengthen their resolve to fight."

"He has every incentive to convince them to surrender."

"You mean the woman, Someris?"

"Yes."

"Doesn't he yet realize she will never be his?"

"He hopes for her, and hope blinds him to the truth."

"Well, even if he doesn't see it yet, you rely too heavily on an old affection for a distant prize."

"I have nursed an old affection for a distant prize for far longer than he," Farimaal replied, looking directly into Synoki's eyes and meeting his master gaze for gaze. "It has not yet deserted me. Anyway, she is not so very distant. We have her."

Synoki stopped pacing. "Here? In the camp?"

"Yes, she came out to meet us in the guise of a messenger as we approached Amaan Sul. She and an old man, one of her advisors I believe. She is currently in our custody."

"Ahhh," Synoki replied, thinking through this new bit of information. "I see. So, he will not only be inspired to do his best, but there are no doubt many inside the city who will not wish to see her harmed."

"Yes, her or her son."

"The boy is not negotiable," Synoki said walking up close to Farimaal. "In this regard at least, my journey was successful. I have gained the knowledge that I sought. The boy is the child of prophecy."

If the news was shocking or impressive to Farimaal, he did not show it. "So it is him, and not Aljeron Balinor."

"Yes, it is the boy."

"Then Balinor is dead."

"No," Synoki said, frowning when Farimaal raised an eyebrow slightly, a visible sign of surprise on the face of one who did not give visible signs. "But I will tell you about him and my journey later. Just remember what I have told you. The boy's life is not negotiable. Whether the city surrenders tomorrow or not, he will die the following morning as a demonstration of the price of rebellion. We will mark their feast day, Midspring, with a victory celebration of our own as the child of prophecy dies before their eyes and mine. Understood? You may barter with the woman, but the boy dies."

"The boy dies," Farimaal echoed.

Synoki grabbed one of the plain wooden chairs nearby and sat down. His rage had largely passed. Farimaal's evenness calmed him. He still did not understand why Cheimontyr had turned away from the city. While Farimaal's motives and actions were not always transparent, Cheimontyr was much easier to predict. Synoki had watched Cheimontyr marching through the hosts of the army with his brothers, going to the front of the line. He had seen the rage on his face and the electrical charge in the clouds and air. He understood better than any what they represented, and he had felt an echo of that power within him and known without doubt that Cheimontyr was preparing to level the city. He had known it, felt it, and hungered for it, but then the giant stood before the gates and did nothing. It was inexplicable, and before the night was through, he would need to pay Cheimontyr a visit to find out what 'not tonight' was supposed to mean. Whatever the explanation, this was but a temporary delay.

He looked over at Farimaal, who remained where he was, waiting for further direction. "Even if they don't surrender to save the woman, I will straighten things out with Cheimontyr, and he will flatten the walls if need be. I learned too late why Balinor had gone to Nolthanin. He was there in search of Sulmandir."

"Sulmandir is dead."

"Apparently not. I saw him fly from Harak Andunin with my own eyes. We have no time to waste. There may be dragons on the way, and if they do not surrender tomorrow, we will press the attack."

"How many dragons?"

"I don't know."

"Even if they do surrender now," Farimaal replied, "we may not be able to let them live and disperse if we know we may still be attacked by dragons. We can't risk the possibility they might regroup and aid the dragons in an attack against us. At least a portion of those who surrender may have to die."

"I don't especially care what you do, so reduce their numbers as much as you wish."

"I will think on it while Rulalin Tarasir carries out his duties," Farimaal said. "Should I send for him?"

"Yes," Synoki said, "Send for him."

Rulalin sat on the floor of his tent, gazing at Soran's lifeless face. He had asked some of the few remaining men of Fel Edorath to bring the body here, and they had, without a word. He knew that he couldn't keep a dead body in his tent for long, but for tonight at least, he would keep Soran with him.

He hadn't seen Soran go down, but he felt guilty and responsible all the same, even though he knew it was stupid to blame himself. Soran was a soldier. Had Soran not been fighting under his command against the Great Bear, he would have been either in Aljeron's custody as an accessory to Rulalin, or fighting with Aljeron's men against the Malekim and Black Wolves, and there had been plenty of casualties in that fight as well. He knew it was stupid, but he felt responsible.

"Captain Tarasir?" a voice called from the entrance to his tent.

"Yes," he answered without turning to see who went with the voice. It wasn't one of the officers immediately under him. It wasn't Farimaal or Tashmiren. It was an unknown voice.

"You have been summoned to Captain Farimaal's tent."

He looked over his shoulder at the man then, and he saw a face he vaguely recognized even though he didn't know the man's name, the upper half of his body poking into the tent. Rulalin rose to his feet, wondering. It must have been late Second Watch at least. "Now?"

"Now."

He nodded and followed the man into the dark camp.

Rulalin entered Farimaal's tent and was surprised to see Synoki sitting a half a span or so to the side of Farimaal in the shadows. He searched his memory for the last time he had seen Synoki. He saw him a few times in the Mountain of course, and when they camped just east of Fel Edorath. And after that, he saw Synoki just after the burning of Col Marena. He couldn't remember, though, if he saw Synoki when they passed through Erefen or beyond, as they swept south across the open plains of Suthanin. No, he had not seen the man at Cimaris Rul or after, because it was there he first realized that Synoki had disappeared from view. He knew of course that in a military operation of this magnitude, there were any number of reasons why he might have missed seeing Synoki in their midst, but he had begun to wonder. He never really understood how Synoki fit into either of the main military hierarchies of Malek's hosts, hierarchies headed by Cheimontyr and Farimaal. Since becoming a captain of the Nolthanim, Rulalin had increasingly realized that Synoki was almost certainly independent of these structures. Whatever he did and whatever his role, he most likely operated directly under and for Malek, and for that reason alone, being summoned before Farimaal and Synoki together told him that this would not be a routine visit, if any visit to Farimaal's tent could be considered routine.

Rulalin entered and stood patiently before Farimaal, waiting to be addressed. He ordinarily would have been more nervous, but Soran's death had produced a somewhat numbing effect. Soran was dead, as were most of the men from Fel Edorath, men whom, theoretically, his treachery had intended to preserve. Though Wylla seemed in some ways to be close at hand, she was in other ways further than ever. Rulalin was weary and tired and not especially enthralled with the wonder of life.

"I am told that your friend fell today," Farimaal said from his wooden chair, looking up at Rulalin. While such a statement from Tashmiren might have carried an edge or note of scorn, Farimaal's voice was free of any obvious emotion.

"Yes, he is dead."

"I am sorry," Farimaal replied. "From all accounts, he was a good soldier."

"He served me well," Rulalin answered. "And by extension, of course, you and our master."

"His death was not in vain," Farimaal continued. "The enemy is defeated. Their attempt on Cheimontyr failed. The war will soon be over."

Rulalin nodded. He had expected it to be over earlier that evening, for he saw Cheimontyr's fury after the attack by the Great Bear was repelled. He was shocked to return to the camp and find the city walls and gates intact.

"You have one last task to perform for us," Farimaal added.

"You want me to go to the city and demand their surrender?" Rulalin felt a cold shudder ripple through his body.

"We do."

"The men I will be dealing with despise me, you know," Rulalin said, as matter-of-factly as he could manage.

"We know, but they are not fools and will surely see the futility of fighting any further. Besides, you know them, and that alone gives you an advantage that we do not have. You will know better than we how to read their mood and make the appeal."

"When am I to go?"

"You are to be at the gate by first light. That will give you several hours to communicate our demands and receive their surrender."

"What are the demands?" Rulalin asked, looking from Farimaal to Synoki, shrouded outside the circle of torchlight, watching closely the exchange between Farimaal and himself.

"The first and most important demand is that they must surrender by an hour past midday. The choice is simple: surrender or be destroyed."

"An hour past midday?" Rulalin asked, his mind quickly processing the implication of the deadline. "You mean to attack the city right away if they don't surrender."

"We will level it, and they should take this into account as they make their decision."

"And the other demands?"

"I will communicate those directly to the representative of the army who returns with you to our camp. When he comes and offers the surrender, he will be told what to do. At that point, I will hold your service complete, and I will extend to you the offer you have requested to come with the Nolthanim when we go north to our ancient home."

"With Wylla Someris?"

"That remains in doubt. She has not cooperated and her life is justly forfeit."

"That may be so," Rulalin said, feeling some life return as he pleaded for Wylla, "but I have lost not only my friend but most of my men in my service to you and our master. Grant me the life of the queen as a boon, I beg of you."

With this, Rulalin dropped to both knees and bowed his head before Farimaal, closing his eyes and waiting for an answer. No answer came at first, except for a low, eerie laughter coming from the direction of Synoki. Rulalin resisted the urge to look up. At last Farimaal spoke.

"I will entertain the idea, but first things must come first. Secure the city's surrender, or the point will be moot. Come back with it by an hour past midday, no later, or nothing you say or do will save her, and you will have no future among the Nolthanim."

"I understand," Rulalin answered, and rising to his feet, he bowed, turned and walked from the tent.

Rulalin sat alone before the massive gates of Tol Emuna. Riding out into the open area beyond the camp of Malek's hosts, he had wondered how many archers from the top the city walls had him lined up with arrow nocked and ready. *Go ahead and shoot,* he thought, *it might almost be merciful.*

Now he sat waiting, having called for the gates to be opened. He had almost choked on the phrase "emissary from Malek," but he imagined the exasperated voice of Soran telling him to get over it and get on with it, then finished his call for the demands of Malek to be heard. Now he waited, wondering if the gates would open or if something large and heavy would be thrown down from the wall upon his head. Of course, a large, heavy object thrown down upon his head would be merciful compared to the things many of those behind these gates would like to do to him. He wondered, not for the first time, if they would respect the conventions of war and refuse this opportunity to take vengeance upon him.

The gates opened. The creaking of the machinery disturbed the quiet of the drizzly morning, and he checked his horse, waiting to see what the opening gates would reveal. No one swooped out upon him, and as the light of the day fell upon the area just beyond the gates, he saw a single rider waiting for him. It was Caan.

He hesitated, but Caan did not, riding out to receive him. He expected anger from his former teacher, but it was not evident in the eyes that were fixed upon him. He found there only sadness, sadness and weariness.

"Emissary," Caan said as he approached, "you come under a flag of truce and will be received as such. You are free to enter the city and deliver your message."

"Caan," Rulalin started, searching for something to say. "I'm sorry."

Caan looked at him for a long moment, then said. "Apologies without change are useless. Don't waste the little time left to me with them, and don't kid yourself that they have meaning. As long as you serve the will of your new master, they are hollow."

Caan began to turn his horse toward the city. "I'm sure this is not the message you have been sent to deliver. Come, let us get this over with."

Rulalin pushed his horse along behind Caan. He was angry. He'd known he would be received poorly, but his former teacher's moralizing annoyed him. What he was doing he was doing for Wylla, to save her life. Caan couldn't see that, and the others here wouldn't see it either. He had been stupid to say he was sorry. It had made him look weak. He was here on behalf of Malek, and unless he got the surrender he'd been sent to secure, Wylla would die. He must not appear weak, and he must be successful.

The ride to the building where Caan said the captains of the armies of Kirthanin were waiting was short. Few people were out and about in the streets in the early morning. Rulalin imagined that with the retreat the previous evening, the night had been long and the activity frenzied. The first light of this new day had brought no hope, only more clouds and rain, a renewed vision of the magnitude of the army camped at their gate, and him, an emissary from Malek, demanding their surrender. He had not made the demand yet, of course, but they would all know why he was there.

He followed Caan inside the building and down a series of hallways. They approached a pair of larger doors, and as Caan reached out to open them, Rulalin braced to see Aljeron.

Aljeron. Rulalin had gone all the way to the heart of Malek's lair to avoid falling into the hands of Aljeron, and now his service to Malek had brought him into those very hands. Yes, Caan had promised that his life would be safeguarded as a messenger come under flag of truce, but Rulalin could well imagine Aljeron finding it too hard to resist this chance to obtain the "justice" he had so zealously sought, especially when confronted with the notion of surrender and the realization that said justice was now finally out of reach.

The doors opened, and Rulalin walked steadily into the large round chamber hall behind Caan. Stopping in the middle of the room before a semicircular table with a dozen or so men, women, and Great Bear, he surveyed them as quickly and nonchalantly as possible. Aljeron was not there. Neither were several of Aljeron's most trusted officers, Saegan and that friend of Joraiem's, Evrim or some such, who had helped press the attack against Fel Edorath all these years. Along with these, Pedraal and Pedraan were missing, and that disappointed him. He had hoped to secure their help in convincing the others that surrender was necessary, for the sake of their sister if nothing else.

He did recognize Corlas Valon, a young officer of his own army from Fel Edorath. For seven years Valon had served him, but he had gone with Aljeron from Fel Edorath even as

Rulalin approached the city with Malek's host. He also recognized Bryar, as hard and warlike behind a table as she appeared on a horse. There was also Joraiem's brother, Brenim, and an older captain of Shalin Bel who had worked closely with Aljeron, though Rulalin didn't know his name. There was a man and woman wearing the colors of Cimaris Rul, and the woman looked like Nyan, one of the Novaana who had been at Sulare with him all those years ago, but he couldn't be sure. The man with her was unknown to him. There was also an older man he didn't recognize and an officer of Tol Emuna as well. All this he saw and processed in just a few seconds, and that was all he was given before the acrimony in the room was unleashed upon him.

"So you've come to gloat, murderer and traitor," Brenim Andira said, slapping the table with his hand as he stood and glared at Rulalin. His hand moved to the handle of his sword. "Truce or no truce, I should slit your throat. If we're going to die anyway, you might as well die first."

"Brenim, sit down." The older man that Rulalin had not seen before put his hand on Brenim's shoulder and held him firmly, and Rulalin could see the younger man straining against the grip. "Let's hear the emissary out."

Brenim sat down, reluctantly, and before anyone else could join in, Rulalin said, "We can waste more time on bitter personal exchanges if you like, or we can get down to business. It's up to you, but you should know that your time is short."

"Meaning what, exactly?" Caan asked, having taken a seat at the table.

"Meaning you have until an hour past midday, until the start of Seventh Hour, to send a representative back with me to surrender."

"Or else?"

"The walls and gates of Tol Emuna will be leveled, and both you and the city will be completely destroyed."

For a moment there was silence, and it was broken, surprisingly enough to Rulalin, by Corlas Valon. "Let them come," he said. "The Bringer of Storms turned away from the walls last night. I say he knows he can't break them down and this is a trick. They want us to lay our weapons down and come out because they can't come in."

"I agree," Bryar spoke up. "We haven't traveled the length and breadth of Kirthanin to surrender now. We fight. If we die, we die. Surrendering can offer us nothing better."

The door behind Rulalin opened, and he turned with the others to see who was coming. He held his breath, wondering.

It was Pedraan. At least, he was pretty sure it was Pedraan. He'd always told the twins apart by their weapons, and this one was carrying none. The twin slid in quietly, shut the door, and took a seat beside the end of the semicircular table. Rulalin looked to the door, half expecting it to open again and see Pedraal come in, for they were almost never separate, at least that's as he remembered them. No one came, and the door remained closed.

He turned his attention back to the gathering. He was about to speak when Caan started. "We will debate the merits of surrender among ourselves while the emissary waits outside the room. For now, we should focus on making sure we have all the information he has come to give us. Is this the entirety of your message?"

"Yes and no," Rulalin said. "It is the entirety of the official message. I don't know why Cheimontyr didn't destroy the walls last night. He answers to himself and Malek only. I would urge you, though, not to believe it was because he couldn't do it. Test his power and you will be sorry, I assure you."

"Of course you do," Brenim sneered. "It's your job to assure us so we surrender and go with you."

"Yes, it is true that this is the job I've been given, but I could not care less about you and this city. If you choose to be fools and refuse to surrender, the city will be destroyed, you will be slain, and I won't care a bit. That's not why I'm urging you to heed the warning and surrender."

Rulalin's voice was hard and cold, just as he intended, and though he saw the anger in the eyes of several swell as he spoke of their demise, no one spoke when he finished. His words had produced the desired effect, he could see, and now it was time to make his move.

"I could not care less about you, but there is someone else whose life means more to me. If you do not surrender, she will die."

"My sister," Pedraan said, rising from his seat. "You speak of Wylla."

"I do," Rulalin answered.

Pedraan stared at him, and deep-rooted enmity burned in his eyes. "What have you been offered for your service, Rulalin? Are you to be my sister's jailer? Do you fancy yourself her husband if you succeed?"

Rulalin met Pedraan's gaze. It was critical that he communicate a desire simply to keep Wylla alive. It was critical that he make it clear that a passion for her life united rather than divided them. "I have been promised nothing, save only a chance to live among the Nolthanim when they return to their ancestral home. I am here to bring Malek's ultimatum and to ask, to beg even, that you surrender. You can't win by fighting, but I may be able to secure Wylla's life if you surrender. That's something we all want, regardless of what else we may disagree on."

"And my nephew?" Pedraan asked.

"He is out of my hands." Rulalin shook his head "But the representative you send back with me can certainly inquire after him. My attempts on his behalf have failed."

"You have made attempts?" the older man inquired.

"I have."

"Why?" Brenim asked.

"Because Wylla asked me to."

The silence of the table was broken as several there whispered among themselves. Caan rose. "It is time to make a decision. The emissary may step from the room."

"I will take him out," the older man said, rising from the table and walking over to Rulalin. There was silence as all eyes watched him approach. Rulalin looked warily at the man but followed him out.

When the doors were shut behind them, the man turned to face Rulalin. "I wanted to thank you for your efforts on behalf of Wylla and Benjiah."

Rulalin, still wary, spoke cautiously, "You're welcome."

The man remained there, examining him, and Rulalin grew uncomfortable. Finally he said, "Yes? Is there something else?"

"No," the man answered. "I just wanted to see you for myself, the man who killed my son."

10

NEGOTIATION

MONIAS REMAINED OUTSIDE the council room with Rulalin only for a moment, but when he stepped back inside, the argument over how to respond to Malek's ultimatum was under way and already quite heated.

"I don't know why we sent him out," Brenim said. "There's nothing to discuss. Surrender was never an option, and it still isn't. What's changed?"

"Much has changed," Turgan said, his deep Great Bear voice commanding the attention of the room, "and we would be fools not to discuss it, whatever we may ultimately decide."

"Turgan is right," Caan said. "We cannot afford to waste time bickering. Where there are many voices, there is wisdom, and we should consider this from as many sides as possible."

"I don't understand why we should," Bryar said, her voice cold and hard, a striking contrast to the passion in Brenim's own pleas. "If we surrender, we will die anyway. Malek won't let us ride from here alive. So, if I'm going to die, I'd rather die fighting than not. Let's take more of the enemy with us into the grave."

"If the choice were that simple," Gilion began, "I would agree with you. If I had to choose between being executed by the enemy and being given a sword to fight against him, even if I knew he was too numerous to defeat, I would take the sword and fight. This is about more than just how we die. This is about the fate of the men and women of Tol Emuna. If Cheimontyr does level the city, the citizens who have sheltered us will die too."

"Better to die with us than be Malek's slaves," Bryar retorted.

"That isn't necessarily your choice to make," Caan replied. "Acknowledging our defeat is not necessarily an act of despair. We have known all along we might not be able to win this battle. Perhaps Allfather will deliver us another way."

"What, with legendary dragons who are nowhere to be found?" Brenim said, his voice betraying his aggravation. "We are what's left of the strength that remains in Kirthanin, and when we surrender, Malek is one step closer to having the world he has so long desired."

"Even if Malek triumphs for a time, there will come a day when Allfather sets all things to right and restores Kirthanin to its original beauty and splendor," Monias said. "Perhaps the time has come to acknowledge our defeat and place our hope in Allfather's eventual victory, to trust that He may mean to deliver Kirthanin by another way. As long as there was hope that the battle might be won, it was good to fight and resist Malek's will. Now that this hope is gone, our goal should be to preserve as much life as possible, and surrendering may well save at least the citizens of Tol Emuna and perhaps also much of what remains of the army."

"But are we so sure that hope is gone?" Corlas Valon said, rising to address them. "I believe what I said a moment ago to

Rulalin. Think about it. We were defeated. We were retreating, and Cheimontyr came marching through the battle lines to the front of the city. We saw what he did to Zul Arnoth, and we have seen him in action since. Why would he not do anything? I say he realized the mighty walls of Tol Emuna were too strong. I say our enemy knows that we can withstand a siege here for many weeks and months, and he wants to flush us out into the open and destroy us. What's more, I say we shouldn't let him."

"And if you're wrong?" Talis Fein of Cimaris Rul said. "The walls of my city were great and mighty too, but the Bringer of Storms summoned the power of the sea and struck them down. Had we not evacuated the city as we saw our doom upon us, we would all be dead. I cannot share your optimism that we will be safe here, no matter how great the walls of Tol Emuna are."

"There may be a third option," Carrafin said. "I've lived here my whole life and know these walls to be strong and sure, but even I could not say with certainty that they will withstand an attack. So, between surrendering and waiting for him to assail us, perhaps there is a third option. Perhaps we should open the gates and march out against him one more time, with everything we have. If we fall, the city will be open and there will be no need for its destruction. Perhaps the citizens will be shown mercy."

"It is not a matter of *if*," Turgan said. "We will fall. Of the entire strength of Great Bear that entered Tol Emuna, now less than a quarter remains. By last estimate, there are only eight hundred of us left. We are weak and decimated, and without us, what is left of our armies will be destroyed by their superior forces."

"Not to mention that if we ride out," Bryar said, "Cheimontyr will have clear shots at us all. Whether the walls can withstand the power of his assault, if we ride forth, we will not."

"We hold onto Rulalin," Brenim said, "and if Cheimontyr attacks the city, we wait for the walls to be breached. If they are, and Rulalin survives the attack, we kill him and stand our ground and fight whatever comes in. We die with swords in our hands like men. If they can't breach the wall, we hang on as long as possible. Who knows, maybe relief and aid will come from another quarter as my father has suggested."

"The city will be leveled and we will all die," Gilion said after a moment. "What's more, Rulalin Tarasir is an emissary and his life is under protection of truce. We need to surrender. A soldier knows when he's beaten."

"You may be beaten—" Brenim began to answer, but Pedraan rose to his feet and interrupted him.

"Enough," he said, hands out as though he could hold back their emotions and calm them by his gestures. "This is all foolishness. We are defeated. Can you all not see that? We did what we could, but we have lost. We have done more than many of us thought we could. We have fought and persevered bravely. Now it is time to accept Malek's terms and walk away. Perhaps Rulalin is right, and maybe some of those we love will be spared and will live to see a better day. As for me, I am willing to surrender and accept my fate, if it might mean that others may live."

"But Pedraan," Bryar began, "like me you have lost a brother in this war. Will you not fight for his memory?"

"You lost your brother fighting against Fel Edorath, not Malek, or is war so much in your blood you can no longer tell the difference between one battle and the next?"

"Pedraan," Caan said, "be careful what you say."

Pedraan sighed and raised his hand to acknowledge Caan's point. "I'm sorry Bryar, that was unduly harsh. Yes, Pedraal is dead, but getting myself killed and the city leveled won't bring him back. Enough is enough. All has been said. We should vote to see what the will of the council is. If it is for war I will fight, though I think it folly. If it is for surrender, I will surrender. If we are evenly divided, I will accept Caan's decision as final."

Silence hung heavily upon the room, and when a vote was called for, only Bryar, Brenim, and Valon voted not to surrender. They looked around, glaring at the others as the vote was taken, but no other hands were raised.

"The will of the council is to surrender," Caan said, looking over all who were gathered there, but bringing his gaze to rest on the three. "Will you abide by the decision of this council?"

"As much as I disagree with this decision, for my part I will abide by it," Brenim said quietly, and Valon and Bryar echoed him.

"Good, then we are decided. All that remains is for me to give Rulalin the news and go with him to Malek's camp while the rest of you begin to make ready for our surrender."

"No," Pedraan said, and all eyes swung to him.

"No?" Caan asked.

"No. I will go with Rulalin while you oversee the surrender of the city."

"But Pedraan—"

"It is my sister and nephew whom they hold. Yesterday, I lost my brother, and today I must do all I can to save them."

Rulalin rode back out through the gates of Tol Emuna. It was fully an hour before midday. They would easily be back in Farimaal's tent before the deadline. He felt great relief, and the image of Wylla journeying with him into the northlands, far from this place, far from the madness of the past, appeared before him. The city was going to surrender. Surely that must count for something in his plea for her life.

And yet along with the relief there was sadness. The city, the last defense, was *surrendering*. Kirthanin was going to bend the knee to Malek. His third attempt at conquest had finally been successful, and Rulalin had played a part in that success, though not a huge part, to be sure. He wasn't so proud as to think his participation had won the victory or would have slowed it had he joined the opposition, but he had helped.

He'd grown up under the shadow of the Mountain, dreaming of fighting against Malek and his hosts like every other little boy in Fel Edorath. He'd dreamed of heroism and valor, not self-preservation and betrayal. Soran was dead now, and there was no longer any need to lie for his sake. Rulalin had sworn his allegiance to Malek to save his own life and perhaps the life of Wylla, and that was the long and short of it.

He looked over at Pedraan, riding silently beside him, his face set like stone upon the open plain between the city and the camp ahead. Pedraan did not have his war hammer, nor a sword or spear or bow, nor even a knife or dagger. The Pedraan he had known all those years ago in Sulare had been interested in only one thing: fighting and learning to fight. He had seen Pedraan on the battlefield in the early campaigns of the war between Shalin Bel and Fel Edorath. The twin was a gory spectacle, his clothes flecked with blood and his great war hammer whirling through the air as he struck down men like a blacksmith would strike his anvil. He and Pedraal both had the ability to dominate the battlefield; they were warriors of the first order. And yet today Pedraan carried no weapon. Even under truce, Pedraan had a right to bear a weapon into Malek's camp. Rulalin had certainly done so, keeping his sword on the entire time he was in Tol Emuna, and he would have expected the same in return.

And what had happened to Pedraal? Pedraan had explained his coming with Rulalin by stating that he was the ranking officer of the Enthanim army, but Rulalin knew that Pedraal was older and the captain of Amaan Sul. If Pedraan now claimed the title of ranking Enthanim, and if he now attended councils and rode as emissary alone, then Rulalin could only believe that Pedraal had fallen.

He looked over the battlefield beside the camp where the bodies of Kirthanim lay intermingled with Malekim and Black Wolves. Perhaps Pedraal lay out there among the dead. Perhaps when the surrender was complete, he would ask Farimaal if the dead Kirthanim could be gathered and buried. He would even volunteer himself and the men under him to do it, provided such a move would not jeopardize Wylla's life.

They approached the camp, and the eyes of many turned upon him and Pedraan as they rode in. He could have gone directly to Farimaal's tent, but he didn't. He took Pedraan first to his own tent, where they dismounted and entered.

Soran's body had not yet been removed. He lay cold and lifeless under the dark cloak that Rulalin had draped over him as a shroud. Rulalin thought his soldiers were going to remove the body that morning, and so he was surprised and momentarily distracted by it. He recovered quickly, acting as though it was nothing and moving to his table to pour himself a drink.

He turned to offer one to Pedraan, who stood beside Soran's body, gazing down upon it, sadness on his face. "Drink, Pedraan?"

Pedraan nodded toward the corpse. "Who is this?"

Rulalin was surprised by the lack of hostility in Pedraan's voice. Of all men in Kirthanin, Pedraan might not have had the best reason to hate Rulalin, but he had reason enough. Joraiem had been his brother-in-law, and the woman made a widow was his sister, the boy made an orphan his nephew. Rulalin had expected nothing but anger and hatred, and the complete silence of the ride and utter stoniness of Pedraan's countenance supported his expectations. But the question Pedraan asked sounded free of any acrimony, hostility, or gloating over the loss of someone obviously dear to him. If anything, there was compassion mixed with sadness in his tone.

"He was a fellow Werthanim from Fel Edorath. He served me faithfully and well for years, and this was his repayment."

"He has reaped what he sowed," Pedraan said quietly, "but I will not judge him, for I don't know what was in his heart. I have loved war too much, the act itself and not what I hoped to accomplish through it. Maybe, like me, he loved it too."

"Will you judge me, Pedraan?" Rulalin asked, handing him his drink.

Pedraan looked up at Rulalin. "What I have against you is not your love of battle. I don't believe you fight because you love it. You fight because you have to. However, you took my sister's happiness and robbed the world of the best man I knew. For that, you will be judged, though not by me."

Pedraan took a drink from the cup and continued. "He was the best of us, you know. Of all the Novaana gathered in Sulare, Joraiem was the best. It wasn't his fault Wylla chose him and not you."

"I know."

"Then why?"

"It no longer matters why," Rulalin said. He knew time was short and didn't want to waste it trying to defend the indefensible. Soon it would be time to head to Farimaal's tent, and he needed to redirect their focus. "We have to worry about more pressing things, like saving your sister's life."

"I'm listening."

"As I told you in Tol Emuna," Rulalin said, sitting down. "I have not been promised anything with respect to her. She has refused to cooperate, and her life may still be in jeopardy. I think that the city's surrender may make it easier for me to plead her case, but if you care at all about your sister, you will help and not hinder me when you appear before Farimaal."

"Farimaal?"

"Captain of the Nolthanim and leader of Malek's hosts, save only the Vulsutyrim under Cheimontyr. Especially as you are her brother, you can only hurt our chances of saving her if you are difficult or demanding in any way. As hard as it may be to swallow your pride, you must, for Wylla's sake."

"Don't worry about me," Pedraan said. "I have no pride left. We're defeated and know it. I'm here to save her and anyone else who can be saved. I won't throw them away in a foolish display of bravado."

"Good."

"You haven't spoken of Benjiah."

Rulalin looked at Pedraan, still standing beside Soran's body. "I don't think there's anything I can do for him."

"Why?"

"Because of what happened at the Kalamin, what he did there. Even though he did it with Valzaan's staff, I think they're afraid of him."

Pedraan nodded. "They should be."

"Why?"

Pedraan seemed to weigh his words. "I just meant that I was there. I saw from the other side of the river what he did."

Rulalin knew Pedraan had kept something to himself, but he just nodded. "I understand. Don't worry about me. I have no desire to see Benjiah killed. I took Wylla's husband and would save her son if I could, but I just can't."

"Then I must see if I can."

"I hope you can."

"Anything you can tell me that might help?"

"No. Farimaal speaks little but observes everything. He is unlikely to be persuaded by argument, and I don't know that there is anything in him that would respond to an appeal to mercy, so don't mistake his lack of emotion and few words for softness. No, Pedraan, I don't know anything that can help you."

"Well, then I guess we should go and see what happens."

Rulalin finished his drink and set it down on his table. He rose and walked from his tent, and Pedraan followed.

Tashmiren stepped out in front of Rulalin and Pedraan as they walked briskly through the camp. He stopped with a sneer, watching the two men approach. Rulalin, looking up at him, barely hesitated as he reached back for Pedraan's cloak to pull Pedraan around the man without a word.

Tashmiren would not be bypassed so easily, and turning, walked more or less alongside them. "Where are your protests of love for Kirthanin and defiance against Malek now, Tarasir?"

Rulalin walked on, and Tashmiren continued. "I remember how you first received me in Fel Edorath, trying to be so diplomatic, but your disgust and disdain were evident. How quickly you changed your tune when there appeared to be no other way to save your own skin. Now you are the herald for our Master's great victory. Things have changed, haven't they?"

Rulalin stopped and turned to face Tashmiren, whose smirking face was almost gleeful. "Yes," Rulalin said, trying to measure his words even though his hatred of the worm was evident. "I have done what I once thought was unthinkable, but in so doing, I may yet preserve the life of one dear to me."

"The woman hates you," Tashmiren answered. "Everyone but you can see that. Or maybe you see it but won't accept it."

Rulalin started walking again, and this time only Pedraan followed. Tashmiren remained behind, calling out, "Whatever reward Farimaal might grant you, you're not really one of us, Tarasir, and you never will be."

"Who was that?" Pedraan asked as they rounded a corner and passed beside another row of tents.

"An arrogant fool who serves as a messenger and mouthpiece for Malek."

"He doesn't like you very much," Pedraan said.

"I'm well-loved in both camps," Rulalin said sarcastically, then added. "Don't let him distract you from what we've come to do. If we save Wylla, it doesn't matter what he or anyone else says."

"He didn't distract me. It's you I'm worried about."

"He's nobody. I've already forgotten him."

They walked on and after a few moments arrived at Farimaal's tent, set apart some twenty spans or more from the other tents of the Nolthanim and their captains. Rulalin hesitated, wiping his sweaty hands on his cloak and looking over his shoulder at Pedraan. "This is it. Ready?"

"As I'll ever be."

Soldiers held them up as they approached, and a man ducked into the tent to announce their arrival. He reappeared a moment later, and the flap was opened so they could proceed.

It was not long after midday, and yet the two torches within the tent were lit, flickering in the semigloom of Farimaal's abode. Farimaal sat sprawled in his wooden chair in his usual spot. Beside him and a little behind sat Synoki. On either side of the tent, watching, stood the other Nolthanim captains. All were here to receive the surrender of Tol Emuna.

As Rulalin led Pedraan to Farimaal, he heard Pedraan gasp the name *Synoki* as he drew near.

"That's right," Synoki said, smiling from where he was seated. "Your memory serves you well, young Someris, but I confess, I never really could keep you and your brother apart. Which one are you?"

"I am Pedraan Someris," Pedraan replied, recovering from his momentary surprise. "Captain of the city of Amaan Sul and ranking officer of the Enthanim. I am come to offer the surrender of Tol Emuna and the Kirthanim assembled there, and to negotiate the terms."

"Negotiate?" Synoki continued, rising and stepping in front of Farimaal. "Where did you get the idea that there would be anything to negotiate?"

Pedraan appeared to Rulalin unfazed, either by Synoki's leadership role here in Malek's camp or by the mocking tone in his voice. "You sent an emissary to solicit our surrender, and the captains of the Kirthanim have tentatively agreed that a surrender would be wise. That is assuming, of course, that the terms are just and fair. If you intend to destroy us and the city, then we have no incentive to lay down our arms. I'm sure you understand, as you sent for a representative rather than sending demands with your own emissary."

"The terms are these," Farimaal began, and Synoki stepped aside. "Tomorrow, every man, woman and child will exit Tol Emuna, deposit their weapons at the place we designate, and assemble on the plain before the city. You will assemble by Third Hour, and the captains of your army will be executed for their treason against Malek. When justice has been done, those who remain will be given instructions and the army will be disbanded. You will do this, or we will destroy the city. These are the terms."

"The city will be spared?"

"If you do as directed."

"The captains will be executed?"

"Yes. As punishment for past offenses, namely leading armed resistance to Malek, and as a warning to any who might consider future insurrection."

"But the rest of the army and the citizens of Kirthanin," Pedraan replied, "they will be spared?"

"Yes."

"That includes the queen of Enthanin and her son, whom I believe are currently in your custody?"

Farimaal did not answer, and Synoki limped closer to Pedraan. The faintest hint of a smile lingered at the corners of his mouth. It was insolent, but with a gravity that Tashmiren's open mockery lacked.

"Ah," Synoki said, "your sister and nephew. I wondered when we would come to them. She is a queen, a leader every bit as responsible for this current rebellion as you and the other captains. Her life is forfeit. He is a prophet of Allfather, and his life is not only forfeit, he will be the first to die. He will die before all of you as a sign that your god has forsaken you and as proof that resistance to Malek and his power is vain."

"He is but a boy, and the staff he used against your army is broken. He can do no more harm. She is a leader of her people, but the army of Enthanin is under my command. Kill me with the captains of Kirthanin to exact your justice, but let her go free. You can show the people not only that rebellion won't be tolerated, but that Malek will not take life unnecessarily."

Synoki turned from Pedraan to Rulalin, and looked him squarely in the eyes. "What do you say, Captain Tarasir? Should the woman and the boy be allowed to live?"

Rulalin returned Synoki's cold gaze, wondering if it was a question or a trap. "It is no secret that when I entered Malek's service I requested the life of Wylla Someris as a reward should my service please him. I have delivered Fel Edorath and now Tol Emuna. I have fought and led as well as I know how. I ask again for the life of Queen Someris."

"And the boy?"

Rulalin discreetly rubbed his sweating hand against his cloak at his side. "May it be as our master chooses."

Synoki nodded slowly and stood still for a moment before Rulalin. He turned his head slightly to take in Pedraan, who stood motionless beside Rulalin. Turning, he walked back to his chair.

"All right," he said as he settled in, looking quite comfortable with where the negotiation was going. "If the city surrenders as directed. If the soldiers lay down their weapons. If the captains give themselves up to face their trials and executions. If everything happens tomorrow as we desire, then the queen will be spared."

"She will be released to join her people?" Pedraan asked.

Rulalin heard the question and swallowed. He understood that Pedraan would not see Wylla's release into his custody as real freedom or escape, but tomorrow Pedraan would be executed and there would be no shield for her but Rulalin. Pedraan would return to the city, and Rulalin would press his claim for Wylla more strongly if need be, but he hoped it would not be necessary.

"We have said she will be spared," Farimaal said in a tone that made it clear that the question had been answered and the subject concluded.

"And the boy?" Pedraan asked, a mixture of hesitation and persistence in his tone.

"The boy dies first, as promised."

Pedraan did not reply, and Rulalin was relieved. He could see that further argument could achieve no good outcome, and he was grateful that Pedraan had seen it as well.

"These are the terms," Farimaal said. "You accept?"

"We do," Pedraan answered, taking a knee. "I offer you the surrender of Tol Emuna and the army of Kirthanin."

Rulalin and Pedraan walked through the camp in silence. Rulalin had been charged with the task of seeing Pedraan back to the city gates. Now they were standing beside their horses, getting ready to mount.

Pedraan stepped back from his and looked at Rulalin. "I would like to see my sister."

"You heard my orders. Directly means directly. We need to head back to Tol Emuna."

"I heard the orders, but I'm asking anyway."

"If I take you to her, they'll know, Pedraan."

"Rulalin," Pedraan said, putting his big hand on Rulalin's shoulder. It wasn't done in a threatening manner, but Rulalin felt awkward as Pedraan's big fingers gripped him, no doubt out of desperation. "Tomorrow morning I'm going to be executed. I doubt letting me say goodbye to my sister matters much to them."

"I'm sorry, Pedraan," Rulalin said. "I can't."

"Look," Pedraan continued. "My brother is dead. In the morning, my nephew is going to die before my very eyes. Wylla is all I have left. I'm all she has left. I need to tell her about Pedraal and Benjiah. I need to say goodbye."

Rulalin stood, agonizing for a moment. Any deviation from the plan could jeopardize Wylla's life. He knew that. It could jeopardize his life. To take Pedraan to her would not be wise.

He looked at Pedraan, and suddenly he didn't care. Pedraan had appealed to him, not as a traitor or an outsider, but as a man. Pedraan was going to die tomorrow, and deep inside him, Rulalin knew he should be the one to die, not Pedraan. Caan had said it. What good did feeling sorry do without change?

"All right," Rulalin said, whispering now although there was no one nearby to hear them. "I'll take you to her, but it can only be for a moment. Bring your horse and follow me."

They walked together, and Rulalin felt an urge to explain his failure to speak for Benjiah before Farimaal and Synoki. Pedraan had dealt with him more than fairly since coming from the city, and it was suddenly important to Rulalin that Pedraan understand.

"Pedraan," he began as they led their horses through the camp, "I would have spoken for Benjiah had there been hope. There is none, though, and I couldn't risk Wylla's life."

At first Pedraan did not speak, but his steps slowed and eventually stopped, and Rulalin stopped beside him. "Has it not occurred to you yet that you've made a lot of really bad decisions on the basis of either wanting my sister for yourself or wanting to preserve her life? I love her too, but there are things, many things, I would not do to save her."

"Yes," Rulalin said quietly in return, "I know I've made mistakes, big ones, but he couldn't be saved and she could be. What's wrong with that?"

"What's wrong with it?" Pedraan murmured. "He's only a boy, that's what's wrong with it. He doesn't deserve to die like this."

"Maybe not, but I can't save him any more than you can. I focused on the life that was within our reach."

"Then don't tell me you're sorry. If you did what you think was right, then why apologize?"

Rulalin didn't answer, and they resumed their course. They came before long to a place where a handful of men captured the previous day were tied and seated on the ground. A handful of guards were posted nearby. Rulalin skirted this area and moved beyond it to the place where Wylla and Yorek were likewise tied and seated. He motioned to the guard to leave them, and he approached with Pedraan.

Wylla looked up, her face tear-stained. She saw Rulalin first, then Pedraan, and seeing him she scrambled up as best she could with her hands knotted securely behind her back and ran to him. "Pedraan!"

"Wylla," he said, wrapping his arms around her as she buried her head against his chest.

For a moment Pedraan just stood and held her close. Yorek rose also and moved closer. Pedraan motioned to him as he held onto Wylla, and Yorek nodded in reply.

"Rulalin, could you untie my hands, just for a few moments?"

Rulalin thought of all the reasons why he shouldn't acquiesce, but he saw the look of pleading in her eyes. He started on the knot, and after a few moments, her hands were free.

Wylla lifted her arms and took Pedraan's face in her hands. "Why are you here, Pedraan?"

"The city has surrendered."

"No!" Wylla said vehemently. "It can't. Tol Emuna is our last hope!"

"We must look elsewhere for hope," Pedraan said calmly. "We are defeated. There is no need for the city to be leveled and its civilians slaughtered."

"They will be slaughtered anyway."

"We are assured they will live."

"Really?" Wylla said sarcastically. "And what guarantee do you have? You trust Malek and his underlings?"

She looked sideways at Rulalin as she spoke, and he felt the sting of the accusation. He did not respond or retaliate but only looked away as though his interest at the moment were leagues away.

"We have no choice, Sister," Pedraan said firmly. "They may not keep their word, we know that. But if we fight on, they will certainly destroy us all. We will risk surrender."

Wylla did not protest further. She put her hands on Pedraan's arms and looked at him closely. "Why have you come alone, Pedraan? Where is Pedraal?"

"He is fallen."

Wylla did not speak or move, but as Rulalin shifted his gaze to her, he saw that the tears which had recently been in her eyes and upon her cheeks had returned. "Yesterday?"

"Yes," Pedraan answered. "He fell defending me."

She nodded. "Then he died doing what mattered most to him, watching over his brother."

"Wylla," Pedraan said, "I came as our emissary to negotiate our surrender." Wylla nodded again but didn't speak. "I tried to secure Benjiah's life as part of the surrender, but I couldn't. They mean to execute him."

Wylla wiped her tears with her hands. "I know. That's what I've been crying about with Yorek. I came to this camp to save him, and I have failed."

"We all have."

Wylla reached out and took Pedraan's arm. "What about you, Pedraan? What about the army and the officers?"

"The officers are to be executed tomorrow following the surrender," Pedraan answered softly. "After Benjiah is executed first."

"Tomorrow, both of you," Wylla said. The words escaped her mouth like a puff of air after being punched. She seemed physically to recoil and crossed her arms upon her stomach as though bracing for another blow.

"Yes," Pedraan confirmed. "I thought you should know, and I wanted to say goodbye."

She stepped closer and threw her arms around his neck, though she had to reach up on her tiptoes to do so. "I love you, my brother. If you go before me like Joraiem and Pedraal have done, and like Benjiah is likely to do, do not forget me."

"I won't, Sister," Pedraan answered. "And I will go before you. Your life has been promised me."

Wylla stepped back. "What do you mean?"

"I mean that I asked for your life, that you be spared, and your life was conceded."

"I am supposed to live? To linger on after all I love are gone? If that is the life they offer me, I don't want it."

"I am sorry, Wylla. I have done all I could."

Wylla did not respond, and Rulalin saw that the time to go had arrived. "Come," he said, "we must be heading back to Tol Emuna. I will resecure you."

"Goodbye, my sister," Pedraan said. "You are a great sister and a faithful queen. Whatever comes tomorrow, know that."

Yorek had come up alongside Wylla, and she leaned her head onto his shoulder as Rulalin and Pedraal mounted.

"Goodbye, my brother," Wylla said as they prepared to ride. "I love you."

Rulalin turned his back to them and rode, and Pedraan rode with him.

Darkness had fallen, and Rulalin sat restlessly in his tent. After seeing Pedraan back to Tol Emuna, reporting to Farimaal, and seeing to the disposal of Soran's body, he'd returned to his tent and fell asleep in the late afternoon. His sleep was restless, troubled with dreams that fled for the most part upon waking, and the fragments he could recall made no sense. Now he sat in silence in the darkness, waiting for the morning that would bring Malek's triumph and Kirthanin's defeat.

He had tried to assure Pedraan as they rode back to Tol Emuna that he would do everything he could to see to Wylla's safety, but Pedraan ignored him and refused to speak on the matter. He even tried to discover why Aljeron had been missing from the council of captains in Tol Emuna, but Pedraan likewise kept his silence. Rulalin could only think that Aljeron must have fallen, if not yesterday, then in some earlier battle, and he had simply been unaware. The thought of his enemy fallen did not fill him with satisfaction and delight as he once imagined it would. He wasn't exactly saddened by the thought, but at the same time, he'd expected to find more joy in it then he did. He was alive, and Aljeron, apparently, was dead. Even so, it seemed to make no great difference to him. He rose and stepped out of his tent.

He had made his plea for Wylla's release into his custody before Farimaal, and he was reasonably satisfied that, provided everything else with the surrender went well, all would happen as he hoped. Of course, Farimaal stopped short of anything like a guarantee, but Rulalin knew well enough by now that Farimaal felt no need to guarantee anyone anything.

He thought of Wylla, somewhere out there in the dark. If he was troubled and restless, he couldn't imagine what she must be going through, knowing that the morning would bring the death of her son and brother. He knew he might not be able to offer much comfort, but if he seriously intended to take care of her from now on, he'd better get used to trying. He set off through the camp to find her.

The camp was crawling with soldiers. Few would sleep tonight. Farimaal had sent word to all the captains that half of every company was to be awake and ready, just in case the surrender was a ruse. Rulalin had assigned officers and men to this duty, but he refused to join them. He no longer cared what happened if they were attacked, so he thought it best to entrust his men to officers who did.

Again he approached the place where Wylla was being held, and again he dismissed the guard, who seemed sleepy and not too pleased about being asked to move from where he was sitting. He did, though, and Rulalin squatted down beside Wylla, who lay sprawled out in the grass.

If he'd thought she was asleep, he was wrong, for she sat up immediately. She peered at him in the darkness. "What is it? Is there news?"

"No," he whispered. A snore from Yorek interrupted them. Rulalin looked over at the sleeping man, then back at Wylla. "I was just concerned and wanted to check on you."

Wylla looked down at Yorek and then leaned in closer to Rulalin. "Can we go off a little distance so we don't wake him?"

Rulalin nodded and rose, as did Wylla. He led her a little bit away until Yorek's snores were unheard and there was no one for many spans in any direction.

"This is better, thanks," Wylla said.

"You're welcome," Rulalin answered. "What is it?"

"It's Benjiah," Wylla said. "He has only one hope, you."

"Wylla, there is nothing I can do."

"You can—"

"I can't. I explained this to Pedraan. They don't care what I think. They won't listen to me."

"I didn't say they'd listen to you. That's not what I meant."

Rulalin stared at her face and saw that she was serious. "I can't help that way either."

"Why not?"

"They'd know it was me. I'd be dead. We all would be."

"Rulalin, just listen to me for a moment."

"It's no good, Wylla," Rulalin said, agitated. "Don't you see? Saving you is all I can do. It is all I can muster, and even that isn't a sure thing. I could still lose you. I can't risk it."

Wylla did not answer directly. She lifted her hands and motioned to Rulalin to calm down. "Just hear me out," she said after a moment. "If he dies, you won't have saved me. The best part of me will die with him. Now will you just hear me?"

"Yes," Rulalin said reluctantly.

"All right. I know it won't be easy, but it is dark and all eyes are focused on the city and their surrender in the morning. Benjiah is under your care. The same way you can send off my guard to talk to me, you can get rid of his. We'll slip away."

"We'd never make it. Apparently Benjiah's death is a big deal to Malek. It's a symbol of his triumph over Allfather."

"They will be busy receiving the surrender of the city."

"Yes, but they'll send Black Wolves and Malekim and maybe even Vulsutyrim after us. There's no way they'd let us get away."

"We'd have a head start."

"Not enough."

"Not if they don't know where to look. We'll go around Tol Emuna and then north and east. We'll go to Nolthanin and hide."

"Wylla," Rulalin said, shaking his head, "we won't make it, and even if we did, even if we somehow got away, they'd find us eventually."

"Maybe, but we could elude them for a while, maybe even for years." At this she dropped down on both of her knees, and Rulalin did not doubt that if her hands were not tied behind her, she would have reached up to him and grabbed him with them. "Rulalin, I am on my knees begging. Do you see? You killed my husband, but I am groveling at your feet. I have nothing left. Don't let them take my son. You say you love me. If you love me, you will free him. You will do this. I will go wherever you want me to go, only free my son."

He stooped and put his hands on her shoulders to help pull her up to her feet. "Wylla . . . "

She shook free from his hands violently. "No. I will not rise until you promise you will do this. Promise. Promise you will help me. I am begging you, Rulalin. Please, you must help me."

He stood for long moment, looking down. At last he nodded. *Apologies without change are useless.* "All right, Wylla. Let's go get him."

11

MIDSPRING

R ULALIN AND W YLLA walked calmly through the camp. He kept her hands tied and held on to her upper arm. If he was stopped by anyone for any reason, he wanted it to appear as though he was treating her like a prisoner. They reached his tent and ducked inside.

"I think you should stay here," Rulalin said quietly. "It'll be suspicious if I approach Benjiah's cage with you."

"Are we near the edge of the camp here?"

"No."

"Then you need to take me. Once his cage is found empty, we'll be on borrowed time. You can't risk bringing him back here to pick me up."

"Then I'll need to find a place to stash you while I approach Benjiah's guards."

"Then that's what you'll have to do."

"Can I trust you, alone and unguarded in the dark?"

"Would I toy with my son's life?"

Rulalin didn't answer. He knew Wylla would not do anything to jeopardize Benjiah. He took a deep breath. "Are you ready to do this?"

Wylla hesitated, and Rulalin could tell something had just occurred to her. "What will happen to Yorek when they find us missing?"

Rulalin looked back at her, blankly. She knew what would happen. Saying it was unnecessary.

"We have to go back and get him," Wylla said, starting out of the tent.

Rulalin took her arm and pulled her back. "Hold on," he said. "You should have thought of that before. I can't take you back there and then leave again with both of you. The fact that Yorek is still lying there asleep is probably the only reason why the guard hasn't raised the alarm yet."

"But he'll die."

"We'll all die. You can't save him, Wylla. You can't save everyone. Do you want to get Benjiah or not?"

"I can't leave Yorek to die."

"He knew when he came here that he might die," Rulalin said.

"He didn't know I might sentence him to that death by sneaking away in the night."

"My guess is that he'd rather you and Benjiah get away, don't you think? If you asked him to lay his life down for Benjiah, do you think he would?"

"I would not ask him that."

"Wylla," Rulalin said at last. "We either leave this tent and go get Benjiah, right now, no further questions and no arguments, or I take you back to Yorek and leave you there."

Wylla stood staring at Rulalin for a long time. "All right," she said. "Let's go get Benjiah."

They stole back outside the tent, gliding quickly away from it. Rulalin was aware of every sound in the night, every cough from nearby tents, every whisper from men standing on guard or going about their business, every buzzing insect winging its way through the air. Moving carefully, they made their way gradually toward Benjiah's cage. Rulalin pulled Wylla aside behind another wagon, this one empty.

"We've got a problem," Rulalin whispered as he looked over the wagon at the cage and those around it.

"What?"

"The guards."

Wylla looked at them. All but one, who stood beside the cage, huddled by a fire a few spans away. There were perhaps half a dozen, which didn't appear to her overwhelming even if there were more than before. "What's the problem?"

"These aren't my men," Rulalin answered.

Wylla looked back at them, and the implication of what Rulalin was saying dawned on her. "But they are Nolthanim and you are a captain of the Nolthanim, right? They'll do what you say?"

"I don't know," Rulalin replied. "My men have been watching him, almost without exception, since the day he was captured. I don't know why they've been relieved or what orders these men have been given. Nor do I know why I wasn't told. I can only imagine that it was decided I couldn't be trusted with him any longer."

"So what do we do?"

"I don't think there's anything we can do."

"You won't even try?" her voice pleaded with him.

Rulalin looked down at her. "Wylla, I love you. Because I love you, I will walk out there and see what's going on, but if I realize this is impossible, then it's over. I'll walk back here and take you back to Yorek, and we'll have to let tomorrow bring what it will bring."

"Rulalin, you can't ask me—"

"I'm not asking; I'm telling you how it is. Now I'm not going out there until you promise me that if I fail you won't do something stupid. If you do, you'll not only fail to save Benjiah, you'll kill yourself and Yorek and me as well. Do you understand?"

"Yes."

"You promise?"

"I promise."

"All right," Rulalin answered, and he looked back at the guards by the cage. "Now stay here."

He walked away from the wagon, circling around until he could approach the fire from a different direction. Then he turned in toward the guards and the cage and did his best to walk at a good but not hurried pace. He wanted to appear official and authoritative.

"What's going on here?" he asked firmly as they looked up. He wanted to control the situation if he could. "Where are my men who were guarding this prisoner?"

One of the soldiers in the huddle stepped away from the fire and moved between the others and Rulalin. His face was familiar, for Rulalin had seen him often by Farimaal's tent.

"Those men have been relieved," he said.

"On whose orders?"

"Farimaal's."

Rulalin swallowed. He'd both suspected and dreaded that this would be the answer. These men were here on direct command from Farimaal, and he doubted there was anything he could say or do to get them to leave their post willingly.

"I see," he said, nodding as he stalled, trying to think of something, anything. "In fact, that's good. I lost too many men yesterday to waste them on a pointless guard duty."

He started toward Benjiah's cage, but the soldier stepped in front of him and held up a hand.

"I beg your pardon?" Rulalin said indignantly.

"I can't let you near him."

"I am a captain of the Nolthanim and don't answer to you," Rulalin said, moving forward again. The soldier drew his sword and put the tip squarely before Rulalin's chest.

"Farimaal commands the Nolthanim, and he told me to let no one near this prisoner, especially you."

The words *especially you* hung in the air. Rulalin knew he was finished and had no wish to overplay his hand. "Easy, soldier," he said. "You could have said as much. Had you told me Farimaal wanted him left alone, that would have been sufficient. Carry on."

He turned and started off. Nothing further was said and no one followed him. When he knew he was out of sight of the guards, he doubled back to retrieve Wylla. He had been worried about how she would react, specifically fearing that she'd race toward the cage in a desperate, final attempt to see her son, only to get cut down by the guards in the process. However, she did nothing of the sort, and when Rulalin took her arm to lead her away, she followed without resistance, walking with him wordlessly all the way back.

When Rulalin left her, Wylla lay down in the grass but could not sleep. The evening was warm despite the intermittent rainfall, but she felt cold and empty. She'd not really believed that they would get away for long, perhaps a day or at best a few weeks. She had hoped at least, however, to release Benjiah from that terrible cage and hold him close again. She had hoped to die with him, fighting for their freedom and survival. To be denied this after finally persuading Rulalin to go along with it was almost more than she could bear. Watching Benjiah executed in the morning would certainly be. She buried her face in the sparse grass and wept.

She lay for a long time, quietly sobbing, and then felt a gentle touch. She was suddenly aware that someone lay beside her. She sat up with a start and turned to see Yorek looking up at her. "Shh," he said, "It's all right. It's just me."

Wylla lay back down, relieved. "I just . . . when I felt you all of a sudden like that, for some reason I thought it might be him."

"It's all right," Yorek said. "Relax. Lie down."

She did lie down. Turning toward him, she allowed him to caress her hair as she rested her head against his chest. A memory of her mother, sitting behind her on the edge of her bed with a great brush, stroking her long dark hair, caught Wylla off guard. There was immense comfort in the memory, as there was immense comfort in Yorek's tender touch.

"Do you want to talk about it?" he asked quietly.

"No," Wylla answered. "What is there to say? In the morning my two greatest fears will be realized. My son will die before my very eyes, and Kirthanin will bow the knee to Malek."

"Both seem likely," Yorek conceded.

"Likely? It's as good as done."

"I admit, it certainly seems that both are inevitable, but neither has happened yet," Yorek said. "Hope remains."

"I can't afford to hope," Wylla replied. "Hope led me here to my death, and you to yours. Hope led me to beg Rulalin for aid tonight while you slept, to abase myself before that murderer and traitor, and for what? My son is guarded tighter than ever and Rulalin wasn't even able to get me through to see him."

"You went to see him?"

"Yes," Wylla replied, hesitantly, even guiltily. "I convinced Rulalin to try to set him free. I thought we might be able to get away and at least have a few days together. It would have meant leaving you here to your fate. It was a terrible thing to even consider. I'm sorry, Yorek."

"Oh, Wylla," Yorek replied, his voice cracked and tearful. "Don't apologize to me. If I had awoken to find you gone from here, with or without Benjiah by your side, I would have rejoiced. I'm glad you tried."

"Even so," Wylla insisted, "it would have been wrong to leave you. At least I will not have that on my conscience tomorrow."

She lay beside him and he said no more. The sounds of men laughing floated on the night air from somewhere far away in the camp. Wylla did not know exactly what time it was, but she would have guessed it was Second Watch. Morning would begin to creep across the sky late in Fourth Watch, so there was little time left. She wondered, as a mother must, if Benjiah was sleeping. Did he know what tomorrow held? Was he aware that his last precious moments were slipping away? Surely he had known the possibility of his doom from the moment he was captured, but he had lived so long in that situation that tomorrow would come upon him unexpectedly.

She wanted to go to him, to sneak somehow past all the guards and reach in through the slats and stroke his hair as Yorek now stroked hers. She was being comforted, but who was comforting him? She wanted to cradle his head in her hands, to feel his soft skin one last time. She knew she couldn't have these things, but she wanted them all the same.

"I wish I could just tell him goodbye," she said.

"I know."

"One of the hardest things about losing Joraiem, about the way I lost him, was that I never got to say goodbye. He was dead when I came to him, lying lifeless and bloody in the sand. He was gone, Yorek. His body was there, but he wasn't, not really. He was gone, and I'd said none of the really important things, the things I needed to have said. I want to say them to Benjiah. I want a chance to tell him goodbye."

"You may never get that chance in this life," Yorek said after a moment, "but I think you will speak to both of them again, when Allfather makes all things new."

"It seems a distant hope."

"At times it does, but distant and unreal are not the same."

"No, maybe not," Wylla replied, "but between now and then is tomorrow, and what tomorrow holds I cannot face."

"You can and will, Your Majesty," Yorek said soothingly. "You have faced many difficult things already. You will find strength to bear what must be borne, even tomorrow."

"We shall see," Wylla said. She rolled over and faced the other direction. She closed her eyes even though she knew she would not sleep. The night would creep along slowly, but even so, the dawn would come too soon.

The morning light found the massive gates of Tol Emuna already open and the surrender under way. The captains had realized that in order to empty the entire city by the appointed time, they would need to begin before dawn.

Pedraan stood by the gates as the soldiers of the armies of Kirthanin passed solemnly through. It had been agreed that Caan would ride out with the first of them to oversee the discarding of weapons and to make sure, as much as he could, that everything went smoothly. Pedraan was to stay and see the army out, and then he would bring up the rear. Next would come the Great Bear, and after them Carrafin would oversee the evacuation of the civilians. So far, everything was going as planned, though Allfather alone knew what the remainder of the day would bring.

By the middle of First Hour, the army was completely out of the city. Pedraan looked up at the thick grey clouds spitting tiny drops of rain in uneven measure. The day was warm, so the moisture on his face and hands and cloak were not especially uncomfortable. It was, despite the dreary cloudiness, not such a bad day. Perhaps one could get used to nothing but clouds all the time, used to the absence of the sun and blue sky. Perhaps, Pedraan thought, but he would not have such a chance. He was a captain of the army and was therefore "guilty" of rebellion. He wasn't going to get used to anything anymore. Today he was going to die.

It had been a long night, beginning with his report to the captains. The meeting was sober. No one was really surprised by the news they would be executed. None of them had expected to survive the surrender. There was more concern about the possibility, some would have said likelihood, that Malek's captains might not keep their word about sparing the soldiers and civilians. This risk was exacerbated among those who had known Synoki from their adventures seventeen years before, now aware that he was a figure of some prominence among Malek's host. Trusting any promise involving one such as him was very difficult.

For his part, Pedraan thought that at least the civilians should be safe. He could not see how Malek would profit by their deaths. Malek wanted to rule the world, and surely that implied someone to rule over. At the same time, he realized that just because he couldn't see profit in the deaths of the people, that didn't mean they'd be safe or escape the day without suffering.

The soldiers, though, had raised their weapons against Malek. He could imagine things going badly for the soldiers once they surrendered and the captains were dead. In any case, he would certainly never know about it, because Malek and his men would be sure to kill the captains first. If they did intend to betray the negotiated terms of surrender, there'd be no authority to object to their treachery.

After the long and difficult meeting, in which they planned the details of the surrender, he left to seek Karalin. He'd found her asleep in the chair of a room where she'd been working among the wounded. She'd tried to wait up for him, but weariness from nursing the injured men and preparing them for evacuation had drained all her energy. His time with her had been hard. He kept thinking there should be some perfect way to express himself, something appropriate to say that would sum up all he felt about losing Pedraal, about surrendering to Malek, about what he'd hoped life would be like with her and how much he didn't want to let go of that dream, but nothing sounded exactly right. He kept trying to explain things that no longer made sense to him, and she kept assuring him that she understood what he meant. She assured him, but he no longer understood it himself and didn't see how she could understand either. In the end, he had only been able to tell her that he loved her and was sorry it had all come to nothing. Then the time came to begin evacuating the army and he'd had to go.

He nodded to Turgan and the Great Bear assembling at the gate, and then he walked out after his men. There was something strangely peaceful about surrendering. From the moment Valzaan had come bursting in on them on that stormy autumn night in Amaan Sul, he felt like he was living life on the edge of the precipice. Every moment, they had teetered on the brink of disaster. Now that they teetered no longer and had in fact fallen over the edge, he felt a distinct sense of relief.

He closed his eyes and imagined the peace of letting go, of ceasing to struggle for balance. He liked the image. He imagined falling effortlessly through the air, knowing that he would soon hit bottom and die, but that at least it would soon be over. He thought of Pedraal's lifeless body, and of the certainty that whatever he had felt when the Malekim killed him, it had not lasted long. Pedraan knew he should worry more about those who would live on after him, about those who would have to live under Malek, like Karalin and his sister, but he found it too hard to muster the energy. They were going to have to figure all that out. He didn't want to spend the little time left to him thinking about that.

Before long, they approached the place where the column of men was being divided into two separate, smaller ranks. Standing at the fork were Vulsutyrim who had apparently been given the job of overseeing the surrender of weapons. They towered over the men passing below them, gazing down with looks of scorn or indifference at the defeated. Pedraan could see the two rows of soldiers being directed past two growing mounds of swords, knives, bows, arrows, and the occasional spear. The sound of additional blades being tossed onto the pile rang out, and he watched as the men ahead of him began to unbuckle their sheaths and swords to toss them in as well.

He had no weapon to add, and as he drew near the pile, a Nolthanim stepped before him.

"Leave your weapons here," the soldier said not so much roughly as definitively.

"I have none."

The man looked doubtful, and he motioned to another Nolthanim, who came over and joined him. "Remove your cloak."

Pedraan did as he was directed, and they examined him closely, finding no hidden blade of any kind. At last they told him to proceed. He stepped back into the steady but slowing stream of men, leaving the towering stacks of useless weaponry behind.

Third Hour came and went. As Pedraan looked around, he could see that the assembled crowd was vast. The army, the Great Bear and the civilian population had all been evacuated from the city and now crowded around the curious scaffold that dominated the center of the plain beyond the two great mounds of weapons. The Great Bear had added their staffs to the piles.

The scaffold was enormous, having been made, Pedraan thought, from planks scavenged from the great wagons the Malekim had pulled across Kirthanin. It was easily a span above the ground with steps on either side. There was nothing upon the scaffold save only two great poles in the center, thicker than any Great Bear staff and easily two spans high, rising into the sky perhaps a span apart.

"What in the world are they for?" Brenim had asked him when Pedraan was brought to the guarded captains near the front of the crowd.

Any hope that perhaps some of the leadership might escape their doom had been dashed pretty much right away. Pedraan didn't know how the Nolthanim knew who each of them was, but they had known. All the high-ranking officers from each of the various armies had been eventually taken into hand by two or three Nolthanim soldiers and escorted none too gently to the front. Bryar and several of the scouts were there, as were a number of the lesser officers that Pedraan would not have considered captains, but who had distinguished themselves in battle.

"I don't know," Pedraan had said in reply to Brenim's question about the poles. "Though I'd bet they have something to do with our execution."

Brenim didn't say anything to that, and Pedraan was left to his thoughts as he examined the poles upon the scaffold. He could see a solitary iron ring on the inside of each, and he guessed that perhaps men were going to be chained to the pole so that their dead bodies could remain on display for all to see.

A flicker of anger that he should die this way, his body exposed before the crowd of friend and foe alike, flowed through him and was gone. There was no use getting angry about it. It could no longer be avoided. If such was his fate, he would receive it as bravely and nobly as possible.

A moment later, a sound in the distance attracted his attention, and he turned to see what it was. At first he couldn't tell, but gradually he realized that something, or someone, was making its way through the assembly. In fact, it was probably many someones, for the crowd was parting to make way.

A pair of Malekim was drawing one of their great wagons through their midst, and something like an enormous box rested on the back. The people around the wagon were pressing to get out of its way, then closing in behind to stare at the box on the back.

It drew near enough that it was only ten or fifteen spans from them, and Pedraan could see now it was not a box. It was a wooden cage, made from solid wooden slats a little less than a span in length and height. It was a cage, and Pedraan could see two hands gripping the slats from the inside. From his angle, he could not see the person attached to the hands, but he didn't need to. Farimaal and Synoki had made clear who was to be executed first, and he had no doubt that his nephew was in that wooden cage.

A great silence had fallen over the whole assembly, and only the creaking of the huge wooden wheels made any noise. Before long, the wagon was brought all the way forward to the edge of the scaffold. The Malekim left the wagon there and disappeared back into the crowd as the Nolthanim who had walked behind the wagon took up positions to guard it. They stood still, backs to the wagon, watching the crowd.

Vulsutyrim moved in among the assembly, stationing themselves at almost even intervals. Pedraan knew they were there to nip any adverse reactions to the executions in the bud. They would be a strong deterrent to anyone with any opposing ideas, as would the vast army of Malekim and Nolthanim surrounding the men and women on the plain. Where the Black Wolves were this morning, Pedraan had no idea, but he had seen none.

He scanned the area around the scaffold beyond the wagon, and he froze when he saw his sister. She was standing with Yorek at the far end of the scaffold, with a prime view of the twin poles. With them was Rulalin, and all of them stood gazing at the cage. Pedraan's heart sank. He hadn't supposed she would be spared the indignity and grief of watching her son and brother die, but she was so close. It was almost enough to make him lose heart. He had been somewhat comforted that Karalin would be somewhere out there in the faceless sea of spectators, since he didn't want to watch her watch him die. He didn't want to look down upon the weeping face of his sister as he left this world either.

He didn't have long to think about this, because a man in an ornate cloak approached the wagon, the man in the camp whom Rulalin had called Tashmiren. At his direction, the cage was opened. Pedraan held his breath as Benjiah was brought out. He looked not quite gaunt, but thin, haggard, and unkempt. He stretched as he emerged, taking a moment to stand to his full height before being prodded to get down off the wagon and follow Tashmiren. They walked to the stairs and ascended to the scaffold. There, a pair of Nolthanim produced two solid chains and bound Benjiah fast to the two poles.

Pedraan winced as he saw it done. The chains were looped through the iron rings, secured above Benjiah's head. Then they were attached to his wrists and pulled so tight that even from where Pedraan stood he could see the strain placed on his nephew's arms. He could see the strain and he heard the gasp of pain as they were secured, the excess chain hanging heavily down from his wrists. The men who secured him then descended, leaving Tashmiren and one other man, a great brute of a Nolthanim who was standing motionless at the rear, on the scaffold with Benjiah.

Benjiah's arms were pulled high and out from his shoulders, but his head was down, his dangling hair obscuring his face. Pedraan watched him, aware there were tears upon his own face. He reached up and wiped them away with his sleeve. He was prepared to die today. He'd made his peace with that. He was weary of the fight, weary of the world. He'd lived long enough and served his purpose, but not Benjiah. *He shouldn't be up there on display like that, waiting to die*, Pedraan thought. *It isn't right.*

But there was nothing he could do. All that was left was to hope that Benjiah's death would come quickly, that he would die with as little pain as possible. Beyond that, Pedraan's only hope was that he would be next.

Benjiah stared down at the wooden planks under his feet. It felt good to be standing, even if it felt like his arms might be pulled out of their sockets at any moment by these chains. His shoulders ached from the tension, but it wasn't the pain in his arms that dominated his thoughts, it was the scene, which he had seen before in his dreams and which had at last come to pass in reality.

He looked down because he didn't dare look up. The poles, the wooden stage or scaffold or whatever it was that had been constructed during the watches of the night, and of course the vast assembly—all were exactly as he had dreamed them. He would not look up, though, and gaze into their faces. He wished to see neither the jeering of his captors nor the tears of his sympathizers. His mother, though, was different. He had seen her out of the corner of his eye as they dragged him from the wagon. He should like to see her clearly one more time, but not yet. He would look for her at the end, but if he found her too soon, he might lose his composure. Now, though, he needed his strength to face whatever it was he was going to have to face.

Tashmiren walked up to him and stood still before him, but he did not look up. "Comfortable, boy?" he whispered, his voice sneering.

When Benjiah did not respond, he continued. "I wonder if you still think your little stunt by the Kalamin River was worthwhile. You didn't save your friends, not really. They are defeated after all, as you can see. And now, well, you will die before them. Was it worth it?"

Benjiah gazed into Tashmiren's mocking eyes. "The look of shock, anger and rage in all of your faces when you found your way blocked and your plan frustrated? Yes, it was worth it."

Anger flashed through Tashmiren's eyes. "Well, I'm glad to see you're not broken already, otherwise this morning would have been so much less interesting. I assure you, before you die, you'll wish you'd never taken up that old fool's staff at all, let alone wielded it against my master."

Benjiah looked down again, and Tashmiren moved away, toward the front of the scaffold. He thought back to the towering wall of earth and the battlefield beside the Kalamin, and he smiled. Yes, thwarting the plans of the enemy had been good, but what had made it all worthwhile was the feeling of warmth and light that had flowed through him as he wielded Allfather's power. That feeling of being embraced, surrounded and indwelt by light, love, and power greater than anything Benjiah had ever conceived of was worth all that had come after. It was worth the indignity of the cage and being subject to his father's murderer. It was worth the long days and nights being toted league by league across Enthanin. It was even worth these poles and this ignominious stage. Whatever came next, he didn't regret it for a moment, and no pain or torture or death would ever make him say otherwise.

"Welcome, subjects of Malek," Tashmiren called from the edge of the scaffold. The sound of his arrogant voice, booming in the quiet stillness of the morning, drew Benjiah's eyes at last. He raised his head enough to see Tashmiren's back.

"My master and yours bids you welcome. Though you have of late been in rebellion against him, he is prepared to show you mercy as you have now come to your senses and are prepared to bow the knee.

"He is prepared to show mercy," Tashmiren repeated, stepping to his right and beginning to walk slowly along the front of the scaffold, "but his mercy has limits, as you would expect for one so greatly wronged. We are here then, to witness the trial and execution of the ringleaders of this rebellion. And, when we have administered justice, to establish the terms by which you will bind yourselves to your new master now and forevermore."

Tashmiren paused, underscoring the assembly's complete and utter silence. Benjiah dared raise his eyes and survey some of the crowd, and a sea of faces stared back, all eyes trained either upon the man who addressed them or upon himself, chained between the two great poles. He lowered his eyes to the floor again, not wanting to see any of the faces in particular.

"Today is Midspring," Tashmiren said, a hint of amusement in his voice. "As I understand it, it is a day when you honor and revere Allfather, a day of worship and celebration. Well, it is appropriate then that you surrender today, for today you acknowledge your true sovereign, Malek. Midspring will be from now on a day when you will honor and revere him, when you will worship and celebrate his triumphant return to the Mountain, where he will rule from now on. Though you may not see it yet, being as you are still trapped in old ways of thinking, there will come a day when you will greet Midspring as the mark of your great liberation, as the day when Kirthanin was at last made what it was always meant to be and united at last under the authority and rule of Malek, the last of the Titans."

The assembly remained silent, and Tashmiren, walking along the scaffold in the other direction, started up again. "But first, before we can look to the future, we must tie up the loose ends of the past. Gathered before me at the foot of the scaffold are the captains of your army. They will be tried and executed for their crimes against Malek in a moment, but first there is other business at hand.

"The boy you see before you"—and here Tashmiren turned sideways and motioned to Benjiah as he paused—"is here brought as a symbol of your rebellion and of your senseless adherence to this outdated worship of Allfather. Though he claims to be a prophet, a servant of this god from days of old, he stands before you in chains. If he were truly a servant of some powerful, supreme being, he would not be here, waiting for death. The fact of the matter is, these ancient stories of Allfather are lies and exaggerations. The Titans were our true rulers of old, and Malek, first among them, our true god.

"For this reason, the boy Benjiah is the first to be tried, for you will all see, once and for all, that there is no hand mightier than Malek's; you will all see and know who your true master is. When his offenses have been enumerated, he will be put to death, and when you see his lifeless body dangling from the chains, you will know his devotion and service, like your own, has been in vain."

Tashmiren began to run down the charges against Benjiah and to describe his offenses to the gathered assembly, but his voice, though as loud as it had ever been, began to fade in Benjiah's ears. He looked up and saw Tashmiren only a few spans away, but he could barely hear the man's words. A great hush had fallen upon his ears.

The scene before him disappeared. He saw only great darkness and a sky full of rain, torrential rain falling in sheets upon an empty plain. The rain fell heavily and then disappeared as an explosion of light blotted out all things with unfathomable brightness. Benjiah closed his eyes but could still see the light as clearly as if he were staring open-eyed at the noonday sun. The light faded, and he found himself back in the cage, feeling the wooden slats with his fingertips. The cage walls fell away, and he rose and walked out into the great white city. The city square was open and peaceful, empty and quiet. He was aware that he was not in fact there in the city, that he was only seeing it as he had seen it hundreds of times before, but this time he hungered for that place, to be there in fact and not in a dream. He knew that he was chained to the poles upon the scaffold, and he wanted to be free.

Peace, child. Your present trials are but for a moment. You will see this place in truth, in body and not in a dream, but not yet. I have given you this glimpse, one more time, one last time, that you may know, even now, in your hour of great distress, that I have more for you to do. Today is not your last.

Benjiah's head jerked up. The scaffold, Tashmiren, and the watching crowd reappeared. The voice, the scene, all fell away, and his senses returned. He saw the real world and heard the echoes of Tashmiren's voice. He smelled the strong scent of spring grass in the rain, despite the odor of the death from the rotting carcasses of war. He was aware of the world in a heightened fashion and to a degree previously unknown to him.

"So," Tashmiren was saying, "having heard the charges that Malek brings before you, have you anything to say?"

Tashmiren stood looking at him, his back not fully turned to the assembly, the perpetual smirk in his face still lingering there. Benjiah had no idea what Tashmiren had been saying, but he could see that Tashmiren thought it was devastating and precluded any possibility of reply.

Benjiah looked at his accuser and then glanced in the direction where he believed his mother might be. He found her face there almost immediately. She was looking up at him with tears in her eyes, and when his eyes made contact with hers, she raised her hands in a simple gesture of greeting, like she was reaching out to touch him.

A song began in the back of Benjiah's mind, a song that he had never heard before, and yet the words and music both flooded him vividly. He began to sing, mouthing the words almost silently. The verse was short, and he soon sang it all the way through. As he did, he saw scattered images of a pretty house with a large wooden veranda, where a man held a young boy in his lap. He saw a battlefield strewn with bodies and men gathering the dead into piles. Among them he saw the same man, now greying, cradling the head of a young man—the young boy now grown, Benjiah thought, probably his son. The man sat in the rain, face blank and worn, water streaming down his beard, singing. Singing this song.

"What did you say?" Tashmiren said, his voice no longer booming as he stepped closer to Benjiah, his eyes threatening.

Benjiah began to sing again, this time loud enough for Tashmiren to hear the words. He sang it through, and Tashmiren said, "What is this gibberish? I asked you if you had a defense for your rebellious actions, and you sing nonsense? You've lost your mind."

Benjiah raised his head and held it high. The light, the love, and the warmth were beginning to flow through him. He felt the presence and power of Allfather, and he sang the song now with strength and boldness so that it echoed across the plain.

> *Peace, my son, and lay you down,*
> *The sun has gone away.*
> *Wake and find the dawn at hand,*
> *Tomorrow is today—*
> *Tomorrow is today.*

His voice faded, and he could hear whispers and stirrings rippling through the crowd. Tashmiren was staring dumbfounded, a mixture of confusion, aggravation, and anger on his face. Benjiah sang the song again, even louder, his voice soaring above the crowd and echoing across the assembly. As he did, he noticed a man with fury in his face making his way through the crowd, limping along as the soldiers parted before him.

He looked up to the clouds and saw there something remarkable. The rain had stopped, and a crack in the cloud cover had opened. Rays of sunshine were streaming through, illuminating the grey morning. The whole assembly looked up. The crack widened, and the light was suddenly so bright that he had to close his eyes. He forced them open again, though, and found that he could see while the others apparently could not. Tashmiren had both arms raised above his head to try to shield his eyes from the bright light, and the people gathered there were likewise overwhelmed by the sudden and dramatic sunlight.

He gazed out over them, aware of golden images far off in the distance, lots of them, visible against the grey clouds that still hung in the sky to the west.

"Behold, he comes!" Benjiah shouted, his voice a roar that filled the sky. With his arms he strained against the chains, adrenaline and energy and joy pumping through his body.

"The Father of Dragons!" he called again. "He comes!"

EPILOGUE

THE KALIN SEIR and their battle brothers slackened their pace, and Aljeron and the others slowed to. They had been moving quickly all morning, determined that this was the day they would reach Tol Emuna. They didn't slow because they were tired, and they didn't slow because they were hungry. They didn't even slow because the rain had stopped. They slowed because the slightest of cracks in the cloud cover, which had been a fixed part of the landscape for the better part of the last half-year, had appeared in the east, in the very direction they were heading.

All eyes looked upward as the faintest trace of blue sky became unmistakably clear. They knew, intellectually, that once it had been a common sight, so common in fact as to hardly warrant any notice, but today it was like looking at a piece of finely wrought gold for the first time. They felt intuitively the wonder of it, and they stood, whispering to one another, marveling at the sight.

Aljeron noticed a warm breeze upon his face. He would have closed his eyes to enjoy the feeling for just a moment, be he didn't want to stop looking at the sky. What did it mean, this change in the heavens? He couldn't guess, but it seemed obvious that the answer lay at Tol Emuna.

He looked over at Valzaan to ask, but unlike the rest, who all stood oriented toward the thin sliver of blue sky, Valzaan was facing west. His blank white eyes appeared fixed upon the cloudy sky that hung there.

Aljeron was puzzled. He didn't know if the prophet was capable of perceiving the slight increase of brightness in the east or not, but surely if he wasn't he would have inquired as to the reason for their halt. Why did he stand facing the opposite way?

"Valzaan," Aljeron asked, stepping closer to him. "What is it?"

Valzaan raised his hand and pointed. Aljeron followed the direction of his finger but could still see nothing.

"What am I looking for?"

"Can you not see?"

"No, I can't."

"They are coming."

"They?"

"The dragons. Sulmandir and his children."

Aljeron felt a tingle of excitement ripple up and down his skin. He peered harder, and he thought that perhaps this time he could make out the appearance of little golden specks against the greyness.

"Dragons," he whispered.

"Yes, they come," Valzaan said reverently. "On wings of gold, they come."

"That's why the clouds are breaking, why sunlight and blue sky are forcing their way through at last."

"The two are related, but the dragons are not why."

"Then why?"

"Because Allfather has decreed an end to Cheimontyr's control of the weather and has wrested the wind and rain from his hand, once and for all."

"Then the Bringer of Storms is dead?"

"No, he is not dead, but his hour draws near. Like Vulsutyr, his father, his doom approaches. He cannot and will not stand before it."

Aljeron looked back to the sky in the west again, and this time there were many, many golden specks, and he could see them clearly now. He wondered what it would look like to stand below them, watching the dragons soar above his head. It would be a sight to behold.

"We should run," Aljeron said.

"Yes," Valzaan agreed. "Let us run. The dawn of a new day is at hand."

Sleeping in his ancient gyre,
Removed from all the cares of men,
He heard his Maker's voice
He made at last his choice
And stretched his wings to fly again.
Rising from his mountain refuge,
Returning to the wars of men,
He'll ride on wings of gold
As the final days unfold
And he won't go home again.

—From "Waking the Dragon"

The End
of the Fourth Book of
The Binding of the Blade

GLOSSARY

Aelwyn Elathien (ALE-win el-ATH-ee-un): Novaana of Werthanin, Mindarin's younger sister.

Agia Muldonai (ah-GEE-uh MUL-doe-nye): The Holy Mountain. Agia Muldonai was the ancient home of the Titans, who lived in Avalione, the city nestled high upon the mountain between its twin peaks. Agia Muldonai has been under Malek's control since the end of the Second Age, when he invaded Kirthanin from his home in exile on the Forbidden Isle.

Alazare (AL-uh-zair): The Titan who cast Malek from Agia Muldonai at the end of the First Age when Malek's Rebellion failed. Severely injured in his battle with Malek, Alazare passed from the stage of Kirthanin history and was never seen again.

Aljeron Balinor (AL-jer-on BALL-ih-nore): Novaana of Werthanin (Shalin Bel), travels with his battle brother Koshti.

Allfather: Creator of Kirthanin, who gave control of Kirthanin's day-to-day affairs to the Council of Twelve. To accomplish this task, He gave great power to each of these Titans. Since the time of Malek's Rebellion, Allfather has

474

continued to speak to His creation through prophets who remind Kirthanin of Allfather's sovereign rule.

Amaan Sul (AH-mahn SUL): Royal seat of Enthanin.

Anakor (AN-uh-core): Titan, ally to Malek, killed by Volrain in the Rebellion.

Andunin (an-DOO-nin): The Nolthanim man chosen by Malek at the Rebellion to be king over mankind.

Andunin Plateau: Wasteland of northwestern Nolthanin.

Arimaar Mountains (AIR-ih-mar): Suthanin's longest range, which runs between Lindan Wood and the eastern coast of Suthanin.

Assembly: The official gathering of all Kirthanin Novaana who are appointed to represent their family and region.

Autumn Rise: See seasons.

Autumn Wane: See seasons.

Avalione (av-uh-lee-OWN): Blessed city and home of the Crystal Fountain. It rests between the peaks of Agia Muldonai and was once the home of the Titans. Like the rest of Agia Muldonai, the city was declared off limits by Allfather at the beginning of the Second Age.

Avram Gol (AV-ram GALL): Ancient ruined port city of western Nolthanim known in the First Age as the City of the Setting Sun.

Azaruul butterflies (AZ-uh-rule): Green luminescent butterflies.

Azmavarim (az-MAV-uh-rim): Also known as Firstblades, these swords were forged during the First Age by Andunin and his followers.

Balimere (BALL-ih-mere): Also called Balimere the Beautiful. The most beloved of all the Titans to the lesser creatures of Kirthanin. It is said that when Allfather restores Kirthanin, Balimere will be the first of the faithful Titans to be resurrected.

Barunaan River (buh-RUE-nun): Major north-south river between Kellisor Sea and the Southern Ocean.

Bay of Thalasee (THAL-uh-see): Bay off Werthanin's west coast.

Benjiah Andira (ben-JY-uh an-DEER-uh): Joraiem and Wylla's son.

Master Berin (BARE-in): Master of Sulare.

Black Wolves: Creatures created by Malek during his exile on the Forbidden Isle.

Mistress Brahan (BRA-HAN): Rulalin's housekeeper and chief steward.

Brenim Andira (BREN-im an-DEER-uh): Novaana of Suthanin (Dal Harat), Joraiem's younger brother.

Bringer of Storms, the: See Cheimontyr.

Bryar (BRY-er): Novaana of Werthanin, Elyas's older sister, who fights for Fel Edorath under Aljeron's command.

Caan (KAHN): Combat instructor for the Novaana in Sulare.

Calendar: There are ninety-one days in every season, making the year 364 days. The midseason feast days are not numbered and instead are known only by their name (Midsummer, Midautumn, etc.) They fall between the fifteenth and sixteenth day of each season. These days are "outside of time" in part as a tribute to the timelessness of Allfather; they also look forward to the time when all things will be made new.

Calissa (kuh-LISS-uh): Novaana of Suthanin (Kel Imlarin), Darias's sister.

Carrafin (CARE-uh-fin): The captain of Tol Emuna, known as the "Captain of the Rock."

Charnosh (CHAR-nosh): Titan, ally to Malek, killed by Rolandes during the Rebellion.

Cheimontyr (SHY-MON-teer): The Bringer of Storms, most fearful of the Vulsutyrim who can control the weather.

Cimaris Rul (sim-AHR-iss RULE): Town at the mouth of the Barunaan River where it pours into the Southern Ocean.

Cinjan (SIN-jun): Mysterious cohort of Synoki.

Col Marena (KOLE muh-REEN-uh): Port near Shalin Bel.

Corindel (KORE-in-del): Enthanim royal who attempted to drive Malek from Agia Muldonai and betrayed the Great Bear at the beginning of the Third Age.

Corlas Valon (KORE-las vah-LAHN): Fel Edorath captain whose troops join Aljeron's to face Malek.

Council of Twelve: The twelve Titans to whom Allfather entrusted the care of Kirthanin. The Council dwelt in Avalione on Agia Muldonai, but frequently they would transform themselves into human form and travel throughout the land. The greatest was of these was Malek, whose Rebellion ultimately brought about the destruction of the Twelve.

Crystal Fountain: Believed to be the fountainhead of all Kirthanin waters, this fountain once flowed in the center of Avalione.

cyranis (sir-AN-iss): A poison of remarkable potency that can kill most living things almost instantly if it gets into the bloodstream. Consequently, the cyranic arrow—the head of which is coated in cyranis—is one of few weapons that the people of Kirthanin trust against the Malekim.

Daaltaran (doll-TARE-an): Aljeron's sword, a Firstblade whose name means "death comes to all."

Daegon (DAY-gone): Titan, ally to Malek, killed by Alazare during the Rebellion.

Dal Harat (DOLL HARE-at): Village in western Suthanin, Joraiem Andira's home.

Darias (DAHR-ee-us): Novaana of Suthanin (Kel Imlarin), Calissa's brother.

Derrion Wel (DARE-ee-un WELL): Town in southeastern Suthanin.

draal (DRAWL): A tight-knit community of Great Bear.

dragon tower: These ancient structures were built in the First Age as homes away from home for dragons who naturally live in the high places of Kirthanin's mountains and prefer to sleep high above the ground.

dragons: One of the three great races of Kirthanin. All dragons are descended from the golden dragon, Sulmandir, the first creation of Allfather after the Titans. All dragons appear at first glance to be golden, but none except Sulmandir are entirely golden. Three dragon lines exist, marked by their distinct coloring: red, blue, and green.

Dravendir (DRAV-en-deer): A blue dragon.

Eliandir (el-ee-AN-deer): A red dragon.

Elnin Wood (EL-nin): Forest of central Suthanin that straddles the Barunaan River, home to the Elnindraal clan of Great Bear.

Elyas (eh-LIE-us): Novaana of Werthanin, Bryar's younger brother, who died fighting for Amaan Sul in one of the first campaigns against Fel Edorath.

Enthanin (EN-than-in): Kirthanin's eastern country. Residents are Enthanim.

Eralon (AIR-uh-lahn): Faithful Titan killed by Malek and his allies during the Rebellion.

Erefen Marshes (AIR-i-fen): Swampland boundary between Werthanin and Suthanin.

Erevir (AIR-uh-veer): Major prophet of Allfather in the Second Age.

Erigan (AIR-ih-gan): Great Bear, Sarneth's son.

Evrim Minluan (EV-rim MIN-loo-in): Joraiem's best friend and close friend to Aljeron.

Farimaal (FARE-ih-mal): Leading general of Malek's, who brought the Grendolai into submission.

Fel Edorath (FELL ED-ore-ath): Easternmost city in Werthanin; the first line of defense against attacks from Agia Muldonai.

Fire Giant: See Vulsutyr.

First Age: The age of peace and harmony that preceded Malek's rebellion. Not only did peace govern the affairs of men in the First Age, but the three great races of men, dragons, and Great Bear coexisted then in harmony.

Firstblade: See Azmavarim.

Forbidden Isle: After Malek's failed Rebellion at the end of the First Age, he was driven from Kirthanin and took refuge on the Forbidden Isle, home of Vulsutyr, the Fire Giant.

Forest of Gyrin (GEAR-in): Forest south of Agia Muldonai, home to the Gyrindraal clan of Great Bear.

Forgotten Waters: Passage across the Southern Ocean from Suthanin to the Forbidden Isle.

Full Autumn: See seasons.

Full Spring: See seasons.

Full Summer: See seasons.

Full Winter: See seasons.

Garek Elathien (GAIR-ick el-ATH-ee-un): Novaana of Werthanin, Mindarin's father.

Garring Pul (GAR-ing PULL): Southernmost city of Enthanin, where the Kalamin River meets the Kellisor Sea.

garrion (GARE-ee-un): Mode of transport common in the First Age used by the Titans and some Novaana. Garrions came in many shapes and sizes, but they all functioned similarly: A dragon would pick up the garrion with his talons as he flew.

giants: See Vulsutyrim.

Gilion Numiah (GIL-ee-un new-MY-uh): Captain of Shalin Bel's army.

Gralindir (GRAY-lin-deer): A blue dragon.

Great Bear: One of the three great races of Kirthanin. These magnificent creatures commonly stand two spans high and are ferocious fighters when need calls. Nevertheless, they are known for their great wisdom and gentleness.

Grendolai (GREN-doe-lie): The joint creation of Malek and Vulsutyr, these terrifying creatures were used to attack the

Dragon Towers when Malek invaded Kirthanin from the Forbidden Isle. The dragons call them Dark Thieves.

gyre: A manmade dragon den built on top of a dragon tower.

Haalsun (HAL-sun): Faithful Titan killed by Charnosh during the Rebellion.

Halina Minluan (huh-LEE-nuh MIN-loo-in): Evrim and Kyril's older daughter.

Harak Andunin (HARE-ack an-DOO-nin): Mountain in Nolthanin whose name means "Andunin's Spear."

Hour: See time.

Invasion, the: Malek's second attempt to conquer Kirthanin.

Joraiem Andira (jore-EYE-em an-DEER-uh): Novaana of Suthanin (Dal Harat) and a prophet, murdered by Rulalin.

Jul Avedra (JULE uh-VADE-rah): Coastal town of Enthanin about midway between Tol Emuna and the Kalamin River delta.

Kalamin River (KAL-uh-min): River separating Enthanin from Suthanin.

Kalin Seir (KAY-lin SEER): The "true sons" or "sons of truth," a loyal contingency of Nolthanim who went into hiding after Andunin's rebellion and stayed hidden for two thousand years.

Karalin (CARE-uh-lin): Novaana from Enthanin (near Amaan Sul), crippled left ankle.

Keila (KEE-luh): A warrior woman of the Kalin Seir.

Kellisor Sea (KELL-ih-sore): The great internal sea of Kirthanin that lies directly south of Agia Muldonai.

Kelvan (KEL-vin): Novaana from Werthanin who died on the Forbidden Isle while battling Malekim and Black Wolves.

Kerentol (CARE-en-tall): Great Bear, elder of Taralindraal.

King Falcon: See windhover.

Kiraseth (KEER-uh-seth): Father of the Great Bear.

Kirthanin (KEER-than-in): The world in which the story takes place. Kirthanin comprises four countries on a single continent. Each country is defined by its geographic relationship to Agia Muldonai.

Kiruan River (KEER-oo-an): Marks the boundary of Werthanin and Nolthanin.

Koshti (KOSH-tee): Aljeron's tiger, battle brother.

Kumatin (KOO-mah-tin): Sea serpent created by Malek under the Forbidden Isle.

Kurveen (kur-VEEN): Caan's sword, a Firstblade whose name means "quick kill."

Kyril Minluan (KEER-il MIN-loo-in): Novaana of Suthanin (Dal Harat), Joraiem's younger sister and Evrim's wife, mother of Halina and Roslin.

Lindan Wood (LIN-duhn): Forest in eastern Suthanin, just west of the Arimaar Mountains, home to the Lindandraal clan of Great Bear.

Malek (MAH-leck): The greatest of Titans whose betrayal brought death to his Titan brothers and ruin to Kirthanin. Since the end of the Second Age and his second failed attempt to conquer all Kirthanin, he has ruled over Agia Muldonai and the surrounding area.

Malekim (MALL-uh-keem): Also known as Malek's Children, the Silent Ones, and the Voiceless. These creatures were first seen when Malek invaded Kirthanin at the end of the Second Age from the Forbidden Isle. A typical Malekim stands from a span and a third to a span and a half high and has a smooth thick grey hide. "Malekim" is both a singular and a plural term.

Marella Someris (muh-REL-uh so-MAIR-iss): Wylla's deceased mother, former Novaana and Queen of Enthanin.

Merias (mer-EYE-us): Captain of the army of Amaan Sul.

Merrion (MAIR-ee-un): White sea birds with blue stripes on their wings that can swim short distances underwater in pursuit of fish.

Mindarin Orlene (MIN-duh-rin ore-LEAN): Novaana of Werthanin, Aelwyn's older sister.

Monias Andira (moe-NYE-us an-DEER-uh): Novaana of Suthanin (Dal Harat), Joraiem's father.

Mound: Central feature in the midseason rituals that focus on Agia Muldonai's need for cleansing.

Nal Gildoroth (NAL GIL-dore-oth): Solitary city on the Forbidden Isle.

Naran (NARE-un): Leader of the Kalin Seir.

Nol Rumar (KNOLL RUE-mar): Small village in the north central plains of Werthanin.

Nolthanin (KNOLL-than-in): Kirthanin's northern country, largely in ruin during the Third Age.

Novaana (no-VAHN-uh): The nobility of human society in Kirthanin who at first governed human affairs under the direction of the Titans but have since adapted to autonomous control. Every seven years the Novaana between the ages of eighteen and twenty-five as of the first day of Spring Rise were to assemble from the first day of Spring Wane until the first day of Autumn Wane. Sulare is commonly referred to as the Summerland. "Novaana" is both a singular and a plural term.

Nyan Fein (NYE-un FEEN): Novaana of Suthanin (Cimaris Rul), married to commander Talis Fein.

Parigan (PARE-ih-gan): Great Bear, lead elder of the Taralindraal.

Pedraal Someris (PAY-drawl so-MAIR-iss): Novaana of Enthanin (Amaan Sul), Wylla's younger brother, Pedraan's older twin.

Pedraan Someris (PAY-drahn so-MAIR-iss): Novaana of Enthanin (Amaan Sul), Wylla's younger brother, Pedraal's younger twin.

Pedrone Someris (PAY-drone so-MAIR-iss): Last king of Enthanin, deceased.

Peris Mil (PARE-iss MILL): Town south of Kellisor Sea on the Barunaan River.

Ralon Orlene (RAY-lon ore-LEAN): Mindarin's late husband.

Rebellion, the: Malek's first attempt to conquer and rule Kirthanin by overthrowing the Twelve from Avalione.

Rolandes (roll-AN-deez): Faithful Titan killed by Daegon during the Rebellion.

Roslin Minluan (ROZ-lin MIN-loo-in): Evrim and Kyril's younger daughter.

Rucaran the Great (RUE-car-en): Father of the Black Wolves.

Rulalin Tarasir (rue-LAH-lin TARE-us-ear): Novaana of Werthanin (Fel Edorath), who murdered Joraiem in jealousy over Wylla.

Ruun Harak (RUNE HARE-ack): A spear given to Andunin by Malek.

Saegan (SIGH-gan): Novaana of Enthanin (Tol Emuna) who fights alongside Aljeron.

Sarneth (SAHR-neth): A lord among Great Bear, one of the few to still hold commerce with men, of Lindandraal.

seasons: As a largely agrarian world, Kirthanin follows a calendar that revolves around the four seasons. Each season is subdivided into three distinct periods, each of which contains thirty days. For example, the first thirty days of Summer are known as Summer Rise, the middle thirty days as Full Summer, and the last thirty as Summer Wane.

Second Age: The period that followed Malek's rebellion and preceded his return to Kirthanin. The Second Age was largely a time of peace until a massive civil war devastated Kirthanin's defenses and opened the door for Malek's second attempt at total conquest. Any date given which refers to the Second Age will be followed by the letters SA.

Shalin Bel (SHALL-in BELL): Large city of Werthanin.

Silent One: See Malekim.

Simmok River (SIM-mock): Nolthanin north-south river that pours into the Great Northern Sea.

slow time: See torrim redara.

Soran Nuvaar (SORE-an NEW-var): Friend and officer of Rulalin.

span: The most common form of measurement in Kirthanin. Its origin is forgotten but it could refer to the length of a man. A span is approximately 10 hands or what we would call 6 feet.

Spring Rise: See seasons.

Spring Wane: See seasons.

Stratarus (STRAT-ar-us): Faithful Titan killed by Anakor during the Rebellion.

Sulare (sue-LAHR-ee): Also known as the Sumerland. At the beginning of the Third Age the Assembly decreed that Sulare, a retreat at the southern tip of Kirthanin, would be the place where every seven years all Novaana between the ages of eighteen and twenty-five were to assemble from the first day of Spring Wane until the first day of Autumn Wane.

Sulmandir (sul-man-DEER): Also known as Father of the Dragons and the Golden Dragon. He is the most magnificent of all Allfather's creations beside the Titans. After many of his children died during Malek's invasion of Kirthanin at the end of the Second Age, Sulmandir disappeared.

Summer Rise: See seasons.

Summer Wane: See seasons.

Summerland: See Sulare.

Suruna (suh-RUE-nuh): Joraiem Andira's bow, previously his father's, whose name means "sure one."

Suthanin (SUE-than-in): The largest of Kirthanin's four countries, occupying the southern third of the continent. Ruled by a loose council of Navaana. Residents are Suthanim.

Synoki (sin-OH-kee): A castaway on the Forbidden Isle.

Tajira Mountains (tuh-HERE-uh): Nolthanin range in which Harak Andunin is located.

Taralin Forest (TARE-uh-lin): Western forest of Suthanin and home to the Taralindraal clan of Great Bear.

Talis Fein (TAL-is FEEN): Commander of the armies of Cimaris Rul.

Tarin (TARE-in): Novaana of Enthanin, Valia's cousin.

Tashmiren (tash-MERE-in): Servant of Malek, originally from Nolthanin.

Therin (THERE-in): Faithful Titan killed by Malek and his allies during the Rebellion.

Third Age: The present age, which began with the fall and occupation of Agia Muldonai by Malek.

time: Time in Kirthanin is reckoned differently during the day and the night. Daytime is divided into twelve Hours. First Hour begins at what we would call 7 AM and Twelfth Hour ends at what we would call 7 PM. Nighttime is divided into four watches, each three hours long. So First Watch runs from 7 PM to 10 PM and so on through the night until First Hour.

Titans: Those first created by Allfather who were given the authority to rule Kirthanin on Allfather's behalf. Their great power was used to do many remarkable things before Malek's rebellion ruined them.

Tol Emuna (TOLL eh-MUNE-uh): Heavily fortressed city of northeastern Enthanin's wastelands.

torrim redara (TORE-um ruh-DAR-uh): Prophetic state of being temporarily outside of time.

Turgan (TER-gun): Great Bear, elder of Elnindraal.

Ulmindos (ul-MIN-doss): High captain of the ships of Sulare.

Ulutyr (OO-loo-teer): Vulsutyrim captor of the women on the Forbidden Isle.

Valia (vuh-LEE-uh): Novaana of Enthanin, Tarin's cousin.

Valzaan (val-ZAHN): The blind prophet of Allfather.

Voiceless: See Malekim.

Volrain (vahl-RAIN): Faithful Titan killed by Malek during the Rebellion.

Vol Tumian (VAHL TOO-my-an): Village along the Barunaan River between Peris Mil and Cimaris Rul.

Vulsutyr (VUL-sue-teer): Also known as Father of the Giants and the Fire Giant. Vulsutyr ruled the Forbidden Isle and gave shelter to Malek when he fled Kirthanin. At first little more than a distant host, Malek eventually seduced Vulsutyr to help him plan and prepare for his invasion of Kirthanin. This giant was killed by Sulmandir at the end of the Second Age.

Vulsutyrim (vul-sue-TER-eem): Name for all descendants of Vulsutyr; both a singular and plural.

War of Division: Civil war that weakened Kirthanin's defenses against Malek at the end of the Second Age.

Water Stones: Stone formations created by the upward thrust of water released from the great deep at the creation of the world.

Werthanin (WARE-than-in): Kirthanin's western country. Residents are Werthanim.

windhover: Small brown falcons that are seen as "holy" birds in some areas of Kirthanin because of some stories that associate them with Agia Muldonai.

Winter Rise: See seasons.

Winter Wane: See seasons.

Wylla Someris (WILL-uh so-MAIR-iss): Queen of Enthanin and widow of Joraiem.

Yorek (YORE-ek): Royal advisor to Wylla.

Zaros Mountains (ZAHR-ohss): Mountain range bordering Nolthanin on the south.

Zul Arnoth (ZOOL ARE-noth): Ruined city between Shalin Bel and Fel Edorath; sight of many battles during Werthanin's civil war.

ABOUT THE AUTHOR

L. B. Graham was born in Baltimore, Maryland, in 1971. He loved school so much that he never left, transitioning seamlessly between life as a student and life as a teacher. He and his wife Jo now live in St. Louis. They would like one day to have a house by the sea, which he wants to call "The Grey Havens." His wife is Australian, which he thinks is appropriate since his grandfather was Australian and his father was born in Melbourne. The fact that he has these Australian connections and that his father grew up in Ethiopia all make him think he is more international than he really is. He went to Wheaton College outside of Chicago, where Billy Graham went, but they aren't related. He likes sports of all varieties, especially basketball and lacrosse. His biggest sports achievement was scoring 7 goals in a lacrosse game when he was a junior in college (a 10–6 win against Illinois State). He and his wife have two beautiful chidren, Tom and Ella, who love books, which pleases him immensely.

Also in the Binding of the Blade series

Price: $16.99
To order, visit www.prpbooks.com
or call 1(800) 631-0094

Forged to kill and wielded to survive,
the blade has bound them all . . .

"It was foretold after Malek's first fall that twice more he would bring war, and that the last time, the very waters of the sea would obey him and fight for him. If this be so, then I cannot imagine how Sulare will escape his wrath. . . ."

Also in the Binding of the Blade series

Price: $16.99
To order, visit www.prpbooks.com
or call 1(800) 631-0094

After one thousand years, Malek emerges
to unleash the full force of his army.

"The master of the Bringer of Storms has poured much power into him, power received from My hand at the creation of the world. His grip on this world will grow stronger, and the shadow he is casting over the world will grow darker. So it is and so it must be. Even so, be strong and stand firm, for you are Mine, and I am with you."

"Powerful storytelling is no small accomplishment, and this alone lifts Graham head and shoulders above most of his competition. Graham's story has depth: substantial people with real problems and emotions, a tale of more than just dragons and wars.
—*Books and Culture*

Also in the Binding of the Blade series

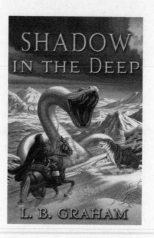

Price: $16.99
To order, visit www.prpbooks.com
or call 1(800) 631-0094

As the rains fall and the floodwaters rise, Aljeron embarks on a dangerous quest across the forsaken land of Nolthanin.

For all of Kirthanin, the days are dark and hope seems far away. And yet, in the midst of their darkness, a ray of light appears when Benjiah takes up Valzaan's staff and enters where all others fear to go.

"L. B. Graham has done a great job in creating an interesting world and story line that many readers will be anxious to read more about."
—www.vnoel.com